The Brass

Compass

By Ellen Butler

Jack —
Couldn't have
done it without
you!

Ellen Butler

Power to the Pen

Power to the Pen
PO Box 1474
Woodbridge, VA 22195
PowertothePen@ellenbutler.net

Trade Paperback ISBN 13: 978-0-9984193-0-5
Digital ISBN 13: 978-0-9984193-1-2

Categories: Fiction, Historical, Thriller & Suspense,
Characters/Female Protagonists, Military, German, WWII

Editing by Blue Otter Editing.
Cover Art by Jennifer Givner.
Cover Photograph by Toni Frissell, [Victoria Station, London]
1951, Library of Congress, item 96506374.

Dedication

To Oscar, a boy with the courage of a lion,

forced to become a man under the darkest of times.

To the Women of the OSS. Your bravery saved lives.

Germany & Surrounding Countries

Unbeknownst to me, my training started as a child, long before the Nazis came to power, before the war, and before my stay at the prestigious Swiss finishing school, Château Mont-Choisi, in the idyllic town of Lausanne. Had my mother realized the path her machinations put me on, I doubt she would have ever let me out of her sight.

Chapter One
Into the Night

February 1945
Germany

"*Was ist sein Name?*" What is his name? The SS officer's backlit shadow loomed over his victim as he yelled into the face of the shrinking man on the third-story balcony. "We know you've been passing messages. Tell us, who is your contact?" he continued in German.

Lenz's gray-haired head shook like a frightened mouse. With his back to me, I was too far away to hear the mumbled response or the Nazi's next question. I pulled my dark wool coat tighter and sank deeper into the shadow of the apartment building's doorway across the street from where my contact underwent interrogation. The pounding of my heart pulsated in my ears, and I held my breath as I strained to listen to the conversation. In front of Lenz's building stood a black Mercedes-Benz with its running lights aglow, no doubt the vehicle that brought the SS troops. None of the neighboring buildings showed any light, as residents cowered behind locked doors praying the SS wouldn't come knocking. This was a working-class neighborhood, and everyone knew it was best to keep your mouth shut and not stick your nose in the business of the Schutzstaffel.

Their presence at Lenz's home explained why my contact at the bakery was absent from our assignation earlier today. I dreaded to imagine what they had done to Otto for him to give up Lenz's name ... or worse, mine. Even though I'd never told Otto my name, a description of me could easily lead the SS to their target.

"*Lügner!*" Liar!

I flinched as the officer's ringing accusation bounced off the brick buildings. A young SS Stormtrooper stepped out onto the balcony and requested his superior look at something in his hand. I should have taken their distraction to slip away into the darkness and run; instead I stayed, anxiously listening, to hear if Lenz would break under the SS grilling and reveal my identity. Clearly, they suspected he was involved in spying and would take him away. They probably also knew he had information to spill and would eventually torture it out of him, which was the only reason he hadn't been shot on sight. It was only a matter of time before he gave me away. My friends in the French Resistance had been directed to hold out for two days before releasing names to allow the spies to disband and disappear. I wasn't sure if the German network applied the same rules, so I remained to see if he would break before they took him.

"Where did you find this?" the officer asked.

The trooper indicated inside the apartment.

"*Zeig es mir.*" Show me. He followed his subordinate through the doorway into the building.

Lenz turned and braced himself against the balcony. I watched in horror as he climbed atop the railing.

"*Halt!*" a bellow from inside rang out.

Lenz didn't hesitate, and I averted my eyes, biting down hard on my cold knuckles, as he took his final moments out of the hands of the Nazis. Sounds of shattering glass and buckling metal ripped through the darkness as his body slammed into the SS vehicle. In my periphery, a neighboring blackout curtain shifted.

"*Scheisse!*" the SS officer swore as he and his subordinate leaned over the railing to see Lenz's body sprawled across their car. "Search the apartment. *Tear it apart!*"

The moment they crossed the threshold, I sprinted into the night.

My breath puffed out in small plumes of smoke as I dodged through alleys, in and out of darkened doorways, moving on the balls of my feet. Silently, I cursed the cloudless sky as the moonlight bounced off the cobblestones, its brightness clear enough to land a plane. Unless waiting at midnight at a drop zone for needed supplies, a spy preferred the inky blackness of cloudy skies. Especially when escaping the enemy.

A few kilometers from Lenz's apartment, I paused behind the brick rubble of a bombed-out building. My gaze searched the area for any sign of movement. Standing alert, I held my breath, attuning my senses to the nighttime sounds, and listened for the whisper of cloth, the click of a boot heel, or heaven forbid, the cock of a gun. The thundering of my heartbeat slowed, and I balled my fists to stop my shaking hands. All seemed quiet … for the moment.

My fingers curled around the tiny film cartridge, filled with information vital to the Allied cause, nestled in my coat pocket. Dropping down to one knee, I slipped the heel of my right boot aside and tucked it into the hidden cavity. The coded message I'd planned to pass to Lenz would have to be burned, but I couldn't take the chance of lighting a fire right now. It would have to wait until morning.

My body cooled from the run, and I blew into my hands to warm them as I assessed the situation. There was no way I could return to the Nazi's home. If my absence had yet to be noticed and arouse suspicion, there was still a distinct possibility the SS would be knocking on the *Oberst's* door at sunrise demanding admittance. I had to assume, even though Lenz didn't reveal me, Otto already had, or would be tortured into doing so. Lenz's suicide did not guarantee my safety. Eventually, the SS, or worse, the Gestapo, would follow up on the slightest possibility that the *Oberst* housed a spy, especially considering his most recent house guests included the Minister of Armaments and War, Albert Speer, along with half a dozen army officers and a pair of naval captains.

Even though, due to his injury, the *Oberst* no longer led troops into battle, he was a brilliant tactician, and his home remained a hot bed of strategic planning. Army leaders had spent hours in his luxurious dining room talking weapons, troop movement tactics, and maneuvers. Though *der Führer* never deigned to visit, on at least one occasion, the *Oberst* had been summoned to consult with Hitler's top military advisors in Berchtesgaden. It was the exact reason why, when the chance for me to imbed myself into his household fell at my feet, I did so without hesitation, despite the high level of risk and against my superior's strong objections.

I tilted my head against the rough brick, and my mind flashed back to the fateful day in November 1944 when I'd been returning to my job as a telephone operator in Stuttgart, acquired for me by a special operations executive—an SOE agent. I carried a small net sack of food I'd purchased using my meager ration cards and watched two giggling children skip down the sidewalk ahead of a thin, gray-haired woman. She absentmindedly called for them to slow down, but her attention was focused on a piece of paper in her hand.

It happened in an instant. The little boy threw the girl's doll into the street, and with a cry, she ran after it. I saw the car's driver hadn't seen the contretemps or the child run into the road. The groceries dropped to the ground as I raced into the street. My fingers snatched the little girl's hood and I yanked. We stumbled out of harm's way as the driver swerved to miss us both. That moment of squealing tires, burnt rubber, and boy's distressed yell was perpetually seared into my mind.

After the children had been calmed and the agitated driver returned to his car, the distraught housekeeper poured out her sob story, no doubt worried that I would complain of her inattention to her employer. In a babbling monologue, with tears shimmering in her sunken eyes, she told me the two motherless children had been foisted into her charge when their last nanny moved to Frankfurt to take care of a sick parent and injured brother. The household was moving to be with the *Oberst*, army colonel, in Oberndorf, Germany. I slowly rocked the little girl in my arms while sympathetically nodding as she explained the situation. Finally, she rounded out her story by asking if I knew of anyone willing to leave Stuttgart and take up the position.

My mind churned at the mention of the colonel and his position in Oberndorf, the home of the Mauser K98k factory, the *Wehrmacht*'s rifle of choice. The housekeeper's plea couldn't have been more perfect. My cover identification characterized me as the eldest of four children, a far cry from the truth. However, I took the initiative to weave a beautiful, nurturing tale about raising my brothers and sister while lovingly comforting pint-sized Klara, as Dagobert, the imp who'd thrown the doll, hid behind Magda's skirts. Five days later, after a nerve-racking investigation, I moved into the household, along with a newly acquired Minox mini spy camera and instructions for passing information to my contact at the *Marktplatz* in Oberndorf.

A rustling sound jerked my attention to the right and sent my heart a-rabbiting. The perpetrator, a tiny four-legged creature, squeaked and darted across the street. A silent breath of laughter puffed out in relief, even as I realized that those few minutes I'd let my guard down could have cost me my life. With renewed determination, I rose and continued my stealthy journey into the night.

Chapter Two
Long Cold Road

I followed one of the less-traveled dirt roads out of Oberndorf that led deeper into the Schwarzwald, Black Forest, and had no manned checkpoints. The lane lay like a ribbon in front of me, bright enough to follow in the moonshine. I quietly padded along a frozen track left behind by the treads of a tank; my body remained tense and ready to jump down into the gully that ran along the side. However, the jolt of fear that drove me through town waned, leaving behind weariness, and it took a grim determination to continue putting one foot in front of the other.

The breeze bit at me, and I pulled the collar tighter around my neck before jamming my hands deep into the coat pockets, regretting, in my haste to get to Lenz's, that I left my gloves behind. Magda had presented them to me on Christmas Eve— a generous gift considering the current rationing conditions. Guiltily, I wondered what the SS might do to her and the rest of the staff.

The harsh February winter still held us in its clutches, which meant there were no comforting chirps of cicadas and crickets, only the wind whistling through the pines, the grate of my soles on frozen road, and the whooshing of my breath to keep me company. I turned a corner and heard the whine of an engine. In an instant, I slid down the gully and hid behind a bush. The vehicle's headlamps arced around the bend, slicing into the trees on the opposite side, and I crouched lower as the *Heer* staff car continued down the boulevard. During the moment of brightness, I checked my watch. It wasn't yet midnight, and I prayed my absence would go unnoticed until morning.

Hours later, my flagging footsteps tripped over a rise on the uneven roadway, and I fell to my knees, scraping my hands as I landed on the frosty gravel. The bitter dryness burned my arid throat with every inhalation. With what little willpower I had left, I pulled myself up, dragged my weary body into the woods, and found a bower, devoid of snow, to curl up beneath. I pulled dead leaves and pine boughs over me for warmth.

Just for a few minutes.

My dreams took me back to an earlier time, when my life lay like a blank canvas of privilege and comfort in front of me.

♠♠♠♠

Spring 1938
Wales, Britain

The trunks had been packed for two days. Returning to my birth country, where I could visit my only living grandmother, settle into a home, and decorate my own bedroom, had me antsy with excitement. Most of all, I looked forward to spending time with my mother, whom I hadn't seen since the winter holiday break. Of my three roommates, my parents were the last to arrive. A day overdue, they had missed the commencement ceremony. Not a surprise, since my roommates' families all lived somewhere in Britain, whereas mine were coming from the exotic African nation of Rhodesia, where my father had just finished his assignment as a minister-counselor at the U.S. Embassy. I sat, for the last time, at the scratched and worn wooden desk, now bare of any personal items, cleaning my 35 mm Argus A camera—a Christmas gift from my mother and my most prized possession. Photos of friends, the school's snow-covered turrets, a broken swing set, the new budding leaves, a bicycle tire, whatever struck my fancy lay in a portfolio at the bottom of my trunk. The school's art teacher took a great interest in my photography, and her last words to me at the end of the term were of encouragement to continue.

A soft knock at the open dormitory door had me turning to find the smiling visage of my beautiful mother. Forgetting all my etiquette classes, I threw myself across the room into her outstretched arms, inhaling her rosewater scent. "Mum!"

"Oh my goodness, look, Edward, my little peanut is all grown up." Her jade-green eyes, which I'd inherited, raked me up and down.

As she did so, I noticed the blue dress she wore hung loose on her frame, and the mink coat seemed to overwhelm her slight figure. Her angular cheekbones, a defining feature, seemed even more prominent, making her look gaunt. Mother always maintained a trim figure, but this was beyond slim. I frowned.

"Hello, my dear, it is good to see you." My father stepped forward and drew me to him in a stiff hug.

"You too, Father" I murmured into his shoulder, noticing that he had lost some of his barrel chest.

"This doesn't look too bad. Not quite the cold, austere type of place I expected in a British boarding school. It's actually quite homey and you seem to have fit right in."

"I suppose so." I gave a wan smile. Following a rocky start, the school had been just fine. After all, I'd been adapting to environments all over Western Europe, while my father worked his way up the foreign officer ladder, moving us from consulate to consulate and embassy to embassy. Adapting to a stuffy, upper-crust boarding school had been tricky at first, but once the girls realized I'd seen much more of the world than they, I'd achieved a type of awed respect. Though I would have preferred to have continued my education with hired tutors and remained with my parents, it had been impressed upon me that Africa would be a dangerous place for a young girl, and Mother insisted on ensconcing me safely in this "homey" environment. When it came to my education, Edward, my stepfather, always bowed to my mother's recommendations.

"Your mother is correct. You have grown taller. No longer my little girl, you have become quite the young lady." He eyed me up and down.

My real father had been killed in a car accident when I wasn't yet two, turning my mother into a widow before her twenty-third birthday. Still young and beautiful and carrying a pedigree from a wealthy New York family, she remarried before my fourth birthday. Even though he never officially adopted me, Edward had been kind and loving in his own way, and at a young age, at my mother's behest, I'd taken to addressing him as Father. He and my mother never had children of their own, and by the time I turned seven, he'd started introducing me simply as his daughter rather than "Marie's daughter."

"I think she's taller than I am, and grown to be quite lovely. But I do miss those blond locks you had when you were little." A hacking cough overcame my mother.

With furrowed brow, he released me and tenderly guided her to one of the unmade beds. The rough mattress ticking scraped against the soft fur of her mink coat as she coughed into a handkerchief. I slid down beside her and rubbed her hunched, convulsing shoulders.

The episode wound down and she waved her hand at us. "I'm fine, I'm fine. Be a dear and point me in the direction of the little girls' room." She dabbed at her eyes.

"Left out the door and straight to the end of the hall," I answered.

Her gloved hand cupped my cheek. "You've acquired an adorable British accent. I won't be but a moment."

Edward watched my mother's exit, and I watched Edward, noticing the deep grooves around his eyes, as his drawn countenance followed her.

His shoulders jerked when I spoke. "What is wrong with her? She looks ill. What happened in Africa?" I didn't mean to sound so accusing, but fear made my voice sharp.

He lowered himself on the bed across from me and removed the gray fedora. "There was fever. We all caught it. Your mother is taking longer to recover."

"When? Why did no one tell me?"

"She did not want to worry you."

"She seems so … thin and fragile."

"I've arranged for her to see a specialist as soon as we return to the States."

"A *specialist*? What kind?" I probed.

"A lung specialist."

"But will she—"

"Enough," Edward cut me off. "Your mother does not like to speak about these things, and I have something important to tell you before she returns." He unbuttoned the top button of his overcoat and rubbed a hand through hair so thinned I could see his scalp. "You'll not be returning to the States right away. We have arranged for you to attend finishing school in Switzerland."

I gasped, "Finishing school?"

"It is a top-drawer facility."

"But … I thought … I was to come home."

"It's only a year. Then you will return to D.C.," he said in a placating tone.

"Aren't I a little old for finishing school? Shouldn't we be looking at colleges?" Actually, I disliked the thought of more schooling, but if college got me back home, I would go in a heartbeat.

"College is a possibility. We can see how things … turn out after finishing school."

"What am I supposed to learn at finishing school?"

"Château Mont-Choisi provides a number of things for a young lady about to be launched into society. Languages—"

"I already speak four languages," I interrupted.

"Dancing lessons." He looked at me sternly and continued as though I hadn't spoken. "A wide variety of sports, such as golf, and you'll be able to continue riding, which your mother tells me is one of your favorite activities, and of course, the etiquette lessons."

"Etiquette." I spat the word out. "That is one lesson I'm sure I've gotten enough of here in this stuffy British school. 'Pinky out when we drink tea, ladies,'" I said in the headmistress's uppity British accent while sipping from a pretend cup with pursed lips.

Edward frowned. "There is more to etiquette than learning how to drink tea. And if your behavior is any indication, it is clear you are in need of it."

"Fine," I said crisply. "Then I would like to go to finishing school in the States."

"Swiss schools are far superior to any of those in the U.S."

"No, thank you."

"I beg your pardon?"

"No," I said with deadly calm and crossed my legs. "I won't do it. I'll tell Mother I do not want to go."

"It is your *mother's* wish that you go. Please do not be

difficult," he said in a soft voice.

"I … I don't believe you." Tears pricked the backs of my eyes, and I bit down on my bottom lip in an effort to hold them in.

"That feels much better," Mother said.

Always the gentleman, Edward rose as she entered the room and discarded her coat on the bed next to me.

"Now, where were we?" Her bright gaze took in Edward's stern look and my shining eyes. "You told her … without me?"

Neither of us spoke. I turned away from them.

She sighed. "I see. Edward, dear, would you give us a moment?" Mother's voice was soft as silk, but steel lay underneath. "Please."

He took his dismissal without argument.

Her dress rustled as she sat on the bed in his place. "Peanut?"

"Why?" The whispered word was filled with hurt and sadness.

"My dearest, I only want what is best for you."

I skewered her with my angry gaze. "Am I that much of a burden on you and Father that I am not allowed to come home? Is my presence so odious I'm to be shipped off to *another* school?"

Her sympathetic features turned to shock at my words, and she reared back as though I'd slapped her. Putting a hand to her chest, she cried, "How could you say such a thing?"

"Last holiday you told me I was going back to D.C. with you. Why am I now being sent away … *again?*"

"Dearest, when I was your age, I would have given anything for an opportunity like this. To attend a Swiss finishing school, and Château Mont-Choisi! Heavens, have you any idea the strings your father pulled to get you in?"

"But … I want to go home," I muttered in a small voice. The tear fell unbidden.

"Oh, my darling girl." She crossed over to my bed and wrapped me in her arms. "Don't cry. This is a chance for you to meet important people. You'll go to museums, learn about art, and see plays at the theater. You can ride horses. It will be fun, I promise you. It will also teach you how to run your own household and servants. You'll learn about floral arranging and cookery. You'll meet grand people. And when you complete the course, we'll have a splendid coming out, and you'll be the toast of Washington society. The crème de la crème will come, and maybe you'll meet a handsome young senator or congressman who'll sweep you off your feet. Doesn't that sound magnificent?"

"What about college?"

"There will be time for that. Once you complete this program, you'll have your pick of colleges … if you're not already married. Dearest, believe me, I'm desperate for you to come home with us now, but when the prospect arose for you to attend Mont-Choisi"—she shrugged—"I simply couldn't allow my own desire to have you close-at-hand outweigh this marvelous opportunity. It's only for ten months. It'll go by in a blink. Oh, and I've completely forgotten, you and I are going shopping in Paris before you begin class. Isn't that a wonderful treat?"

I couldn't resist her excited gaze. Ten months wasn't so long, and some of the things sounded like fun. I'd always enjoyed our museum days when we lived in Vienna and Rome. So, I allowed myself to return her smile. "When do we leave for Paris?"

♠♠♠♠

A clicking sound brought me awake, and it took me a few moments to recognize the sound was the chattering of my own teeth. An uncontrollable shiver shook my frame, and with stiff muscles, I pushed to my feet, stamping them to get rid of the numbness. I'd pulled my arms inside my coat to stay warm, and now I clumsily wrestled them back into their sleeves. The forest remained dark, but the road turned gray in the shadowed dawning light, and my pendant watch pointed to five-fifty. My stomach rumbled with hunger, and my tongue seemed to fill my dry mouth. I found a patch of half-melted, undisturbed snow and scooped a handful to quiet the thirst. Needling pins in my feet announced the return of blood flow and reminded me it was time to get moving.

German nursery rhymes spun through my head, and the quiet ticking of my boots against the hard ground accompanied the ditties like a drumbeat. Half a dozen kilometers later, I came to a crossroads. The flaking white paint on the wooden sign pointed directions to nearby towns—Stuttgart to the east, Schweiz to the south and Freudenstadt twenty kilometers northwest. Freudenstadt was the capital of the district and one of the larger towns in the Black Forest. It would be easier for me to hide and perhaps make contact, but it was also one of the first places I would expect the SS to look for me. Dornstetten, a few kilometers east of Freudenstadt, was a quaint small town built during the Middle Ages. I'd been there twice on day trips with the children. The SS and *Heer* presence was less pronounced in these smaller towns ever since the Allies had pushed closer to the Maginot Line that paralleled the Rhine River and more men had been put on the front lines. Moreover, the bus to Dornstetten-Freudenstadt should be passing within the hour.

I faded back into the woods to wait out of sight, and fished a small compact from my purse to see what damage my night on the run had wrought. The Tyrolean fedora was sadly mashed on one side, but with a little tweak here and there, I formed it back into some semblance of order and hung it on a broken branch. The comb caught on snarly knots, and I blinked away the sudden tears as I pulled the teeth through my dusky curls. Along with the shadows beneath my lashes, smudges of dirt marred my face, and my hands were soiled with dried blood from my late-night stumble. A handkerchief took care of most of the mess; powder and fresh lipstick took care of the rest.

The green bus rumbled to a stop in front of two basket-carrying, middle-aged *Frauen*, and I merged in behind them to board. The bus was only half-full, and I slid into an unoccupied seat near the back.

The goose bumps receded, and the gentle swaying of the bus must have rocked me to sleep, because I woke with a start when the bench shifted and another Frau joined me. She frowned and didn't acknowledge my existence, so I turned my attention to the other embarking passengers. A pair of young SS Stormtroopers came down the narrow walkway; they bypassed three empty seats to fill the one right in front of me. The second one glanced over his shoulder, and to my displeasure, our eyes connected.

He smiled and tipped his hat, "Fräulein."

My ears burned and I racked my brain, trying to remember if I'd met this handsome young man at the house, but his face didn't ring a bell. I acknowledged his greeting with a stiff nod, returned my attention out the window, and worked to steady my breath.

The bus meandered its way toward Dornstetten, and the men spoke in muted tones. I only caught snatches of the discussion over the noisy engine, but I could feel the soldier's gaze intermittently focus on me. I remained rigidly upright, my muscles taut as a bowstring and my stomach churning with acid. It wasn't the first time I'd drawn admiring looks from a young man, or older ones, for that matter.

He once likened me to Ingrid Bergman.

In the spy business, looks had gotten a number of women out of tight spots, my own included. On this occasion, I wished I looked like the frumpy, middle-aged Frau seated next to me, to whom the troopers hadn't given a second glance.

A few more stops, then the bus finally came to a juddering standstill in the center of town. Passengers filed off, but I didn't move until the SS troopers' images disappeared from the reflection in the window. Travelers continuing on to Freudenstadt remained on the bus while others disbursed as they exited; however, the two soldiers stood on the street corner in animated discussion. I fell into line behind my seatmate and used her girth to shield my getaway, slipping around the back of the bus.

"Fräulein."

I continued my pace, pretending I hadn't heard.

"Fräulein, *bitte bleiben sie stehen.*" Please, stop where you are.

There was no way I could ignore the command in his voice. My feet hesitated, and I looked over my shoulder.

"*Sie haben ihr Taschentuch verloren.*" You dropped your handkerchief.

It was a ploy. Immediately, I recognized the handkerchief the soldier held in his hand couldn't be mine because it was pristine white, whereas my own filthy handkerchief lay stuffed at the bottom of my purse. This smiling blue-eyed boy was becoming a dangerous nuisance, and he needed to be dispatched. Even though, officially, I had this morning off, eventually Magda would look for me when I didn't come down for breakfast. I had limited time to get what I needed in Dornstetten before moving on.

"*Vielen Dank, Sturmmann.*" Thank you, soldier. I plucked the handkerchief from his outstretched hand, and as he opened his mouth to further the conversation, I proceeded to convulse with a hacking cough that soon turned real from the dryness and thirst I suffered. I will give the young man credit, he had impeccable manners. He wiped the revulsion from his face so quickly I might not have seen it if I hadn't been watching for it. I finished the coughing fit, wiped my mouth, and stuffed the handkerchief into my pocket.

"Pardon. You were saying?" I croaked with my Bavarian German accent.

"*Auf Wiedersehen,* fräulein." He tipped his hat, turned on his heel, and set off at a smart pace.

The ploy worked and I strode across the *Marktplatz* of half-timbered buildings. Women wrapped in woolen cloaks and head scarves gathered around the shops, waiting for them to open. A door squeaked and a squat man wearing an eye patch stood in the entrance to the butcher's. The women filed in and queued, waiting to fill their empty baskets with whatever was available today.

Quietly, my knuckles rapped against the baker's door. A moment later, an apple-cheeked frau, her apron covered in flour, answered. "We don't open for another hour, miss. Best move on to get your other rations and come back later."

I'd remembered the stout merchant from my last trip. She'd given Klara and Dagobert each a raisin cookie, a rare treat for them. Her kindness was the reason I'd chosen this shop. The fact that it was empty pleased me even more.

"Yes, I know, Frau...Hardebecke." Her name unexpectedly popped into my head. "I was wondering if I could beg the use of your toilet. It was such a long trip on the bus…"

She eyed me up and down for a moment. I must have succeeded in looking sufficiently desperate, or the fact I knew her name tipped the scale. With a sigh, she swung the door for me to enter. Warmth and the smell of yeast and fresh bread washed over me.

"Through those curtains and on the left. There's a sink for you to clean up across the hall."

"Thank you, Frau. God bless you." I clasped my hands penitently in front of me.

She blushed and waved me away. "Go on with you. I've got to finish up."

I slipped behind the black curtain and found myself in a short hallway. To the left was the toilet and the right a small room for washing. Furtively, I slunk down the hall until it opened into a large, dark-paneled room. A bulky desk covered in papers and a ledger sat in the center. Bookcases flanked the desk and candles were scattered throughout the room. The baker must have used it as her office, but I didn't find what I was looking for. It'd been a long shot. Her phone, if she had one, must have been upstairs or in the main shop. Most phones to be found in this town were either in very public locations or sitting at the local headquarters office.

I rinsed out my soiled handkerchief and, using the sliver of lavender soap, washed the rest of the dried blood off my hands before cupping them to drink deeply. The water tasted rusty, but I didn't care. It cooled the rawness in my throat and filled my belly. There was no mirror, so once again I took out my compact and used the wet handkerchief to wipe away a bit of dirt I'd missed in the woods.

Frau Hardebecke stacked dark, crusty loaves of fresh bread into a basket as I returned to the main shop area.

"*Danke.* It smells delicious."

She looked up from her work. "Have you *Marken* for bread?"

"Yes, of course." Luckily, I hadn't handed over my *Marken,* ration coupons, for the week to Cook. A handful of half-used booklets of the *Reichseierkarte* remained in my possession. I pulled the *Marken* out of my purse, handed it and the appropriate amount of *Reichsmark* into her flour-dusted hand.

To my relief, money would not be a problem. The coat I wore had been given to me by my SOE contact. "Wear it anytime you step out of the house," he'd said, gruffly pulling it closed and buttoning the top button. A secret pocket had been sewn inside the lining, which held a substantial amount of forged *Reichsmark.* "For bribes," he'd said, and I had thought no more about it … until now.

The baker tucked both into her apron pocket, broke the bread in half, and passed one of the halves across the counter. "Where is your basket?"

Blast! I should have nicked a carrier somewhere along the way. All the other ladies on the bus and waiting in line had them. My purse wasn't large enough to store the supplies I'd need. "I … I haven't got one. I … mean I need to purchase a new one."

She tut-tutted, then bustled beneath the counter before returning with a small shopping basket. A blue-checked towel lined the bottom. "Here."

"How much?" I reached into my purse.

"*Nein. Nein,* take it. I have too many," she insisted.

I should have argued, but I didn't have the time. There were other shops I needed to visit, which likely had long queues out the door by now. The SS would catch me standing in line if I didn't get moving.

"*Danke,* Frau Hardebecke. You are an angel," I said with

feeling and meant it.

She jerked her head. "You'd better line up at the butcher's next. I hear he has venison today."

I thanked her again and exited. Two hours later I'd used as many *Marken* as I could and had filled Frau Hardebecke's basket. Along with the bread, it held a hunk of hard cheese, smoked deer jerky, two bottles of local bier, a withered turnip, a potato, and marmalade. Living in a rural area had its benefits. It was rare to find anything but horse meat in the cities, but the forest provided meat for hunters and more space to raise chickens for eggs.

My next stop would likely be out of the district, and the *Marken* I held would be useless. A small *gasthaus* across the square caught my eye. It ran a café, and I debated using more of my *Marken* to get an *Ersatzkaffee* before moving on. The drawback, the little restaurant sat right next to city hall, the SS command post. However, I'd already been in the small town long enough for a few shop owners and residents to take note that I was a stranger among them. My presence here was not going to go unnoticed, so a few more minutes probably wouldn't make a difference. I stepped off the curb, onto the street, when the blare of a horn drew the attention of every pedestrian in the square.

A septuagenarian herded a forlorn pack of nanny goats, with full udders and jangling bells around their necks, across one of the intersections leading out of the *Marktplatz*. The car honked again, and the old man steered a straggling goat out of the way. The vehicle zipped past the flock with one last rude blast, and then whipped into a parking space in front of city hall. My blood ran cold as the SS officer from Lenz's apartment stepped from the Volkswagen, a downgrade from last night's Mercedes. He did not glance my way as he strode, his shiny black boots clicking against the cobbles, into the building.

I stepped back, staggering against the lip of the curb, and would have lost my balance if a passerby hadn't caught my arm and saved me and my basketful of rations from a nasty tumble to the ground.

"*Danke*," I muttered before making tracks up the closest side street.

I had tarried too long in Dornstetten. Perhaps one of the children had woken early and come for me. Or maybe the SS Officer was at the colonel's house at dawn. Or missing breakfast had emboldened Magda to find me. Whatever the case, he was here. And somewhere inside that building was a young, blue-eyed Stormtrooper who could positively identify me. It wouldn't take long before they would fan out into the *Marktplatz* asking questions and following pointed fingers.

The street headed south, and I found myself alone among the stone and timber homes. A dog barked, and a door opened behind me. My pounding heart hitched a beat as I ducked down a shadowed alleyway between a pair of three-story homes. Coming out the other side, I paused. In front of me, a frau's laundry snapped in the chilly breeze. On it hung a faded, wren-brown head scarf, similar to those many of the local women wore to stay warm. I scanned the area before trotting up to the line and snatching the still-damp, indistinguishable scarf. A quick glance down the rope revealed no gloves or mittens; I was out of luck, and there was no time to pilfer other laundry lines.

I finally came to the end of the charming homes with the forest ahead; in between lay two hundred meters of open ground, browned with dead grass and patches of melting snow. Running might draw attention, so I set out at a fast walking pace and lengthened my stride to cover the distance quicker. A few minutes later, I slipped into the comfort of the concealing trees.

Chapter Three

Down the Rabbit Hole

I hiked through the woods with grim determination to put as much distance between Dornstetten and myself. A kilometer out of town, I stuffed my identifiable fedora into a hole of a passing tree and covered my hair with the ugly scarf.

I'd made it a fair way into the woods before I heard the dogs. It seemed far off and might have been only two of them, but I couldn't take the risk and set about laying a false trail. It took extra time that I could have used to get farther away, but it was more important to get the dogs off my scent. I started by going about in a wide circle, then weaved in and around a thick stand of trees. One of the best ways to throw off the dogs would be to walk through one of the many streams passing through the area, but the small ones I came upon were frozen. My next option was to go up.

I'd been an avid tree climber as a child. As a young teen, I remembered my mother yelling at me to come down out of the big oak in our front yard and berating me for my "unladylike" behavior. The muscles might have been out of practice, but with dogged persistence, I climbed up, basket tucked high under my arm, and carefully crawled across a sturdy branch. I didn't look down or give myself time to think before leaping across to a branch on an abutting tree. The entire tree shook with my weight as I clawed at the rough bark. The dogs' howls were now consistently in the background and less than a few kilometers away if I had to guess. Once the swaying stopped, I slowly crawled to the trunk, identified another solid branch that hooked up with the tree next to it, and took another death-defying jump.

I shimmied to the ground and, praying I'd done enough to confuse the trail, set out at a jogging pace heading north. An hour later, I no longer heard the bark of the dogs.

My travels came to an abrupt halt at a razor-wire fence line. Using the brush and trees as cover, I followed the barrier north until the forest thinned and revealed a barren field. In the middle of the field rose three concrete mounds covered in green camouflage. From my vantage point, I could barely make out a white sign that read *ACHTUNG MIENEN!* I guessed it was some sort of bunker, only I couldn't see an entrance from where I stood. Each concrete bunker had a large black swastika painted on the side. In the northeast corner stood a large barbed wire gate with a paved road leading to the installation. Sandbags surrounded a machine gun nest, covering the gate. A variety of military vehicles including two camouflaged tanks, transport trucks, and a handful of cars were parked inside the fence under the overhang of trees, and leaning against the bumper of a troop transport truck stood an enlisted man smoking a cigarette. He stared at the sky as though he hadn't a care in the world.

Reconnoitering the bunker north would have me hiking kilometers out of my way. Depending upon how far south the fence line ran, I would have to cross a river and risked running into another village. There was no way I'd willingly cross the road leading to the bunker during daylight, so I decided the best course of action would be to stop and remain hidden until nightfall.

I slunk back into the forest, distancing myself from the

installation. Deeper in the woods, I found a well-concealed bower beneath an evergreen tree. One of its roots stuck up out of the ground like a giant's bent knee. I lowered myself on the perch and uncovered the basket. While the chewy bread coated in apricot marmalade and a slice of hard cheese slaked my appetite, it was the chilled bier that settled the anxiety roiling in my stomach.

The respite was welcome, but thoughts I'd held at bay while I navigated my way through the forest now bounced around my conscience like one of Dagobert's rubber balls.

What gave Otto away? Were we observed passing our notes, or was he careless leaving them to be found? Why was the SS and not the Gestapo at Lenz's? The Gestapo's network of neighborhood spies was well known. What led the SS to Lenz's home? Did I say something? Behave in an abnormal manner?

Interactions with Otto in the past month ran through my head. Our conversations were always brief, spoken in code when I had information for him. He palmed my communiqués as I passed him money and ration cards. Any responding information would be passed back inside the bread. *Did I slip up? Did an observer note the regular conversations about the weather and report it? Am I responsible?* That last question gnawed at me, incessantly grinding away like a rat chewing through a block of wood.

Magda. I squeezed my eyes shut. Magda, an innocent in the churning underground of espionage. Magda, the matriarch of the household, who had innocently poured out her problems and taken me under her wing like a daughter. I couldn't wipe the vision of a pair of Stormtroopers escorting her from the house, fear marring her kindly features as she was led to the car. She'd been with the colonel's family for close to ten years. *Would he protect her or be angry at her betrayal? How would she react under interrogation?* The thought of the angry visage of the Nazi screaming at Lenz, interrogating poor Magda, her white hair coming loose from its chignon, dread and anxiety writ in her faded eyes, made me nauseous. I rubbed at my own eyes in an attempt to block out the awful image.

It was terrible enough Lenz and Otto had been captured, perhaps by my own mistakes; however, they both knew what they were getting into. They recognized the risks and the repercussions. Magda had been nothing but kind and an innocent, and I had drawn her into a swirl of intrigue of which she knew nothing. It became a relief when the sun set and I forced myself to close those thoughts in order to focus on the task at hand.

The night darkened, and before the moon rose to its zenith, I headed warily northwest, finding relief in the shadows of the vegetation. The woodland came alive with noises; branches cracked, broken by animals or the breeze, I did not know which. It kept me on edge, regularly slowing my steps as I paused to listen. Finally, I came upon the road that must lead to the bunker. It wasn't straight, instead winding and curving through the overgrown trees, and from the direction which I approached, the front gates couldn't be seen. I searched the night sky for lights but saw none. It seemed the Nazis wanted to keep their installation secret, which was fine by me. If I couldn't see them, I surmised they couldn't see me.

My own journey was no longer the quiet padding it had been along the frozen lanes of last night, and I prayed the snapping twigs blended with the forest sounds. In the distance, booms of exploding bombs met my ears. The Allied advance through France kept the nightly shelling commonplace, although the trees played tricks on my ears, and I couldn't be sure if the noise came from the east in Stuttgart or farther north. I hoped the explosions helped to cover my own noise.

My initial thoughts fleeing Oberndorf had been to head south, to try and cross into Switzerland and get to Zurich, an area I knew well from my finishing school days and one that promised help. However, I soon realized, if I navigated my way south, reached the border, and could outwit, cajole, or flirt my way past the German border guards, without proper papers, the Swiss would turn me away and send me right back into the hands of the Nazis.

Switzerland had been flooded with refugees before the war broke out in earnest. After Germany invaded France, limitations of resources made the government become quite strict with their refugee policies. When I accepted the nanny position, I'd been warned that I would be in the belly of the beast, and that, unlike my former missions in occupied France, the Office of Strategic Services had no organized escape routes from the town of Oberndorf and a limited network of spies. As far as I was aware, I'd been the only OSS operative in the area. Even the agent who had gotten me the phone operator job remained behind in Stuttgart.

The Germans I'd dealt with were sympathetic to the Allied cause, having lost relatives or friends to the camps, but I'd never been introduced to any other contacts besides Lenz and Otto. One assumed there was a network of assets and operatives connected to Lenz, but we'd been kept apart, compartmentalized, for everyone's safety. I now cursed the very secrecy that was supposed to keep me safe as it would lead to my downfall. Papers—with a new identity that would have allowed me to board a train to Switzerland—along with a silk map, remained hidden behind an oil canvas of a mountaintop landscape hanging in the nursery of the colonel's home. As I was unwilling to travel farther into Nazi territory, my fleeing steps instinctively took me in a northwesterly direction away from the Neckar River.

The clear moon only provided intermittent light, and I stumbled my way through the dense timberland, regularly tripping across roots hidden by snow and darkness. When I dropped into France, we'd been given Benzedrine pills to reduce appetite and combat fatigue. What I wouldn't give for a couple of those little yellow pills right now.

Distracted by a rustle of underbrush, what I'd been dreading happened; I slipped into a rabbit hole and something popped. I bit down on my lip, cutting off a cry of agony, and tasted the salty tang of blood as I collapsed on the hard ground. Tears sprung to my eyes.

After the initial agony passed, I loosened my bootlaces to massage the site of the strain, which had already begun to swell. Pushing to my feet, I tested the injury. The ankle seemed able to bear weight, with moderate teeth-gritting, leading me to believe it wasn't broken. I convinced myself the pain was nothing I couldn't handle, so I re-laced the boot as tight as tolerable and gathered my things to limp along at a turtle pace.

By the time the darkness grayed into predawn, my eyes ached with the grittiness of fatigue. The winds had calmed and the scent of oncoming snow drifted through the air. My ankle had swollen so much that I'd lost the feeling in the toes of my left foot, and the ache of the sprain that radiated up my calf caused muscle spasms. The basket I carried dragged at my arm, heavy as a typewriter, but its meager rations were so important to my survival I daren't let it go. I spied a small hut, its white siding flaked and chipped enough to show the brown boards beneath. The front door faced east. I cautiously navigated my way around to the south, tucking myself behind a thicket of frosty underbrush, to wait and see what signs of life would stir with the sunrise.

After twenty minutes, my knees and muscles had stiffened from crouching beneath the frigid, weak winter sun. No smoke rose from the tiny chimney, and in the lightening sky, a woodpile took shape along the front. A layer of undisturbed snow lay across the top. The fatigue and pain spurred me to creep closer to take a look. I gathered a handful of pebbles with my numb fingers and tossed them. They rained against the weathered door, and I held my breath as they rattled to the ground. Nothing. Growing braver, or perhaps more desperate, I threw a rock the size of a pecan. The *thwap* resounded through the forest, and a small animal scrabbled back into its hole.

I snuck up to the miniscule front window and furtively peeped in. I couldn't see a thing through the filth. The lock was broken and the hinges squealed in protest as I pulled the door. To my relief, the scent of stale air with a hint of old burnt wood greeted me. Across from the door was a small stone hearth, with a cot next to it. A plain wooden table with two chairs stood beneath the dirty window, and a petite shelf housed clay mugs, wooden dishes, and random utensils. A pot and kettle rested on an iron grate inside the fireplace, and a thick layer of dust covered everything. It wasn't much, but in my now exhausted, shivering state it looked like a reprieve from heaven.

An hour later, I huddled in a chair next to the crackling fire, unshod feet propped up on a settle, a mug of hot water gripped in my hands. Wrestling the boot off my injured foot had been a painful process that I didn't look forward to repeating any time soon. I'd packed some snow around the swollen joint and wrapped it with the towel from my basket.

Two pairs of antlers hung above the mantel, and I figured the tiny building must have been a hunting cabin. The wooden plate sitting on my lap held half a boiled potato and a few bites of the cheese. I dunked some of the hard bread into the water to soften it. The hunger that had been gnawing at me since the wee hours of the morning was barely appeased by the paltry meal.

Admittedly, rationing had become stringent for the Germans; however, working in such a prestigious household allowed for special dispensation, and our cook often received extra ration cards or "gifts." Even though the Germans complained about the strict rationing, they knew nothing of hunger. Nothing like what I'd witnessed and experienced during my time in France, where the Germans had systematically stripped the French of all their prime meats, vegetables, and wines, practically starving the population. Some might say my position in the colonel's house could be described as a cream-puff assignment. They'd be correct … if it weren't for the extreme danger of being caught and shot in the head.

The mug clunked to the floor, and I jerked out of a semi-consciousness to slide onto the cot and pull the blanket up to my shoulders. The crackling wood reminded me of the fires in our rooms at finishing school, and I fell into a restless sleep riddled with reminiscent dreams.

♠♠♠♠

November 1938
Château Mont-Choisi

A log shifted and the fire hissed. Visina snored quietly into her pillow as I stared up at the ceiling. I was more than halfway through my sentence at the Château, although, if I was honest, the program wasn't so bad. Last month, I danced with Laurence

Olivier during one of our outings to Geneva. The point of finishing school was to build confidence, and it certainly achieved its aim. I'd feel comfortable running a large castle or preparing for a diplomatic formal dinner party. Mother would be so proud.

The day had gone like any other day, floral arranging and cookery in the morning, swimming and riding in the afternoon. It had been an exhausting afternoon, but my mind wouldn't settle into sleep. It kept going over and over the events of the evening.

Following dinner, four of us had gathered in Camilla's cozy room to listen to her radio. She'd twirled the dial and settled on the National Swiss radio station broadcasting in German.

"Can't we find something else? My German isn't good and I'm so tired of hearing about the terrible Nazis," Isabella complained.

However, Camilla and I stayed her impatient fingers. The correspondent was reporting on the aftermath of what would be labeled *Kristallnacht*, the night of broken glass. A night in which paramilitary and civilians attacked Jews and Jewish businesses, breaking windows, burning synagogues, ransacking and demolishing buildings. Anything to do with the Jews seemed to be on the list. So far fifty fatalities had been reported, and thousands more were incarcerated by the Nazis.

When the report ended, Camilla, with a shaking hand, flicked off the radio. "Ladies, I'm not feeling well. Please give me some privacy."

Isabella and Visina, taken aback by her abruptness, rose and stalked out of the room without a second glance.

I closed the door behind them. "Who? Who do you know in Germany?"

Camilla pinched her lips and stared hard. "I don't know

what you mean?"

"I lived there too, Milla. Don't shut me out. I fear for those I knew."

She raised a still-trembling hand to her blond brow.

"Come now, you know me, I'm not one of the gossips around here. I can keep my mouth shut."

"Friederich," she breathed.

"Who?"

"Friederich Dantzig. We met in Vienna, two years ago. He plays the violin for the symphony. It … it was a fling, an April-May *affaire*. Mother was so angry when she found out because he is Jewish. She raked me over the coals and told me to forget him. But … we still correspond in secret."

"Where is he now?"

"Berlin."

I sat on the love seat next to her and held her hand. Ever since the *Anschluss* of Austria, the news from Germany became more and more disturbing.

"Father says they are preparing for war … again."

"I know." I rubbed her hand. "Adelene was called home to Paris. The French are shoring up the Maginot Line."

Camilla's frightened brown eyes stared at me. "What will happen to us?"

"Shh … we are safe. Nothing is going to happen."

"That is easy for you to say. Your home is all the way across the Atlantic. What can the Nazis do to you?"

I patted her hand but had no reassuring words to provide. She was correct. Half of Europe and an entire ocean created a barrier between the U.S. and Hitler.

After leaving Camilla, I penned a letter to Father asking if he'd heard about the attack on the Jews and what the Americans were doing about it. The disturbing report had brought to memory a little girl in Munich, Sacha, one of my girlhood friends. While we attended a Protestant church, Sacha went to synagogue. Religion meant little to me at that time, and I only had good memories of my mischievous playmate. I remember Sacha and I climbed the fig tree in her yard to get away from her annoying little brother, Elijah. We received a dressing down from her mother for throwing figs—not because we threw them at Elijah—because we were wasting the fruit. I wondered if she was still there or if her family had fled from persecution, like so many others. I'd read, in the Swiss newspaper, of trains filled with Jewish children traveling to countries beyond German borders, to Belgium, France, and Britain.

The thump of footfalls pulled me from my thoughts of Sacha and Camilla and her secret beau. The steps stopped outside the room, and a brief rap tatted against the door before it swung open.

"Mademoiselle Lily, *se réveiller.*" Miss Lily, wake up.

The lantern swung above me and I squinted against the light. "*Qu'est-ce qui ne va pas?*" What is wrong?

Augustine, the housekeeper, pulled back the eiderdown and spoke quickly in French. "There has been a telegram from your father. Your mother is unwell. You are to dress immediately for travel."

Nothing Augustine uttered could have woken me more quickly than *mother* and *unwell.* I rose from bed and pulled off my heavy cotton nightgown in a blink. The coughing episodes that nagged Mother during our shopping trip to Paris, and her subsequent denials that it was something to be concerned about, played over in my head. Father had written a few weeks after they returned to the States assuring me her health was improving.

One of the maids, Berthe, I think, arrived carrying my valise.

"What's going on?" Visina whispered.

Augustine shushed her and told her to go back to sleep.

"How am I to get home?" I pulled up my stockings.

"Your father has made arrangements. Once you're dressed, go to the headmistress's office. She will provide you with everything you need to know."

Augustine worked quickly to help me into a pale gray wool travel suit while directing Berthe on the appropriate clothing to pack in my valise. "Here, *mon petit*, take your heavy coat. It will be cold on the ship."

I traversed the dark, silent hallways to the headmistress's office, where she explained my travel arrangements. A car would take me to Geneva, where I would get on a flight to Paris. An American family stationed at the Paris embassy happened to be transferring back home and had tickets on a cruise ship leaving Le Havre, two days hence. My father had been able to secure me passage, and the family would chaperone me to New York.

The flight from Geneva to Paris went smoothly, and an embassy vehicle picked me up from the airport where the driver told me that the Caton family had already left for Le Havre. He would not be taking me to the embassy but would drive straight to Le Havre, where a hotel room had been arranged for me until the ship left. I was pleased by this information; the farther west I traveled, the closer I got to my mother.

The Catons turned out to be a kind family. Julia was in her mid-twenties and mother to a pretty little five-year-old girl named Elise. I estimated Henry, Julia's husband, to be in his mid-thirties. He spent his days reading reports and smoking in the men's lounge. The only time I saw him was during dinner, when we dined at the captain's table. I couldn't blame him. Two days into the crossing, Julia and the nurse they'd brought to watch after Elise succumbed to the rocking of the ship. I ended up spending my days walking the decks and having tea parties with Elise to keep her occupied while the ladies lay miserable in bed. I didn't resent having to look after Elise. She was a spirited little girl, and keeping her occupied served to keep my own mind from dwelling on the fears that would sneak up on me when I was alone.

The fourth night on the ship, I dreamed of Mother. She was her beautiful old self again; her eyes sparkled like the sun on the Aegean Sea, her cheeks had filled out, and her smile could entice birds to sing. She and I were having a picnic next to the river Danube, and she told me how much she loved me and how proud she was to be the mother of such a lovely young lady. She told me that Edward would need my help and asked me to watch out for him. I promised I would. Then she proceeded to give me fashion advice. I awoke from the dream refreshed, and for the first time since that dreadful night at the Château, the gnawing in my gut dissipated. I considered the dream an omen—that my mother had turned a corner and her health was on the upswing.

On the seventh day, our ship docked in the bustling New York Harbor. Mr. Caton escorted me to the train station, where he pressed a gold and cloisonné bracelet into my hand. "A gift, for taking care of Elise."

Father sent a car to pick me up at Union Station in D.C. The trip from the station to my parents' new home in Georgetown took less than thirty minutes. It was past nine when I finally arrived. A young, apple-cheeked maid answered the door and ushered me into the front hall.

"My little world traveler, you are a sight for sore eyes." Edward, wearing a black suit and no tie, stood in a doorway on my left. Though he'd gained some weight since I saw him in

England, the haggard look around his mouth hadn't changed, and his eyes were bloodshot, rimmed in red. "I'm so glad you have arrived."

He came over and pulled me into an unexpectedly tight embrace. I returned the hug.

"How was your trip?" he asked as I handed off my rain-dampened coat and gloves to the maid, who promptly disappeared through a green baize door.

"Long," I sighed.

"Come into my study. Let me get you a drink. Would you like a brandy or sherry?"

"Sherry, please." I stared up at the staircase, wanting to protest and insist on seeing Mother; however, my etiquette training kicked in, and I followed him into the large study, surrounded by mahogany bookshelves. Two burgundy velvet wingback chairs rested by a fireplace, and I sat in one of them, enjoying the warmth emitted by the burning logs.

"How was the trip with the Catons?"

"Fine. Mr. Caton gave me this bracelet for taking care of his daughter after the nanny and Julia became seasick. But please, don't hold me in suspense, tell me how Mother is getting along?"

Edward handed me the sherry and sat across from me. "My dear…" He swallowed. "About your mother … she … she passed away," he choked out.

"What?" I said in a high-pitched voice.

"I am sorry. It … it happened three days ago."

"Three days?" that silly high voice squeaked out.

"Yes, on Thursday. The funeral is tomorrow."

The glass slipped from my fingers. Its contents spilled unheeded onto the Axminster rug. The air must have been sucked from the room, because I couldn't breathe, couldn't think, couldn't move. Edward clasped my numb hand and spoke to me in words I didn't comprehend. A wailing sob bubbled from below, agonizingly working its way up my chest, until finally, I sucked in a breath and allowed the untamed cry to burst forth.

I awoke abruptly. A chill pervaded the room, the fire burnt to embers. Peaks and valleys of late-afternoon sunlight filtered through the clouds and into the window, chasing away the unhappy memories. I rubbed my eyes and stretched stiff muscles. The drapery of fatigue had been removed by sleep, and it was now time for me to formulate a decisive plan.

My options were limited. Without papers, Switzerland was a no-go; I'd never make it over the mountains or through the checkpoints without help.

Heading east, farther into Germany, turned my stomach. My identification card was now useless, even dangerous. I lit a candle and watched the paper crinkle and blacken around the edges where the flame licked at it. Anneliese Kruse disap-peared beneath the sparks, and I tossed it away into the fire along with the message for Lenz. My last connection to the nanny's life floated gracefully up the chimney in a cloud of smoke.

I could remain in this hut in hopes that the Allies would eventually overtake the area and not shoot or bomb me on their way in. The hut was warm and had some provisions. A chest beneath the cot revealed a rifle with one bullet in the chamber, which I could use to find food. However, regular smoke could draw the enemy's attention. My boots stood side-by-sided, like silent soldiers, next to the hearth. The information on the film hidden within held viable intelligence that the American forces needed. No. Staying put in this bungalow was not a practicable option. As much as I dreaded to admit, I needed to move.

But move where? The only choice seemed to be west, toward the front.

My last eavesdropping mission led me to believe the Allies were pushing through the eastern-most edges of France toward the Rhineland. Hitler had commanded his generals to send additional troops and armored divisions to fortify their position to keep the Allies from crossing the river into the Fatherland. The front, a constantly moving line, was probably one hundred to 150 kilometers away. If I could get back into France, I still remembered names that could reconnect me with French intelligence. Hell, I could walk into an Allied encampment, surrender myself, and hope my superiors back in Paris could sort it out before I was shot or imprisoned. I needed to find transportation if I wanted to get the vital information to the proper people before it was too late.

Unfortunately, all my plans were delayed by two factors. First, due to heavily falling snow. Second and more frustrating, I couldn't get my boot over the swollen ankle. I spent the evening packing the injury with icy snow and propping it up on the chair, tricks I'd learned after a nasty tumble from a horse when I was a child.

Dinner consisted of a hard-boiled egg, apricot marmalade, and more hot water. Afterwards, I covered up the window with a blanket, snuffed the candle, and carefully banked the fire so it would burn through the night. I probably should have put it out; staying the night increased my risk of detection, and the fire was dangerous. However, its warmth balanced out the frigidness wrapped around my foot, and I hoped it would dispel the soreness plaguing my throat. The only good the snow brought was the hope that it covered any sort of trail the dogs might track.

In the flame's glow, I fingered the miniature brass compass at my breast. It had certainly saved my life the past two days, guiding me like a beacon away from danger. Lenz, a jeweler by trade, had mounted the clasp and provided a chain so I could wear it as a necklace. I'd told him it was my father's and, since it was made in Switzerland, not something that would give me away. It was just another one of the lies I'd told.

Oh, it was true, the manufacturer was Swiss, but it was never *my* father's.

He gave it to me. I remembered our exchange as clear as if it were yesterday. I'd given him my St. Christopher medal, the patron saint of travelers.

"To keep you safe," I'd told him.

He pulled the scratched and well-worn compass from his pocket. "I jumped into Normandy with this. It was my father's. He used it in World War One."

I'd pushed it back at him, insisting he needed it more than I, but he folded my fingers around the cool metal.

"Keep it. The military issued me a new one when I jumped into France. You can give it back the next time we meet."

Was it any wonder that I dreamed of *him* that night?

Chapter Four
City of Light

November 1944
Paris, France

Raucous laughter filled the air. A mixture of American and British servicemen crowded around outdoor tables, enjoying coffee and camaraderie. An army sergeant slapped the back of an English airman, and I smiled at the lighthearted group, voyeuristically enjoying their moment of pleasure—for once the tensions of war not uppermost in their minds. The sun warmed my face on this unseasonable autumn day as I approached the outdoor Café de Flore on the Boulevard St. Germain. A breeze tickled my legs and flirted with the hem of my lightweight coat, and I adjusted my hat forward to shade my eyes. Patrons crowded the outdoor café, enjoying an alfresco lunch. I searched in vain for an open table, finally alighting on a dark head bent over a book all alone at a table on the outer edge of the restaurant. The olive-brown uniform declared him to be an army captain, and an empty chair sat across from him. Unwilling to give up my plans to eat outside at my favorite restaurant, I squared my shoulders and approached the lonely soldier.

"Pardon me, Captain, would you mind if I joined you?" Two piercing, marine-blue eyes fringed with black lashes met mine, and a slight jolt ran through my body. I gave a hesitant smile. "You see, all the other tables are filled."

The beautiful eyes glanced away, surveying the crowded restaurant, then he rose and indicated the empty seat. "By all means."

While I situated myself, removing gloves and placing them beside my handbag, the captain waved at the waiter.

"*Bonjour,* Mademoiselle Lily," he said, punctuating with a click of heels.

"*Bonjour, Philippe.*" With perfect, albeit countrified French, I proceeded to order an egg salad sandwich and a café au lait. Philippe gave a precise bow and ambled off. My gaze returned to my ruggedly handsome tablemate.

His brows puckered in puzzlement. "You *are* American, correct?"

"Yes, indeed, Lillian Saint James, from Washington, D.C." I extended a hand.

"Charles McNair, of Milwaukee. My friends call me Charlie," he replied with a slight Midwestern accent. The hand was rough but warm, and it sent an unexpected shiver up my arm. Surprise flashed, and his gaze darkened but was quickly masked as he released my fingers.

"Thank you for allowing me to join you."

"It's my pleasure."

"What were you reading when I interrupted?" I indicated the forgotten book.

"*The Sun Also Rises,* by Hemmingway."

"Ah, yes, the self-indulgent, beautiful Brett drags a jaded Charlie Barnes gaily across Europe from Paris to Pamplona with their motley group of friends," I said, gazing around the Parisian café. "Apropos, I suppose, considering where we are … and the title character, of course."

"I wouldn't know. I've only finished the first chapter."

I waved to the book. "Feel free to carry on as if I'm not here. I don't wish to disturb your reading. I simply couldn't give up spending lunch outside on a day like this."

"Actually, I am more interested in knowing what Lillian Saint James, from Washington, D.C., who speaks French like a Parisian and apparently reads Hemmingway, is doing here."

My lips lifted. "Oh, I think Philippe would argue with you. My French is definitely not Parisian. And call me Lily. Like you, I'm here to eat my lunch."

"That is not what I meant." A finger drummed the table. "What is a beautiful, young Ingrid Bergman look-alike doing here in war-torn Europe instead of safe at home in America?" He tilted his head. "Are you a nurse?"

I wasn't wearing a uniform, but it was a good guess on his part. I had been known to don one when the situation demanded it. Most of the American women in Europe were nurses, typists, or secretaries for the War Department. Since the OSS had yet to give me a new assignment, I had the novelty of time on my hands. The day had been so beautiful—and Colette tempted me with a new dress and petite bow-bedecked hat— I'd taken to walking the Paris streets for fun.

I told none of this to my tablemate, instead allowing the standard-issue reply to roll off my tongue. "Just trying to do my bit. I'm a photojournalist for a newspaper." I'd told that lie at least a dozen times to strangers and friends alike, but on this occasion, telling the lie to a solemn Charlie McNair made me uncomfortable.

Beyond the beautiful eyes, Charlie sported high cheekbones and a slightly crooked nose that looked like it had been broken at one time. His uniform fit over a stocky frame of compact strength, and I estimated his age to be late twenties. Although he might have been younger, either the elements or anxiety had etched premature crow's feet. The war aged everyone early.

Laughter erupted again from the rowdy table of GIs and distracted my tablemate.

Philippe returned, placing a drink and sandwich in front of me.

"*Merci*," I murmured.

"*Bienvenue*, you are most welcome." Philippe eyed Charlie but didn't deign to offer a refill on the coffee. With a Gallic shrug, he walked off.

"So, Captain, what does that fancy patch on your left shoulder signify?" I deftly diverted the conversation away from myself.

"Hundred-and-first Airborne, and that is a Screaming Eagle," he said with pride.

I'd known the answer when I asked, but for appearance's sake, I allowed my eyes to widen. This wasn't the first paratrooper I'd run across. Their tactical fighting skills became legendary after D-Day. "So you signed up to jump out of perfectly good airplanes?"

This brought a slight smirk. "Yes, ma'am, I did."

I paused, debating whether or not to ask my next question. "Did you jump on D-Day?"

The smirk vanished. "Yes, ma'am, I did."

"I see." My first assignment had been dropping behind enemy lines into France a few weeks before the invasion of Normandy, something I trained for with British SOE agents and French Resistance fighters. Though my middle-of-the-night jump had luckily been onto a quiet pasture with two other agents, it had been nerve-racking to say the least. Not an adventure I wished to repeat. I couldn't imagine witnessing the chaos and fear during the actual invasion as men jumped from planes pelleted by antiaircraft fire. At the time of the incursion, I'd moved farther inland to help French Resistance fighters blow up important railway supply lines. Absentmindedly, I stroked a scar on my left wrist, a memento of the day.

"Did you parachute into Holland?"

"Yes, I did. It was a perfect day for a jump." He wiped his mouth with a napkin. "Unfortunately, the mission didn't turn out quite like we'd hoped."

I could tell he was one of the types who enjoyed the rush of jumping, so I encouraged him. "Tell me what it's like to jump out of an airplane flying hundreds of miles per hour."

Pushing his book away, he leaned back to ponder the question. "Well … you see, it starts out with all this noise. The plane engines roaring, the wind buffeting through the open door, and men lined up ready to pile out, one after another. Your heart is racing and blood pumping. It is noisy chaos." His gaze flicked up to the fluffy clouds above. "Then it's your turn, and before you know it, you're out the door with the plane zooming away. We jump using a static line, so the chute is pulled when you leave the plane. When that chute deploys, it's as if someone suddenly turned a switch." *Snap* went his fingers. "It's silent … that is, if you don't have antiaircraft fire shooting up your ass." He cleared his throat. "Pardon my language."

I waved away the expletive. I couldn't have explained it better. He captured the moment perfectly … well, except for the utter fear that you might lose your breakfast on your way out of the plane.

"Your heart slows, and for a few short minutes, you float carelessly in the breeze, enjoying a view only seen by the birds. On a perfect, sunny day there's nothing to compare it to."

I found myself poised, sandwich suspended in the air, and my mouth half-open as he spoke. Charlie's gaze returned to mine and I returned to earth.

I laughed and shook my head. "You almost had me going there for a moment, Captain. I was actually thinking it would be fun to jump out of a plane strapped to nothing but a thin silk chute."

Finally, my tablemate cracked a full-on smile, his even, white teeth flashed, and I skipped a breath. "Call me Charlie, and it is fun. Someday, I'll take you."

Knowing someday was unlikely to happen, I humored him. "Sure, Charlie, maybe someday."

A patron from behind rammed his chair into mine, jostling my arm and spilling my coffee.

Charlie passed me a napkin. "Are you all right?"

Wiping the drink off my hand, I nodded. "Yes, the coffee's cooled. I'll be fine."

He looked to the offending perpetrator and with firm command spoke. "Corporal, I believe you owe the lady an apology."

The corporal glanced up. "Huh?"

"That's, huh, Captain."

Immediately, the corporal stood and saluted. "Sorry, Captain, what's the problem?"

Charlie pointed to the mess. "You owe the lady an apology."

The corporal did a double take and let out a whistle between his teeth. "I'm so sorry, ma'am, did I do that?" he said in a thick southern drawl. "I am such a klutz. Here, let me help you clean that." He pulled out a red handkerchief from his pocket and began ineffectually patting at my arm.

His other two companions decided to get in on the act. "Nice move, Billy Ray, we bring you to a ritzy joint like this and you spill the dame's drink."

"Why don't you come on over here and let us buy you a

fresh one to make up for our friend's clumsiness?" the other private suggested.

As a young, attractive female in a dense male population, I'd gotten used to being propositioned by servicemen from all walks of life. Deflecting passes was a skill I'd mastered, but this time I didn't have to.

"Gentlemen, the *lady* is with me. Corporal, now that you've apologized, I suggest you stop manhandling her and return to your seat." Charlie frowned and crossed his arms.

The corporal's ears flamed red. He returned the handkerchief to his pocket, mumbled another apology, and shuffled back to the table.

Charlie resumed his seat. "Now where were we?"

"I believe I was about to ask what you are doing in Paris. Is the 101st stationed nearby?"

"In Mourmelon. I'm on a forty-eight-hour pass."

"First time in Paris?"

He nodded.

"And are you enjoying it?"

He shrugged. "I arrived only a few hours ago. But since Lily Saint James sat down, the day is looking up."

"So you haven't walked the Champs-Elysées? Or seen the Eiffel Tower? Notre Dame? *Non*?"

"*Non.*"

"Then when I'm finished, I'll take you to see them."

"I wouldn't want to impose."

"Nonsense." I flicked my hand in dismissal. "I'm waiting on a new assignment, so my workload is light, and I've got some time on my hands. Besides, I feel honor bound to show a distinguished officer such as yourself the highlights of *gay Paree.*"

"Well … if you insist…"

"I insist."

Due to fuel rationing, there were few cars on the road that weren't military vehicles. Many of the civilians still used horse carts, and bicycles were prevalent. The occupying Allied forces were working hard to restore all train services. Luckily, the Métro, within the city, remained operational and was used heavily by everyone. The subway covered a large portion of Paris, was in good running condition, and it had stops close to many of the tourist sites. Unlike London, Paris had come through the war relatively unscathed, never having felt the full force of the Luftwaffe bombs. The major sights remained untouched in their glory, and it wasn't much different from I'd when visited with my mother in the spring of 1938. We took the Métro to the Eiffel Tower, and I pointed out a few of the buildings that sustained machine gun and mortar damage from the skirmishes between French Resistance fighters and the German army.

As we crossed the bridge over the Seine to see the Cathédrale Notre Dame, I explained Paris's eighteen arrondissements or neighborhoods.

"So this is the famous Notre Dame." He pronounced it *no-ter dame* like the college, as he took in the crenellated Romanesque architecture.

"Careful, the Parisians will turn up their noses at you for saying it that way." I repeated the proper French pronunciation.

He rubbed his chin. "How about I let you do all the talking."

I grinned at his boyish charm. "Deal."

"Do you think they have a resident hunchback living in the bell tower?"

"I'm not sure. Shall we go find out?"

He offered me his arm and we climbed the steps together.

Afterwards, we found ourselves strolling the Champs-Elysées; my hand rested lightly on Charlie's arm while we enjoyed the beauty of the waning fall sun. It was almost surreal how normal and comfortable I felt with him. For a few hours, we allowed ourselves to forget that a war raged not far away, and men at the front were dying.

"Where did you learn French?"

I shrugged and answered with nonchalance, "My father was a foreign service officer for the State Department. We moved around a lot. I spent most of my childhood living around Europe."

"Do you speak any other languages?"

Gazing down the street at the distant Arc de Triomphe, I weighed my answer. It wasn't so long ago my life had been an open book. Since the war, I'd gotten used to watching every word, and it took a moment to realize that I was in Allied-occupied Paris. Charlie was one of us, and I wasn't on a mission behind enemy lines. Even though I'd lied about my purpose for being in France, today I wanted to just be the girl of yore and share the truth with someone. "In addition to French, I speak German and Italian, and I can probably get along in Spanish. Although my Spanish gets jumbled up with Italian."

"Where are your parents now?"

"My father lives in D.C. My mother passed away before the war."

"I'm sorry."

I shrugged, chewing my lower lip. Time had tempered the terrible ache of missing her. However, the loss remained a weight on my heart. She was a difficult subject for me to speak about.

He came to a halt, my hand dropped away, and I turned to see the lines of his face, serious with sincerity. "I'm sorry. It's difficult to lose a loved one."

It had been a long time since I'd thought about my mother's

death, even longer since receiving another's sympathy over the loss. "Yes, I miss her. My biggest regret ... I wasn't there when she passed away." I sniffed, pulling a handkerchief from my coat pocket to dab at the unexpected tears.

Charlie offered his arm again and we continued walking. His silence spoke volumes; he wouldn't push for answers but was ready to listen if I was willing to talk.

The story came easier than expected.

"I was at a finishing school in Geneva. My parents were back in Washington. I had wanted to return to the States as well, but my mother insisted I complete my education. She hoped I would return to D.C. to marry a senator or congressman and take my place among Washington society. She was preparing me for a political life not much different from her own."

"She wanted what was best for you."

"I suppose. But that type of life was never for me, flower arranging, table settings, serving afternoon tea, etiquette lessons ... bah." I sighed. "Oh, I suppose it wasn't all bad. I met some nice girls, kept my languages sharp ... but life as a pretty little doll on the arm of a politician never held much of a draw. Though I did love the sports ... riding, golf, tennis ... and the dancing. Did you know I once danced with Laurence Olivier?"

Charlie raised his brows in disbelief.

"It's the truth. We took an outing to Geneva for the weekend and he was there."

The gloaming sun threw pinky-orange streaks across the clouds, and I paused to admire Mother Nature's beauty. "They kept it from me ... her illness."

"What did she have?"

"Tuberculosis. She was infected with it in Africa, at my stepfather's last embassy station. I should have known. She was so thin and frail when they came to pick me up from the English boarding school where they'd left me. By the time my stepfather summoned me home, it was too late." I shrugged.

Charlie's warm hand curled around my fingers gripping his bicep, and we ambled wordlessly down the pathway toward the Triumphal Arch, an architectural monument affiliated with important military parades throughout history. A few years ago, German troops proudly paraded through, establishing their dominance over France. It was only a few months ago, Allied and French forces, along with French Resistance fighters, marched through the mammoth monument celebrating the release of Paris and its people. The joyful day had branded itself into my memory.

"I was furious at Edward for waiting so long to tell me she was sick. I blamed him for her death. Sick with despair, I lashed out at him. Said awful things. Later, I realized there wasn't anything he could've done. He got her the best medical care money can buy. We didn't speak for months. Then the war came, and I left." I sighed at my childishness.

"Have you forgiven him?"

"Yes, I suppose I have."

"Are you on speaking terms?"

I nodded. "After my first assignment, the harsh realities of war were brought home. I have grown up enough to know now that he is all I have left. We cannot continue to be at odds. He worries and keeps telling me that I don't need to be here. He threatens to have me returned Stateside."

"Could he do that?"

"Oh, I think he could. There is a legend in our family that General Eisenhower once dandled me on his knee. And of course, my father knows the vice-president. I imagine one phone call could have me shipped back home like that." I snapped my fingers. "But … it's more now. I have a real chance to serve my country and help the cause ... help these people. To make a difference. I think when he realized I was serving my country, not just behaving like a petulant child, he stopped arguing. I know he doesn't want to lose me but"—I shrugged my shoulders—"he understands. We all have to make sacrifices for the war effort."

"Aren't there other photojournalists that your newspaper could send over? Let you go home for a holiday? How long have you been here?"

My steps paused, and Charlie's innocent gaze turned to me. Immediately, I realized my mistake. I'd told him my cover story when I sat down at his table, but just now I'd been speaking the truth, referring to my job with the OSS.

"A while," I hedged, not wishing to add more lies.

"Why you?"

"The languages. I can speak to everyone."

"Of course."

"What about you? Who did you leave back at home? Do you have other brothers serving?"

"No. I have two younger sisters. One got a job in the factory. The youngest sister works at my parents' general store."

"So, you're the prodigal son. You have family that worries about you."

"I suppose."

"Of course they worry. They just don't want you to know they worry." I kicked at a stone. "Do you miss them?"

"Every day."

The smile had disappeared, and his face took on a melancholy frown, as though he looked at Paris through different eyes, no longer a fun tourist destination but a city forced upon him. I blamed myself for allowing the conversation to turn gloomy. I'd never told anyone about my mom and strained relationship with my stepfather. Charlie had made it so easy. As a matter of fact, it was too easy to be myself around him, and as much as I enjoyed not watching every word, it was also dangerous—bad spy craft, as the Brits would say.

I opened my mouth to suggest parting ways.

"How would you like to join me for dinner? A gesture of appreciation ... for showing me the sights."

"Oh, that's not necessary."

"Nonsense." He turned those beautiful peepers on me. "It's the least I can do."

My will melted beneath his gaze.

He took me to the officers' club, and following dinner, I took him to a dance club where GIs with money were welcomed.

Prostitutes lined the bar, and I steered Charlie away to one of the tables on the far side. Smoke hung heavily in the air, the floor crowded with young French girls flirting mercilessly with soldiers, many looking for more than a free drink—the possibility of catching themselves a wealthy American serviceman. We danced for hours. Charlie spun me around with fast swings and pulled me close for the slow, gliding waltzes.

At one point he whispered in my ear, "How do I compare to Laurence Olivier?"

"Your moves are matchless." It wasn't a lie. On the dance floor, Charlie and I fit like puzzle pieces.

Charlie allowed no other man to dance with me until a lieutenant colonel asked to cut in. With reluctance, he handed me over. The lieutenant colonel gazed down at me with hungry eyes and leaned in a little too close for comfort. His breath reeked of liquor and his feet stumbled unsteadily.

"*Bonjour.*" I smiled at him and proceeded to speak nothing but French. All of his come-ons were deflected with an innocent raise of my brows and another spate of French. At one point he tried some bad German. To which I laughed and shook my head. *"Non, je ne parle pas Allemand."* No, I don't speak German. It was perhaps not nice manners on my part; however, I had no interest in spending more than the required dance with this man, wishing only to return to the arms of my captain.

The clock tower rang two in the morning by the time we left. Charlie insisted on escorting me back to my apartment in the fifteenth arrondissement.

"Come up for a nightcap?"

He hesitated, looking up at the old stone apartment building with its wrought iron balconies jutting out in a random pattern. "I shouldn't."

"Why?"

He removed his hat, ran a hand through his hair, and plopped it back on his head, then gave a heavy sigh. "I won't want to leave."

Since dropping into France, I'd been put into positions where I had to behave like a flirtatious hussy to get past checkpoints and misdirect inquisitive soldiers. That wasn't how I wanted it to be with Charlie, but something in my gut warned me—I'd never see him again if he left now.

I was not ready to have this man walk out of my life.

I drew in a breath and took his hand. "I don't think that will be a problem."

He trailed me up the stairs.

I lost my innocence to my captain that night. The act went against everything that had been drilled into me by my parents, the Church, and instructors at my finishing school. I recalled lectures about loose women and sleeping with men who were not your husband. Somehow, in the midst of war, when life could easily be stolen in the exhalation of one breath, none of the lectures mattered. Intuition told me my life would likely end at a young age, and the homilies seemed insignificant. With every caress, Charlie touched something deep inside me. Joy, an emotion so simple yet so far removed from my state of being that I hadn't experienced it in years, flowed through me like the swift waters of the Danube.

The next morning, we shared eggs and toast in the tiny kitchenette. And, the smell of strong coffee steeping in a percolator always reminds me how I watched him sip from the chipped rosewood china cup. I snapped a profile of him with my camera. When I pulled the viewfinder down, Charlie met my searching green gaze, replaced the cup on its saucer, and pulled me onto his lap. We spent the morning making love, obsessed with each other. He explored every inch of my body, stroking the pale skin with gentle fingers.

His tender playfulness had my lonely heart falling shamelessly in love with him, and our passion filled gaping emotional holes in my life. For those hours, we lived in our own private soap bubble. I was no longer Lily the spy, and he ceased to be the army captain. The little French apartment became a safe haven away from the guns, war, and death that raged not so far away.

My roommate, Colette, a former member of the *Résistance Française* and now an agent for the Free French Intelligence, did not return that night. I later discovered she'd been sent on assignment. I liked to think she would have approved of my choice. Her own first-time experience had been quite different from mine, having lost her virginity to a brutal invading SS soldier at the tender age of sixteen, and the reason she joined the Resistance.

It was late afternoon when Charlie and I emerged from the apartment to seek out sustenance. An army private striding down the street toward us drew in one last puff of his cigarette, threw down the butt, and stepped on it. He snapped a salute. "Captain."

Charlie returned the salute and made to walk on, but I recognized the writing on the envelope he carried.

The private placed a package in my hand. "You need to report by oh-nine-hundred tomorrow."

The captain's look of surprise and consternation would forever be ingrained in my memory as I took the documents. "Thanks."

The runner pivoted, stuffed his hands in his pockets, and ambled off.

I sighed, dreading Charlie's questions and knowing I'd have to feed him more lies.

"Your next assignment?" Charlie watched the private's retreat.

"I suppose so. They must have found me a military escort to my next location," I added as an explanation for the unorthodox delivery of the documents. The private must have been new, his handoff poorly done.

"Then this is … good-bye?"

"Not necessarily. I have until oh-nine-hundred tomorrow. What about you?"

"My train leaves at ten-hundred."

We wasted not a moment of our time together.

Chapter Five
On the Move

February 1945
Germany

By morning the swelling and the storm had receded. I tore the dusty, white-linen valance hanging above the window into strips, and after wrapping my ankle, I was able to get the boot over it. The small chest, about the size of a footlocker, revealed not only the World War I bolt action rifle that kept me company through the night but also a pair of navy mittens, a pair of men's trousers, and a beat-up brown rucksack. I filled the rucksack with the rest of my rations and my handbag. A search through the small dish cupboard revealed a tin of sardines, a tube of cheese, and some crackers, which were also added to the sack. I pulled on the trousers, tucked up my dress, and tightened the oversized waist with the belt from my coat.

The morning sun shone bright enough to filter through the pines and bounce off the three inches of fresh snow covering the ground. I estimated the temperature hung around the freezing mark when I set out that morning. The soft snow made the going slow, but worse, it laid a track. I soon broke off a pine branch and used it to obscure my trail. This area of the Black Forest was littered with streams and rivers. Most of them were frozen, and I successfully crossed over on foot, but it took time to scout some of the larger streams to make sure the area was uninhabited. The Nazis built many of their dreadful work camps outside small towns, so I had to be careful to avoid stumbling into one.

There was a work camp not far from the weapons factory in Oberndorf. Ironically, the men were forced to construct the weapons that built the army that subjugated them to begin with. I'd been stunned when I'd found out about the appalling practice. Some were their own German people the Nazis considered "undesirable," others were gypsies or healthy men and boys from France or Belgium. The Nazis basically enslaved each country's inhabitants that they'd invaded. However, a recent conversation I'd overheard between the colonel and Minister Speer led me to believe this workforce was treated rather well compared to the camps they'd built for the Jews in Poland. The colonel had at least insisted on daily meals to keep the workforce alive and so they could churn out their monthly quota of fifteen thousand guns. Speer spoke further about the Polish camps, referring to them as Hitler's "final solution." Unfortunately, I'd heard Magda approaching and had to abandon my hidey hole, so I missed the rest of the conversation.

The path I took headed uphill in a westerly direction north of Baiersbronn, where I would have to cross one of the major roads heading out of town. A train whistled in the distance. I debated heading closer to Baiersbronn to see if I could find some sort of transportation, when the grind of an engine met my ears. I stuffed my gloves into my pocket and swung the gun off my shoulder as I hid behind some shrubbery. Two staff cars and a motorcycle with sidecar roared past at a fast clip, and a few minutes later, trucks filled with soldiers lumbered into sight. I slunk down farther as tanks squeaked and rumbled past followed by lines of troopers marching on foot. All in all, I estimated two battalions paraded past.

I waited until the sounds of their engines and footsteps

could no longer be heard. Taking the plunge, I ran across the road and slid down the embankment on the opposite side; my feet slammed into the rails of the train track, jarring my injured ankle, and I slapped a hand over my mouth to muffle the cry of pain.

The track looked well used, the grease on the rails fresh from a recent train. I picked my way across and scrambled back up the verge into the cover of trees. The passing caravan had put me off any thoughts I might have had about going into Baiersbronn, and I hustled as fast as my injured ankle allowed over the hill and down the valley. My hop-along flight soon came to a standstill when I ran into the Murg River.

The banks were frozen, but in the center of the green river, water gurgled and flowed around the treacherous rocks. Using the flat of my hand to shield my eyes from the bright sun, my gaze swept up and down the gorge, eventually alighting upon an old-fashioned, manual cable car. The metal basket hung in the center about fifteen meters above the river and looked only large enough to hold one person.

I climbed the treacherous ladder to the icy platform and halted at the top. Half a dozen homes across the river came into sight. They were a less than a kilometer away and clustered around a bridge. An army motorcycle, looking remarkably like the one that passed me, was parked outside one of the homes. Anyone watching would be able to see the cable car. I could wait and cross at the bridge after dark, but sunset was still hours away and I needed to keep moving.

The rusty pulleys groaned as I hauled the cage toward the platform. The cable caught twice, and I had to hang on it with my full weight to get it going again. My feet slipped, and the cable dropped from my hands as I reached out for the railing to save myself from tumbling off. Finally, I drew the basket even with the platform. I took one last look at the homes before climbing into the bucket and letting go. The car whizzed across the river, whining with disuse. I feared the high-pitched squeal could be heard as far away as Vienna and breathlessly watched for curious figures to come running out of their homes. The cage came to a halt about three quarters of the way across, and I quickly grabbed the guide cable before the car could slide backwards and continued to pull it to the far side. I heard the rumble of trucks in the distance. Fear gave me added strength and swiftness, and soon I successfully reached the far side and scrambled down.

My relief upon reaching terra firma was almost euphoric. However, I kept glancing over my shoulder to make sure nobody was watching. My obsession with what was behind must have been the reason for almost walking directly into what was in front of me.

He wore a brown coat and carried a weapon slung across his shoulder, wispy white hair tossed in the breeze, and his piercing eyes gave me a start. I'm sure I made quite a picture in my overly large trousers carrying a gun and rucksack. I'd tucked my hair up into the stolen brown scarf, and I imagined my cheeks were bright red from exertion, but that didn't exactly explain why his brows knit in an angry glare. Perhaps he was the owner of the cable car and didn't appreciate strangers.

I decided to brazen it out. *"Guten Tag."* Good day.

I nodded and moved to pass around him, but his hand whipped out and grabbed my arm in an unexpectedly firm grip.

"Du bist früh dran." You are early.

Early? What is he talking about? I shook my head and tried to pull away.

He glanced over his shoulder before pulling me closer and

said in an undertone, *"Haben sie eine Zigarette?"* Do you have a cigarette?

"Nein." I wrenched my arm from his grip. "I haven't got any cigarettes." This fellow was just the type I expected to be a Gestapo snitch, and the sooner I was away, the better.

I took five long strides before pulling up short at his next softly spoken word.

"Jude?" Jew?

Slowly, my head turned on its axis. He'd pulled the semiautomatic gun off his shoulder and held it in his hands, though he didn't point it at me. With an unforgiving squint, I answered his question, *"Nein, mein Herr,* I am not a Jew."

He shifted uncomfortably and seemed unsure what to do.

So, I turned the tides on his impertinence and, with raised brows, asked, *"Sind Sie Jude?"* Are you a Jew?

His head jerked and he coughed. *"Nein, fräulein."*

"Auf Wiedersehen," I said, between clenched teeth, before carrying on without a backwards glance. It took all my willpower to force myself not to limp. My shoulders remained stiff with tension as I prayed this stranger wouldn't shoot me down.

When I'd gotten far enough away, I slowed my pace and the limp returned. I'd been hoping to find a place to stop and have something to eat and drink after the cable car undertaking, since the effects of this morning's breakfast—the other half of the potato—had already worn off, but now I trudged determinedly onward, putting as much distance between myself and the inquisitive old man as possible. I climbed higher into the hills, my pace slowing even more as the woods grew thicker and was often blocked by compact undergrowth that forced me to circumnavigate to a less dense pathway.

Chapter Six
Franziska

An hour later, after turning my interplay with the old man over and over in my mind, it occurred to me, in my fear and desperation to get away as quickly as possible, I might have misread the situation.

What if he wasn't a Gestapo snitch? What if he was part of an underground railroad for Jews? He said I was early. Who had he been expecting? Did I miss an opportunity for help?

A downed tree limb blocked my path, and I couldn't summon the energy to climb over it. Instead, I dusted off the snow, plopped down on the damp branch, swung the backpack off my shoulders, and rooted around for something to eat and drink. I'd refilled the empty bottle of bier with water and took a few slugs before gnawing a piece of the deer jerky. The meat would hopefully give me the energy to keep going, because for the last kilometer, I'd actually begun thinking I should ditch the film and turn myself over to the Nazis. Once past Baiersbronn the terrain had gotten steeper and more mountainous, and I felt as though I'd barely made headway. My ankle throbbed, cold permeated the outer layers of my coat, seeping into my bones, and I might have foolishly passed up the best chance at getting out of this godforsaken country.

Ever-gnawing hunger in my belly likely gave rise to these fatalistic thoughts, and the salty deer jerky did little to thwart the hunger, so I dug out the tube of cheese. I'd no idea how old it was, but the seal hadn't been broken and I took a chance. It had a fine, grainy texture and the taste was on par with glue. The best thing I can say about it, it filled the hole in my belly.

A whickering sound met my ears, and I froze with the tube of cheese suspended in the air.

There it was again, along with the unmistakable sound of a hoof stomp.

The food must have revived my survival instincts. I slid off my perch and crouched down, grabbing the weapon at my feet. Both the SS and the *Heer* had cavalry divisions, and a number of battalions still used horses for hauling artillery. There was only one round of ammunition in the gun, and I prayed I wouldn't require more than that.

The whickering came again to my right, but I couldn't see past the scree of brush. I slid into the cavity beneath the dead branch and shifted the weapon, ready to defend myself. The clop of the horse's hooves must have been dampened by the snow, because suddenly shaggy white socks, dirtied with mud, walked directly into my line of vision. I listened for the creak of a leather saddle when abruptly a large brown nostril came down to my level. My heart leapt to my throat, and I jerked back, rapping my head against the hard branch. The horse let out a nicker and warm breath blew at my face.

Petrified by fear, I remained in my hollow, waiting for a pair of boots to jump to the ground or a simple demand to show myself. Neither of those things happened, and I finally noticed there were no reins attached to the beast's bridle.

Gradually, I stuck out my head.

A large draft horse, bred for size and strength and usually used as a beast of burden, stood in front of me. Its dark brown coat showed a few bald patches, and as I pulled myself up out of the dirt, he backed up a pace, giving a snort and a shake of his head.

"Whoa … it's all right. There's a big boy." I crooned nonsensical German phrases. He allowed me to approach and take hold of the bridle; my mittened hands stroked his long neck. Gently, I blew into his nostrils and he gave another soft nicker. I hadn't been around horses since finishing school, but I remembered my equine etiquette.

"Where did you come from?" I whispered.

The fellow seemed placid enough, and although dirty and perhaps a little thin, in fairly good shape. I removed the mittens and ran my hands down his forelocks, searching for broken skin. His coat was dull and rough, clotted with mud in places, but finding no injuries, I encouraged him to walk in a circle while I watched for any sign of a limp. His gait appeared fine. After a second pass, I led him over to where my rucksack lay and dug around until my hands landed on the soft, round turnip. Cutting the root vegetable into smaller pieces with a pocket knife, I held my hand out flat. The soft, whiskered lips tickled my palm.

When my mother died, in my anger and pain, I stopped attending services and turned my back on God. After witnessing some of the atrocities the Nazis inflicted on the French, I questioned even the existence of God. Nonetheless, in the past few days, I'd sent up whispered prayers, and perhaps God had been listening, providing me with shelter when I needed it most, and now a mode of transportation.

However, my journey was not turning into smooth sailing by any stretch of the imagination. This horse was a typical workhorse, likely used for hauling supplies, and had probably never been ridden before. That and the fact there was neither saddle nor reins had me thinking God had a bad sense of humor. I'd ridden bareback a handful of times, but never on such a broad-shouldered horse and always with reins. If I hopped up on his back with no way to control him, one of two things might happen. We'd either go trooping off wherever the horse pleased … or he'd immediately throw me and I'd be dealing with a broken head in addition to the twisted ankle.

I emptied the rucksack, searching for some sort of rope to use as reins. In one of the side pockets, I found a hank of twine, less than a meter long and much too thin to be of any use. I tossed the backpack aside with a huff and began searching the woods for other options. The horse followed a few steps behind as I canvassed the area before returning to where I started. I stared grumpily at the useless bag.

Shoulder straps! Made of leather and adjustable, they just might be long enough.

"Come on. Give me some luck," I mumbled, unbuckling the bottom of the straps and holding the length from the bridle to the neck. It would be a little short, but beggars couldn't be choosers, and I went about cutting the leather out of the top loops. The twine came in handy for making a new strap for the pack.

Finally, with a makeshift harness in place, I led the horse— who I'd taken to calling Franziska because of the similarity to an overly wide cook we once had when we lived in Vienna— over to the fallen branch, which I used as a mounting block. I thanked the saints for providing me the trousers as I tossed my leg across the large breadth of Franziska's backside. He eyed me with a questioning tolerance while I arranged myself and the reins. I leaned forward and gave him a gentle kick.

He didn't move.

I kicked harder.

Franziska stomped a foot and tossed his head, almost yanking the reins out of my hands and unseating me.

I racked my brain for the verbal commands I'd learned

during my riding days in Switzerland; visualizing the trainer in the ring, it unexpectedly came to me.

"*Schritt*," I commanded, pulling out the word so it sounded like shaare-itt, and flapped the reins.

His weight shifted beneath me.

"*Tay-rap*." I tried another one. Not that I wanted to trot, but I figured whatever got him moving.

I let out a curse and kicked him.

Franziska moved forward about three steps, then came to a halt. I was fairly certain he just decided to move forward on his own, not due to my foul language.

Okay. This horse is not used to riders, so how do I get a horse used to pulling munitions to move forward? I'd once seen a farmer in France ploughing a field; he'd whistled at the horse when it was time to turn at the end of the field.

I gave a sharp whistle, flicked the reins, and we were off!

Franziska had a sure-footed, loping walk and a gentle rolling canter, which I preferred, but I had difficulty keeping him striding at that pace. He kept slowing into a bone-jarring trot. Eventually, I gave up and reduced him back down to a walk. Even so, we covered distance at least four times faster than my previous limping pace, and Franziska's broad back allowed me to prop my injured foot up, reducing some of the pain and pressure from the tight boot. Once an hour, I allowed Franziska to graze on whatever he could find that wasn't covered with snow. At one of the streams, I used a heavy stick to break through the ice to let him drink. Every so often, the crack of a falling branch would rend the air. Luckily, Franziska seemed unfazed by the random noises and continued his steady pace up and down the steep hills.

The horse's gentle, warm presence provided me a sense of security. I had no idea why it should. I was fairly certain he belonged to one of the military regiments, and my having him constituted thievery, adding one more reason for the Nazis to hang me … in case they didn't already have enough reason to do so.

A few hours later, the scent of a wood fire drifted past, and I immediately gave a soft clicking noise, which I'd learned was a signal for Franziska to halt. I sniffed the air and desperately strained to hear the sound of voices.

The gun lay across my lap for easy access as we walked into the campsite.

Three surprised faces stared up at me as they scrambled to the far side of the small fire, where two rabbit-sized carcasses roasted on a wooden spit; the tempting smell had my stomach rumbling. Two men and a boy wore ragged coats that puffed out at odd angles. A crinkling ruffle sounded when they moved, and I assumed they'd insulated their clothing with paper.

As I observed them, the tallest, with a protuberant nose, withdrew a knife from his jacket pocket. The boy, who couldn't have been more than twelve, shuffled behind him. Their eyes looked unnaturally large in their thin faces with protruding cheekbones as they warily watched me.

Franziska shifted and they drew farther back. The knife rose higher, poised to strike.

"Brrrrr." I rolled my tongue behind my teeth to soothe the horse, patting his neck. Then I returned my own weapon to my shoulder.

"Guten Tag." I murmured.

The man with the knife didn't move, but the shorter one on his right, with a graying beard, lifted his chin. I evaluated the situation and debated my options. I didn't like the looks of that knife, but the warm fire beckoned to me, and it had been years since I'd ridden a horse for any length of time. My backside could use a break.

"May I warm myself by your fire?" I asked in German.

No answer.

"Sprechen Sie Deutsch?" Do you speak German?

Their eyes darted between each other before returning to me.

"Ja." The short man spoke and let out a dry cough.

Finally, a response. "I am not here to harm you."

The short man seemed to relax and moved forward a step, but the knife holder held out his arm blocking the shorter man's approach. His face remained taut with anger and fear. The blue trousers that stuck out below their dark coats were similar to the men who had been forced to work at the factory, and, except for the boy, their faces displayed beards.

"Ich bin kein Nazi." I am not a Nazi, I said in my most soothing voice.

Still, no welcoming overtures. Like me, they were obviously on the run, and I understood their hesitation to greet a stranger riding a horse and carrying a weapon, even if it was a woman. Who was to say I wasn't a Gestapo spy sent to inform on their location? To my left stood a crudely constructed lean-to made of sticks, bark, and pine branches. Beside the fire sat two tin cups and what was obviously a military mess kit, most likely pilfered on their run.

"Never mind," I mumbled beneath my breath. *"Schritt, Franziska."* I whistled to the horse. He lumbered forward a few steps.

"Warten Sie." Wait. The short man pushed the knife holder's arm out of his way. *"Englisch?"*

My blood ran cold at my foolish mistake. However, I saw the man's hopeful expression and clicked at Franziska to pull him up. *"Ja."*

It was as though the spigot turned on full force. German babbled at me, and eventually I held up my hands to pause the flow. The short man approached the horse and helped me off while the boy went to hold his head. During the ride my ankle stiffened, and I was thankful for the help. Had he not given me a hand, it would have been a hard landing. As it was, I hobbled painfully over to a dead log fireside and held my hands toward the warmth.

"How did you find us?" The knife had disappeared back into the coat, but the man's expression remained wary, and he stayed on the far edge of the fire.

"Smelled it." We spoke in German.

The fear was back as eyes darted around.

"It is better to have a fire during the day, but you should really have a lookout. We are fairly deep into the woods, still I believe there is a village not too far away."

"About twenty kilometers that way." The short man pointed over his shoulder to the west.

"Is there *Heer*? *Waffen* SS? Gestapo?" I asked.

"*Ja, Heer. Gestapo?*" He shrugged his shoulders as if to say, "Who knows?"

I understood. The Gestapo was like ivy, growing in all directions, invasive, eating away at the foundations of German cities and towns.

The boy sat on a rock to my right and asked, "What is the name of your horse?"

"I call him Franziska."

"Franziska?" His face crunched up in thought. "But, fräulein, that horse is a boy," he said with such gravity that, for the first time in weeks, I smiled.

"You are correct. But he reminded me of a cook we once had when I was a girl about your age."

"Where did you get him?" knife man asked. "Stolen?"

"Actually, Franziska found me. We wandered into each other, you could say."

"He is strong, like a *Wehrmacht* draft horse. For hauling the big guns."

"Probably so." I didn't like how knife man's pugnacious eyes studied my mount. Rationing forced many Germans to survive on horsemeat, and though I understood the need to use whatever food could be found, I had no plans to allow my newfound friend to become dinner. His use as my transportation was far too important, and I made a mental note to keep my new companion within sight. I slipped the weapon off my shoulder, laid it across my lap, and removed my mittens. I had no interest in shooting anyone, but if I, or my horse, were threatened…

"Where are you headed?" the short man asked.

"*L'Alsace.*"

A look passed between the two older men, but the little boy gasped, "*Nein, nein,* fräulein, you shouldn't go there. It's too dangerous for a pretty girl like you."

"The Gestapo is not kind to spies." This from the knife holder.

"I do not imagine they are kind to Jews who have escaped the work camps … either."

No one moved. Eyes darted back and forth, but it was the boy's actions that affected me the most. He shrank away with a look that could only be described as too knowing for one so young. The inquisitiveness in his eyes went flat, and the animated expression smoothed into an impersonal drawn countenance. Upon observing his reaction, I immediately regretted speaking so baldly.

"How did you know?" the short one asked in quiet tones.

"I've been living the past few months in Oberndorf." I nodded at him. "Your clothes gave you away."

"I told you we should have stolen those uniforms," the knife holder snapped at the older man.

I had taken the man into dislike and wildcatted to the older man's defense. "That might have been fine for the two of you, but what about the boy?"

The dark glance he gave the urchin led me to believe the boy was with them by the grace of the older man. It was clear he saw the young one as a liability.

"Theft would have been noticed," I continued calmly, glad the child had been watching me and didn't notice the man's calculating look. "You would be better off going into town and acquiring some regular villager clothing. The beards are good if you didn't have them when you were at the work camps." I looked directly at the knife man's curly hair and full lips. His overly large nose was only accented by the hollow cheeks. "Your features are very Jewish. It would be best for you to stay behind."

"What have the Jews ever done to you?" he snapped at me.

"Not a thing. But I think we all realize *Der Führer* has deemed otherwise, and it puts you in danger." I looked toward the shorter man with the blue eyes. "Your features are far more Arian. If anyone needs to go into the village for supplies, it should be you and the boy. Children often go unremarked and can slip under the noses of the Gestapo," I said, remembering a nine-year-old French boy who had a knack for being in the right place at the right time and was able to provide the Resistance with intelligence he'd "overheard."

The man's laughter turned into a coughing fit. When it ended, his eyes crinkled with a genuine smile. "She is very astute, Jako. Thank you, child, you speak the truth. I am Gregor, that is Jako, and the little one, Dieter."

"You are Jewish," I stated.

"*Nein*, I am a Protestant minister."

"Minister?" I frowned. "I don't understand. Why were you taken to the camp?"

"My sermons on embracing *all* of God's children, including Jews, were deemed subversive."

My brows rose. "You're lucky to be alive."

"Much like you, I couldn't stand by and do nothing."

"Who is to say I am doing anything?"

"You are an English spy, no? Behind enemy lines. I do not believe you are here for the fresh air." He shifted and coughed again.

I didn't correct their assumption that I was English. The less anyone with whom I came into contact knew about me, the better. "What camp did you escape?"

He named a town I'd never heard of.

"Outside Frankfurt, we were assigned to a work group and sent to build Luftwaffe airstrips, for landing the planes."

"Even the boy?"

The boy listened attentively to our conversation as he slowly rotated the rabbits; fat dripped and sizzled on the burning wood.

"Even Dieter." He went into another coughing fit.

"You are ill, Gregor, and need medicine." I stated the obvious.

"Have you any?" Jako asked in a clipped manner, leaning to the side, as if to see through the dark leather of my rucksack that I kept strapped to my back.

"Unfortunately, no." My gaze returned to Gregor. "You are a minister. Have you tried approaching the village cleric? He might be able to help you. Give you shelter, medicine."

"Perhaps me, but what about my friends?" His hand arced through the air, encompassing Jako and Dieter.

"There's got to be some sort of resistance or underground that can help them get to safety."

"The Gestapo is unrelenting, and with the Allies moving closer by the day, villagers are not so willing to put their own families in danger. We cannot blame them. Though they may be willing to help a Protestant minister ... a Jew?" He shook his head. "The Nazis have put normal German people into untenable positions."

"I know," I whispered. The guilt over seeing the gaunt workers being herded like sheep from their barbed-wire-enclosed barracks into the factories every morning was something I had had to live with on a daily basis in Oberndorf. I used my intelligence gathering as a justification for my direct inaction to helping them.

"They have special treatment for spies ... if they aren't shot on sight. You should be careful. They can be particularly brutal with women," Gregor said.

Jako had picked up a stick lying by the fire and began whittling with the knife.

I nodded. "So I've been told." A few days after dropping into France, I hooked up with a group of French Resistance fighters outside of Le Mans. While we discussed sabotaging key rail lines inside the dank depths of a root cellar, a middle-aged fighter named Reynaud, whose wife and children were killed during the initial German invasion, pulled me aside. I can still remember the distinctive smell of his Gauloises cigarette. Its smoke wafted around us as he explained in no uncertain terms the type of treatment I would experience should I fall into the hands of the enemy. His dark eyes remained hard and unrelenting, and I didn't blink once as he spoke. The lecture, a shock to my then naïve sensibilities, stayed with me. Do not mistake, I didn't enter this war unprepared.

During my time in England, I was taught how to use a knife, familiarized with the varied weapons from German, Italian, British, and American armies, trained in hand-to-hand combat—with limited success—and had been given munitions training. I'd been woken in the middle of the night by men in German uniforms. Buckets of ice water were thrown at me along with interrogation questions as I stood in nothing but my nightgown. It had all been part of the training.

Nevertheless, Reynaud's words brought home, for the first time, that I would likely meet my death in a country that was not my own, and there remained a distinct possibility my demise would be gruesome and unimaginably painful at the hands of the enemy. Being shot in the head suddenly became a far more palatable way to go, and it was down in that dark room— between the smell of cigarettes and earth—that I decided I would try to provoke the enemy into shooting me immediately if I was ever caught.

"How far away did you smell the fire?" Jako flicked a shaving into the fire.

"Not far, maybe twenty meters."

"Have you a plan?" Gregor asked.

"Get to the front. Find a friend. Try not to get shot."

A log shifted amidst a shower of sparks and Gregor kicked it back into place. "The last is perhaps the most important."

"And the most difficult."

"Do you have help?"

"Once I cross the Rhine."

Jako gave a disbelieving snort. "You still have long way to go." He leaned forward, placing his elbows on his knees, and eyed me.

"It shouldn't be too difficult with Franziska." I gripped the gun in both hands and stared him down.

"The rabbits are almost done," Dieter chirped. "Will you eat with us, fräulein?"

Jako's eyes slid away. I had perhaps won this round, but I didn't trust him, and I'd come to the realization that I would gain no more information from this disparate crew. I did not believe Gregor would allow harm to come to me, but I doubted his ability to overpower Jako should he make a move toward the horse. And I had no interest in using up my single shot of ammunition by gunning down an innocent man who had already endured Lord only knew what kind of torments and was simply trying to survive. I also needed to make a plan for the night. The temperatures would be plunging, and I needed to find some sort of shelter; it would not be the tiny lean-to across the way with a boy and two men.

"*Nein, meine Kleine,* I must be moving on."

Dieter's face fell.

"Come, now, stay and eat with us. You have a long road ahead of you and will need your strength," Gregor enticed.

Jako's mouth flattened, most likely displeased at having to share his paltry catch with another mouth. As welcome as the meal would be, I hadn't interest in lowering my guard enough to eat around Jako and his deadly blade. I still had provisions in my pack, and besides, I imagined my portion would come out of Gregor's or Dieter's share, both of whom needed the nourishment more than I.

"Must you go already?" Dieter's pleading eyes seemed to beg for another friendly face.

"How about I stay for a few more minutes while your dinner finishes cooking?" I smiled at the imp and was rewarded with one in return.

Jako harrumphed.

"Who taught you your German? You have no accent," Gregor asked.

"I lived all over Europe when I was a child."

"Hasn't that made your … position difficult? Even more dangerous?"

He voiced a fear that I'd struggled with during my ship ride over to England. "You mean, did I ever run into someone who knew me as a child?"

Gregor's brows rose.

"Once. I looked very different when I was younger … knock-kneed with a narrow face and very blond into my teens." I glanced down at my canvas-covered knees thinking back to that alarming encounter in the colonel's house. The children and I had just walked in the door—I remember I'd gotten down to one knee to help Klara with the buttons on her coat—when the colonel stepped out of his study followed by Herr Heinberg. I rose as the colonel proudly introduced the children to his guest. It took me only seconds to recognize Heinberg, he'd grown a mustache and grayed around the temples, but the moment he bent to shake Dagobert's hand … I remembered. Fear shot through me like a lightning bolt. I stepped back from the tableau to distance myself, but the colonel insisted on introducing me. I waited for Heinberg to recognize me … call out … have me arrested. Instead, a gleam of male appreciation lit his face, and I knew I was safe.

"There was no flicker of recognition. The men never notice; it is the women I fear."

Jako's hollowed gaze narrowed as he studied me. "You are saying women are more observant, *ja?*"

I lifted my chin. "Perhaps."

"That is why they make excellent spies." Gregor held out

his hands and leaned closer to the heat of the fire.

"Who was he?" Dieter asked.

My gaze shifted back to the boy. "The man I recognized?"

He nodded.

"When I knew him, he was an insignificant government worker. He is now an important man in the Nazi Party."

Gregor helped Dieter remove the rabbits from the spit, laying them on a large, flat rock, and while Jako began cutting up portions, I decided it was a good time to take my leave. Gregor did not renew his entreaty to remain. I thought he had finally picked up on Jako's dislike of me, or perhaps he realized it was not safe for me to remain with their little coterie. The lad followed me to the horse, and I showed him how to hold his hands together to give me a much-needed boost onto Franziska's back. Once situated, I whistled him into his teeth-clacking trot to get away from Jako while he was still occupied with his meal. I couldn't take much of the uncomfortable jouncing, made worse without stirrups, so once we'd gotten far enough away and I knew we hadn't been followed, I slowed the horse back down to a walk.

Chapter Seven
Noah's Animals

Twilight fell, Franziska summited a hill, and we came out upon a verge to find a tiny village nestled in the valley. I didn't see any factories and wasn't sure if the village even had electricity. Like Gregor said, I saw no sign of a military presence, no trucks, cars, or motorcycles. As a matter of fact, I couldn't identify a main road into the hamlet, though there must have been one. Small, single-story dwellings with thatched roofs dotted most of the landscape, and I imagined, in the springtime, the acreage would be carpeted with verdant grass. In the center of the little town rose a white church spire. Picture perfect.

Had I been on foot, I would have snuck into the chapel after dark to seek sanctuary and escape the elements for the night. However, sneaking my enormous companion into a tiny town church seemed laughable, not to mention ill-advised. I searched for another option, and my gaze alighted on an outlying farm. A figure exited the barn carrying a lantern. The clothing identified the form as a woman. She navigated the snow-covered ground to a two-story brick house; the light disappeared as the wooden door shut behind her. I contemplated the gray weathered barn.

Darkness drew in swiftly, as it does in the winter months. Franziska and I waited patiently while the village quieted for the night. Lights flickered here and there, doors opened and closed, a dog barked, the scent of hearth fires drifted through the valley, and stars began their twinkling dance in the night sky.

I approached the barn from behind, hoping the structure would cloak Franziska's clopping steps. Our footprints created a path behind us, but it couldn't be helped. The moon rose; its light was alternately blocked and unobstructed as shadowy clouds drifted past. When we reached the barn, I hooked Franziska's reins over a nearby tree limb and snuck around the side to a normal human-sized door. The rusty metal latch squeaked when I lifted it, but the rough-timbered door swung silently into the barn. A chicken clucked and I heard the rustle of shifting hay. A quick flick of my lighter showed an average barn. Holding the light up high, I perceived a couple of goats, some chickens in racks up above an overhang, and a donkey's muzzle poking out of the stall directly in front of me.

The scent of hay, earth, and manure blended together in the cozy space. The barn brought welcome warmth from the outside temperatures that continued to plunge; I was relieved to be out of the bitter wind that had picked up after sunset. Further investigation revealed three unused stalls covered in straw. I found a pitchfork leaning against a post and took a few minutes to freshen the hay before leading Franziska through the door. It was tight, his mid-section barely fit through without scraping the sides, but I daren't open the large barn doors as they were in the direct line of sight of the house.

I didn't worry about the goats or chickens, but I feared the donkey would kick up a fuss. The bray from the creature would be heard like a foghorn across the valley. It was a tight corner, and Franziska and the donkey came nose to nose. The donkey stomped, and as soon as Franziska's rear end cleared the opening, I quickly pulled him down to the berth at the end. The donkey kicked the side of his stall and gave three quick snorts. Franziska snorted and shook his head up and down, his mane flying in different directions.

A soft lullaby that I used to sing to Klara at night when she cried for her mother filled the chamber with my mezzo-soprano voice. The song calmed Franziska, but the donkey shifted restlessly in his box and gave off a snorting whinny that threatened to turn in to a full-fledged, teeth-grinding bray. Once I loaded Franziska into his stall and closed the door, I went back to calm the donkey, using shushing noises and singing quietly. Above me the chickens rustled in their nests, and one of the goats gave a bleat. I strove to calm the environment that could, any moment, erupt into an all-out symphony of agitated animal racket that would surely bring the farmer and give me away.

My heartbeat pulsed in my ears, and I clenched my fists in an effort to maintain my own calm. The donkey was at the heart of the animals' edginess, so I tugged some fresh straw out of a hay bale and held it out to the restless creature while speaking German nonsense in a singsong voice. He seemed to grow less nervous as I stroked his nose, and taking the straw out of my hand, he turned away to masticate his treat. Pressing unsteady fingers against the pounding at my temples, I quietly made my way back to Franziska.

He'd found the fresh hay in the hayrack and was already eating. I pulled him back for a moment to remove the bridle, then allowed him free access to the meal. I didn't want to use up the fluid in my lighter, so I moved about the barn by the light of the moon shafting across the floor from the open door and a window in the front of the structure. However, when I closed the door through which Franziska and I had entered, the darkness almost completely closed in. Even with the window and my night vision, I had to feel my way down the walkway, back to where the horse stood.

My toe kicked against something hard that skittered into a nearby post. I bent forward, sweeping my hand back and forth, until my fingers contacted uniform metal prickles that I recognized even in the darkness. Franziska's head turned only once to look at me as I stroked the curry comb through his pelt before continuing his meal. A shiver of pleasure rippled through his muscles. I brushed by touch, skimming my other hand behind the comb, feeling for encrusted clumps it might have left behind. I think by the time I'd finished, most of the matted dirt had come clean, and having taken care of the horse, I was finally able to sit on a bale of hay to eat.

I had to use the lighter in order to find the tin of sardines in the rucksack. The residual tension of the day's events also had me opening the second bottle of bier. The alcohol warmed my belly, and the salty fish tasted satisfactory even though they were served on a flavorless stale cracker.

Finishing the last of the bier, I went outside and made my way to the back of the barn, where I found undisturbed snow to fill the bottle and relieved myself for the night.

The quiet, soothing sounds of the barn—rustling, a snort, animals breathing—relieved me. Franziska lay down among the straw, and I curled up against his back, wrapping myself with a small blanket, by the smell, I assumed belonged to the donkey.

How on earth did I end up here? The nonsensical thought flitted through my head. It was foolish because I knew exactly how I'd gotten here.

Chapter Eight
Getting Here

Spring 1942
Washington, D.C.

"I don't think you understand; the committee must take this situation seriously. Jews are disappearing by the dozens and we are doing nothing about it." My heels echoed against the marble floors while I walked double time to keep pace with the long-legged sixty-five-year-old politician.

"I've already addressed this issue."

"But, Senator, if you would just take a moment to read the letter." I shook said piece of paper.

The senator came to an abrupt halt in the domed rotunda of the senate office building, and I slid past him before coming to my own clumsy stop. "Young lady, there is simply no way I'm going to waste the committee's time with a letter from some childhood school chum of yours. I don't care who her father is related to."

His condescending tone flicked out at me like a whip and I flinched. I don't know why. I should have been immune to it by now. The senator's bullheadedness and refusal to listen to the opinions of any of the women in his office were legendary. For the most part, we'd learned to circumvent his prejudice by providing our opinions and advice to his chief of staff, a man who displayed an open mind and softer touch, and some of us had seen our ideas floated upriver to the senator and eventually the Senate Foreign Relations Committee, which the senator chaired. It was exactly what I should have done, but his chief of staff had traveled to the home office in Georgia for the week, and I deemed Camilla's fervent plea urgent enough to go directly to the senator.

"We are fighting a war on two fronts," he continued in his harsh tone. "We've got boys in the Pacific fighting the Japs and over in Africa fighting Nazis. Right now we have to pull together and support our soldiers. The committee doesn't have time to listen to a schoolgirl's fearful ramblings."

"She is an adult woman, and her father is a viscount," I said through clenched teeth with barely controlled irritation.

"I don't care who her father is. We simply don't have the means or manpower to investigate the, frankly, farfetched allegations she's making."

My expression must have shown my disconcertment, because his tone and face softened and he placed a fatherly hand on my shoulder. "You remind me so much of your mother—she passed her beauty and grace to you. I'm sorry, but there's nothing more I can do."

My shoulders deflated.

"Now be a good girl, and when you get back to the office, send Ruth over to the Capitol. I've some dictation for her." He patted my cheek, then turned and whooshed out the glass door before I could utter another sentence.

At five o'clock, I handed in my resignation to Ruth. Gray hairs escaped the chignon of her normally perfect coiffure, and her blouse revealed deep wrinkles built throughout the day. She removed her glasses, rubbed tired eyes, and sighed. "Are you sure you want to do this ... now?"

I glanced away from her disappointed expression. "I'm sorry, Ruth, I've got to do something more."

"What are your plans?"

"I … I'm not sure yet. I have heard the newspapers need photographers and reporters. I'm pretty good with my camera." I shrugged.

"Well, I'm disappointed you're leaving. Of all the young girls in the office, you're the only one gutsy enough to take on the senator when he's in one of his moods."

Thinking of my afternoon interaction with him, I grimaced. "I don't have quite the knack you do."

"Pshaw." She pushed her chair back and came around the desk. "You've got gumption, girl, and I'm sorry to lose you." She pulled me into her motherly embrace. "Let me know if you need a reference."

Unexpected tears rose and I cleared my throat before answering, "I will, Ruth. You take care of yourself."

The wheels of politics moved too slowly for my taste, and if I was personally going to make a difference for the war effort, I'd have to step outside my comfortable and sheltered lifestyle. As I walked past the Supreme Court on my way home, I paused to stare at the magnificent pillared building. Above the Corinthian columns, deep grooves engraved into the marble portico read, "Equal Justice Under Law."

Where was the justice in a man like Hitler?

It was time for me to fight for those whose country now trampled justice under its feet. I squared my shoulders and decided morning would find me at the local recruiting office.

A few hours later, my roommates and I stood around our secondhand coffee table, glasses in hand. "Jane, drink your champagne, and stop staring at me like I've grown a turnip out of my ear." I indicated with the bottle. "I know it will not be what I'm used to, but if I can manage the pitfalls of an English boarding school, I'm sure I can handle basic training for the

WACs." I laughed as the rosy liquid bubbled over the rim of the bowl-like glass and ran down my fingers.

"That's not what I'm worried about," Jane mumbled.

"Then what?" I snapped, irritated Jane wasn't showing the support I'd expected. The boxy brown dress she wore hung loosely off her shoulders because she'd recently lost weight, and her lipstick had been chewed off. And, looking closer, I could see the dark circles that had built under her eyes. Work must have been stressful at the law firm where she worked.

"It's just that ..."

Evelyn, southern sweet and always the peacekeeper, interrupted, "Don't fuss, darling, Jane is simply upset that you'll be leaving us. That's all it is. Honestly, I am too. I'm going to miss you." She clinked her glass against mine.

Jane opened and closed her mouth, took another sip, then her mouth quirked. "Evelyn's right, we are going to miss you."

"Thank you, ladies. I'll miss you too." I swallowed back a lump of sentimentality. "But ... after Milla's letter." I shook my head. "It's time I did something more for the war effort."

"I have an idea." Jane perked up, a beautiful smile transforming her face. "One of my co-workers is having a party. Let's change into some fancier togs and go out."

"A wonderful idea." Evelyn swallowed the last of her champagne and put her glass down with a firm clank. "I've got a new green dress that I've been dying to wear. Lily, you should wear the black and white, and borrow my spectators." Evelyn had a sharp eye for fashion, and we'd gotten used to accepting her advice because it invariably hit the mark. "And Janie, you always look chic in your blue cocktail dress. Since I took it in last week, it should fit perfectly on your figure."

An hour later, a cab dropped us off at an apartment building on Wisconsin Avenue, the first of three stops we'd make that night.

The next morning, I awoke with a fuzzy mouth, blurry headache, and Jane irritatingly shaking my shoulder.

"Wake up."

I rolled away, pulling the pillow over my head. "Go away, Janie."

"We need to talk before Evelyn returns." She snatched the pillow off my face.

"Why?" I groaned. "Where did she go?"

"To the bakery. Here"—she shoved a mug in my face— "have some tea. It will make you feel better."

Once she'd gotten me into a coherent sitting position, drinking the hot beverage, Jane explained that her boss, Mr. Barden, wanted to speak with me before I joined the army. I tried to bring his face to mind, but all I could remember was a nondescript man of average height. No remarkable features stood out, although some of my lack of memory could possibly … possibly be blamed on the champagne.

"Why? What business is it of his? Is this Edward's doing?"

"It has nothing to do with your stepfather," Jane assured me. "If you are determined to serve your country, there are better ways than joining the military." She grabbed my shoulders and shook. "You must understand, with your knowledge of French and German, you can do so much more than march around in military uniform and become a nurse. If you trust me, you'll take the time…" Jane's impassioned speech ended abruptly when the apartment door closed.

Evelyn sang out, "I have cinnamon rolls. Wake up, dearies."

The fact Jane refused to speak further with Evelyn in the apartment aroused my curiosity, and since I was in no particular rush to get to the recruiting office, I agreed to let her take me to the Willard Hotel that afternoon to meet her boss for lunch.

We'd walked around the Capitol building to catch the streetcar running down Pennsylvania Avenue. The crowded trolley forced Jane and me to stand at the rear holding on to the loops overhead. However, something wasn't right. The hairs on the back of my neck had been standing at attention since before we boarded. At the Sixth Street stop, I waited until the bell chimed, an indication that the lumbering vehicle was moving on, before grabbing Jane's hand and yanking her off the back steps at the last minute. The bumper of the trolley whisked past the tail of her coat, sending it swinging.

"Lily, what on earth are you doing? We could have been killed and now we're going to be late to the meeting." She pulled her hand out of mine and checked her watch.

As she spoke, I locked eyes, through the glass of the trolley's window, with a pinched-faced stranger who must have rushed to the back. Raising my hand, I flagged down an oncoming taxi.

"Get in, Jane. I'll explain once we're in the cab." Jane seemed relieved that I'd acquired another, faster, mode of transportation so quickly, and slid in beside me without further comment until I directed the cabbie to turn right on Sixth street and stay straight until hitting G Street. Once we rounded the corner, I relaxed and turned to my irritated and confused roommate.

"Mind explaining why we are taking the scenic route?" she drawled and crossed her arms.

I sighed and adjusted my hat. "You're not going to believe this, but I think we were being followed."

Her brows rose.

"There was a man lighting a cigarette, across from our apartment, when we left. He followed us for a block, turned, and then picked us back up in front of the Supreme Court building. He dogged our steps all the way to the streetcar and then got on after we did."

"Perhaps he just wanted to ride the trolley."

"Maybe, but every time I looked at him, he looked away and he stayed at the front of the streetcar ... until our untimely exit. He must have rushed to the rear, and he gave me a deadly look as the street car pulled away. You didn't notice him?"

Jane made a moue with her mouth and tapped her chin in thought.

"You don't believe me? You think I'm being unreasonable?"

She blinked and shook her head. "It doesn't matter. We're safe, and even taking your roundabout way, we should arrive on time." She leaned forward to direct the cabbie to turn left on Fourteenth Street and drop us at the Willard.

The taxi pulled to a halt in front of the limestone staircase at the stroke of twelve, and a negro porter opened our door. "Do you ladies have luggage in the trunk?"

"No, we are here for lunch," Janie responded.

We climbed the red-carpeted steps into one of the finest and oldest established hotels in Washington, D.C. Jane gave her name to the maître d', and we followed him to a solitary table in a cozy nook. Jane's boss rose to his feet as we approached.

"May I take your coats, ladies?" the maître d' asked.

We removed our gloves and wraps, handed them over, and settled ourselves, Jane on my left and her boss directly on my right.

"What would you ladies like to drink? Wine? A cocktail?

"I'll have a coffee with cream," Jane responded.

I followed Jane's lead and declined the wine. "Coffee as well, sugar, no cream."

"And you, sir?"

"Another scotch on the rocks." Barden indicated the glass in front of him, empty but for a few chunks of ice.

"Very good, sir." The maître d' bowed himself off and we were finally left alone with Jane's boss. And alone we were indeed. The only other patron sitting near us was a businessman in a dark suit three tables away. The rest of the patrons were grouped at tables near the front of the dining room.

"So good of you to join us today." He smiled. The smile didn't reach his eyes, but that was not what stood out. He studied my face and form as if viewing me under a microscope, his gaze acute and sharp.

I didn't recall him regarding me so astutely the night before, and I refused to allow the scrutiny to unnerve me. I straightened my spine and threw back my shoulders, meeting his bold gaze. "Thank you for the invitation, Mr. Barden."

The waiter arrived and placed salads in front of us.

"I pre-ordered. Forgive my presumption, but I figured you ladies might be late."

Nothing about this man's bearing seemed to give any indication that he was actually apologizing, rather the words were simply platitudes. For some reason, his attitude got under my skin.

I picked up my fork and spoke before Jane. "Not at all, I was just telling Janie this morning that I was due for some vegetables and"—I stabbed a piece of iceberg lettuce, probably cut from the core of the head—"white lettuce. Have you taken the liberty of ordering our entire meal?" I batted my lashes and gave a *Mona Lisa* smile. "Or are we silly little girls allowed the rare treat of ordering for ourselves?"

I felt rather than saw Jane's jaw drop at my rudeness, but my comments finally broke through the overconfident veneer.

Mr. Barden relaxed his posture and chuckled. "Jane, you never mentioned how charmingly blunt your roommate was."

My face flamed and I curled my lips in.

"I … uh … I apologize Mr. Barden," Jane muttered.

"No, no need to apologize. Waiter, please tell us your specials and bring menus for the ladies. They will be choosing their own entrees.

The stiff, white-coated waiter—who shifted nary a brow at the conversation that just passed before him—bowed. "*Oui, Monsieur.* Today the chef has prepared a savory duck a l'orange, grilled flounder with broccoli and cauliflower florets, and squab in a brown sauce."

I recognized the man's accent as French and answered in his native language. "What comes with the duck?"

"Petite peas with creamed onions," he responded in French.

"I'll have the duck."

"*Oui,* and for you, *Mademoiselle?*"

"I'll take the flounder," Jane replied, taking a sip of the coffee that had just been placed at her elbow by a different waiter.

The first waiter looked at Mr. Barden. "I'll stick with the filet and potatoes."

"Very well." The waiter exited our nook.

"Jane tells me you speak multiple languages. Tell me about them."

"I speak French, German, and some Italian. Although, we were so young when I lived in Italy, my Italian is rather parochial."

"Where did you learn your German?"

"In Bavaria, Germany, and Vienna, Austria. Why?"

"And your French?"

"Lyons."

"Mm-hm." He nodded, tapping his blunted nails against the tablecloth.

"So when you speak, it is the French of France."

"Yes, of course, what else?"

"Not the French of New Orleans, or from school."

Realizing what he was getting at, I smiled. "Yes, I see. No, I didn't learn in a schoolroom … well, no, that's not exactly true. I suppose you could consider the Swiss finishing school a classroom. However, I never got my fingers rapped for my accent by Madame Dubois."

"Madame Dubois?"

"She taught flower arranging."

His cheek quirked up.

"Why do you ask? Are you interested in my translation skills for your firm? If so, I'm sorry to inform you that you are wasting your time. I am determined to join the army, if they'll have me, to do my part for the war effort. I tried to explain that to Jane this morning." I turned to her, but she wouldn't meet my gaze, instead keeping her profile toward me. Barden simply continued to watch me with a contemplative expression.

"She successfully identified and evaded the tail you put on us this morning," Jane said, ignoring my comments.

"Did she really?" He crossed his arms and leaned back. The intensity from before returned.

"Tail? You saw it too, didn't you? I knew there was something off about that fellow." I pointed a finger at her. Then I realized what had been said, and my finger faltered as I looked back to Barden. "You had a man tailing us? Whatever for?"

"What if I told you I wasn't a lawyer?"

I tilted my head as I tried to figure out what kind of game we were playing.

"What if I told you I worked for a special government department that needed people like you?"

"To be honest, I would tell you that I had already worked in a government office—a rather nice one, as a matter of fact—and had no plans to return to a desk. Things are happening in Europe that the United States simply doesn't understand. Hitler isn't just expanding his empire; he's persecuting an entire race of people he's deemed as less than human. I need to help those I once knew in Europe, and I think the only way I can do that is by joining the military."

"What if I told you could do that in my department?"

"And what department would that be?"

"Coordinator of Information office."

I shrugged. "Never heard of it."

"It's new. Have you heard of MI6?"

"British Secret Intelligence? Yes..." I was rather surprised he had. MI6 was a national secret, and I only knew of it due to an overheard conversation at one of our duty stations in England.

He tilted his head.

"You mean this Coordinator of Information office is going to become the American branch of the British Secret Service?"

"Not a branch of ... our own."

My gaze swung to Jane and for once she looked me in the eye. "You're not a secretary for a law office?"

"No."

"What do you do then?"

Her eyes darted to Barden. He nodded and she turned back to me to answer, "Intelligence."

The picture began to clear, as if a rainstorm had passed overhead and the clouds drew apart. "When you told me that I could serve my country … this is what you meant? Spying?" I said the last word in a hoarse whisper.

Jane's brows rose.

I sipped my coffee and digested the ramifications of the offer in front of me. Camilla's letter came to mind and my brain traveled no further. This was how I would help my friend. This was how I could obtain the justice I so valiantly sought. "Mr. Barden, what if I told you I had a letter in my possession that I thought could be useful to your office?"

"I'd be very interested in seeing this letter."

I set the cup down so firmly it clanked against the saucer. "Where do I sign?"

Four days later, I reported to a ramshackle office in Rosslyn, Virginia, and thus began my training as an agent for what would become the Office of Strategic Services.

Chapter Nine
The Naiveté of Youth

February, 1945
Germany

A girl's soft, whispered voice wended its way through my dreams, her questions unclear, and in my vision, I leaned forward over the prickly hedgerow of our house in Bavaria, straining to hear the words she spoke. A whicker brought me out of my nighttime hallucinations, and the voice became clearer as I woke from the depths of sleep.

My living heater had risen sometime in the night, and I'd coiled into a ball beneath the miniscule blanket to stay warm. The sun had yet to rise, though the darkness had eased, casting the barn into an ashen light. Franziska was back at the hayrack, his stall door open, and to his right stood a girl I estimated to be no more than eight or nine, stroking his neck. A long, dusky braid hung down the back of her navy coat, and she continued to whisper softly to the horse.

I pushed myself into a seated position, and the braid swung out as the girl jumped away from Franziska with a small cry of alarm.

"*Guten Morgen.*" Good morning, my rusty voice ground out. I yawned and stretched, subtly burying my weapon deeper into the straw.

"I did not see you there." The child had put a hand to her throat as she watched me.

"*Mein Name ist Anna.*" My name is Anna, I said with a friendly smile. "I am on my way to see my aunt in Heidelberg. She is ill." The lie rolled off my tongue as cleanly as soap off a newly washed dish. "The snow covered my trail and I got lost. It was late and we sought shelter in your barn for the night. What is your name?"

If she thought my attire odd, she didn't comment on it. Instead, her attention returned to my four-legged friend. "My name is Gertrud. Is this your horse?"

"*Ja.* Do you like him?"

"He is quite large, isn't he? What do you call him?"

"Franziska."

She gave me a sidelong glance but didn't question me further.

"You're up early, aren't you?" My watch told me it was barely half past five.

She gave the horse one last pat, then picked up a metal bucket that I hadn't noticed before. "It is time to milk the goats and collect the eggs. My chores."

"Ah." I rose on stiff legs and limped forward as I followed her to the pen that held three goats, all with heavy udders.

She poured grain into a small trough, then opened the gate and allowed one of the goats out. The goat went directly to the trough to begin feeding. Gertrud looped a collar around its neck and pinned it to a ring on the wall, then sat on a small box. Soon the tinkling of milk spray against the metal bucket could be heard.

I rotated my ankle to stretch out the stiffness and watched her pull the teats. The pain level had reduced, and I could put all my weight on it with far less discomfort than yesterday.

"Would you like some?" She looked over her shoulder at me.

I shrugged.

"There's a cup over there." She used her chin to point.

My eyes followed the area she indicated and found a tin cup hanging from a post of an empty stall. I wiped the inside with the corner of my coat before handing it to her, and after a few squirts, she returned it. I'd never drunk raw goat's milk; it had a warm, creamy texture, sweeter than cow's milk. Normally, I wouldn't have a problem with it, especially knowing the nourishment it provided would help sustain me through the next steps in my journey. Unfortunately, it clashed with my late-night meal of sardines; goat's milk didn't go well with the oily-fishy aftertaste that curdled on my tongue. However, I didn't wish to insult Gertrud and stalwartly swallowed, but I had a hard time not gagging as it went down.

"Good?"

"Mm…lovely," I murmured, using my sleeve to wipe away a few drops that dribbled down my chin. "Don't you have brothers or sisters to help with the chores?" Farms like this usually had a brood of children to help run it.

"It used to be my brothers' chore, but two died in battle, and the youngest just left to fight the Russians. So, now it is mine."

"I see."

"My *Mutti* says to me, 'Gertrud, you are no longer a baby, you are a big girl, and because your brothers have gone off to fight and become heroes, you must do their chores.'" She returned to the task at hand. "After all, we all must do our part to bring about a New Order in Europe. My *Vati* says we must do as the Nazis say because the *Der Führer* is dangerous, even though *Mutti* tells him to hush. But I think the boys at school look handsome in their uniforms, and I want to do what I can to make Germany the greatest country in the world. If that means the Jews must leave, then so be it." She shrugged and continued pulling the goat's teats.

"How many men from your town are in the war?"

"Lots! We have Waffen SS and *Heer* soldiers, and even a Luftwaffe pilot. Have you heard of Hans Geffen? *Nein?* He has been shot down twice and survived. He is our local hero. He is very handsome," she said with a giggle.

"Well, you seem like a good daughter. Your parents must be mighty proud of you," I said with a smile I'm sure didn't reach my eyes.

Gertrud's little speech told me all I needed to know. This village, at the very least this farm, was submissive to the Nazis and their Nationalistic propaganda. It was not a safe place for me to look for assistance. I now regretted suggesting Gregor come into town to ask for help from these people. Gestapo or no, this town had children and husbands at the front whom they would support at any cost. Jews were unwelcome, and a spy was likely to be hung from the local church steeple.

I determined to make preparations for an immediate departure. First order of business, keep Gertrud talking and delay her chores. "Tell me about your schooling. What is your favorite subject?"

As Gertrud chattered about her schooling preferences, I returned to the stall to pack up my rucksack and put Franziska's bridle on. Unfortunately, the ankle, though better than the day before, still slowed my movements down. After buckling it in place, I looked up and found Gertrud watching me, the bucket of milk hanging at her side.

"Are you leaving?" She tilted her head.

"Have you finished the milking already? My, that was fast." I readjusted one of the bridle clasps.

"Yes, but I must collect the eggs. Aren't you coming in for breakfast?"

"*Nein*, I don't wish to be a burden to your *Mutti* and *Vati*. Besides, I must continue on to my aunt. Like your parents need you, my aunt needs my help to take care of her children."

"Where is your saddle?"

Luckily, having taken care of two children for the past few months, I was ready for Gertrud's inquisitiveness and had a lie prepared. "We donated it to the cause, of course."

She sighed. "Johann, my brother, took our horse and the saddle, and the Waffen SS took the other two, so I haven't one to give you."

As we stood talking, the barn became noticeably lighter, and soon the pink rays of dawn would be upon us. I needed her to return to the chores so I could slip the gun out from under the pile of hay where I'd hidden it. I feared her reaction should she see me picking up the weapon, yet she seemed in no hurry to carry on with her business.

"Your *Mutti* is waiting. Shouldn't you get to those eggs?"

Gertrud shrugged. "She isn't up yet. Not until the cock crows."

Internally, I grimaced. Just what I needed, a chicken alarm clock announcing the break of day and possibly my getaway.

"Perhaps you can show me how it's done?"

"It's easy." She plopped the bucket down right in front of the stall's exit. "Follow me."

I shifted the bucket aside with my foot and followed her to the chicken lofts. A ladder I hadn't noticed lay on its side. Gertrud placed it against the wooden header, hung a basket on her arm, and climbed up to the chickens. I took a step back and froze when Gertrud turned, smiling proudly, with a speckled milk-chocolate-colored egg in her hand.

"Here, take one." She bent down and held it out.

"*Danke*," I murmured.

"Would you like to try?"

I shook my head. "I'm afraid of heights."

This made Gertrud giggle. "*Mutti* is too." Her demeanor suddenly turned serious. "But how do you ride your horse?"

The girl was too quick for her own good. "Oh ... I'm afraid of that too, but it can't be helped. We must do what we can for the war effort, even if we fear it."

She nodded with the gravity of a thirty-year-old, then resumed her egg collection. I returned to Franziska's stall to retrieve the gun and to wrap the egg up so it wouldn't get broken in my backpack. I filled the tin cup I'd used for the goat's milk with hay and lay the egg in the nest. There was no mounting block; instead I lined Franziska against the wall and climbed atop the stall door. It put me at the perfect height for mounting him. I threw my stiff leg over his back and slowly lowered my sore rear end and tender thigh muscles. My breath blew out in a few short pants as I adjusted to the discomfort.

Saddle-sore was a misnomer. It was just as painful without one. "Gertrud, can you open the barn door for me?"

Children are notorious for wanting to be helpful to adults, and from my discussion with this little girl, I had little doubt she would do as I asked without question. She climbed down the ladder, skipping the last three rungs to jump to the ground, and bounced to the big barn door. It must have been well oiled because it barely made a noise as she swung it open. Coming abreast of the child, I pulled up and leaned down to place a few *Reichsmark* in her hand.

"For you. Thank you for the milk and egg. Shh ... don't tell *Mutti* and *Vati*." I winked.

Gertrud's face lit up and she happily tucked the coins into

her apron pocket. "*Danke*, fräulein." Then she clicked her heels together, stood at attention, and shot her right arm out in a stiff salute. "*Heil Hitler.*"

Having become immune to this address that had become equally used as a greeting and farewell throughout Germany, I returned her salute with a tepid one of my own. "*Heil Hitler.*" The cock's screeching crow rent the air and had me practically jumping out of my skin. Franziska hardly blinked, simply tromping forward into the new dawn rays.

"*Auf Wiedersehen.*" Gertrud waved as we clopped away.

I waved and glanced one last time over my shoulder before entering the gloomy forest. Gertrud stood at the door of the farmhouse, and it looked as though she was speaking to someone. I suspect one of her parents had come looking for their delinquent daughter. Knowing Gertrud's vociferous nature, I prayed the money I gave her was enough to buy her silence and keep the wolves at bay.

A good night's rest and fresh hay made Franziska frisky, and I gave him enough head to take us cantering into the windblown hills.

Chapter Ten
Dogfight

Another frozen stream lay in our path; the late-morning sun's rays bounced off the glassy ice. I whistled Franziska to a halt and drew my leg over his rump, landing with most of my weight on my good foot. Gertrud's early-morning chores had given me no time for eating or washing up. The brook ran fluidly beneath the thin layer of ice, which broke easily under Franziska's weight. I emptied the tin mug of its treasured egg and filled it with the crisp mountain water. The liquid quenched my thirst, and after draining two cups full, I refilled it and left it on a wide, flat rock while I gathered kindling and wood to light a fire. Franziska helped himself to the stream, and I offered some straw that I'd taken from the barn, but still full from his morning meal, he took only a small amount before turning away. I fastened his reins to a nearby tree branch, though I'm not sure it was necessary. Franziska showed little interest in wandering far from me.

The fire caught and smoke soon snaked its way upward. To my relief, the flame was small enough that the smoke dissipated amongst the pine-needle-covered branches above. I gently dropped the egg into the water-filled cup and placed it on the flames. Soon the liquid boiled merrily over the edges as the egg bounced around the tiny container. The small blaze blackened the outside of the cup, but I didn't care. Its blessed warmth and the anticipation of a meal that wasn't oily fish or dry meat had me thanking the heavens for small favors.

Seven minutes later, I wrapped a mitten around the handle to pull the vessel from the dissipating fire, and utilizing a bone-white stick, worn clean by the weather, I flipped the egg out into my covered palm and rolled it back and forth to cool it before peeling. The egg was cooked to perfection. A hint of softness in the center kept it from being too dry. I remembered another time when my roommate had watched, with a skeptical eye, as I boiled my morning breakfast into a shameful rubbery ball. After my third attempt, Evelyn laughingly took pity on my wretched culinary skills and taught me the secret to making the flawless soft-boiled egg. I sent up a silent thank-you to Evelyn as I swallowed the last bite.

From my coat pocket, I pulled out the pristine-white handkerchief, provided to me by the young Stormtrooper on the bus, and plunged the cloth into the still-warm water, then used it to vigorously wipe down my face and hands. The heat soothed my puffy, fatigued eyes, and I held it there, enjoying the calm it brought. I pulled the scarf from my head and unwound the braids, combing through the wavy curls they had created. My hair was due for a wash; it was dirty from the trip and my own natural oils. I used the warm water, drawing it through with the comb, hoping its tines would draw out some of the grime. After re-braiding it, I tied the scarf around my neck, Girl Scout–style, to allow my hair to air dry. I picked up the handkerchief again and stared at the material, running my fingers over the damp cotton fibers.

Dornstetten seemed a lifetime ago.

My perilous journey was now into its fourth day, and every moment that I paused to rest or eat made the information in my boot and head less valuable to the Allies. The attention to ablutions suddenly seemed silly. I swiftly jammed the hankie into my pocket and doused the fire with one last cup of water.

Less than an hour later, Franziska and I came upon a street running east-west, and I decided to take my chances with it. It would leave us more exposed, but the road would be faster than going up and down through the sylvan foothills.

The monotony and quiet were unexpectedly broken by three German Luftwaffe planes followed by American fighter pilots that soon engaged in air combat. The planes zoomed around, in and out of sight, and the *rat-a-tat* of machine gunfire, like hail on a tin roof, could be heard throughout the forest.

A *boom-boom-boom* rent the air, sending Franziska bucking and shying. My hands pulled on the reins, and it took all the strength my legs possessed to stay atop him. The bunker from which the flax gun was shooting couldn't have been more than a kilometer away and came from behind me in the forest I'd just bypassed. I must have missed it by meters. Unbelievable that I hadn't seen it, and sheer luck that a patrol hadn't caught me as I passed it.

Franziska was finally under control when an American plane banked above me. A metallic screech had me flinching as the right wing ripped apart under enemy fire. The engine burst into flames before flying out of my sight, but I could still hear the roar of the aircraft as it plunged earthward. An explosion rocketed through the air, shaking the ground, and a plume of black smoke trailed into the sky. The acrimonious stench of burning metal and fuel filled the atmosphere. Sounds of the dogfight and the flax gun shifted south, and as Franziska and I rounded a corner, I could have sworn I saw a canopy from a parachute drift down among the trees not too far ahead.

We were still fairly deep into the forest, but the road had begun sloping downhill. I had a feeling we would be out of the rolling hills and valleys of the Black Forest and into the flats of the Rhineland before nightfall, which meant I'd be running into more populated areas and German fortifications.

I spurred Franziska into a canter and we crested the next rise. What met my gaze had me pulling and whistling Franziska up short. He skittered sideways and nipped at my pants, showing his displeasure with my rough treatment of his mouth. I absentmindedly patted and soothed him as I took in the sight. In the middle of the road hung the American pilot, his parachute and its ropes twisted among the canopy of trees. His head hung limp, helmetless, as blood dripped from a cut on his forehead— drip, drip, onto his boot and from his boot to the ground. His suit had been ripped and torn, and his left leg was bent at an odd angle, the foot wound up in one of the ropes. Protruding from the top of his right boot was the wooden hilt of a knife. It dangled, just on the edge of the boot, as though the pilot had been in the process of retrieving it before passing out.

Tentatively, I gripped the toe and gently shook his leg. The knife toppled from its precarious perch, missing Franziska's shoulder by millimeters, and clattered to the ground. It only took a moment to dismount and fetch the knife. Pulling Franziska to a tree stump, I remounted.

Many of the ropes were too high for me to grasp, even on Franziska's back. If I'd had stirrups, I would have been able to stand to reach them, but I was no circus performer, and there was no way I would dare to climb on Franziska's back and attempt to balance. With one hand, I held the reins, and with the other, I stretched and sawed at any rope that came within my touch. Franziska wasn't an overly fidgety horse, but he did have a tendency to shift at just the wrong moment. Finally, I cut the cord wrapped around the pilot's left leg, and he shifted down. One last tug, and the silk parachute ripped asunder and the airman fell to the ground.

I slid off the horse and did not bother to tether him.

Throwing my mittens aside, with shaking fingers, I searched in vain for a pulse.

"No, no, no, no," I fervently whispered.

I swept aside the longish bangs. The gash on his forehead didn't seem to be enough to kill him. Granted, it bled a fair amount, but it wasn't all that deep. It looked like something he got falling through the trees. I'd patched up worse when Dagobert had jumped from his bed a la Tintin. Neither could the broken leg have taken his life. I unzipped and pulled apart his leather jacket to find his clothes covered in congealing blood, and the answer to my question. A two-inch piece of metal shrapnel stuck out of his chest. Even if I had been a heart surgeon, I doubt I could have this man's life.

An inside pocket revealed the photo of a pretty blond girl with a sunny smile. I flipped it over, but there was no inscription. Tears came unbidden as my bloodstained thumb glided across the raised letters of his dog tags.

David O'Leary … Christian … A positive blood type.

My blood type.

Powerlessness threatened to overwhelm me. I fell onto my haunches against the hard ground and covered my mouth with the back of my hand to suppress the sob expanding in my chest and rising up my throat.

There was no reason to cry. *It's not as though I knew him.*

Death ran rampant through the war. But for some ridiculous reason, I'd gotten it into my head that I could save this pilot. As though his plane crashing practically on top of me was a sign from above that I could save a life. As though I could be heroic—a foolish thought.

Franziska brought me back to earth by nosing my shoulder. It was just a ghost of a sound drifting across the wind, but the horse's senses were far better-attuned than mine. The rumble of a vehicle reverberated in the distance. Someone had probably seen the parachute and was coming to investigate.

There was no time for this superfluous breakdown.

Swiping the tears away, I snapped off one of David's dog tags, dropped the knife next to his out flung hand, and took a precious few moments to relieve him of his snub-nosed .38 revolver, holster and all, and shoved everything into my coat pockets. If there had been time, I would have searched the body for more necessities, but already the engine's noise grew closer.

Franziska must have sensed my panic and wouldn't stand still. We went round in circles, like a child's dreidel, as I tried to pull myself up. Finally getting ahold of his mane, I heaved myself onto his back and threw my leg over. The roar of the truck was almost upon us, just one or two more curves before we'd be in sight. I whistled and kicked, whipping Franziska into a galloping frenzy that had us flying down the hill and around the corner. Gripping one of the reins, the other having dropped free, and his mane with both hands and tightening every muscle in my knees and thighs, we thundered down the road. I crouched low and stuck to him like a cocklebur. The noise of Franziska's hooves covered my own gulping sobs.

Chapter Eleven
Oskar

Evening approached and with it the comfort of nightfall. Franziska and I had taken to the trees again to bypass a checkpoint along the road and circumnavigate a German encampment. Both of which had me traveling much farther north than I wished.

After tethering Franziska and leaving what was left of the hay, I stealthily made my way to the outskirts of the town of Bühl in hopes of finding another place to spend the night. Steel-colored clouds had rolled in through the day. They hung heavy in the sky and the scent of snow drifted in the air. Disappointment flooded my system, chilling my blood like a cold bath. Instead of another sleepy town, there was a heavy military presence encamped in the surrounding fields and bustled through the narrow streets. Reality settled in—taking the slower, roundabout way through the forest had spared me much of their presence, but it was only a matter of time before I ran into the war machine, especially approaching this close to the front lines.

My heart sank further as I watched two more infantry battalions roll into the small town and set up shop. Officers shouted orders, men scurried around, more tents went up, and industrial-sized kitchen pots filed into a church; it wasn't too long before a chow line formed. Patrols would be sent out in the night. It was likely there were already two- and three-man patrols scouting the woods right now. I'd have to be very careful.

During all the activity, I continued to survey a little farmhouse in the southwest corner of the village. The company never approached, and during the time I surveilled the location, neither did it show any civilian activity. Even amidst the Nazi army, it seemed a prime location for me to hole up for the night. Although, I wasn't so sure Franziska would be sharing it with me. It would be difficult for me to sneak him into town unremarked.

I returned to Franziska with a heavy heart and apprehension in my soul. It was time for me to take the next steps to get into France. My journey would only become more perilous, and traveling through the populated area along the Rhine on his back was simply too dangerous for both him and me.

"You have been an excellent companion, my good fellow." I removed the bridle. "But I'm afraid our journey together ends here." I laid my cheek against his neck.

He shook his head as if relieved to be shed of the restraint. However, I could have sworn his eyes looked at me in askance, saying, "What's next?"

He watched with interest as I began my own trans-formation. To my disappointment, the men's pants had to go. I would miss their comforting warmth, but they made me look out of place. The dress, wrinkled beyond repair, was well covered by my now grimy coat. I hoped through time, and with the help of gravity, the wrinkles would even out. I retied the belt, which I'd been using to hold up the pants, around the coat to keep it closed over the dress. Luckily, the coat's dark coloring hid most of the dirt, and its length covered the dress. Unfor-tunately, there was little I could do about the smell of horse and every other scent that clung to me.

I re-covered my head with the scarf and debated what to do with the rucksack. It was out of place for a woman to carry such an item; however, it housed too much that I wasn't yet willing to part with. For the moment, I decided to retain it. Eventually, I'd probably have to ditch it and return to carrying the purse that currently lay squashed at the bottom. I eyed the faux brown alligator skin, then reached down and pulled it out, repacking it with my handkerchief, mirror, comb, and other sundry things I might need, including what was left of the deer jerky. I rested it at the top of the food and drink for easy removal. The American airman's sidearm, removed from its case, remained in my coat pocket, but I determined the rifle with its measly single bullet had to be left behind. The weapon was too visible, not to mention illegal, for me to carry without a permit. I buried the pants, bridle, and rifle under a downed tree, covering it further with sticks and dead leaves.

Franziska nosed my hand and I laid a cheek against his. "I'm sorry, Franzi, but this is where we must part. It is simply too dangerous for you." I kissed his muzzle. His long lashes blinked and the big brown eye viewed me with interest.

Twilight fell, and with a slap to his rump, I sent the reluctant horse on his way. I had to wait for him to move off on his own, because every time I walked away, his plodding footsteps soon followed. I didn't blame him. Depending upon who found him, he'd either be conscripted back into the military ranks or turned into a meal. I shuddered at the thought, but it couldn't be helped; our fates were no longer entwined.

I returned to my earlier hiding place in time to watch a three-man patrol enter the woods about two hundred meters east of my location, the flicker of their flashlights becoming brighter as the light waned. My mind quickly reviewed the hiding spot where I'd left the weapon and clothing. I reckoned it would be difficult to find in the daylight and nearly impossible at night. Of course, my biggest concern was for Franziska's safety. I closed my eyes and mentally shouted, "Run, Franziska, run!" After all, we had formed a close bond in the past few days. Who knew?—maybe he was tuned into my mental warnings.

I shook my head. Maybe I was losing my mind.

Darkness fell, and I made my move in fits and starts across the field before the moon rose, waiting apprehensively for a shot to ring out and strike me down as I stole behind a rock wall, a bush, a broken cart. The scent of cigarette smoke brought my dash to safety to an unforeseen halt, and I remained leaning against the listing farm wagon. My gaze combed the area for the owner. The soldier must have shifted into my line of sight, because as he took a drag, the red glow lit up, giving away his position. I could barely make out the two dark shadows leaning against one of the covered transport trucks—one of a dozen lined up. I remembered seeing it in the daylight, painted in camouflage greens and browns

The strike of a boot heel crunching against a rock in spitting distance had me hunkering down to the ground and mashing myself as close to the cart as humanly possible. If the wheel hadn't been broken and the cart listing, I would have crawled beneath it. As it was, I held my breath.

The officer approached the two men and they saluted. *"Zigaretten?"* A flame lit up his face, and the cigarette glowed red as he sucked in the smoke. The officer pulled papers out of his pocket. "New orders. Take the truck to Rheinau, tonight."

He turned and I couldn't hear the rest of the conversation, but the gist seemed to be a particular division was low on ammunition and supplies were being requested.

A flashlight switched on, and the three men hovered over a map as the officer pointed and gave directions to the small town on the Rhine River. Everyone saluted and the officer walked away.

One of the enlisted men finished his cigarette and dropped it to the ground. "Let's get this suicide mission done," he said before swinging himself up into the front seat. His partner soon followed.

My feet pounded against the ground, gaining speed, as the truck rumbled past. I gripped the tailgate with one hand, my toe got hold on the bumper, and I launched myself into the back of the truck, rolling hard up against the corner of a wooden box.

Ouch! I rubbed my shoulder. There would be a bruise there tomorrow.

The truck came to a halt, and I flattened myself beneath the bench where soldiers usually sat. A brief conversation between the checkpoint guard and the driver ensued before the gears shifted and grinded and we continued our bouncing journey.

An hour later, I slipped out of the back of the truck as it stopped in line at another checkpoint. The third since we left Bühl. Each a test of my nerves. Each had me breaking out in a cold sweat. The paperwork must have been in order; no one bothered to search the back of the truck at any of the stops. However, the checkpoints were nothing compared to the Allied strafing run the driver wildly dodged by driving off into a ditch that almost upended us. The heavy boxes were thrown around, and had I not been beneath the bench, one of them would have undoubtedly crushed me. I think the incident took ten years off my life.

We had turned south a few kilometers back. No illumination could be seen; even the transport truck driving away remained lightless, although the shadow of darkened buildings silhouetted against the backdrop of the sky. Ducking beneath my coat, I risked using my lighter to check the compass and orient myself.

Fat flakes of snow drifted down to land on my shoulders as I set off in a westerly direction. The Rhine was close—I swear I could smell the river waters from here—and I debated finding a place to hide until daybreak, but something drove me to get into France tonight. Being this close to the front lines meant that I'd have to be careful, not only of the *Heer* and SS but also the Volkssturm, civilians given the authority to act as Germany's National Guard.

Five days ago, my intelligence led me to believe that the Allies would be pushing through the Maginot Line and across the Rhine within the week. I figured by now my friends would be just on the other side of the river.

Rounding the corner of a building, I ran into my first obstacle. We bounced off each other with an "oof." I stumbled over the rubble and almost lost my footing.

The dark figure fell to the ground. "*Halt. Wer geht da?*" Who goes there?

I could have laughed at the clichéd question if the flashlight hadn't suddenly blinded me. "*Schalten Sie das Licht aus!*" Turn out the light, I commanded. "Do you wish for the entire British Army to see us?"

The light flicked off and the teenage boy rose.

"Who are you? What are you doing here?"

"I am Anna. Who are you?"

"Oskar." He gripped my arm and pulled me through the open door of the dilapidated building.

I didn't resist.

"It is my job to patrol this neighborhood district." Once in the bowels of the building, he flicked on his flashlight again, raking me with it before pointing its beam at the floor. "I don't recognize you."

"I ... I don't live here. I am on my way to France." My mind worked furiously to concoct a plausible story. "M-my sister was working as a teacher ... in Alsace, and we haven't heard from her in months. Mother begged me to find her and bring her home ... before the enemy captures her." I said the last in a frightened whisper.

"Do you have travel papers?" He wore civilian street clothes instead of the brown *Hitler-Jugend* uniform I would have expected from someone so young. Was he Volkssturm or something worse, a Gestapo spy? Or simply a boy trying to keep his home from being invaded by the enemy?

I shook my head. "*Nein*, they burned in a bombing raid."

"Where are you from?"

I froze. Not a single German town came to mind.

"I said, where are you from?" he demanded, waving his Luger at me.

"Freudenstadt." The name blurted out of my mouth. "I have been on the road for many days." The moment that name came out of my mouth, I instantly regretted it. I should have chosen someplace farther away from Oberndorf.

"You should return there. You are walking right into the frontline battle. It is lucky you have not been shot."

You have no idea. "My mother is distraught and it is important that I find my sister. See, I have her picture here." I pulled the photograph of O'Leary's girlfriend out of my pocket. My other hand remained shoved deep inside its pocket, tightly gripping the pilot's weapon, with my index finger wrapped around the trigger.

He looked at the photo, covering his flashlight so that the glow filtered through cracks he made with his fingers. "She is very pretty."

"When I think of the horrible things that could happen to her..." I shuddered.

"You realize she is probably dead," he said, not in a harsh way but rather a matter-of-fact tone.

"She is my sister ... I can't give up. I have to take a chance."

"How will you get past the *Siegfriedstellung* and cross the river?" He returned the photo.

"I ... I don't know." In my flight, I'd forgotten about the Siegfried Line, a wall that had been built during World War I and rebuilt before Hitler invaded France. It consisted of a combination of bunkers, water-filled trenches, and concrete triangles sticking up from the ground like teeth, built to be tank barriers. In the months since the Allies landed in Normandy, the wall had been reinforced as a last line of defense against the invading army. "I thought I could hire someone to take me. I ... I have some money." I looked at him through my eyelashes, and even through the dirt and filth of the past few days, my feminine wiles must have been working because I distinctly saw his face flush in the low light.

"How much?"

I named a sum that was respectable but not outrageous.

He hesitated and seemed to be wavering between the call of the money and his job, which should be to turn me in to the local police. I prayed he would take the money. I had no interest in shooting an innocent boy, but if it came to it, I wouldn't hesitate to use the weapon to save my own life.

"Follow me, and stay close. Don't talk."

He turned, but I caught his sleeve. "Where are we going?"

"To the river." He shrugged off my hand.

We picked our way through debris-strewn streets of a residential part of town, some of the homes blackened and burnt to a skeleton of what they once were, others with shattered windows missing large chunks as if a giant had taken a bite out of them.

He came to an abrupt standstill, barring my way with his arm. "Wait here," he said and disappeared around the end of the building.

I heard a quiet murmuring of voices and laid my head against the rough wooden siding, allowing my eyes to close for a moment. I wasn't sure if Oskar was aiding me or taking me to the police station to turn me in, but I couldn't pass up the possibility that he had been swayed by my sob story and took pity on my plight. Besides, I still had the .38 wrapped in my hand ready to pull it out at a moment's notice.

"Come on. No time for sleep. You wish to see your sister?"

My eyes snapped open to find Oskar unexpectedly close.

We wound through dubious side streets until we reached a patch of trees, and then mounds of concrete were in front of us. Oskar must have known where the bunkers were, because he wove us in and out, ducking behind this one and that, through some barbed wire that had already been cut, and we tiptoed between flooded trenches. Clearly this path wasn't a first for my new friend as he remained surefooted, moving us quickly without a backward glance. A hundred meters past the wall, the river opened up in front of me.

The frigid waters of the Rhine darkly snaked northward as it made its run downhill from the Alps through the valley of the Rhineland and would ultimately culminate at the mouth of the *Nordsee*. My guide paused, searching the darkness before starting down a set of steps onto the embankment. He motioned me to my knees, and we followed the bulkhead, crawling like babies until coming upon a short dock. The end of the dock revealed a dark shape that took the form of a low-slung wooden rowboat.

"You pay now."

"Whose boat is this?"

"It was my uncle's. He was killed in battle."

Speaking of battle, shelling could be heard to our north, and in the distance rose the glow of angry fire.

I looked at the tiny boat, then back at Oskar. "I'll pay you half now, half when we reach the other side."

He shook his head. "You'll take the boat yourself. Straight across is a beach. Pull the boat up to the trees and hide it. Understand?"

"Yes."

"You will need to watch out. There are patrols and soldiers. It is very dangerous once you cross over."

"What about the boat? Don't you need it?"

"Hide it, and bring your sister back with you. At midnight, three days from now, I'll signal with the flashlight if it is safe to cross. Three short flashes. You understand?"

"What if I haven't found her by then?" As soon as the question popped out of my mouth, I realized how silly it was, but a master stroke to allay any fears Oskar might have had of my intentions.

He shrugged. "Three days. That is all I can promise. The radio transmissions say the enemy is moving forward every day. We are not sure if the military can hold this position."

"Why are you helping me? You could get into big trouble for this … if the Gestapo finds out…" I didn't have to finish my sentence; we both knew what the Gestapo was capable of.

For a moment he didn't answer. "I have a little sister. If she were in trouble … I would do anything to save her."

Guilt over dragging this innocent boy into my lies clawed at me. "If anyone asks, you don't know what happened to the boat. Say it was stolen, and don't come back. The signal is too dangerous. Stay away."

I pressed the money into his hand.

"I will be here. Three days." Then he helped me down to the rickety boat.

My feet landed in a puddle of water. "I think it's leaking."

"Row fast."

I gazed up at the boy to find white teeth bright against the darkness.

"It's not leaking. It's a boat. There is going to be water." He showed me how to lock the oars into place. "The current is strong. Row upstream to counteract it. You want to land straight across; it is the safest location. Do you see that bridge? Do not allow the boat to drift that far downstream. There are big lights and machine guns on that bridge and they will shoot you. Understand?"

I gulped and nodded.

"*Viel Glück*. Remember, beware of the current. Upstream." He wished me luck, pointed with his finger, and gave a shove with his boot.

He wasn't kidding. By the time I reached the far side of the river, my arms were limp as cooked spaghetti noodles and my hands like raw meat. Even with the mittens on, I could feel the burn of painful blisters rubbing against the rough material. I barely had the strength to navigate the last few meters, and the berthing was anything but quiet. One of the oars whacked against a jutting rock, jerking it out of my hand and slamming into my breast. I couldn't hold back a yelp of pain as I clutched a hand against the injury. There was little time to process what happened. A moment later, the boat grated against the sandy bottom and came to a standstill. The other end still bobbed in the wake of the tide, and, fearful that I'd be pulled back out into the current, I clambered out the front and pulled with all my might on the bowline to tug the vessel out of the water far enough ashore. After it was almost completely out of the river, I collapsed onto the pebbly sand on my hands and knees.

My breaths came out in shallow pants between clenched teeth, and I fought against the misery. My body was so overwhelmed by pain and exhaustion. Feet wet and cold as ice cubes were in direct contrast to my hands hot with blisters, my arms and shoulders burning with fatigue. As I drew in each breath, my chest throbbed, and the ache in my head that started during the chaotic truck ride ratcheted up another notch. My gut twisted and I heaved. There was so little left in my stomach it was mostly bile. When the retching finished, I rested my head against the boat's frame, stretched my feet out, and pulled off the mittens to blow gently across the blisters. That tiniest bit of pain relief calmed my nerves. In a few minutes, my muscles relaxed and my breathing leveled out. The dampness of sweat now cooled against my feverish skin.

Eventually, I dozed listening to the flow of water, the creak of another boat moored nearby, and the grate of my own vessel against the sandy shoreline. No explosions, gunshots, or mortar fire could be heard. For once the war was quiet, almost peaceful.

The initial comfort of cooling perspiration turned into chilly goose bumps, and a shiver ran through my body, bringing me fully awake. Sunrise couldn't be far off, and I wanted to be farther inland, past the Maginot Line, when it did. Knowing I'd never return to it, like poor Oskar believed, I left the boat and crawled up the short beach once again into the relative comfort of the trees.

Except for the fact that I was in France, I had absolutely no idea where I was. The current had been much stronger than Oskar led me to believe, and I was a kilometer, or more, downriver from where I'd started. Either the machine gunners Oskar mentioned had been asleep or they simply weren't expecting someone to cross from Germany into France. The enemy would be expected to come from the opposite direction. What fool would be heading into the fray?

I walked, or stumbled would be a better way to describe the next period of time. Too exhausted to try to find a footbridge, I'd gotten soaked up to my thighs walking through a canal that ran parallel to the Rhine. The freezing waters bit at my skin, and the fluffy, innocuous snow flurries that had drifted down from the skies through the night turned smaller and began falling at a steady rate. My body shook and shuddered and my teeth chattered uncontrollably. My mind began to drift in and out of reality as I dragged my frigid, shattered frame onward, finally collapsing in a doorway of some sort.

I heard an exclamation and responded in the same tongue. "*Aide-moi!*"

There was heated whispering, and then my arms were pulled above my head and my body dragged over the threshold before the door closed with a snap. The next bit was a blur, recalled only in snatches of memory. A stooped figure helped me down a flight of stairs into a windowless room lit by a small, glowing brazier. Callused, work-worn fingers grasped at my coat, and I was stripped of my wretched wet clothes. A scratchy warm blanket wrapped around my body and weak tea forced down my throat, much of it splashing on the blanket.

"*Merci,*" I remember mumbling right before the bliss of oblivion enveloped me.

Chapter Twelve
Cat and Mouse

I didn't come out of sleep slowly by drifting into consciousness. I bolted straight up with a start and completely disoriented. A frisson of fear shot through my body as I searched for familiarity. Beneath me lay a pallet covered with muslin ticking. Rough bricks covered the floor, and a damp, earthy smell led me to believe I was below-ground in a cellar. Except for my necklace, I was naked beneath the blanket. A little coal stove gave off enough warmth to comfortably heat the chamber. Further investigation revealed my coat hanging on a nail above the heater and my other clothes scattered across a drying line strung the length of the narrow room. The coat was almost dry, only damp in a few places. My nylon underthings were dry to the touch, and I put them on. The dress dripped wetly on the bricks below, not just at the bottom but all over. I had a feeling my hosts had taken it upon themselves to clean the miserable thing.

I shook my hair. The braids had been released and it curled damply around my ears. Holding my hands in front of the brazier, I turned them back and forth, revealing pink skin, a little raw, but cleansed of the sand and grime. The angry blisters, still painful to the touch, glistened with some sort of greasy balm.

How long have I been here?

My question was soon answered as the door opened and footsteps clunked down the stairs. I scrambled to pull the blanket back around my shoulders.

The head remained bent, watching every step, holding the rickety handrail in one hand and an oil lantern in the other. It didn't look up until reaching the bottom. When the stooped figure beheld me, it drew to a halt.

The word crone came to mind—hands gnarled and swollen with arthritis that came from age and hard work. The wrinkled face peering at me, protruding between hunched shoulders like a turtle out of its shell, decried her many years on this earth.

"You are awake," she stated in a wheezy voice. Her French accent was of a country dialect and I had difficulty understanding it.

"*Oui*. Where am I?"

"Not far from Drusenheim. Who are you?"

"I am searching for my sister. She was a teacher in Alsace." I pulled the blanket tighter to my shoulders.

Her sunken black eyes stared, giving little away. "Come, child, let us not mince words. You washed up on my doorstep soaking, exhausted, without papers, and carrying nothing except this gun in your coat pocket." She held the weapon with two fingers, by the grip, upside down.

Nothing? My eyes searched the tiny room for the rucksack, my lifeline throughout this ordeal. It wasn't to be found. *Did she take it? Where did I see it last?* I'd removed it to row that dreadful leaking boat across the river. But I slung it on my back when I set off into the woods. *Didn't I? DIDN'T I?* I had no recollection of its weight pulling on my shoulders as I staggered through the night, and I could picture it sitting across from me on the short bench spanning the craft's stern.

There were no identifying papers and the purse generic enough. The rucksack, a simple brown leather affair, its only identifying mark the initials H.H., held nothing that would tie me to it. Still, the boat was bound to be found, and leaving the materials behind was ill-done. I must have been out of my head last night to have allowed it to happen. *Thank heavens the gun was in my pocket.*

"This is not a German weapon. Who are you? A remnant from the *Résistance?* Perhaps a Jew? You needn't be afraid. I am no friend of the Nazis."

Still, I hesitated to come clean with this woman. She looked harmless enough, and my own experiences showed a majority of the French were anti-Nazi; however, there were some who'd accepted German occupation, even going so far as to turn on friends and neighbors to curry favor with the new regime and save their own skin, especially in this region. Hitler had annexed it first, conscripting Alsatian boys and men into the German army, and the Gestapo had tentacles everywhere.

"Are the Germans still here?"

"So far. The British and Americans have been moving from the north and west, French army from the south, but you are sitting in a pocket that the Germans have yet to surrender."

I closed my eyes and clenched my teeth in frustration. If only I'd floated farther upriver, I might have landed in the arms of the American army. Or if I'd crossed farther south, I could be celebrating with the French, perhaps enjoying a bottle of wine with one of my *Résistance* pals. Instead, bad luck had me washing ashore right in the middle of what was left of German-occupied France.

"Where were you going? Perhaps I can help."

"To find my sister."

The wrinkled face wrinkled even more as she made a moue of distaste. "Get dressed." She tossed the gun onto the sleeping pallet, then slowly retreated up the stairs. I waited until the door clicked shut, then made a beeline for the weapon. The chambers remained fully loaded.

Next to the mattress lay a pile of neatly folded clothes consisting of a black sweater with a few moth-eaten holes around the neckline, a pair of black knee socks, and a brown skirt that fell to my calf. The photo of David's sweetheart lay on top of the stack. My leather boots had been left sitting at the end of the bed, next to the stove, and though they were still damp on the inside, I pulled them on and laced them over the knit socks. A quick check of the secret pocket inside my coat revealed the remaining *Reichsmark* and David's dog tag.

With a sense of dread, I slid the heel of the boot aside and found the cavity damp but not full of water as I had expected. The film cartridge fell into my hand, and I shook it, listening for the slosh of liquid. Nothing. Perhaps the film was not ruined after all. My heart lightened. The possibility that the intelligence could be salvaged provided me the incentive I needed to keep moving forward with my plan. Gently, I placed the dog tag on top of the film and slid the sole back in place. The rest of the pockets were empty, the mittens nowhere to be found, probably left behind with the rucksack. I shrugged on the coat and returned the gun to its original location before climbing the steps.

The door opened to reveal a dark entryway of stone floor and what must have been the doorway where the old woman had found me. To my left and right were unlit passageways—the glow of the cellar brazier didn't reach past the top of the steps—and I hesitated, squinting into the darkness, trying to decide which way to go. A soft shuffling sound on my right had the hair on the back of my neck standing on end, and I stepped quickly in the opposite direction.

"Is that you, young one?" The old woman's voice carried hollowly down the passage, and even when she came around a corner and her lantern shed light, my heart remained tippy-tapping in my chest. Her disturbing witch-like looks were not made to set one at ease. "Follow me."

I followed the shuffling figure down a narrow hallway. This was the strangest house I'd ever seen, consisting of long halls covered with timbered walls, some showing blackened scorch marks, and no doorways leading into other rooms as expected. Finally, the woman drew aside a heavy curtain to reveal a room, not much bigger than the cellar I'd just come from. In it sat a wooden table with two long benches on either side. Another brazier, similar to the one in the basement, sat in a corner, and an old iron stove took up the center of the room. A copper teakettle and blackened pot each sat on a burner. There were no visible windows and the walls were made of packed dirt.

My heart no longer pounded—it had stopped completely—and I'm fairly certain all of the blood drained out of my head, for, at the table, drinking from a brown earthenware mug, sat a young German *Feldwebel*, sergeant first class, from a Panzer division if my eyes didn't deceive me. And sitting at his elbow was a weapon I knew well, the Mauser K98k.

"Meet my grandson, Masselin. He is going to help you … find your sister." The lips pulled back to reveal an unpleasant gap-toothed smile.

Swell.

"Have a seat." He indicated the bench across from him. "*Mamè*, get our guest something to eat. She looks … peaked. *Grand-mère* tells me you are searching for your sister. What is her name?" He laid the cup down and rested his hand on the butt of the gun.

His weapon lay too close for comfort. If I made a move, it would turn into an old western-style quick-draw shootout, and though I had been trained with handguns, I had not done so with this exact model; I wasn't so sure I'd win. Additionally, I had no idea if Masselin had friends nearby, in this strange house, to back him up. I decided it would be prudent to get a better lay of the land before making my next move.

The old woman shuffled over to the stove, but my gaze remained on the man across the table as I lowered myself onto the hard bench.

"H…h…" I cleared my parched throat and tried again. "H-helga. Helga Gersbach." Gersbach was the surname I recalled from the documents taped to the painting at the colonel's house. Helga came out of thin air. I committed both to memory instantly. This lie was now my cover and I would need to remain steadfast to it.

"Show him the picture." The gnarled fingers plunked a steaming bowl of soup in front of me.

Reluctantly, I pulled the photo from my pocket and slid it across the table.

He studied the photo. "Very pretty. *Très belle.* And you are …?"

"Ilse … Ilse Gersbach."

"I don't recall a girl by the name of Gersbach working as a … what was it you said?" the sergeant quizzed.

"Teacher," I said between clenched teeth.

"Teacher." He tapped a long, narrow finger against his chin. "What about you, *Mamè*, do you recall anyone named Gersbach teaching around here?"

"*Non*," the old crone replied.

"She worked farther south, closer to Strasbourg."

"Well, I'm sorry to tell you, Ilse, but that area has been captured by the French army. If indeed your sister was there, she is likely in their hands now. Who knows what has happened to her. Perhaps she is providing comfort to the enemy. Such a pretty girl…" He shrugged.

I didn't reply to his insinuations, but I couldn't help allowing my eyes to slide away from his obsidian gaze. He'd gotten his dark eyes from his wretched grandmother, if indeed she was his grandmother. We were playing a game of cat-and-mouse, and we both knew I was the mouse.

"Please, eat your soup." He indicated the pottery dish at my elbow. "Never turn away a meal, I say. Not in such uncertain times." He shifted, and the play of the light softened his sharp, hawk-like features, almost making them look pleasant, maybe even handsome.

I didn't argue. He was correct. If I had any chance of getting away from him, I would need my strength and my wits about me. The soup tasted well-salted, with grains of rice, indeterminate vegetables, and a piece of gray meat bobbing around. It was the most difficult meal I've ever had to force down my gullet. He examined me, sipping from his mug, as I chewed the tasteless meat, swallowing with a painful gulp. It burned a path to my stomach, but I didn't stop until only a thin layer of broth lay at the bottom of the bowl. My tablemate didn't speak as I ate. At some point, I heard the old woman shuffle through the curtain, leaving me alone with her grandson, who, finishing his beverage, pushed away the mug and, removing his hand from the weapon, folded his arms in front of him.

It was the perfect opportunity to extricate myself. *Maybe I wouldn't even need to shoot him. Perhaps I could simply brandish it ... use it to threaten his poor grandmother's life.* My hand slid off the table into my lap.

"Your French is very good ... *für eine Deutsche.*"

I shrugged, replying nonchalantly, *"Meine Großenltern waren Schweizer."* My grandparents were Swiss. "We visited often and learned the language." The indifference was forced. I'd made a tactical error speaking the French of France to the old woman and continuing with this soldier. I should have adopted a German-accented French. As a native, Masselin would eventually realize this.

"Finished?" The woman had returned on silent feet and spoke at my shoulder, startling me enough that I jerked.

The soldier's question had thrown me off, and his hand again rested on the weapon. I'd missed my moment to escape. "*Oui*, thank you it was … filling."

She removed the bowl. "Can you help our guest, Masselin? Surely there is something you can do? Someone you can speak with?"

"*Oui, Mamè*, do not worry, I will help your beautiful little guest find her sister. Come." He rose and held out a hand to help me. "It is time we went."

Those long fingers were not ice cold, as I expected, but quite warm; however, their strength was undeniable as they clamped around mine and pulled me upright.

Chapter Thirteen
Friend or Enemy

Upon exiting, I realized the reason for the strange home; it was a shelter, or bunker, built into the earth.

"My grandfather constructed it during World War One." Slinging the rifle over his shoulder, Masselin answered the unasked question.

Our breaths hung in the steely, frigid air, and a thin coating of powdery snow disguised the landscape, giving a crisp crunch beneath our feet as we walked. "Where are you taking me?"

"To my superiors, of course. They can help you locate your *Schwester.*" He gave more emphasis to the last word.

I pulled my hand from his grip, retrieved the gun, and leveled it at him. "Unfortunately, I'm afraid this is where we must part. I have no interest in meeting your superiors or experiencing their … hospitality. I'll find my sister on my own."

He eyed the revolver and smiled. "Now we come to it. That is a very pretty weapon you are carrying. American … no? Have you any idea how to use it?"

I cocked the hammer with my thumb and continued to keep it steadily pointed at his chest.

"Indeed." His brows knit. "How does a pretty girl come to be carrying a weapon such as this? I ask myself."

"Not that it is any of your business, but I found it on a dead pilot."

He tilted his head, scrutinizing me, and asked in a lazy tone, "And how did you become so adept with it?"

"A single girl must learn to protect herself in times of upheaval. I have no interest in providing comfort to the enemy."

"But who, Mademoiselle, is your enemy?"

My eyelids closed to slits. "Anyone who gets in my way."

"Quite the mercenary, I see." A smirk drew across his face. "Okay, I believe you are looking for your sister. I even believe the story of how you acquired the gun. Now, please put it away unless you want to get shot by one of my brethren."

"I feel more comfortable with it out." I'd been sidestepping around him as we spoke, and he'd rotated with me, keeping a sharp eye on the weapon. "If you would be so kind as to turn around, put your hands up, and get down on your knees, we can both be on our way."

"And let you bang me on the back of the head with it?" He shook his head with a tsk. "I do not think so. It would be counterproductive for the both of us and probably give me a wretched headache. Now, do you wish for my help finding your sister … or not?"

The verbal sparring with this man was stretching my nerves to the limits. I couldn't haul off and shoot him for fear of bringing his friends down upon us. Moreover, the Maginot Line could not be far away, and I needed help getting past the French bunker system. The first line of defense against the Germans, now used by the Germans against the Allied advance. I couldn't tell if he would really help me or if he was manipulating me. His grandmother had been helpful, providing clothes and food. But Masselin was an enigma. Whose side was he on? I wavered, lowering the gun a bit.

"Mademoiselle, you really haven't a choice. One shout from me will bring more soldiers than you can handle, and you'd never make it past the Maginot Line without me. If I am to help, we must go." His eyes darted furtively left and right. "*Now.*"

A decision had to be made. As a spy, I'd learned that sometimes I had to put my life into the hands of others. As much as it irritated me, I had to trust Masselin. I uncocked the gun, shoved it back into my pocket, and indicated, with my other hand, for him to lead the way.

We hadn't gone more than a dozen meters before our party of two expanded to four. Masselin had been helping me over a ridge when a pair of soldiers flanked us.

They saluted one another with offhand "*Heil*" as if they'd done it a thousand times and gave little thought to the words being spoken.

"Sergeant, how was your *Grand-mére*?" The young *Gemeiner*, private, addressed us in French. He wore little round glasses and his slight figure came up to my chin.

"She is well. What are you doing here?" Masselin's face didn't change from its insouciant mien. However, I couldn't help noticing the subtle stiffening of his shoulders, and the grip on my hand tightened almost painfully before being released.

"Patrol." The private eyed me up and down. "Is this her?"

"Her? Who do you speak of, my friend?"

"The spy the SS is looking for. They are saying a British spy has been sending radio transmissions. Although they reported her farther north." He adjusted his soldier's cap.

Masselin laughed. "Calm your imagination, Gilles. *Mamè* has a penchant for taking in strays. The fräulein washed up on her doorstep in the middle of the night looking like a drowned kitten."

"She has papers?" the other soldier, a *Gefreiter*, a corporal, asked. This soldier was a different kettle of fish from the private, he was a few inches taller than Masselin's six feet, and a puckered scar ran across his left cheekbone from nose to ear. The scar, still pink from healing, was obviously a war injury. But it wasn't the scar that made me distrust him on sight. His dark eyes, set too close together, held a look of pure malevolence, whether directed at me or Masselin, I couldn't be sure. It sent a chill down my spine.

"Burned in a bombing raid." Masselin shrugged.

"Fräulein, you are in the middle of a bad situation. What are you doing here?" Gilles addressed me in German.

"She is looking for her sister, a teacher farther south. She's gone missing," Masselin continued in German.

The private shook his head. "A bad place to go. Your sister is probably dead. You should return home."

"She is aware of the danger and apparently ready for it." Masselin's gaze swept me up and down, pausing for a moment at the pocket secreting the gun.

"Taken in by another pretty face, Masselin?" the corporal grumbled in French. He took a drag on the cigarette dangling from the side of his mouth.

"*Non,* I promised *Grand-mére* I would help her young friend." He refused to look my way, and I cocked my head, still wondering about his motives and my safety. When it came down to it—would he help me or save his own skin?

"How can you be so sure this isn't the spy they are looking for?" Smoke blew out the corporal's nose. "She fits the description." He spoke the last in German and his cold stare rested on me.

My stiff fingers curled around the cold grip of the gun in my pocket, and Masselin's jaw clenched.

"*Non,* they said she had black hair … and a limp. Remember?" Gilles interrupted in French.

I sucked in a breath but schooled my features not to react. My wrenched ankle had improved since leaving the ramshackle hunting box days ago, but after a few hours of walking, no doubt the limp would return. I had no idea where they'd gotten the black hair.

"Quiet, you fool," the corporal admonished in the same language.

Gilles clamped his mouth shut.

"She speaks French," Masselin said dryly.

Both the men froze and turned to stare.

"Almost better than you, Lars," he addressed the corporal.

"A strange girl, with no papers, who speaks French and German." Lars removed the cigarette. "And do you speak English as well?" he asked in stilted and highly accented English.

I refused to rise to the bait, instead returning his hard stare with an innocent one of my own. "Would you like to see the photograph of *meine Schwester?*" I pulled the photo out of my left coat pocket, leaving my right hidden with the weapon.

Lars glanced at the photo and grunted. "It proves nothing."

Gilles stepped in front of Lars to see. The older man towered above the skinny private. He took it from my hand and squinted down at it. "Strong family resemblance, don't you think? Same eyes and nose." Holding it up to Lars, he pointed with a dirty finger.

Lars refused to look at it; his gaze remained steady on me.

Masselin snatched the photo from the private and handed it back to me. "Enough. Granted, Ilse is not where she should be, but who is? Clearly, she doesn't meet the description of this spy you've heard about, what, third-, fourth-, fifth-hand?"

"We were briefed this morning. They're calling her the Black Widow," Gilles whispered.

Masselin's eyes sliced to me, then quickly away. "And, Gilles, do you believe this your spy?"

Gilles shook his head. "*Nein.*"

"But it is not up to Gilles, or you, Sergeant," Lars said in a silky voice.

I went to pull the gun out of my pocket, but Masselin's hard grip on my elbow stayed my hand.

"And it is up to you … *Gefreiter*?" Masselin said, reminding the man of his lower rank. "She is a German. Do you suggest we subject this innocent to an SS interrogation? Throw her to the Gestapo dogs?" he snarled.

The corporal's eyes narrowed; he gave a calculating stare before answering, "*Nein*."

"Then what are you suggesting?"

"Simply bring her back to headquarters. If her story is true … perhaps we can help the young lady find her sister … or failing that, return her home."

Not for an instant did I believe Lars's intentions toward me were so benign.

Masselin's jaw flexed, and his fingers dug into my flesh so hard I almost cried out.

"Unless, for some reason, you object?" Lars stared down his bulbous nose at his superior officer.

Masselin barely hesitated, "*Nein*. A trip to headquarters would not be untoward."

My heart dropped. Masselin was an enigma no longer; this man would be my downfall. My trust had been ill-given. I fought his tight grip, trying to pull the weapon out, but his greater strength barred me from doing so. My hand was jammed so far down I couldn't even manipulate the position of the weapon to get it pointed somewhere other than at my shoe.

"Gilles, finish your patrol. The corporal and I will take the lady back to headquarters."

Gilles' kindly eyes surveyed each of us. "Be careful," he

mumbled before taking off in the direction from which he'd come.

"Lead the way, Corporal."

The soldier hesitated, obviously disliking the thought of having Masselin at his back.

"I insist," Masselin purred.

Lars gripped his weapon tightly before turning and walking in the opposite direction of Gilles.

Masselin released my elbow. His breath brushed my ear. "Not now."

Conflicting emotions warred within me, but we walked not more than a dozen steps before encountering a squad of soldiers. Masselin had basically warned me that I was surrounded. If I was to get out of this mess, it would be with flirtation and savvy talk, not with a gun. We loaded into the back of a transport truck along with half a dozen soldiers.

Chapter Fourteen
Interrogation

Sunlight peeked through the slits of the dark curtains covering the window of the second-floor room where I found myself sitting across from *Hauptmann* Müller. I guessed the captain was the commanding officer of this Panzer unit. His slouching posture and drawn features spoke of heavy worries and fatigue. His expression wasn't hard, yet neither was it yielding. The candle on the table between the two of us flickered, creating grotesque shadows on the wood-paneled walls. We'd retained our coats because the barren fireplace remained unlit and there didn't seem to be any other sort of heating source; however, the room provided more warmth than the outdoors. Two soldiers stood behind me; I'd been separated from Masselin and Lars.

I hadn't been searched, and the weapon remained in my pocket, but the odds weren't looking good for making a successful escape using the gun. Fear had my stomach in tight knots and my mouth arid. I licked my lips in an effort to disperse the bone dryness.

"Zigaretten?" Müller held out a half full pack.

I took one. *"Danke."*

Normally, I wasn't a smoker; I found the taste wholly repulsive. However, in the past few years, I'd found it to be an excellent socially acceptable habit that created opportunities for targeted introductions in addition to allowing me the excuse to loiter in places I otherwise shouldn't. The benefits outweighed the costs and I'd inured myself to the disgusting flavor. It took all my efforts to hold the ciggy steady when placing it in my mouth.

The officer flicked a match and leaned forward to light mine before lighting his own. I took a drag and blew it out. The bitter Turkish flavor disconcerted me, but I schooled my features to remain bland, then crossed my legs and sat back in the chair with what I hoped to be an air of insouciance.

He cupped his cigarette working-class style between his cracked and callused fingers. "Now, fräulein, why don't you tell me your story." His blond hair, oily from lack of washing, swept across his high forehead, and he pushed aside several slick strands that fell into his eyes.

I told my cover story with calm deliberation. When I got to the part about my sister the teacher, I slid the worn photograph across the table.

The captain set the butt in his mouth, picked up the photo, and leaned closer to the candle to study it. He then did what no one else had done; using two fingers, he tucked the picture into his pocket.

"That is a very interesting story." He removed a small notebook and a pencil from the same pocket. "How old is your sister?"

The girl in the photo looked to be about eighteen or nineteen, but I would be carrying around an older picture if she hadn't been home in a few years. "She'll be twenty-one in April."

"The exact date?"

"April tenth." My fictitious sister took on my mother's birthdate.

The soldier scribbled down the information, then studied me.

Down went another puff of smoke and out I blew it, up toward the ceiling.

"But, fräulein, you can hardly be more than twenty-one yourself."

"Twenty-four," I said truthfully, tapping ashes onto the floor.

"Not yet married?" His smile dimpled and gave him a boyish look even though I'd estimated his age to be early thirties.

"*Nein.*" I allowed my features to soften.

He blinked. "Surely, a girl such as you must have a sweetheart."

"*Nein.* The war…" I dipped my head, gesturing with my hand.

"Yes, the war has taken many good men." He cleared his throat. "Where did your sister go to school?"

And the interrogation began in earnest. Back and forth we went, the captain smiling his kindly smile and writing down my responses in his notes as the lies piled up around me. I wasn't fooled by his approachable demeanor for an instant. Behind the smile lay calculating eyes, of indeterminate color, that missed nothing. The questions weren't spoken harshly or done at gunpoint. To anyone listening, it would have sounded like an affable conversation between a lady and interested beau. However, the hair on my neck stood on end, well aware of the two sentries behind me and the fact that outside the door was a platoon of well-trained killers. We finished our cigarettes, then the questions began to repeat themselves, an interrogation tactic I'd been trained to expect. The same questions, phrased differently, were tossed at me to see if the story would change. It took all my concentration to keep the lies straight, and I think I did a fair job of it, but I was uncertain if the captain bought the falsehoods I sold.

Raised voices drew Müller's attention. One of them sounded like Masselin, and I couldn't catch all of the conversation, but I'm fairly certain I heard my name. My interrogator excused himself, taking his notebook and one of the sentries with him. He directed the other to watch me. Moments after he left, the loud voices quieted.

It was time to make a move. I shifted my chair to view the soldier behind me and smiled. Before I could entice him closer, the door reopened and in walked Lars.

His reappearance did nothing to ease my state of mind; quite the opposite, as a matter of fact. He sauntered over to the table, put a boot against the side, and gave it a hard shove. The candle flickered wildly, fell off its precarious perch, and extinguished as the table shot past me, slamming against the wall. The move caught me off guard, and I couldn't help the instinctive fearful cringe. The other soldier let out an exclamation of surprise.

"Remain where you are, Private." Lars gripped the chair and dragged the back legs along the wood floors before stopping directly in front of me, close enough to see in the dim light. He sat so close our knees touched, and I automatically shifted mine to the side and crossed my legs.

"You've got everyone fooled. Don't you? The girl with the pretty face has Masselin, Gilles, and even our captain under your spell. But I know better." He tapped his nose. "Girls like you are nothing but a tease. Using men's cocks to get what you want and then moving on once you get it."

Uh oh, some girl broke his heart, and I'm about to pay the price. "I don't know what you're talking about, Corporal. I think you are looking for something that isn't there. I simply tell the truth."

"The truth? What is the truth?"

"I told you, my sister—"

"You are a spy."

"*Nein.*"

"You are the Black Widow everyone is searching for."

"Where is my black hair?" I ran a hand through my light brown locks.

"You colored it."

My brows rose. "The limp?"

He stared down at my feet, then gave a shake of his head. "Why do you speak so many different languages?"

"Many Germans do, even you."

He leaned forward and unbuttoned the top buttons of my coat. Finding the chain attached to the little brass compass, he used a single finger to pull it out. It dangled there, gently swaying while he studied it. "An interesting choice for a necklace."

I knew if I seized it out of his hands, he was wily enough to realize it meant something to me, and he'd take it. Instead, I folded my arms across my chest and glowered at him. To my relief, he dropped the chain.

"Good German girls do not lose their papers and travel halfway across the country to find their fictitious sisters." He pushed aside my arms and undid the buttons down to my waist.

I realized immediately he planned to use sexual advances as an intimidation tactic. All I had to do was bide my time.

"Why don't you tell me what you are really doing here." He pushed one side of my coat off the shoulder and ran his hand along my collarbone. It was a lover's move, and I involuntarily shuddered with revulsion.

"What is wrong? Would you prefer Masselin?" He leaned in, his sour breath fanning my face and puckered scar conspicuously at eye level.

My countenance must have betrayed me, because that hand clawed into a fist, and the rip of my sweater filled the room. He pulled the knit down, past my breast, revealing the slip beneath. I slapped his hand away. His face twisted and he grabbed at the exposed breast, squeezing it cruelly.

I cried out and scrambled backwards, toppling the chair as I rose. My hand impulsively pulled out the gun and pointed it at my attacker. "Get back," I uttered in a hoarse voice.

The door erupted into the room and Masselin burst through. He took in the scene and cursed roundly before holding up his palm and calling out, *"Nein, warte!"* No, wait!

Lights exploded, pain ripped through my head, and I fell to my knees. I'd forgotten about the soldier behind me.

A sharp, throbbing heartbeat pumped at the back of my skull, and I couldn't move my hands to reach behind and pull away whatever was causing the agony. Jumbled voices slowly took shape into language, and I struggled to open my eyes.

"We haven't determined she's the one they're looking for. She doesn't fit the description of the Black Widow." The voice spoke in German.

"Maybe she's a Jew."

There was a disbelieving snort. "Look at her. She is no Jew. She looks like she could be your sister."

Gunfire and mortar shelling exploded close enough to shake the building at its foundation.

"Then who the hell is she?"

"She may be exactly who she claims to be."

"Who cares? We don't have time for this. Give her over to the SS or Gestapo. Let them sort it out. The enemy comes closer. They've crossed the river."

"There is no one this close to the front lines in the area to hand her over to. I'm not calling the Gestapo until I'm sure of her story. If she's not the Black Widow and we claim she is..." The voice trailed off.

"Right."

Excruciating pain overwhelmed my efforts to wake, and I spiraled back into the abyss.

When I came around the second time, the throbbing had dulled to a raw ache that was no longer focused solely on the back of my head. It had spread to the front of my temples. My chin lay slumped forward onto my chest, and in addition to the grating headache, my neck had become so stiff it took a Herculean effort to raise it. I groaned as the muscles agonizingly contracted and pried open my eyes. The room spun, and I shut them again, waiting for the dizziness and nausea to pass. When the lids reopened, I found myself tied to the arms of a chair from wrist to forearm. The bindings were tight enough to hold me—I flexed my fingers—but not cruel enough to cut off the circulation. My fingers weren't white from the rope but rather the cold. The coat, my lifeline, was nowhere to be seen, my pendant was missing, and the rip in the sweater hung loose, revealing a good portion of my shoulder and clavicle as well as the straps of my slip and bra.

The room hadn't changed much. The table remained against the wall where Lars had shoved it, the yellow candle had been replaced onto its holder, and the flame wavered low in its socket. *They must have brought in a different chair to strap me to.* The arms were thick and heavy; the back of the chair was tall, ending at the base of my neck. I wondered how long I'd been sitting in the hard seat, because my backside was stiff and had gone numb along with my lower legs. The wood creaked as I stretched out my knees and ankles, jiggling them to wake the deadened muscles.

The creak and my movements must have alerted the guard outside the room, because the door popped open, and the soldier who had struck the blow regarded me.

"You're awake. *Sehr gut.*" He disappeared.

The candle guttered out, throwing the room into complete darkness. No sun peeped around the heavy curtains. *It must be nighttime.* Fear spread through my body like wildfire and turned my fuzzy brain back onto high alert. It was also at this time that the feeling began to work its way back into my numb limbs. The sensation speared me like a thousand needles stabbing my legs. I stomped my feet to relieve the discomfort until the door reopened.

My favorite captain carried an old-fashioned oil lantern. Its soft glow gave the room a cozy feel, and the brass was darkened with age; he placed it on the table, knocking aside the dead candle.

"Fräulein." With slow deliberation, he picked up the overturned chair, turned the back toward me, and straddled it while making a tsking sound with his tongue. "You have not been honest with me."

I smacked my tongue, running it against my parched lips in an effort to work up some saliva. My answer came out as unintelligible garble and turned into a gasping cough that racked my poor, battered body.

The captain realized my distress, and to my surprise, he pulled out his flask and poured some of the metallic-flavored water down my throat. I gulped at it greedily, but he only allowed enough to whet my whistle, rather than slake the thirst, before pulling away.

I crossed my legs and gave him a wide-eyed glance, "What do you mean, Captain? I have been truthful with you from the start."

"Then how do you explain this?" He removed the airman's weapon from his coat pocket and, resting his left elbow on the back of the chair, pointed the revolver at my forehead. "Smith and Wesson .38, Victory model. American-made, carried by British and American soldiers ... and their spies."

Müller was incorrect. Most agents carried small fighting knives. On one occasion, I'd been given a stinger, a one-shot .22 caliber weapon, disguised as a cigarette, and Colette had once proudly demonstrated a lipstick stinger made by the SOE. If a spy carried a sidearm, it would be an automatic .32 caliber Colt pistol. I'd trained with one; it was widely used by the OSS because it hid easily in a pocket and was unlikely to get snagged on clothes upon removal, unlike the barrel gun with hammer that was currently pointed at me. However, I considered it ill-advised to point out his erroneous suppositions.

On the other hand, here it was—the chance I promised myself back in the cellar in France to force my captors into shooting me and get it over with. I could spit into his face. Explain exactly why OSS spies didn't carry the type of weapon he held in his hand. Something as simple as speaking English. Provoke an attack. Bring this farce to an end before the real torture began.

Nonetheless, even with my tender, dizzy head, sore neck, and stiff limbs strapped to a chair, something kept me from provoking that attack. I stared down the barrel of a weapon, made by my own government, yet some innate stroke of human nature deep inside kept a flicker of hope alive that I would be able to talk my way out of the situation or that Masselin would eventually come to my aid. The possibility that I could sleep my way out of the predicament actually sounded preferable to death. I'd always thought, when the time came, I would be brave and fearless. Look death in the eye and meet it head on. I almost laughed at my foolishness. I was too alive, not yet ready to give up. The motivation to survive clung as strongly as a barnacle to the hull of a boat.

I didn't spit into his face; instead I raised my chin proudly. "I found it on a dead American pilot and took it. They are not hard to find these days. I'm sure you know the bombing raids are constant, and our brave Luftwaffe fights to maintain control of the skies and fight off the cowardly American murderers." My voice might not have been steady, but I stared past the cold steel directly into my captor's eyes without flinching or blinking. I forced my leg to stop bouncing despite the painful bee-like prickles swarming their way up my legs.

"You know you are required to have a permit for this weapon."

"It is a recent acquisition, and I haven't had the time to complete the paperwork," I answered softly.

"Why would a girl like you need a weapon like this?"

"For the exact reason your corporal forced me to pull it out. The mission to find my sister has been fraught with danger, and as a young woman alone … I felt it behooved me to have one in case the enemy pigs tried to take advantage. I had hoped a military officer such as yourself could help me find her. Instead, I am tied to this chair like an animal."

"And the money?"

My crossed leg gave an involuntary jerk.

"Such a clever little pocket. We tore the coat apart looking for other hiding places…" He shrugged but the gun didn't waver.

I lifted my chin. "It seemed a safe way to store my money in case my handbag was lost or stolen … which it was."

A sickly smile drew across his face. "You have an answer for everything, fräulein. And so many *Reichsmark*. Tell me, how did a young woman such as yourself acquire so much money?"

I knew I'd given almost half of my stash to Oskar. There was still a fair amount of money left, but nothing outrageous. "*Mutti* and I have been saving, and when there is so little food and dry goods to purchase … the money adds up over time." I continued to meet his gaze.

"Yet it is my understanding, with rationing, all the prices have gone up."

I didn't bat an eye. "*Ja*, in the cities, but I told you we live in a smaller village. The inflation has not been as marked." After all, I'd been able to afford food in Dornstetten a few days ago, and towns with military installations, such as Oberndorf, seemed to have better control over the price increases.

"I wonder, do you know how to handle a weapon such as this?" He drew his finger along the muzzle and tapped the cylinder.

I shrugged. "I imagine you squeeze the trigger, just like any other gun."

"You would be correct." He cocked the gun. His hand didn't waver and my heart plummeted.

So … this was how it would end, without any provocation at all. I drew in a breath, closed my eyes, and exhaled. The room went silent. My muscles relaxed, and the anxiety I'd been carrying exited my body like an eagle rising in flight. I felt it lift from my shoulders. Soon, I would meet my maker and see my mother. I'd once read a soldier described his near-death experience like a picture show passing before his eyes at high-speed. I waited for the movie to begin, but only one face came to mind. A soldier. Charlie stared down, holding me close as we rotated around the dance floor. "Our dance isn't over yet," he said. His voice rang in my ears so clearly it was as though he'd spoken aloud in this room.

The captain's chair shifted, the memory dissipated, and my eyes flickered open. The weapon now pointed at the ground and he'd replaced the hammer. His head tilted. "Why were you smiling?"

I mashed my lips together.

"I have pointed my weapon at all sorts of men. None of them acted as you have."

"I don't know what you mean."

"You are … unafraid … of death?" He said it like a question rather than a statement.

"My soul is innocent, and I am ready to meet my maker. Can you say the same, *Hauptmann*?"

"We both know you are no innocent. Why did you smile?"

"Why didn't you shoot?"

He sighed and shifted, running a hand through his greasy locks. "Fräulein, let us say for a moment that you *are* the innocent you claim to be. If I believed your story, you have still broken many laws. You left your district, without papers, crossed into a military stronghold, carried a gun without a permit, and pointed that weapon at a soldier in the Third Reich." He held up a finger for each of my transgressions.

"He attacked me!" I defended. "I only meant to frighten him into leaving me alone. Do you think I would have been foolish enough to shoot a soldier with dozens of his comrades-in-arms filling this building?"

He stretched his neck, tilting it side to side, then rotating it in a circle. "*Sieben*," he mumbled so softly I wasn't sure I'd heard him.

Seven? "Pardon?"

The drawn face snapped back into position as though realizing he'd spoken out of turn. His jaw clenched, and his eyes swept the length of my body, returning to the bared flesh just above my left breast.

He'd hidden his awareness of my femininity well, but for the first time, it occurred to me that the captain might be susceptible.

I straightened my shoulders and pushed my small breasts forward. "Come now, Captain, you don't think an insignificant girl such as myself could betray my country? *Nein*, we must purge Germany of her internal enemies, maintain the Aryan race, and stand strong against aggressors of *das Vaterland*." I spouted the Nazi propaganda from rote. During my training in Britain, I'd been given issues of *Der Angriff*, Goebbels's German propaganda newspaper, to read. The disturbing content was not easily forgotten. "Can't we untie these silly ropes and have a drink together?" I gazed at him from beneath my lashes and ran my tongue across my upper lip from one side to the other. "You know, a drink."

His scrutiny followed my tongue. "Ilse, you are a puzzle, one that I have every intention of solving." The look could only be described as predatory.

"Maybe we can solve it together. Without…" I glanced down at the bindings and back up at Müller with my brows high.

A cute little-boy smile peeped at me. "Well…"

Finally, we are getting somewhere.

"Tell me, Ilse—"

The door opened and the private stuck his head in. "Captain, you are needed in the radio room."

I could have screamed at the private's timing.

Reluctantly, the captain rose, taking the lantern on the way out, leaving me in the icy darkness.

I pulled desperately at my bindings, twisting my hands to no avail. The rough twine bit into the soft flesh at my uncovered wrists, and I grunted in frustration at my inability to loosen the restraints. After a few moments, my sight adjusted and I could barely make out the lines of the table and chair. The pale skin of my hands looked ghostly in the dimness. Though my vision was hampered by the blackness, my hearing capabilities seemed to heighten, and I became attuned to every sound. The creak of the chair, the rasp of the rope on my skin. Footfalls thumped along the planks above me and I halted my efforts. A moment later male voices spoke, and I could have sworn I heard the crackle of a radio. I strained to make out what they were saying; however, the ancient floorboards were too thick to allow anything more than deep-voiced rumblings.

"*Hallo*! Is anyone there?" I called as loudly as my scratchy throat would permit and clapped my heels against the ground.

Nothing. The private must have left his post.

The chair was a heavy wooden affair, but I tried to stand, thinking I could bash it against the wall to break loose. I rocked back and forth trying to get leverage to rise, but the depth of the seat worked against me, as did the overall weight and the manner in which I was tied. Since I couldn't seem to go forward, I pushed backward. The chair tipped and I pulled my head forward to keep from slamming my injury against the ground. The freefall began only to be halted with an abrupt crack. Unladylike curses spewed forth. I hadn't realized how close to the wall I'd been and was now hung up on something, perhaps a chair rail. Now, I hung ignobly at an eighty-degree angle against the wood paneling, ineffectually kicking my feet like an overturned beetle in an effort to displace the chair and make it move one way or the other.

Chapter Fifteen
The Enemy

The door hinges squeaked, and I paused my struggles. The beam of a flashlight swept the room, caught my embarrassing position, and the owner of the torch let out a surprised grunt.

Is it the captain? Or Masselin? My heart jumped with hope.

A silhouette approached and suddenly my chair slammed back down onto all four legs.

"Well, well, what have we here? There is no napping for traitorous spies."

The jarred landing served to increase the pounding in my head, and I closed my eyes to stave off a wave of nausea.

"Look at me!" he shouted.

Unhappily, I recognized the voice, realized what it meant, and mentally kicked myself for not provoking Müller into shooting me when I had the chance. My lashes opened to find my nemesis returned. He held the flashlight upward, throwing his face into an eerie relief. The room spun and I couldn't focus.

"You are the Black Widow! I know it."

"*Nein,*" I whispered, hanging my head to stop the spinning.

"*Ja!* You are the Black Widow."

"*Nein.*"

"*Ja!* You have delivered messages to the enemy."

"*Nein!*"

"*Schwarze Witwe!*" Black Widow. He spit out the words like they left a nasty taste in his mouth. "Where have you hidden the radio you used to do so?"

"What?" *Radio? I have no idea what he's talking about.* I'd done many things for my government, but handling a radio was not one of them. I had never been trained to do so. Radio operators were considered one of the most dangerous positions in the spy community. They moved around on a regular basis because it didn't take long for the enemy to zone in on their position. Some of our best intelligence came from these brave men and women, and we'd lost so many of them.

"Did you leave it with Masselin's grandmother?"

My head shot up at that, but before I could answer, the whirling overwhelmed me. I leaned forward and vomited. To my regret, Lars had quick reflexes and jumped back in time. Most of the mess ended up on my skirt and the floor.

"*Du Schwein!*" You pig! He backhanded me.

It felt like my eye would explode from the socket, and I screamed. My head flopped against the chair like a ragdoll, and I went inert, hoping against hope that he'd leave me alone if he thought I'd passed out. I should have known better. The scent of smoke was my only warning. A searing pain pierced my shoulder where he held his cigarette against the bared flesh.

Tears flooded my eyes. I shrieked and kicked with all my might. My aim was off and I hit him in the upper thigh instead of the sensitive manly parts. He recoiled and dropped the cigarette; it landed in my lap and I jiggled my legs until it rolled off onto the floor.

"You are the woman! You are the spy they are looking for! I know it!" He came at me, his outstretched hands going for my throat, but I got my knees up in time to kick at his chest. Delivering a shot with my heel to his sternum, it held him off, but I was only able to push him back a few steps, and his next attack disconcerted me. Instead of going for my throat like before, he grabbed my left foot and tried to wrench the boot off. The laces were too tight, and all he achieved was to drag me and the heavy chair halfway across the room. The bindings tore into my flesh. With one arm he held my foot while the other reached down and withdrew a blade.

Kicking and squirming, I doubled my efforts to get away, but it only took a moment for the knife to slice through the laces. He stumbled backwards as the shoe tore free. I tried to push myself away, but the damn chair was too heavy, and he was upon me before I'd gotten half a meter. He chopped at the laces and flung the other boot across the room, then turned to me. Our heavy breathing filled the chamber and hammered in my ears. In the melee, Lars had dropped the flashlight, which rolled across the floor. It now shone upon the wall, its wavering beam delivering a macabre appearance to our life-and-death struggle, like something you'd see in an old horror film.

His silhouette with the knife rose above me. "Treacherous spy, confess! Tell me you are the Black Widow."

"*Nein, nein!*" My voice cracked and my chest heaved with exertion.

"*Das ist genug.*" That is enough; the captain's stern command broke through our fight.

Lars didn't move, and the lighting was such that I couldn't see his face, but his stance hesitated, as though debating whether or not to heed his superior officer's demand.

"Corporal!" Müller barked.

The blade lowered. "It is her. I know it."

"Get out."

Lars scooped up his flashlight and the door slammed behind him.

Müller surveyed the room and audibly sighed as he placed the lantern on the table and pulled it close, then he righted the chair that had been knocked down and sat across from me. His nose wrinkled with distaste. "You've been ill."

The sour stench of sickness clung to me. He grabbed the lantern and held it between us, and I flinched away from the light exposing the battered cheek. His thumb gently stroked the bruise, and I winced.

The captain sucked in a breath. "*Was ist das?*" What is this? He pointed to the still-stinging burn.

Our eyes met, and I bit my lips to keep from collapsing into a sobbing muddle.

"Private," he called over his shoulder.

The door opened.

"Send in the medic."

"He's not here, sir."

The officer's gaze swung back to me. "Then bring me an aid kit. Fill a clean sock with snow and bring it here. Also, get me a blanket."

We waited in silence for the soldier to carry out his orders.

He moved with slow deliberation as he bandaged the burn mark. I cringed away when he held the snow-filled sock against my bruised cheek.

"Don't move away. I promise it will help."

I nodded but couldn't help flinching back when he put it on again.

He sighed and sat back, scrutinizing me. "I'm going to cut your arm free so you can hold this yourself."

He freed my left hand and handed me the sock. I alternated holding it on my cheek and the knot on the back of my head. After the snow melted, I tossed the sopping cloth onto the table.

"Ilse, I have a blanket for you." He held it up. "I want you to remove your skirt so it can be cleaned. Do you think you can do so with one hand?"

I gulped. The smell was revolting but the idea of removing

any more of my clothes seemed even more repellant.

"I can do it for you if you prefer."

It would have been the perfect opportunity to reengage our flirtation from earlier, but the attack had sucked the inclination out of me, and I simply couldn't muster up the energy to be alluring. "*Nein.* I'll do it," I said with resignation. "Can you turn around?"

"I am afraid not. You have proven yourself a force to be reckoned with, even with two hands tied down." I wasn't sure how much of the battle with Lars he'd witnessed, but something had forced his wariness of me to return.

Wriggling in a silly half-crouched stance, along with the discomfort of having the captain watching, I was able to drop the skirt to my feet, revealing the thin slip beneath. I kicked it aside and snatched the blanket from him, quickly wrapping it around my legs as best as I could, and returned to my seat.

Müller retied the rope around my wrist before he picked up the dark wad and passed it to the private. I couldn't make out the entire conversation, but I did hear the word wash and thought perhaps the captain indeed planned to have it cleaned—after it had been searched for secret pockets, no doubt.

"Now, fräulein, let's get back to this elusive sister of yours. I've been trying to track down anyone by that name, and so far … nothing."

"Do you think she's dead, or has been captured?"

"I'm beginning to doubt her existence at all," he grumbled.

"The photograph?"

"A photo is easy to come by. Especially from a woman as capable as yourself."

I didn't respond. It seemed we'd returned to square one—back to the interrogation.

"Which begs the question … who are you and what are you doing here?"

"In other words, am I the Black Widow?"

"Contrary to our friend Lars' theory, I don't believe you are the Black Widow. So, Ilse, who are you?" He removed a flask from an inner pocket, twisted off the cap, and took a swig. I watched his Adam's apple bobble as he swallowed. He held the metal canteen toward me.

"*Was ist das?*" What is that?

"*Schnapps.*"

The cheap booze blazed a trail down my throat, landing hard on my empty stomach. It wasn't long before its warmth spread outward, dimming the pain and providing an unexpected relaxation of my limbs. It also seemed to bring my mind into sharper focus.

"It will go much easier if you just tell me the truth."

"If you don't believe my story, why don't you turn me over to the Gestapo?"

"Do you wish me to do so?"

"Of course not, but neither do I wish to be fodder for that sadistic animal," I snapped.

"Trust me, Lars is nothing compared to what the Gestapo will do to you," he stated in a matter-of-fact tone.

Even though I'd been warned by my Resistance friends, I wasn't so sure. The Gestapo would handle me with cold calculation. For some reason, I enraged Lars. I knew if he had another chance to come at me … I began to wonder if the captain was using Lars to play a little game my training operative referred to as the hot/cold routine to break me down and force a confession. It was an intimidation tactic—first send in a "friendly" interrogator to create a rapport, then send in a "cruel" interrogator to instill fear. The team would swap in and out until the suspect confessed to one or the other.

His jaw relaxed and his mouth softened. "Now, you can trust me. Just tell me who you are."

"I told you, my name is Ilse Gersbach. *Meine Schwester,* Helga, was teaching down near Strasbourg. She has gone missing. We have not heard from her in months. My mother asked me to go look for her." I fell back on my training—stick to the story, deny all other allegations.

"You see, that is where I have a problem. Your mother might have already lost one daughter. Would she place another into the hands of fate, possibly losing both her little girls in the process? What mother would purposely put her child into such a situation?"

"As you said, I am resourceful. Always have been. Mother was distraught. I insisted I could find Helga. Maybe you could say I didn't really give her a choice. So, she filled my pockets with money and gave me her blessing. Is that so difficult to believe? That the hope of finding her youngest child is worth the risk?"

He regarded me and we sat in a silent staring contest.

"Tell me about your childhood." He made a show out of retrieving and lighting a cigarette. Only this time he didn't offer one to me. "Where were you born?"

"Stuttgart."

"Your French was learned ..."

"My grandparents lived in Lausanne, Switzerland. We visited often. It is where I learned to speak French." Not true, but the months I'd spent at finishing school gave me enough knowledge of the area to provide relatively accurate information should we delve deeper.

"Our friend Lars is under the impression you learned to speak French in Paris."

I didn't bat an eyelash. "He is misinformed."

"And what about English? Where did you learn your English?" He spoke the question in English.

When he switched languages, I could feel the change and did my best to give him a blank look. It was that way every time languages switched. Some of my friends explained that they could switch between different languages as easily as a sailboat gliding through water. For me the change was more abrupt, like changing a record on the turntable. The drop, the click, and then the needle engaged. This could be a disadvantage when trying to follow multiple languages at once. However, it came in handy during interrogations when my questioner was trying to force a slipup.

"*Englisch? Ich spreche nicht Englisch.*" I don't speak English.

He blew a cloud of smoke in my face. "Tell me a fact, Ilse."

"Pardon?"

"Tell me a truth, about yourself."

My stomach burbled and I said the first thing that popped into my head. "I despise tapioca."

This brought a half smile to the captain's face. "I believe you have told me the truth." He stubbed out the cigarette on the boot of his heel and rose. "We aren't finished. Private."

The private entered. "Sir?"

"Wait with the lady. Do not let the corporal in the room."

"Yes, sir."

He left the lantern behind and the private at the door, rifle at the ready. Upon his return, he ordered the private to stand guard in the hallway. He dragged the table in front of me and placed a wineglass filled with water and bits of melting snow floating on the top like miniature icebergs.

"I'm going to tie your feet to the legs, then release your hands."

"Is that really necessary, captain? I did not attack you before when you released me."

"It is necessary. If you try something, the private has orders to shoot you dead. Do you understand?"

Once my ankles were tied to the legs, he untied my hands. I scooped up the glass and drank ravenously. The cold water sluiced down my raw throat, providing much-needed relief against the strain from shouting at Lars. He pulled a packet of field ration crackers out of his front pocket and laid them within reach. They were dry and stale, and I dipped them in the water before swallowing them. It was relief to put something on my empty stomach. I considered throwing the glass at his head but realized it would be foolish. The private, who hadn't thought twice about bashing me with the butt of his gun, would surely follow orders to put an unremorseful end to me.

Müller patiently smoked while he waited for me to finish, then he retied the bindings and departed. He left the lantern behind but didn't see fit to remove the ropes around my ankles.

Even with a little bit of food in my stomach, my energy had been sapped. I rested my aching head on the table. My eyes drifted shut, and I wondered what horror was in store next. I skimmed the edge of sleep; strange dreams of running through thick mud swirled around me.

Chapter Sixteen
Hope

"Ilse."

A hand gripped my shoulder.

"Ilse, wake up."

My eyes, gritty with sleep and raw from fatigue, cracked open. Masselin stood at my elbow and stared down his long, straight nose at me.

"*Connard.*" I grumbled the epithet as I peeled my cheek off the table. Pale fingers of the sun reached around the curtains, adding to the lantern's glow. I have heard it said that things always looked brighter in the light of day. The sight of Masselin gave me cause to doubt the cliché.

"*Je regrette, ma chérie.*" I regret this, sweetheart. His thumb softly stroked across my jawline beneath the bruises, but his touch still had me flinching. "This is not what I had planned."

He'd spoken in a whisper and I answered him back in the same low tones, but my quiet response was filled with bitterness and resentment. "*Non?* I wonder what your precious *Grand-mére* would have to say about my treatment."

Masselin frowned at my words. "She would be very angry with me."

"I should have shot you when I had the chance."

"Why didn't you?"

I stared stonily. *Why didn't I?*

"You are a tough girl, but it is not so easy to shoot someone point-blank. Is it?"

He wasn't wrong. It was far easier to shoot someone in the heat of battle and from a distance than to look someone in the eye and pull the trigger. Everything about Masselin had me questioning his motives. Would he help me now, or would he choose to play it safe to save his own skin?

A footfall could be heard in the hallway and Masselin's head snapped to the door. He placed his fingers at my lips in a quieting motion. The tread continued past our room. When the sergeant's attention returned to me, he spoke in low, urgent tones, "I haven't much time."

"Then untie me." I pulled at the twine.

"Not yet. Lars is still here. The enemy is surrounding this position as we speak. Soon Lars will be sent out to fight. When he is gone, I can release you. I have found a place for you to hide until it is safe."

"No, don't wait, let me go now." I tugged harder at the ropes. "If Lars gets another shot at me, he'll surely kill me."

Masselin's bangs flopped in his eyes as he shook his head. "*Non*, he needs you alive. He is an informant for the Gestapo. He is hoping to leverage you to get off the front lines and become one of them. But he is still not sure that you are the spy they are looking for, and if you don't turn out to be who he claims … it would not go well for him."

None of Masselin's explanation surprised me. There had been a frantic disorder to Lars' interrogation tactics—his desperate insistence that I was the Black Widow still resonated in my memory.

"I have to go. I sent your guard on an errand but he will soon return. Do not lose hope, *ma chérie*. I promise I will be back."

"Masselin, wait, I can—" The door closed behind him before I could finish the thought.

Minutes later the faithful watchdog returned. Checking on the prisoner, he glanced around the room as if to assure himself no one hid in the corners. He looked me up and down, then smoothly shut the door without a word.

At least I knew Masselin was on my side and planned to release me from this nightmare, but for the moment, my situation hadn't changed. Even though I was wrapped in the blanket, the frigid winter saw fit to seep its way into my bones and my unshod toes were numb with cold. The throbbing pain from the injuries on my head had eased off, but fatigue slowed my thinking, and the bruise on my cheek had swelled enough to partially obstruct my vision.

I spent the next hour listening to gunfire and tank shelling, optimistically waiting for my champion to return and set me loose. The door swung inward and all my hopes were dashed.

I don't know how long Lars toyed with me as the sound of the fighting drew nearer. Probably no more than twenty minutes, but it seemed a lifetime.

The sweater lay in tatters around my waist, and the slip, hanging by a single strap, looked as though it'd been through a sausage slicer. Three new cigarette burns blazed a trail down my arm, although, to my surprise, he had yet to cut me with the knife—the removal of my clothes had been completed with surgical precision as he held me still by the throat. The sharp blade lay on the table, against the wall, at his elbow. His first move upon entering the room, like before, was to dramatically shove the table away, leaving me vulnerable and helpless under his siege in the middle of the room.

For the life of me, I couldn't figure out why he was here, torturing me, instead of fighting with his colleagues. *Did he defy his orders? What drove his obsession?* From the sound of the fighting, soon we would both be shot or blown up.

As if my thoughts had brought the gods down upon us, an explosion suddenly rocked the house. The blast left me disoriented and my ears ringing. A chunk of plaster fell onto Lars, but his reflexes had him moving fast. Footfalls and raised voices could be heard coming from the first floor. He dashed away the bits of ceiling and was upon me in a flash. Jamming the sock the captain had used on my bruises, which was still soggy from the snow, into my mouth, he knotted it tightly around the back of my head, and then he pulled the door open and slipped behind it, effectively making me a target for whatever came up the stairs.

I stared with wide eyes—waiting.

The black nose of the M1 came into view first. The soldier carrying it walked on cat feet, making no sound. Lars didn't show any indication that he'd heard the enemy's approach. I looked from the soldier's confused face to Lars, who stood holding a finger to his lips with his left hand and a Luger trained on me with his right. Back and forth my eyes frantically darted. I quaked with dread, waiting to see whose bullets would tear through me first.

The American must have sensed what my mind screamed at him. In a flash three bullets ripped through the door—*bang, bang, bang*—and Lars slumped, face first, to the floor.

"You okay, Sarge?" a voice from the hall whispered.

The army sergeant made some motions with his hands, then stepped over the threshold. His soot-blackened face scanned the room before approaching me. The uniform hung loosely off his average frame, and the stripes on his shoulder identified him as a first sergeant. The Screaming Eagle patch at his shoulder sent a thrill of recognition through me. He smelled of gun powder and sweat, and he fumbled, one-handed, with the knot until the gag dropped away.

"It's bloody good to see you." My voice sounded gruff and gravelly.

His face registered surprise. "British?"

"American, actually. The colloquialism is a leftover from too many years at a British boarding school."

Another sergeant entered the room.

"What took you so long?" I asked.

"I didn't realize we were late." The new soldier, a big, burly fellow with dark hair, chomped on an unlit cigar. "Who are you?"

I rubbed my wrists as the first sergeant moved to cut the ankle ropes free. "Call me Lily."

"What the hell are you doing here?"

My cold fingers felt good against the bruising at my neck. "I'm an agent for the Office of Strategic Services. I've been trying to make it to the front lines but was captured a day or two ago. I'm not really sure."

The cigar shifted from one side to the other, but other than that, the soldier gave no outward show of surprise at my revelation. "This is First Sergeant Glasswell. I'm Thompson, but everyone calls me Tank."

I could understand why. His presence seemed to take up half the room.

"Hey, Sarge." A diminutive private stepped into the room, laid eyes on me, and stopped short. His gaze zeroed in on my chest.

The other two had seemed immune to my state of undress, but the new soldier's scrutiny brought my condition to the forefront. I crossed my arms and flushed with embarrassment.

Tank's brow furrowed as he scrutinized the burns along my pale skin before snatching up the blanket that Lars had left crumpled on the floor and draped it over my shoulders.

"What is it, Whiskey?" Glassman asked, stepping in front of me.

The private snapped out his trance. "I cleared the other two rooms. Nothing," he said with a thick Boston accent.

"Ma'am," Sergeant Glasswell addressed me, "do you know what's upstairs?"

"I think the radio room is directly above us."

"Is there anyone up there?" Tank asked.

Not a creak of the floorboards or crackle from the radio could be heard. "I remember footsteps earlier. I kind of lost track during..." I shrugged and looked away, shame burning on my cheeks. I cleared my throat. "I've been led to believe there were seven men billeted to this building, but I imagine most were sent out to defend the town. I would guess one, maybe two men upstairs."

"I'll go, Sarge." The private headed out of the room.

"That's Wisnewski. We call him Whiskey," Tank said.

"Go with him." Glasswell turned to me and grasped my elbow. "Let's get you out of here."

"Wait." With the sergeant's help, I rose to my feet, took a step, and fell to my knees, my fingers barely brushing Tank's pant leg on the way down.

Tank paused.

"Wait, don't kill him." I peered up at the burly soldier on all fours. "I need him alive. I need to know what he knows. I need to know what he told them."

He turned and bolted out the door.

Glasswell cradled his weapon against his right side, hooked

my right arm around his shoulders, and, encircling my waist with his left arm, managed to heave me up onto stiff, tottering legs. There was a shout from above, scuffling, a shot, and a thud.

Glasswell dropped his arm from my middle. "Tank! Whiskey!"

I would have fallen again had I not curled my fist around his heavy canvas coat. Instead, I listed against him like a boat taking on water.

"We're fine, Sarge." Tank's muffled voice floated down from above.

"Damn, I really wanted him alive," I muttered.

"You're ice cold. Let's see if we can find you some clothes." His hand returned to my waist and he guided me back to the hard seat.

"The German's coat, on the back of his chair." I stretched my fingers, crossed my legs, and bent to massage my numb toes. The pressure sent angry sparks of pain through my foot, which I welcomed with relief. I'd once seen the results of frostbite on a resistance fighter who'd spent too many freezing nights in the elements. His blackened toes were not something I'd soon forget. The fear of removing the socks and finding something similar abated as sensation returned. A tearing sound pulled my attention to the sergeant, and I found him stripping the epaulets and insignia from the heavy overcoat.

"Don't want you to be mistaken for the enemy," he said with one last rip and dangled it in front of me.

"Thanks." Using the arms of the chair, I pushed to my feet and slipped the wool over my shivering frame. My fingers were so stiff from cold and disuse I couldn't thrust the thick buttons through their holes. Without a word, Glassman pushed away my hopeless hands and buttoned them for me. The enormous coat swallowed me, falling below my calf, but I didn't care, I was too desperate for the heat it would provide to my frigid, quaking body.

"Do you want his boots? They'll be too big on you... We could stuff them."

I shook my head. "Mine are in the corner, but I could use his laces."

He pulled the dead man into the middle of the room, flipped him over, and went to work removing the laces. I tottered over to my boots on legs as wobbly as a newborn colt. While we took care of the shoe situation, I noticed the surrounding sounds of fighting had dissipated and only single rifle shots were scattered here and there.

Minutes later, Glasswell assisted me to my feet again. "Let's get you out of here."

Lars' body lay blocking the threshold; Glasswell stepped over him and turned to help me, but I ignored his outstretched hand, instead glowering down at my tormentor. His glazed, sightless eyes stared up at me, the 9 mm Luger still gripped in his hand. The darkened reminders of our little chat that would leave indelible scars burned painfully with every shift of the woolen coat. His actions instilled terror that would haunt my dreams for years to come. Anger and fury filled my tightening chest, my breath sped up, and I lashed out with a kick to his ribs. To my utter frustration, he was so heavy, and I so weak, his motionless form barely moved. Something snapped, and with an outraged screech, I bent down, wrenched the weapon out of his inert grasp, and put two bullets into his blood-soaked chest. I can't say that it relieved the swirling tempest in my body, but it did seem to alleviate the feelings of helplessness.

I gazed up to find Glassman's startled countenance gaping, his weapon at the ready and aimed ... at me.

"Sorry about that, Sergeant." I allowed the gun to rotate

forward on my pointer finger and held the butt out to the stunned soldier. My hand no longer shook.

"*Glass!*" Tank's voice called out as he thundered down the stairwell.

"*We're fine,*" Glassman returned.

The footsteps paused.

"We'll be up in a minute," he said over his shoulder.

Tank's tread retreated up the stairs and the soldier's gaze raked my face. "Is he the one ... who did that to you?"

"Yes."

His jaw clenched as he studied me and the weapon I dangled from my finger. "You know how to handle that weapon?"

"Yes."

"Then you had best hang on to it. You might need it."

I tucked the Luger into my pocket, stepped over Lars, and followed Glassman upstairs. In the hallway, we came upon the German private who had been guarding my door, slumped against the wall, bleeding out from a bullet wound to his neck. The radio room turned out to be a cheery rose-papered bedroom bright with sunshine. A double bed with a dirty white eyelet cover was shoved up against the left wall, and a round drum table with a pair of matching shield-back chairs assembled in the center of the room—an interrupted card game scattered across the table. The game's pot held a small pile of *Reichsmark*, and on top lay my compass pendant, the chain spiraled around it like a snake. The needle rotated and danced, searching for north, when I picked it up.

Against the left wall sat a mahogany rolltop desk with a German radio and an Enigma machine. Tank riffled through papers scattered across the desktop. Next to the radio, tied to another chair with the same twine they'd used on me, and what looked like a dirty sock jammed into his mouth, sat Captain

Müller. Private Whiskey stood relaxed, with his gun trained on the captain's heart.

"We caught this one for you, ma'am." Whiskey grinned at me, proud as a peacock with his tail feathers fanned.

"Glass, come look at this." Tank waved at the first sergeant. "Kraut papers. Can you make anything out of it?"

Glassman shuffled through the documents.

"Spy girl, you speak Kraut?" Tank asked.

"Of course." I tucked the compass into my coat pocket.

Müller's gaze narrowed and he grunted, pulling at the restraints as I bypassed him.

"Hey now." Private Whiskey pushed him back with the tip of his M1. "We'll get to you in a minute."

I shuffled through the missives. Two large maps were obviously troop movements, including military installations across the Rhine. One stack I identified as the daily Enigma transmissions by its weather report. There were also memorandums providing directions from Hitler to fight to the last man and instructing troops to blow up the bridges as they retreated and basically burn everything down to the ground—a trick he'd learned from the Russians. I shoved everything into a leather satchel I found sitting on the bed and handed it to Glassman.

"I imagine your commanding officer will want to see this and the Enigma machine. I need to speak with the prisoner."

Tank pulled the sock out of Müller's mouth. My gaze surveyed the room—the card game, the radio messages, the pair of chairs at the table, back to the captain. The bloody wretch had been here the entire time. He must have known exactly what Lars was doing to me one floor down and done nothing to stop him. I fingered the compass, then I reached back and let fly. My hand connected with his cheek; the contact reverberated up my arm and flung his face aside.

Ow! His stone jaw left my digits stinging. Breath whistled through my teeth as I flailed my hand in the air, shaking out the pain.

The captain's face rotated back to me. He smirked, called me a rude German epithet, and spit at my shoe. Tank reached past me. His fist connected and, with a dull crunch, broke Müller's nose. The smirk disappeared and our prisoner cried out as blood flooded down his face.

"You shouldn't be disrespectful to the lady," Private Whiskey scolded Müller.

"Next time leave the heavy hitting to us, ma'am." Tank chewed his cigar and grinned.

It was too painful to smile and I had to bite my lip to keep from grinning back. "Thanks."

"Clean him up so she can ask her questions." Glassman tossed the dirty sock at Tank. "Be quick about it. We need to report back … and she needs medical attention."

I got comfortable at the card table and enjoyed listening to Müller moan beneath Tank's callous ministrations.

"What did you tell command? Did you tell them you had the Black Widow?" I spoke to him in German.

His eyes flashed at me. "So, you admit, you are the Black Widow?"

I squinted, debating my answers. *Maybe if I'm honest with him, he'll tell me what I need to know.* "No, I am not. I don't know who she is. If they think it's me, they'll stop looking for her. Did you tell them I was the Black Widow?"

While I spoke to Müller, I heard Whiskey whisper to Tank, "How do we know she's really one of ours? She speaks awful good Kraut."

"Did you see the burns?" Tank grunted.

Müller just glared at me, his mouth set in a mulish scowl.

I don't have time for this. I fisted my hands in frustration. "Let me explain something. If you cooperate and answer my questions, I'll make sure you will come to no more harm. Captured as a prisoner of war, you will receive the appropriate treatment under the Geneva Convention." I let that sink in. "If not, I will tell these men you are a high-ranking member of the Nazi Party and that you ordered the murder of hundreds of French citizens at Oradour-sur-Glane."

His eyes flickered at the mention of the French town.

"I see you've heard of the atrocities committed there. I will recommend they turn you over to the French government. Immediately," I said through gritted teeth.

"You cannot prove I was there. Those were SS, not *Heer* troops."

"Do you think you'll survive long enough in a French prison waiting for the facts to be sorted?"

"As a prisoner of war, the only thing I am required to provide to the enemy is name, rank, and number."

"*Hauptmann,* you are speaking in front of three paratroopers who jumped into Normandy and survived the past month surrounded by the enemy in the forests of Bastogne." I had a feeling that Tank and Glassman fit into the category I just placed them. Private Whiskey, on the other hand, looked like more like a fresh-faced replacement, but the captain didn't know that. "They are immune to the hellishness of war. Do you think any of them would hesitate to beat you into submission or shoot you in the head, without compunction, if I asked?"

He didn't respond.

"They didn't like Lars' handiwork. The big one was pretty angry."

I tilted my head toward Tank.

Müller eyed the beefy soldier from head to toe, then turned back to me. "A compromise then. I will answer your questions if you answer some of mine."

I scowled at him. "Fine."

"Are you a spy?"

"*Ja.*"

"British?"

"American."

A flash of disbelief crossed his features.

"Now answer some of mine. What did you relay to your superiors? Who did you tell them you were holding? Did you tell them you had the Black Widow?"

"Lars told the Gestapo he had the Black Widow, but I did not confirm it. We had orders to transfer you tomorrow. What about your sister?"

"A lie. Did you give them a description of me?"

"Not exactly. Lars wasn't willing to tell them. You don't fit the Black Widow's profile. He lied."

The tension in my shoulders ebbed and I relaxed against the wooden shield behind me. The Black Widow, whoever she was, would be safe for a while longer.

"Who are you?"

I pinched my bottom lip, debating my answer. "Just an insignificant girl who took care of some German children."

His eyes flared and recognition flittered across his features. "*Das Kindermädchen?* You? The Nanny? But … I … I don't understand, they said she fled south, to Switzerland."

So, they were looking for me. "Did you tell them Masselin found me at his grandmother's home?"

He looked down.

I uncrossed my legs and leaned toward him. "What did you tell them?"

He didn't answer.

"*Sags mir!*" Tell me! My fist slammed against the table, making the cards and Private Whiskey jump. The two seasoned soldiers remained casual in their stances.

The German shook his head. I ground my teeth in frustration. Glassman shifted impatiently.

"Need some help?" Tank raised his brows.

I zeroed in on the stump hanging from his mouth. "Tell me, Sergeant, do you happen to have any more of those lovely cigars?"

He hesitated a moment before reaching into a pocket and withdrawing a fat stogie. "Would you like me to light it for you?"

"Please."

He went through the process of cutting off the end, then fired it up before holding it toward me.

"Thank you." I took the smelly cigar between my thumb and forefinger. "The captain looks warm. Would you mind dispensing with his sleeves?"

"I'll do it," Whiskey volunteered, retrieving the knife strapped to his calf.

Müller glared at me beneath his furrowed brow as Whiskey worked. I clamped the cheroot between my teeth, making sure not to take a drag. At the tender age of sixteen, some of my boarding school friends and I had gotten ahold of a box of Cuban cigars. We'd snuck into the basement, in the middle of the night, and lit up. It didn't take long before we were all choking and gagging on the foul things. I wasn't willing to make the ignoble mistake of vomiting in front of the treacherous captain again.

"All set, ma'am." Whiskey returned the blade to its scabbard.

I rose. "Herr Müller, do you know what it feels like to get burned by a cigarette? First, the signals race to your brain, and you automatically flinch away from the pain, but when you're tied down, there's nowhere to go. Then you can hear the sizzling, and then the smell. Now, tell me about Masselin's grandmother."

He glared at me mutinously. "How can you justify this? I bandaged your wounds. I was not the one who gave you the burns."

"*Nein*, you are the commanding officer. *You* … allowed … it to happen," I hissed. "Just as these gentlemen will allow it to happen."

His alarmed gaze whipped from one soldier to the other, landing on Glassman. "*Stop her,*" he shouted in English.

Glassman shrugged.

The cigar sizzled against his bicep, and the scent of burning flesh overrode that of the tobacco. He gritted his teeth for as long as he could stand, then let out a bloodcurdling roar.

I removed the stub. "Tell me about Masselin's grandmother."

His head hung forward and he mumbled something.

"*Lauter.*" Speak up.

He shook his head and I pressed the cigar against his skin again.

"They went to the shelter she was holed up in … she … it…" The top of his head shifted side to side.

"*Schweinehund.*" I whispered the epithet and collapsed in the chair.

"We need to wrap this up," Glassman said.

"I'm finished." I handed the cigar back to Tank.

"What should we do with him?" the private asked.

"Whatever you want. He's of no more use to me." I rose and exited the room. I barely flinched when the shot followed my departure.

Tank found me staring down the gloomy staircase. "Need a hand, doll?" Before I could answer, he slung his rifle over his shoulder and scooped me off my feet. My arms automatically wrapped around his neck. Upon our descent to the main floor, he navigated around a dead German soldier. His foot jarred the inert form, and the head flopped back to reveal Masselin's blank visage. Unexpected pity filled me; at least he wouldn't have to be told about his grandmother. I pulled the thick collar up around my ears and tucked my head into Tank's neck.

Chapter Seventeen
Secrets

Clusters of American soldiers milled around the village square as houses smoldered in the background. The distinct acrid tang of smoking wood, rifle munitions, building dust, and coppery blood hung heavily in the air. German soldiers had been assembled, weaponless—guarded by a dozen Americans—in the center of the plaza. They sat quietly on the cobblestones as others were herded, from side streets at gunpoint, hands in the air, toward the gathering. A collection of wounded soldiers congregated at tables of a partially bombed-out café and were being treated by a pair of medics.

Tank's appearance, carrying me, stopped nearby conversations. Questions were tossed at him.

"Hey, Sarge, who you got there, another Kraut prisoner?"

"Tank? Who is that?"

"Tank, who's the Jerry?"

Tank ignored the questions and carried me over to the impromptu first-aid post. An army jeep pulled up, and, stepping in front of other waiting soldiers, he slipped me into the front seat. Two able-bodied soldiers heaved a groaning man, with blood-soaked bandages wrapped around his thigh, onto the stretcher strapped to the hood of the vehicle.

"C'mon, Sarge. You're sending a Kraut over me?" protested a private with a dressing wrapped around his forehead.

"Take her back to the aid station with you. She needs medical attention." Tank spoke to the driver, then turned to the protesting soldier. "And she's not a Kraut. You two take the back." He hooked a thumb over his shoulder.

One of the medics pushed through the crowd. "What's the problem? Sergeant, these men have been triaged. I haven't seen this man"—he did a double-take—"woman. Who is she? What's wrong with her?"

"She's one of ours and she's been through hell at the hands of the Krauts, Doc."

"It's not a problem. If you point me in the direction of company HQ, I'll walk." I swung a leg out intending to alight. "I need to speak..." *Whoa.* The ground shimmied and shifted.

Tank shoved me back in place. "You can barely walk, much less see through that left eye. And when was the last time you ate?"

I pressed two fingers against my temple. "It's been awhile."

The medic began to fire questions at me, surrounding voices rose; it was too much. I couldn't keep up with all the arguments and squeezed my eyes shut.

First Sergeant Glassman's dulcet tone intervened, "What's the problem, gentlemen?"

The voices turned off like a spigot.

"Doc, let her go ... please."

"Whatever you say, First Sergeant." The medic returned to his duties, and the two injured men piled in back without further discussion.

Glassman handed me the leather satchel but addressed his comments to the driver. "Get this bag to Captain Devlin. He's going to want to see what's inside."

"Who is Captain Devlin?" I asked as the car jerked into gear and zipped off down the road so quickly I had to grab the handle attached to the dashboard to keep from falling out.

"Intelligence officer," the driver replied.

"Do you know a Captain McNair?"

"You mean Major McNair? He's at battalion HQ."

I didn't ask any more questions for the rest of the ride because I spent it gritting my teeth against each bump and knock, which sought to exacerbate every bruise on my body. Even so, I couldn't dismiss the wings of joy that beat in my breast, fluttering happily with the knowledge that Charlie was alive and close by. I reached inside the coat pocket to assure myself his compass remained firmly nestled there. Finally, we jerked to a stop in front of a squat one-story school building. The GIs in the back seat got out, and a pair of orderlies retrieved the poor fellow on the hood. I remained in my seat.

"This is the aid station, ma'am. Do you need help getting out?"

"Where are you headed next?"

"Got to drop off these papers at HQ, then I'll go back to pick up more of the wounded."

"Take me to with you to HQ."

"Ma'am, my orders were to drop you off at the aid station."

"I have important information for your intelligence officer, Captain Devlin."

"Whatever you have, ma'am, you can give it to me. I'll make sure he gets it."

"*It* ... is in here." I tapped my forehead. "Let's go."

"Ma'am, my orders were to leave you at the aid station."

"I don't give a damn about your orders. I have intelligence that is important to the success of the Allied advance and the security of the United States."

The fellow had the cheek to roll his eyes at me, and my patience snapped.

"Listen up, soldier," I snatched a hunk of his coat placket and jerked him forward until we were nose to nose. "I didn't spend the past week dodging Nazis, sleeping in the cold, and getting slapped around by a misogynistic monster just to have the intelligence I've been guarding become useless because it didn't get to the right people in time." His eyes had grown wide as I spoke through clenched teeth. I released him and he fell back against his seat. "Take me to your intelligence officer. *Now.*"

He shrugged. "Suit yourself, lady." We zipped through the town, dodging groups of meandering GIs and trucks. "Who did you say you were?"

"I didn't." I could have sworn the drive was even more harrowing than the one that brought us to the aid station, and I wondered who had the audacity to give this fellow a license in the first place. "I'm with the Office of Strategic Services."

He flashed a blank look but I didn't deign to explain. "Someone worked you over good, eh?"

"Watch the road!"

The horn blared, sending chickens scattering in all directions—we missed one by millimeters—then he swerved back into his lane to dodge out of the way of an oncoming truck. Finally, the hair-raising ride ended as we drew to a stop in front of a hotel building that showed relatively little scarring on its façade and only a few broken windows. The driver yanked on the hand brake and hopped out, snatching the satchel from my grip.

"Wait here. I'll see if the captain is in."

Before I had a chance to protest, he strode through the front doors.

My own dismount out of the Jeep was not so quick or agile, and I followed him at a hobbling pace. The lobby bustled with life. A coterie of soldiers sat in a group of leather club chairs to my left, loudly debating the merits of the Yankees versus the

Red Sox over a game of cards. On the right, three soldiers at the check-in desk sorted boxes full of cigarettes and K-rations into piles. Another soldier wandered around calling names and passing out mail. Other soldiers came and went through the front door, blindly moving past me as if I didn't exist. My driver was nowhere to be seen.

The mailman passed in front of me and I laid a hand on his forearm. "Excuse me, can you tell me where I can find Captain Devlin?"

"Room two-oh-six, I think." He didn't glance up from the envelopes sifting through his fingers.

At the far end of the foyer rose the grand staircase, the golden carpets worn and dirty from muddy boots and lack of cleaning but its elegant design and woodwork apparent despite the careworn appearance. A pair of soldiers stood to the right of the stairs, in front of a birdcage elevator, deep in conversation. The beautiful but daunting staircase mocked me. "Does the elevator work?"

"Not if you want it to go up. Timmons," he called out and headed over to the card players.

Two-oh-six—the brass numbers were much like the staircase, worn and discolored but still claiming the former elegance of the aging hotel. I raised my hand to knock; the door swung inward before my knuckles touched the oak wood.

"What are you doing here? I told you to wait in the Jeep," my driver said.

"Corporal, who's that?" a disembodied voice from inside the room asked.

I pushed past the rude corporal and walked into the suite. A sofa and high-backed chair sat in front of a crackling fire. To the right, littered with papers, was a cherry dining table big enough to seat eight. The other half of the room was taken up with a large bed. A hatless, brown-haired captain stood at the foot of the table with his hands on hips. To his left sat a bright-eyed private, who looked not more than a day over eighteen, tapping diligently on his typewriter.

"Captain Devlin?"

His brow furrowed and he squinted at me. "Yes. Have we met?"

"No, sir. My name is Lillian Saint James. I am an operative with the Office of Strategic Services. I have information that your commanding officers are going to want to see."

The driver dogged my steps. "I'm sorry, sir. Would you like me to—"

But the captain waved him off. "It's fine, Corporal." He shook my hand. "You must be the impertinent lady Jones, here, said wouldn't stay at the aid station. Are you all right? You look as though you have been through the wringer."

"I'm fine."

"If you are speaking of the papers Jones dropped off, we're looking into them." He indicated the empty bag on the chair, its contents already strewn across the table.

"*I* am speaking about the film secreted in my boot heel, which provides exact locations of munitions factories, a couple of recently built Luftwaffe airstrips, and two static U-boat locations, including one patrolling the New England coast."

The typing stopped.

Delivering this information directly to the military, without going through the proper chain of command, was a breach of protocol and would likely land me in a bathtub full of hot water, to put it mildly. However, my body would soon give out, and I hadn't the time or energy to seek out my people, who probably assumed by now that I was dead and had written me off. Additionally, I felt that turning the materials over to the frontline troops might improve the likelihood that the intelligence could be used sooner rather than later. Beyond all of these justifications, in the back audience of my brain, there rang a small voice that had been growing to a roar ever since I saw the Screaming Eagle on Sergeant Glassman's shoulder.

"Who did you say you were?" Devlin asked.

"Lily Saint James, code name Fleur-de-lis. I've spent the past few months undercover as a nanny for a colonel overseeing the work camp at the Mauser rifle factory in Oberndorf, Germany."

"Corporal, you're dismissed," the captain said sharply over my shoulder. The door closed with a snap. "Did you say Fleur-de-lis?"

"Yes."

He scratched at the stubble along his jaw. "I was under the impression you were a man."

"I am surprised you have heard of me at all. You were likely led to believe I was a man for my own security." The room started to sway as my limited strength threatened to give out. "Captain, do you mind if we sit?"

"Yes, of course, I apologize." He led me to the high-back wing chair, and I gratefully sank into its plush red-velvet seat, reaching my feet toward the warmth of the fire. "May I take your coat?"

"No." I waved him off, but the cuff fell back to reveal the bruises and rope burns at my wrist. His gaze missed nothing and I self-consciously tugged the sleeve back in place. "Thank you, I prefer to keep it on."

"You look half-starved. Let me get you a drink. Sherry or"—he sniffed the clear contents of a decanter sitting on the sideboard behind the sofa—"apple ... gin, I think?"

"Probably *schnapps*. I'll take the sherry."

"Karp, go scrounge up a hot meal for Miss Saint James."

"Yes, sir."

The sweet alcohol soothed my abused throat, but my hand shook as I sipped. I silently blessed the captain for not filling the glass to the brim, and, resting my head against the soft fabric, I closed my eyes.

"Tell me, if you were in Oberndorf, how did you end up here?"

"A few days ago I watched my contact, a German sympathizer, throw himself off his own balcony to avoid being captured by the SS," I explained in a flat voice. "I believed my cover to be in jeopardy if not already compromised. It was too risky to return to the colonel's home to pick up my exit papers, so I headed into the Schwarzwald."

"Jesus. How long have you been on the run?"

"Seven or eight days?" I opened my eyes to find the captain literally sitting on the edge of his seat. "My mind is a little fuzzy. I think I was captured two days ago. First Sergeant Glassman and Thompson stormed the building where I was being held and ... well, you understand. Basically, I owe my life to those men. Which reminds me, the Germans seem to think there's another female spy around here. They called her Black Widow. Have you heard of the code name? Do you know anything about her?"

"No, you'll have to ask your own people. Information is ... filtered to us. The only reason I recognized your code name is because I read it on a report. Frankly, you're the first OSS agent who's been this forthcoming. The rest of your lot seem to skulk in smoky corners and never answer any direct questions."

"I would be doing the same thing now if I hadn't made such a bloody mess of it." I rubbed my temples. "I am not looking forward to seeing my superiors. And when I do, I have a feeling they're going to spend the next month debriefing me before sticking me uselessly behind a typewriter with the rest of the secretarial pool."

"You seem competent. I'll take you as my secretary."

I allowed a wan smile to cross my face. "I'm not quite ready to be put out to pasture. Besides, I figured coming directly to you, we would cut through a lot of the … filtering. You *are* an intelligence officer?"

"Put your mind at ease, I'm intelligence. Are you … army?"

I finished the sherry and held out my glass for more. The fire had finally warmed my feet. The warmth, along with the sherry, was spreading through my body and seeping into my chilled bones. "No, civilian. I'm not even sure who to report to around here. My German contacts are dead, and the last SOE agent I had contact with was in Stuttgart. As far as the home office knows, I'm dead too. You could say I'm at loose ends." He refilled my glass and I sipped more of the sweet wine. Tension ebbed from my shoulders, and relaxing against the plump cushions had calmed the nagging ache in my head … or maybe it was the sherry.

Devlin rested his chin on his fist and stared at me with an incalculable look.

"All right, so I do have an idea who I should report to."

"You mentioned film."

"Yes, right-o." Reluctantly, I placed the half-drunk sherry on the coffee table. "I used a Minox mini camera. Do you have a viewer or developer for the film?" I slid the boot heel aside and out fell David O'Leary's dog tag. The raised letters scraped roughly against my fingers. I'd forgotten I put it in my boot.

"What have you got there?"

"Three or four days ago, I witnessed an air combat, not far from Bühl, and came across a downed pilot. I tried to help him, but…" Tears pricked my eyes and I licked my lips. "C-c—" I cleared my throat. "Can you make sure the family is notified?"

"Of course." He pocketed the dog tag.

"Here's the film. I pray the canister is watertight because we took a couple of unwanted baths together. If it's ruined, I can show you what I remember, but there was a fair amount of information I simply didn't have time to read."

"Can you tell me what you remember now?"

Sighing, I retrieved the sherry and swallowed it down. "No time like the present. Pull out the maps."

Karp returned carrying a tray. "Some of the fellows were making K-ration stew in the kitchen." He sniffed the bowl. "I think the mystery meat is potted ham. I also got you a biscuit and coffee, ma'am. I put some sugar in your coffee. The boys make it pretty strong."

"Thank you, Private. Leave it on the sideboard if you would, please. I'll get to it in a moment."

"Karp, go find Peterson and send him to me. Let him know I need to develop Minox mini film. Get me Lieutenant Grimes as well … and send in the major if you can find him. After that, take a break and get yourself something to eat."

Sergeant Peterson arrived bearing a negative viewer, although it was for much larger film, and he set to work trying to rig something for the tiny Minox film. Lieutenant Grimes joined us as Devlin and I pored over the maps. I was able to remember and identify a few of the munitions factories and airstrips. However, the details were unclear in my mind— whether due to the fact that it'd been at least a dozen days since I'd seen the materials hidden in the colonel's safe or the utter exhaustion threatening to overwhelm me, I did not know. The scent of the coffee now filled the room and my stomach grumbled at its siren call. I was about to ask one of the men to hand it to me when a voice interrupted us.

"Jake, I heard you were looking for me."

The oxygen in my lungs whooshed out and my heart skipped a beat. There he stood at the opposite end of the table. He'd lost weight since I'd seen him last—who hadn't? The lines around his eyes had deepened, and telltale circles spoke to his lack of rest. The faded memory I'd held in my mind's eye was merely a black-and-white picture show; it didn't do him justice. Having him in front of me was like stepping over the rainbow into the Technicolor glory of Oz.

His gaze dusted past me to Devlin on my right, and I realized just how different I must look compared to our last meeting. "What's the problem?" he asked.

"It looks like we've come into some valuable intel. I'd like you to meet—"

"Charlie?" The word came out as a hoarse whisper and those piercing blue eyes rested on me. The room went silent, and I self-consciously tugged a coil of hair forward to cover the bruising.

Recognition flared. "Lily?"

"You've met?" Devlin asked.

"Good god, what happened? What are you doing so close to the front lines? What idiotic newspaper sent you and your camera to this godforsaken place, and why are you wearing that ratty German overcoat?"

I licked my dry lips. "Charlie—"

"Newspaper? What newspaper?" Devlin's questioning gaze raked me up and down, but I couldn't take my eyes off Charlie.

"She's a photojournalist," Charlie explained.

"I'm not ... exactly a newspaper photographer," I whispered.

"What? What do you mean?"

"I—" The explanation stuck in my throat and I waited, hoping someone else would explain the situation, but nobody came to my rescue, and expectancy hung heavy in the air. "I'm an agent … for the Office of Strategic Services." It came out in a shaky undertone.

His mouth turned down as I spoke. "So, when we met…"

"Photojournalism was my cover in Paris."

"Paris?" Devlin muttered under his breath.

"She's a spy," Grimes clarified.

Charlie crossed his arms. "Thank you, Lieutenant, I am beginning to understand."

Grimes blanched under the derisive gaze.

"And what is an OSS agent doing here at my headquarters?" His icy glare returned to me; its chill wrapped around my heart like a vise.

This wasn't how I'd pictured our meeting—looking like a ragged street urchin, surrounded by his men and unable to explain what Paris meant to me. Powerless to assure him that our time together was not a lie or a simple wartime affair, and how much I'd wanted to tell him exactly who I was and what I was doing for the war effort. He seemed to tower above me, so I shoved my chair back and, using the table as leverage, pushed myself to a standing position.

"She is sharing intelligence with us." Devlin shifted closer and the fabric of his sleeve brushed against mine.

"You should see this, Major. She's identified munitions factories and new airfields." Grimes pointed to the marks we'd circled on the map.

"If Peterson can get the viewer work—"

"It's working," Peterson interrupted Devlin. "You'd better take a look at this, Captain. The first two shots are damaged, maybe we'll get more once they are developed, but this third shot is a partial, and the fourth … holy mackerel! There's a ding-danged U-Boat sitting off the coast of Rhode Island."

Grimes and Devlin maneuvered around to the coffee table, where Peterson had set up shop. Charlie and I didn't move. His arctic mien held me immobilized, and my mind begged to know what he was thinking, but there was no way I'd ask in front of his men.

"Charlie, you're going to want to see this. So is Regimental and probably the navy," Devlin said.

Finally, his intractable gaze released me from my stupor, and as I turned, the room shimmered, a ringing filled my ears, and darkness tunneled around me. My arms felt floaty and detached while my legs became leaden weights.

From far away, I barely heard my own voice above the din, "I'm sorry, gentlemen, I believe I need to—" My legs collapsed. Strong arms wrapped around me before I hit the hard floor.

It was strange. I could feel the soft comfort of the sofa beneath me and hear voices speaking. Someone pulled the coat aside. There were gasps, and questions tumbled over each other.

"Holy Mother and Mary, who did this to her?"

"Is that a cigarette burn?"

"Take a gander at her neck."

"Who did you say found her?"

"She's so thin. Grimes, get a medic." That was the only voice my mind recognized. I think I tried to push the hands away. "Shh, it's all right, Lily. Don't move. It's all right."

No, no, don't look. It's ugly, my mind cried, but I couldn't force the words beyond my lips; eventually the ringing turned into a roar and the darkness pulled me into the void.

Chapter Eighteen
Lost Compass

"Come on, doll, wake up. Doc says you need to eat some soup."

My eyes opened to find a most unlikely nurse at my side. Tank sat next to the bed, his big hand wrapped around a bowl and the inimitable cigar clamped between his teeth.

"Where am I?" I croaked. My arms were trapped under a poufy eiderdown cover that weighed on me like an anvil.

"You're still at the hotel. The captain and major decided it would not be a good idea to put you at the hospital with the rest of the wounded."

"I've got to get up. I have information for your intelligence officer. Where are my boots? There's important information—" My arm finally obeyed and popped free from beneath the blanket. A white linen sleeve with a lace and embroidered cuff covered the burn marks but was a little too short to cover the fresh bandages at my wrists. I struggled to sit up.

"Whoa ... slow down. Captain has the information. It's already worked its way up to Regimental. Your boots are under the bed, empty of their cargo." He winked.

I sighed as memories sifted back into consciousness, including the unfortunate interaction with Charlie right before I uselessly passed out.

"What am I wearing?" I peeked under the covers to find myself devoid of clothing—bra, slip, socks—all removed to be replaced by the linen nightgown. I'd been stripped and bandaged. *Who removed my underthings?*

"One of the fellows discovered it in the wardrobe in his room. He was going to send it home, but when the major found out about it, he commandeered it. Probably left behind by a guest who had to leave in a hurry."

"Remind me to thank the soldier who donated it." Weak winter sun filtered through the sheer curtains at the window, illuminating the ornate wardrobe, writing table, and desk chair. A scratched and worn army-issue footlocker stood between the desk and door. "Who do I have to thank for giving up this room?"

"The major. He's bunking with Captain Devlin. Here, let me help you sit up. Doc says you're dehydrated and need fluids."

I couldn't argue with that assessment; my mouth was as dry as a cat's tongue. He drew me forward and plumped the pillows, arranging me into a sitting position, before handing me the bowl. I couldn't believe how weak I felt. My hand shook so much most of the warm broth didn't make it into my mouth; instead it dribbled down my chin and onto the covers. Tank didn't say a word. He retrieved the soup and began feeding me.

"How did you end up drawing the short straw?"

The cigar stump shifted sides. "What do you mean?"

"Babysitting duty."

"Actually, I got here about fifteen minutes ago. From what I have heard, there's been quite a parade of folks dropping by check up on you. The major, Whiskey, Peterson. The captain's been in and out a few times. Seems he's got something to show you when you wake. First Sergeant Glassman stopped by too. He chewed out Jones for not leaving you at the hospital, but the way Jones tells it, you refused to get out of the Jeep. Seems you've got a bit of a stubborn streak. Sarge said he should have carried you in, and because he didn't follow orders, Jones has been put on KP for the week."

I gave a guilty cringe. "How long have I been out of it?"

"'Bout eighteen hours. Doc says you probably have a concussion from the bump on the back of your head. How did you get that?"

I swallowed the broth. "Rifle butt."

Tank frowned and said no more until I'd finished the entire bowl, then he handed me a biscuit and a mug filled with a fizzy orange drink. "Doc said this would be good for you. And Whiskey left you a chocolate bar."

The biscuit was hard and rather tasteless, but the sugary orange drink made up for the biscuit and seemed to help steady my hands. "Thank you, Sergeant." I gave him a wobbly smile. "You can go now. I'm sure you have better things to do than babysit me."

"Can't. Got orders to stay with you until the doc returns."

"Well, I wouldn't want you to disobey orders and end up on KP with Jones."

I relaxed against the pillows, fiddling with the silk ribbon at my neckline. Something was missing. I flattened my hand against my collar, then reached inside the gown, but my hunting fingers didn't find the metal links they sought. The memory of my compass pendant sitting atop the pile of cards floated past. *Did I put it on?* No, the pendant was tucked into the pocket of the coat. "Tank, do you know what happened to the German overcoat I was wearing?"

"No, ma'am, can't say as I do."

Panic gripped me. I shoved aside the sheets. "I need to find the coat."

"Now hold up. Don't go getting yourself into a twist. We can get you a new one if it's missing. Sawyers said we just got a whole shipment of winter gear in yesterday."

"*No.* You don't understand. I must find *that* coat. It's imperative." Tears stung my eyes and I mashed my lips together to hold back a sob.

"Okay, calm down. Calm down. I'm sure it's around here somewhere. Let me check the wardrobe... Here it is." He laid the wool across my lap. "Now what is so important about *this* Kraut coat?"

I checked the left pocket but came up empty. Foolish of me. I flipped it over and dug around the rough lining of the other pocket; my fingers closed around the precious compass and relief flooded my system, warming me better than the bowl of soup. I withdrew the pendant, draped the chain over my head, and patted it in place.

Tank remained at the foot of the bed, watching my dramatic performance with a puzzled expression until the necklace rested on my chest, then his mouth turned down and a look of regret crossed his features. "Did your sweetheart give that to you?"

I chewed my bottom lip with no idea how to answer. Tank had been protective, gentle, and kind to me since finding me strapped to that chair. I remembered how he carried me down the stairs, but my heart belonged to another. And though there was nothing lover-like in my last encounter with Charlie, even if I'd lost him, I was unwilling to give up his talisman. Its bearing had saved my life.

"Is he an agent like you?"

I shook my head.

"In the service?"

"Yes," I whispered. A knock at the door saved me from answering further. "Enter."

The door swung open to reveal First Sergeant Glassman.

"You're looking much better." He came to stand next to the bed. "The eye doesn't look quite so gruesome."

"Gee, Sergeant, you really know how to boost a girl's confidence," I drawled, provoking a grin. "Thanks to Tank, I'm feeling much better. Which reminds me, I never properly thanked *you* for saving my life back there. If it hadn't been…" I shuddered at the thought of what might have happened.

"No problem, ma'am." He gave a deprecating shrug. "If it hadn't been for your wild-eyed signal, I might have been the one shot in the head."

I reached out and took his rough hand into mine and gripped it tight. "Thank you, First Sergeant. I owe you one."

Glassman blushed.

"Well, there is something you can do for me." Captain Devlin stood in the open doorway carrying a handful of papers.

Tank saluted; I released Glassman and sat back against the pillows as he entered. "At ease. Gentlemen, can we have the room?"

The men took their leave and Devlin closed the door behind Tank. "Madam, tales of your heroics and beauty are running rampant through the company, and half the men are smitten with you without even having set eyes on you. You'll have them all at your feet once they actually see you."

I dismissed such blatant flattery, especially because I knew in my current state I must look like hell. "What can I do for you, Captain?"

"Call me Jake."

"Very well, what can I do for you, Jake?"

"My translator has come down with dysentery and is currently spending his time at the latrines." He held up a sheaf of papers.

A few I recognized as documents I'd encouraged Glassman

to take. "Yes, of course. Do you want me to read them out loud or type them up?"

"Read." Jake seated himself in the chair vacated by Tank. While he sorted through the documents, I straightened the counterpane and shoved the German coat aside. He pulled forth one of the documents and laid it in my outstretched hand.

"This looks like a command from the general field marshal directing troop movements." I broke off a piece of the chocolate bar and popped it in my mouth. The sweet cocoa was an indulgence I hadn't tasted in a long time, and I savored the treat as my eyes skimmed the paper.

"That compass looks familiar."

I paused mid-chew.

Jake steepled his fingers and gave an enigmatic smile.

The chocolate, now as tasteless as chalk, tumbled down my throat. "I beg your pardon?"

"The compass you are wearing around your neck. He used it to orient himself the night we jumped into Normandy. He once told me it was his father's."

Possessively, I tucked the pendant beneath my collar.

"You're the girl. The girl from Paris."

I didn't rise to his bait.

"It's funny, I haven't seen the compass since his trip to Paris. And while he was there, he acquired a new trinket. It looks to me like a St. Christopher medal. Yours?"

Once again, I was put into a position where I had no answer, and even if I did, I'm not sure I would have provided it. My training held me in a tight grip. I'd already told this man too much. I refused to allow him to goad me into a confession about Charlie. Especially if Charlie hadn't seen fit to explain it to his friend himself.

"Would you like me to continue?" I crossed my hands piously over the document.

"Don't worry, he'll come around. He feels duped ... betrayed. But you and I know it's all part of the job. Deep down, he knows it too."

I wasn't so sure. I looked to my next meeting with Charlie with a sense of eagerness and trepidation. Since Jake had opened this door, I couldn't hold back my next question. "Is it possible to see him?"

His brows rose and a half smile crossed his features. "I can let him know you're asking."

Chapter Nineteen
The Lucky Talisman

"I will be back in an hour. If you finish up and are looking for something to occupy you, there is a file next to the typewriter that needs to be translated." He buttoned the top two buttons on his shirt. "You know how to type?"

I smiled wryly at Jake. "Yes, Captain, I know how to work the typewriter."

"Good girl," he said absently, in such a manner it made me feel like he was praising a favored pet, as he searched for his hat.

Indeed, in the past few days, Jake Devlin seemed to have taken on the role of big brother. Truth be told, I liked him. Jake had the charm that comes from living the life of old money. He reminded me of the men I grew up around and worked with on Capitol Hill. Not only did Jake have an appealing charisma, he was highly intelligent without being condescending. As I had been patronized by so many men in my career, it was this humbling trait that had me valuing Jake's opinion above all others ... except one.

He patted his pockets as he visually scanned the room.

"Jake." I scooped the hat off the coffee table. "Catch." It wheeled across the room and he snatched it out of the air one-handed.

"Thanks."

"It's cold. Don't forget your coat," I tutted. The door banged shut and I sighed in the peaceful silence. What a difference a few days made. My strength returned bit by bit. The headache, my constant companion since I left Oberndorf, finally abated, and the damage wrought by Lars was slowly healing. This morning the bathroom mirror revealed the ugly bruising around my eye had lightened to a purple edged in yellow. I suppose I'd been lucky that he hadn't hit me with his fist and broken my cheekbone. The bruises at my neck had also faded to a dull ochre, the handprint no longer distinguishable in its outline, and today was the first day it didn't feel as though a painful walnut stuck in my throat every time I swallowed.

I adjusted the apron of my dress—a classic black, with red and white embroidery, German dirndl, handily acquired by Sergeant Peterson, who was better known as the battalion scrounger—and settled myself into the red-velvet wingback chair that I'd occupied only a few days ago. I pulled the photos out of the manila envelope and began sorting them across the low table. The strong coffee left a bitter taste and I added another lump of sugar. The door to the suite opened and closed. I peeked around the side wing of the chair expecting to see either Jake returning or his orderly, Private Karp. Neither man appeared.

Charlie, humming "Moonlight Serenade" and wearing only a pair of olive trousers and a towel slung around his neck, went directly to the antique washstand and mirror next to the wardrobe. He proceeded to work up a lather and soap his face with a shaving brush. I froze, the coffee cup halfway to my mouth and my shoulders stiff, as I shamelessly watched, knowing full well he did not realize the room was occupied. I should make some sort of noise to alert him. Yet I couldn't tear my eyes away, and I voyeuristically observed the muscles ripple beneath his skin while the razor rasped down the tender flesh at his neck. My tummy fluttered and my breath came out in shallow puffs. A new scar, still pink with healing, curved along his shoulder blade and undulated as he shaved.

I hadn't seen Charlie since our disastrous reintroduction. Though I'd had a parade of visitors come to my room in the past few days, Major McNair was not one of them … at least not while I was awake. I did not know if his neglect was due to work or disgust, but I'd been reluctant to request Devlin, or any of my other visitors, to send Charlie to me. Now … here he stood, and all the eloquent apologies that I'd thrashed out in my head over the past two days incoherently scattered, and my brain exited like a vaudevillian actor booed offstage.

He wiped the residual soap off his face and combed his damp hair into place.

The time had come. I swallowed and steeled myself. "Hello, Charlie."

He spun around to face me.

"Or should I call you Major McNair?" Fortunately, I managed to return the coffee cup to the saucer without spilling. "Congratulations, by the way, on your promotion."

He flipped up the lid on the footlocker that had been in my room the first day but disappeared as I slept, and drew out an olive drab T-shirt, which he pulled over his head. Then he opened the wardrobe and yanked out a Class-B gabardine shirt. His fingers quickly worked the buttons as he came around the sofa and took the seat opposite mine.

"Lily, you're looking"—blue eyes swept up and down my ridiculous costume, resting briefly at the bruises on my neck, and followed the chain that disappeared beneath the poufy white blouse—"much restored."

"I'm on the mend. Would you care for a cup of coffee?" I didn't wait for a response, instead reached for the pot and extra cup. I held both in an iron grip to keep my hands from shaking under his intense scrutiny. "We seem to be out of saucers."

He took the cup without glancing at it.

I licked my lips. "I'm sorry, Charlie." The apology surged forth with zero finesse. "I'm sorry I lied to you in Paris."

His jaw flexed. "Was any of it true, or was I just part of the cover?"

Stung by the accusation, I closed my eyes. "Journalism was the cover, but the rest ... it was all true. Everything. My mother's death, the relationship with my stepfather, the dinner, dancing ... our night together. All of it." I wrung my fingers and whispered, "It was all true."

Charlie didn't respond. My gaze flicked up from my hands to find a frown marring his profile as he contemplated the fire. He rose, snatched the poker off the stand, and stabbed at the embers. His movements, so abrupt, had me shrinking into the chair. My reaction, caught in his periphery, seemed to anger him further, and the poker dropped back into its metal cleft with a clang.

I purposely relaxed my fists and reached for the comfort of the coffee, cooled and now skimmed over. Following my lead, he returned to his seat and picked up his own beverage.

"Why Fleur-de-lis?"

The unexpected question startled me. The coffee went down the wrong pipe and I choked. Charlie handed me a cloth napkin as I coughed. "I beg your pardon."

"Jake told me it's your code name. How did that come about?"

"Oh." I wiped the last of the spittle from my lips. "My name, the fact that I speak French, and the birthmark. You know." The memory of Charlie stroking the flower-shaped stain at my hip had me flushing.

His fingers tightened around the mug. "How did they know about the birthmark?"

"Medical records."

His grip relaxed. "I would have worried had I known."

"Then it is probably best you did not."

"How long have you been in country?"

"The orders I received in Paris."

"No, I mean how long have you been here in Europe?"

"I shipped over to Britain in late forty-three to finish my training. Dropped into France a week before Normandy with French Resistance and SOE."

"What do you mean you 'dropped in'?" His brows drew down.

I remembered his lovely parachuting story from the Paris café and chewed my lip at the foolish mistake.

"Did you parachute into France?"

The napkin coiled around my fingers. I couldn't take my eyes off it. "I trained at Manchester."

"My blathering ... you must have thought me a fool." He laughed ruefully.

"No! Good heavens, Charlie, no. You were ... lovely." It was on the tip of my tongue to tell him that little speech had me falling tops over tails for him, but I held back. "Do you have any idea how I have savored our time together? Dreaming about the two of us in Colette's dinky Paris apartment? Those treasured memories kept me going through the freezing nights in the Schwarzwald. We promised ... promised to meet up at the end of the war, and I was determined to hold up my end of the bargain. When things got bad ... I would close my eyes and pretend I was back at the club, dancing in your arms. You remember."

His jaw flexed at that, but I detected a softening around his eyes and plowed onward. "You came to me in my darkest moments. For a time, it allowed me to forget about the bitter cold wrapping around me, and the pain…" I raised the back of my hand to my cheek.

"I don't know you."

"But you do, Charlie. *You* know me better than anyone in the world." I laughed at the irony. I'd poured my heart out to a man I spent a weekend with in Paris, and no one knew me better. Having spent much of my life hiding my true feelings, hiding who I really was, hiding … always hiding, at school, at home, even my Washington roommates didn't know about the rift I'd caused between my stepfather and myself. And why would they? I'd always been so reticent to talk about anything personal or close to my heart. Or perhaps it had been ingrained by the etiquette lessons at the British boarding school and Mont-Choisi.

There had never been another man in my life. Not like Charlie. No one knew me better. Had connected with me at such a primal level, and yet here he sat, staring at me like he spoke to a stranger. It was a knife to my heart and made me realize that, through my own lies and secrecy, I couldn't force a reconnection.

Perhaps it would be best to let him go. Retain Paris as a beautiful memory, a weekend two souls, desperate for intimate human contact, united, but only for that miniscule moment in time. Maybe I wasn't allowed more. After all, who was I but a disgraced agent who got her team killed and endangered an innocent woman? The depressing reality of my shame bore down on me.

What had I been thinking?

"Here." Disgust at my own ineptitude had me withdrawing the compass from its resting place between my breasts and pulling it over my head. "I believe we said we would return our tokens when next we met."

The necklace swung from my forefinger.

Recognition flared across his features, but he didn't reach to retrieve the talisman. "Keep it." He cleared his throat.

I continued to hold it out.

"It's brought you luck."

"Lucky or not, it is *your* father's. I always meant to return it. No time like the present."

He crossed his arms. "I want you to keep it. Besides"—he shifted uncomfortably and his eyes flashed over my shoulder— "I've lost your St. Christopher medal. Sorry."

It saddened me to realize the talisman I'd given him was gone. Lost, like our connection. However, he was correct, the compass brought me luck, and knowing it might come in handy again, I draped it over my head. It would be my remembrance of him and a time when I felt cared for.

"Thank you."

Private Karp entered, interrupting our tête-à-tête. "Morning, Major," he saluted, "Morning, Miss Saint James."

"Private," Charlie responded.

"Captain Devlin asked you to join him at the briefing."

"Very well. We'll pick this up later." He rose and left the room.

"Your eye looks much better today, ma'am." I'd told the private many times to call me Lily, but the military seemed so ingrained, or perhaps it was my advanced years compared to his nineteen that kept him from calling me by my first name.

"Do you think so?" I rose to view it in the mirror so recently used by Charlie. The bruise didn't look much different from a few hours ago, when I'd studied it under the dawning light.

"Yes, ma'am. It was much more swollen the day you arrived.

Looked like someone had put you through a meat grinder, I told my buddy Sims." He flushed at my raised brows. "Not to say you still didn't look pretty. I mean, you are a good-looking dame … I mean …"

I decided to put him out of his stuttering misery. "Yes, Private. I understand. I am sure I looked a disheveled mess when I arrived."

"Sergeant Thompson said you'd had a bad time of it. Said he killed the Kraut who did that to you."

A shimmering flash of sunlight glinted off a piece of metal and caught my gaze. "Indeed, he did."

Dog tags hung off the towel bar, and I reached down to see to whom they belonged.

McNair, Charlie, AB positive blood type.

It wasn't the tags that paused my fingers. In between the two tags hung my St. Christopher medal. A long scratch with encrusted black dirt marred its surface. The chain was missing and the golden ring that originally curled through the pendant had been replaced with a larger ring of steel, wide enough to accommodate the thick silver chain on which it now hung.

He lied to me.

I touched the compass. It seemed Charlie was as unwilling to part with my talisman as I, his. Perhaps we weren't as far apart as I'd imagined.

"Private Karp, the major forgot his dog tags. Could you deliver them to him? And when you do, let him know *I* found them."

Chapter Twenty
Operation Pony Express

"Karp, sort out those maps at the end of the table and get them properly filed," Devlin ordered. "I'll be back in an hour."

I packed a manila folder in the file box and closed the lid as Devlin exited. The unit had received orders—in forty-eight hours the 101st would be heading west, back to Mourmelon, France, where everyone expected to regroup and train for a jump into Berlin. I'd been in the room when the welcome orders were announced to leadership. There wasn't a man in the paratroopers who wasn't looking forward to getting off the front lines. They'd been on since December when Brigadier General McAuliffe sent them into the Ardennes Forest to shore up the Tenth Armored Division. They went in under-supplied, without proper clothes, ammunition, or medical supplies. I'd heard the stories how, when requested to surrender by Wehrmacht command, General McAuliffe replied, "Nuts." It was the stuff of legends, became a byword for the paratroops, and was oft heard whenever a soldier lost a card game.

They didn't realize how lucky they were. American commanders made an effort to rotate units off the front lines. These days, German soldiers only got off the front lines through good connections, injury, or death.

I'd received orders of my own on the same day as the 101st. My presence, which I had assumed Charlie or Devlin ... or someone ... had informed command about, was discovered by Lieutenant Colonel Kincaid quite by accident.

Devlin, Glassman, Peterson, and I had been sitting around the dining table, playing poker, in a heated debate over the tactics for crossing the Rhine River, a barrier that seemed to have stalled the forward momentum of the Allied invasion. I'd bluffed everyone into folding and was raking up my winnings when Kincaid unexpectedly walked in. The men jumped to their feet like they'd sat on a firecracker, and I rose in deference to the uniform. Kincaid, who had been at regimental HQ, noticed my presence immediately. It would have been tough to miss me in the ridiculous dirndl alone, but that morning I'd also braided my hair in German fashion to match the outfit and give the boys a laugh. The lieutenant colonel took exception to my presence and proceeded to chew the lot of them out for allowing a Jerry call-girl into a room holding classified documents. None of the men dared interrupt the diatribe. However, I didn't wish to have my headache flare up from the yelling, and I interrupted the lieutenant colonel mid-tirade.

"Excuse me, Lieutenant Colonel ... I'm sorry, I don't know your name."

His mouth hung open for a moment before snapping out, "Kincaid!"

"Well, Lieutenant Colonel Kincaid, I realize my clothing is misleading, however I am the American agent your troops rescued last Tuesday. So, you needn't worry. I'm part of the war effort. I have the appropriate security clearance," I blithely assured him with a self-deprecating smile.

Kincaid's eyes bulged and he sputtered, "What in tarnation are you talking about, missy?"

The fact that Jake ever so gently shook his head, and Glassman was biting his cheek in an effort not to laugh, clued me into the fact that perhaps Kincaid had not been told about my rescue and subsequent translation services that I'd been providing his battalion for the past week. My lips flattened, unsure how to go on.

The captain came to the rescue. "Sir, I believe you were told about the film provided to us by Fleur-de-lis."

"I heard," his gruff voice grumbled out like he chewed rocks for dinner.

Jake nodded at me. "May I introduce Lillian Saint James?"

"You mean to tell me this dame is Fleur-de-lis?"

I offered my hand. "At your service. Please forgive the clothes. My own were … destroyed and one of your men was able to supply this … outfit." For some reason Kincaid's gruff voice and frowning demeanor put me on edge. It also made me realize I should have made my own efforts to leave the 101st days ago and reconnect with the OSS secret intelligence division.

"I wasn't aware the agent was still here." He begrudgingly shook my hand.

"Yes, well … there has been a bit of recovery." *I'd been dragging out my stay because Jake had been welcoming and made me feel useful.* "Then Captain Devlin asked for my help and I couldn't very well say no." *No. I refused to lie to myself. I remained because of Charlie.* "Anything for the war effort. Right, Lieutenant Colonel?"

I smiled brightly at the officer, but my revelations had the effect of turning Kincaid's face into a thundercloud, and I realized I'd allowed myself to babble while caught up in my own thoughts.

"I see." He bit down on the two words. "Would you mind giving me a moment with my men, Miss Saint James?"

"Not at all."

I mouthed "sorry" at Jake before escaping the tense chamber.

A while later, Glassman found me and communicated that the OSS had officially been notified of my survival and location. I wondered who would be paying for the oversight in failing to notify leadership that they were housing an agent who'd gone MIA. I also wondered if Jake would be spending time on KP duty.

Once informed of my survival, OSS issued orders for my return. I was directed to hitch a ride with the 101st as far as Mourmelon, then continue by train to Paris, where who knew what kind of reception awaited me. My own limited belongings could be packed in a matter of minutes; they consisted of a hairbrush, bobby pins, toothbrush, nightgown, overcoat, shoes, and the dreaded dirndl. Today, after begging Peterson to scrounge up a less outlandish outfit, I wore a pair of fatigues cinched with a random black leather belt, olive T-shirt, and camo field jacket. Since there wasn't much for me to do, I'd offered to help Karp pack up the "office."

Three men I'd never seen before entered through the open door. One of them, a corporal I didn't recognize, pointed at me. "There she is, gentlemen. You need anything else?"

"No, Corporal. Thank you," said a short, bald man wearing a dapper brown suit.

My hands paused their work, assessing the newcomers as they raked me with their eyes, taking in my odd clothing. Karp, too, stopped what he was doing and seemed stymied by their appearance.

"Lillian Saint James?"

The singsong lilt surprised me; I hadn't met any Irish RAF pilots. But my gaze was drawn to his companion. His appearance could best be described as unassuming; someone you wouldn't notice in the crowd.

"Private Karp, I bet you're wondering what a Royal Air Force Pilot and an SOE agent are doing at our doorstep." I said.

The agent hardly batted an eye. It was the pilot who confirmed my suspicions. "Well, there you go, mate. Sniffed out by one of your own kind." He guffawed and clapped the brown-suited man on the back.

"Private." The suit adjusted his little round glasses. "May we have the room?"

Karp's eyes zinged back and forth between the men and me.

I nodded at him. "Go ahead … and close the door behind you, please."

"Have a seat." I indicated the sofa. "May I offer you a drink? Sherry? Schnapps?"

Both men declined, so I folded into my favorite red chair, crossed my hands decorously in my lap, and waited.

The RAF pilot cleared his throat, but it was the soft-spoken agent who began, "There is a situation and we'd like your help."

"Anything to help the cause. By the way, I'm Lily Saint James, but you already know that … and you are?"

"Captain Fitzgerald, ma'am." His chilled hand folded firmly around mine. "And this is Mr. Blaus."

Mr. Blaus, whose name I sincerely doubted, made no move to do the niceties; instead he carried on the conversation, patently ignoring the introductions.

"We have received word of a missing RAF pilot who was able to find sanctuary outside of Sankt Blasien, in the Schwarzwald." Blaus spoke in the dulcet tones of the British upper class.

Captain Fitzgerald unfolded a well-worn map, marred by coffee rings and ink blotches, and put his long finger on a tiny town about seventy kilometers north of the Swiss border.

"I am vaguely familiar with it. I believe there is a monastery there, which has been converted into a hospital. There is also an Adolf Hitler Gymnasium. Your pilot did not land in an auspicious location. I'm surprised he could find someone to hide him. The Jesuits were run off in thirty-eight? Thirty-nine? Hmm … he's not far from the Swiss border. Why hasn't he tried to make a dash for it?"

"He does not speak German, he has no papers, and … he's injured," Captain Fitzgerald replied.

"How bad?"

"We are unclear, but 'making a run for it' doesn't seem to be an option at the moment." The pilot rubbed his elbow.

"Why haven't you sent one of your agents to bring him over the border? Or sent one of your network of sympathizers to help?" This I aimed at Mr. Blaus.

"We haven't an agent in that area, and we are afraid the network has been compromised. There have been some unexplained arrests recently."

"In other words, you don't know who you can trust."

"Nor an agent we can use without compromising other delicate operations."

"How did you obtain this information?"

"Third-hand."

In the espionage business, it wasn't unusual to gain information through the proverbial grapevine; it was always a risk that someone in the grapevine was feeding misinformation or working for the other side, hoping to entrap an agent or entire ring of agents. "How do you know it's not a trap?"

"We are certain. It's our man."

"What do you want from me?"

"We understand you made it through the forest."

"Yes, but I started in a different location than your pilot, farther north, not so close to the Swiss border. I had some knowledge of the area, speak German, was clothed like a native, and had help getting across the Rhine. None of which your man has, and in the end, I still got caught. It is only by the grace of God, and the 101st, that I sit here before you. He'll never be able to get across without help. I can tell you what I know, but unless you send someone in, I don't like his chances."

Fitzgerald nodded in agreement during my monologue. "That is precisely why we are here, to get him help."

"You mean help from the 101st?"

"Not exactly," Blaus replied.

"I'll tell you what I can." I shrugged. "But your intelligence runs deep and probably knows far more than I. My own ring of intelligence in Oberndorf was limited, and at least one of them is dead."

"Miss Saint James, how would you recommend we stage a rescue if you were in this situation?" the captain asked.

"It's a particularly snowy winter if you haven't noticed. Does he ski? If so, tell him to strap on and let fly." My levity was met with blank stares. *Ah, the British sense of humor was lacking these days.* "First, he needs proper clothes to disguise his … Englishness, if he hasn't already been provided with some. I would send in an agent to pass him the clothes and appropriate papers. Do you have a letterbox set up in the area? Since his injuries seem to hinder his mobility, trotting him across the border may be difficult. I would suggest you get him to the nearest train station and out through Switzerland. It's the easiest way to move. You could always try a car, but acquiring one legally could be tricky, and an illegal vehicle would make an escape nerve-racking, to say the least. There is also the petrol consideration; you know it is severely rationed nowadays. The train is definitely safer. It was my original exit plan."

I turned back to Blaus. "And undoubtedly the exit plan for many your agents in that area. The key will be papers and visas that pass muster, an appropriate cover story, and the ability to get this to him. If he doesn't speak German, he'll need some sort of help getting across the border." I fingered the compass and mused, "There are so many displaced foreigners in Germany these days. Does your pilot speak any languages, Flemish, Dutch, Serbian?"

"He's fluent in French," Fitzgerald volunteered.

"With an English accent, no doubt."

Both men nodded.

"Your ideas have merit," Blaus said, seeming to assess my simple plan.

My gut was telling me that they weren't here to listen to the ideas of a recently disgraced agent. "However, I'm sure I am not telling you anything you haven't already thought of, so let us speak frankly, gentlemen. What exactly are you doing here, or more to the point, what do you want from me?"

"Our assessment of the situation is similar to yours, and we'll need to send in an agent ... or two in order to rescue the man."

Something didn't add up, and I tapped my lips with a finger, evaluating the two men in front of me. "Why ... would you risk two agents to save this one pilot? Why not leave him hidden until the Allies break through into Germany? It can't be much longer."

The men shared a look.

"The risk of leaving him there is too much, and allowing this man to get caught is simply not an option," Fitzgerald replied.

"Why not? Hundreds of planes have gone down behind enemy lines. POW camps are full of Allied troops captured by the enemy. Who is he?"

Again the look and no response.

Gears grinded in my brain and clicked like a bolt sliding into its pocket. "Wait a minute, he's royalty, is he not? Lord something-or-other has put you in this position."

Blaus didn't blink, but Fitzgerald tugged at his collar.

"Does the family know?"

Nobody moved.

"Never mind, 'need to know.' You're probably keeping it under wraps until he's either rescued or confirmed dead. And if the Nazis get ahold of him and realize who he really is, they *will* use him." I shuddered. "So, are you asking me to train the unlucky chap going on this suicide mission?"

"Not precisely." The captain again tugged on his collar.

Blaus stroked his chin and studied me with an inscrutable stare.

I raised my brows, waiting for an explanation. It took a moment for realization to hit, and I released a bark of disbelieving laughter. "You're proposing *I* do it?"

"We requested help from our counterparts at the OSS, and your name came up. Stories abound about the lovely Miss Saint James. You are a skilled agent who has taken on many a *nom de guerre* and still managed to get out of sticky situations. I am told the information you have provided the cause has been invaluable." Blaus's voice slid over me, slippery as a snake, in an effort to play to my vanity.

"Gentlemen." I crossed my legs and sank farther back in my chair. "I don't think you understand the situation. My cover is blown, nonexistent, shot down like your man. The Germans call me *Das Kindermädchen*, the Nanny. I'm sure the Gestapo has provided my photo to every border guard from north to south. Going back in is not only a suicide mission for me but also an ugly death for your man if we are captured together. The cuts and bruises from my last mission are still healing." The bandages had been removed from my wrists, and I pulled back the cuffs to reveal the remnants of the rough scabs and brown bruises left behind from the cords.

Fitzgerald's Adam's apple bobbed as he swallowed, and he gave another ill-at-ease tug at his collar.

Blaus didn't deign to glance at the injuries. "The eye has almost healed and you will be provided with ample disguise, proper papers, transportation, and a partner."

"I have orders to return to Paris. I am to depart with the 101st." Even as I said it, I knew I had no interest in returning to Paris to have my hand slapped, or possibly to be fired and sent home in disgrace. My mind turned over the possibilities of getting back into Germany to help poor Little Lord Fauntleroy out of the situation. The thought of sneaking back into Germany frightened me.

In reality, my Oberndorf contacts were dead—possibly due to my own blunders—and I should be honored that anyone was willing to work with me again. On the other hand, it occurred to me that my past mistakes made me the perfect agent to carry off this mission. My history made me disposable, and if I failed, the reports would reflect their man's death could be blamed on American ineptitude rather than British. It was clear the SOE had no plans to send someone else to retrieve the pilot. Either I successfully removed him or ... who knew what would happen to the chap. As much as I feared returning, I simply couldn't find it in myself to callously refuse to help. It wasn't lost on me either that, if successful, this mission could provide me a chance at redemption.

"Once you are out, I can fly you directly to Paris," Fitzgerald said in a reassuring tone.

I could have laughed at his confidence. "Where are these orders coming from? SOE, OSS?"

Tug, tug went the captain. "Well, ma'am, strictly speaking, this is a volunteer operation. The OSS granted permission to contact you."

"In other words, you're asking me to *voluntarily* go on a suicide mission, and my own government sanctioned it."

Nobody responded.

Suddenly, an unpleasant thought formed. Perhaps *I* was being a little too trusting. I had never met either of these two men, and they weren't OSS, nor American, for that matter. Fitzgerald's uniform and Irish brogue had gotten the pair into the building. Did the corporal who brought them up ask any questions? Blaus I'd immediately pegged as an agent, but for whose side? Was this entire story a setup to get me out of the comforting embrace of the Allied military and back into Germany? Were the Germans so desperate to capture *das Kindermädchen* that they'd send agents into the lion's lair?

"Mr. Blaus, if that is your name, I'd like to see some bona fides. You too, Captain. I've just realized that you are asking me to go on a dangerous mission, you are not a part of my organization, and frankly, I don't know who the devil you are."

Fitzgerald's eyes widened as though insulted by my insinuations, but Blaus allowed what must have been his version of a smile. Two corners of his lips rose the tiniest fraction of a millimeter. "Very good. I've been wondering when you would ask. We have been speaking for twenty minutes." He reached into an interior pocket and pulled out an envelope. "Inside you will find a directive allowing you leave to take this mission. In addition, you will find the number of the local RAF command post and names of those who can vouch for Captain Fitzgerald. As for me, Mr. Smythe assures me that your favorite ice cream flavor is strawberry."

Strawberry ice cream was a code word I'd used with my SOE contact in Stuttgart. Strawberry meant safe. I took the envelope and flipped through the two pages before tucking it beside me, to be studied and reviewed later, outside of watchful gazes.

Well, if I am disposable, at least I can try to get one more person out of the hellhole.

"Who is my partner?"

"A male, around six foot, who speaks German."

"Don't forget dark-haired," said Fitzgerald.

"Hair can be changed," Blaus blandly responded.

"Wait a minute, let me get this straight. You're not sending an SOE agent with me? I'm supposed to dig up an OSS agent to rescue *your* man? You're asking me to risk two American lives?"

Blaus cleared his throat. "At the moment, our resources are limited."

"What is the timeline for the rescue?"

"The timeline is short."

I narrowed my eyes. "Clarify short."

"He must be retrieved within the next few days," Fitzgerald emphatically stated.

"What is your plan to get me in country?"

"We were thinking a night drop."

I laughed. "Have you lost your mind? We'll be shot down as soon as we cross the border."

"Into Switzerland, then," the captain said.

My laugh turned into a gasp. "Don't be foolish. We've bombed Zurich. Accident or not, the Swiss are not happy with the Allies, and they are no longer escorting random planes flying into their airspace to their airfields. They are shooting them down. It's a foolish risk." My gaze turned fully onto Blaus. "I am surprised you would even suggest something so hazardous."

"We are confident we can make a safe drop," Blaus said in a matter-of-fact tone. "The drop zone is a farm just across the border."

"Let us say, even if I can locate another agent in the area willing to go on this insane mission, what if he doesn't have jump training?" I shook my head. "Forget it. We enter Switzerland by train or on foot, and we train into Germany. Our visas will have to be for business. But what kind ... and who can I find to accompany me?" I stared sightlessly, picking at a hangnail, and speculated out loud, "If I can locate Luc, he was a *Résistance* fighter I once worked with, maybe…"

Blaus cleared his throat. "May I point out, you are sitting in the heart of an elite fighting force. Jump trained. Weapons trained, and seasoned in the field."

I gritted my teeth. "None of them are trained in espionage and even less likely to speak German."

Blaus reached into a different pocket and withdrew a small scrap of paper. "I have a list of four potential candidates who speak the language. Three meet the height requirements."

"No."

"But—"

"I said no. I will not return behind enemy lines, a marked woman, with an untrained operative. Nor would I ask any of these men to go AWOL and risk internment, or worse, for some Lordy-Lord of the British Empire. I'll go alone before I risk a single hair on any one of these men's heads," I said with quiet vehemence.

"They wouldn't be considered AWOL. These men have permission from General McAuliffe," said Fitzgerald.

I think my mouth hit the floor. "McAuliffe approved this mission?"

"He approved the use of one of his men to help with an RAF rescue mission."

"In other words he has no idea what his man is getting into."

"Need to know," Blaus explained.

"More like, didn't want to know," I muttered.

Blaus shrugged. So, they wanted me to ask a weary soldier—who was supposed to be returning to the relative safety of Mourmelon, a reprieve from the front lines—to give up his seat on the next truck heading west and go with me into the Nazi stronghold. I ground my teeth and we all stared at each other.

"Let me see the list."

I almost hoped that Jake would be on the list. His German was passable, but he didn't meet the height requirements. I recognized only one name, Sergeant John Feinberg. His parents immigrated to the States after WWI. He had a narrow face, distinct overbite, wiry physique, and according to the intelligence, he spoke the language like a native. We'd shared an early-morning breakfast together last week. He was another Normandy vet. His family owned a garage and gas station in Toledo, and his brother had been sent home six months ago after losing his leg in Italy.

None of the other names on the list rang a bell, but I knew putting my finger on any one of them could mark the soldier for death. Did I go with the man I knew, or pick a stranger who might have had a girlfriend or wife and young child at home? In the end, I chose Feinberg, because he looked German and seemed to be the type of guy who wouldn't flinch in the face of a Nazi border guard.

Later, when I approached him with the proposal, Feinberg never hesitated. "So, it's a rescue mission?"

"Yes, but there is a high risk we could be captured or killed." I enunciated every word.

"I see."

"If we are captured, our government will disavow any knowledge of our mission. No one will come to our rescue. Your dog tags must remain behind. You will not be going in as a serviceman, you will be entering the country as a spy, and, if captured, we will be executed for espionage or worse."

"You've done this before?"

"Not a rescue like this. No."

"But you were in Germany and got out. Right?"

"Yes, but I didn't escape unscathed."

"I heard about that." His head bobbed.

He confirmed what I already feared; my anonymity had become nonexistent.

"When do we start?"

With that, Operation Pony Express was born.

A few hours later, my hair had been colored a muddy brown with gray streaks and pulled back into a tight bun. My eyebrows were darkened and thickened and a pair of black-rimmed glasses added. The glasses, along with strategically placed makeup, covered the remnants of the bruising and went with the new suit and shoes I found hanging in my closet.

I trimmed the sergeant's hair and he shaved his scruffy beard for the photos Blaus needed to complete our identification, ration, licenses, and proof-of-residence cards. The Germans were obsessed with paperwork, and the SOE had already prepped the documents, which was why the person accompanying me needed to meet certain requirements. Back in November, the OSS gave me three weeks to prepare and memorize my backstory before dropping me into Austria. Granted, Pony Express was to be an in-and-out mission, but it was still minimal time to memorize our back stories and provided me one more cause for heartburn.

Blaus supplied John with a suit, tie, overcoat, and Swiss watch. All had been either brought out by other agents or replicated with an eye for detail. Both the SOE and OSS had costume departments to rival the largest Hollywood production. The clothes were apt for Feinberg's new role as a Swiss banker intent on meeting with Nazi Party members interested in opening new accounts. I would be posing as his secretary. We were both Swiss-born citizens.

I fell asleep memorizing my cover story.

Chapter Twenty-one
The Rescue

The ropes bit into my wrists as I struggled against them. A dark figure loomed in the corner, sniggering at my hopeless exertion. The red tip of the cigarette burned bright as he sucked in the tobacco, and smoke slithered out his nose like an escaping soul. He stepped into the circle of light emanating from the old oil lantern and leaned toward me. Captain Müller's breath brushed my cheek.

"Now it is your turn, fräulein," he sneered, then pulled the cigarette from his mouth and pressed it against my flesh.

I screamed and screamed, pushing at the figure.

"*Lily, wake up!* It is okay, you're safe. You are safe."

I drew out of the depths of the nightmare to find strong hands at my shoulders and a dark figure above me.

"Ch-Charlie? Is that you?"

Warm arms wrapped around me and my face buried into a familiar chest. The lingering nightmare's aroma of cigarettes dissipated as his musky scent enveloped me.

My fingers gripped his biceps with relief. "Charlie, oh, thank God, it is you. I was back in that filthy room, tied to that chair," I babbled.

I'd spent the last week working hard, staying up late, and falling into bed exhausted, which had probably kept the nightmares at bay.

"Shh, it's okay. You are safe. I've got you. I'll keep you safe." He rocked me and mumbled the soothing inanities. "They will never touch you again."

Even as he spoke the comforting words, I realized the reason for the nightmare likely stemmed from my upcoming mission. A mission that Charlie was not privy to. Jake had been told that my plans were changed and I wouldn't be catching a ride with him in the morning. Feinberg, sworn to secrecy, was spending his last night bunked with the RAF pilot.

I'd lied to Charlie in the past, and it had caused a gulf between us, which had yet to be fully repaired. He had treated me with cordial respect since I found the St. Christopher medal, and a few times I'd caught him staring at me with an unfathomable look, but he'd been called up to regimental HQ and we'd not gotten time alone again. Our conversation remained unfinished. If we were to get back on track, I simply could not hide the truth from him again.

"Charlie, there is something I must tell you."

"Sh, I'm sure whatever it is will keep until morning."

"No." I pushed him away. "It won't. I'm leaving at oh-six-hundred on another mission."

He ran a finger through my colored locks. "I wondered what inspired the new style."

"I didn't want to leave without saying goodbye."

"Where are they sending you?"

I chewed my lip. "I don't want to lie to you anymore."

"You are going back in?" He frowned.

I sighed.

"Jesus. You know we are moving closer every day. Why are they putting your life at risk? If they catch you…" He pulled me to his chest so tight I could hardly breathe.

"Charlie … Charlie." I tapped a shoulder and his arms relaxed from its smothering hold. "I can't tell you more. But know it is important." A*t least it's important to the King of England.* "And it shouldn't take but a few days."

"I don't want you to go." He ran a gentle finger down my cheek and across my chin. "Must you?"

His tender plea brought the sting of tears to my eyes. "Truly, the mission is not so dangerous."

"I'm sorry. I know I shouldn't have asked. I just…"

"Oh, Charlie—"

His lips came down hard upon mine, and I stroked the supple skin on his naked back, wishing I could stay cloaked by his warm body forever.

Charlie didn't leave my bed that night. Our lovemaking wasn't Paris's languorous and tender coupling. It was desperate and unforgiving, between two people who had no more nights left. The desperation fueled our passion and he drove into me almost frantically, like he wanted to climb inside my soul. Little did he know … he'd already done so.

The memories of our joining taunted me as the train swayed, its repetitive motion mind-numbing enough to relax me into a false sense of security.

It turned out to be a good thing that we'd chosen a paratrooper, because we ended up having to make a jump. It was the easiest and quickest way to get us to Thonon les Bains, once a bustling tourist town on the edge of the Lac Léman, known on the Swiss side as Lake Geneva. Transporting into Switzerland by boat, crossing the frigid waters under cover of darkness cut out having to obtain or create another set of false papers to get into Switzerland. It would give the illusion we'd originated in country and hopefully keep us off the German intelligence radar. Switzerland housed a hotbed of spies from all sides, and new entries were monitored closely.

We picked up the visas to get us into Germany in Bern, Switzerland. The SOE had an office in Bern, and Blaus arranged for a package to be left at a prearranged dead drop. The package contained paperwork, codes for meeting our contact in Germany, and for identifying our RAF pilot. It was also in Bern where we caught the train to Zurich. From Zurich, we boarded a different train to take us north into German territory. Though Germany sent regular trains through Switzerland to provide supplies to their forces in Italy, few passenger trains traveled across the Swiss-German borders these days, and it was the reason our timeline had been so tight. We could not afford to miss the train going in, nor its return coming out.

It all sounded so easy when discussed in front of a roaring fire, sitting comfortably ensconced in a velvet chair. Now, in the relative luxury of a first-class cabin, watching the stark, snowy Swiss countryside streak past the window with the German border looming closer, I wondered if I'd been skillfully brainwashed back in France. How else could I justify agreeing to this cockamamie mission?

Feinberg tugged at his coat sleeves and shifted again. Normally, agents traveling on the same train didn't sit together. My refusal to leave Feinberg, an untrained agent, on his own was part of the reason Blaus tied our cover stories together. If we'd been alone in the compartment, I would've provided words of reassurance. However, a gentleman in a natty brown coat and black fedora joined us during the Zurich stop, and our limited conversation, by nature, turned inconsequential. I pulled a copy of *Neue Zürcher Zeitung*, a Swiss newspaper, out of my large tote bag and offered it to my partner. He unfolded the paper without comment.

It wasn't long before the landscape no longer soothed me, and I dived back into the bag to retrieve a copy of *Buddenbrooks*, by Thomas Mann, a novel I picked up at a shop near the train station. However, I soon found that I couldn't concentrate on the bourgeois storyline, and my eyes scanned the pages without actually reading them.

A few differences stood out from the last time I was in country. First, I had the necessary papers for my return to Switzerland. I also carried the British pilot's papers secreted within the lining of my bag. Second, a small white pill of cyanide nestled in a broach pinned to my dress. John had also been given one. Instead of keeping it in my handbag, I'd foolishly secreted the pill that I'd been given when I moved into the colonel's home in the spine of a copy of *Mein Kampf*. Having no interest in repeating the mistakes of my last capture, I was confident I'd have the wherewithal to swallow the pill should it become necessary.

The drawback to our plan—the train didn't stop immediately over the German border to release us close to our quarry. We couldn't debark until Tuttlingen, overshooting our destination by eighty kilometers. We'd be forced to backtrack, and it put me far closer to Oberndorf than I would have preferred.

Barbed wire fencing flashed past the window. The train slowed and soon came to a halt. We had crossed the border. An SS Stormtrooper and dog stood outside our window. It only took a few minutes before the train began moving again, but I knew that didn't mean we were safe. The stop allowed the German police to board. Officers would soon be visiting every car, checking IDs and visas and questioning passengers. Being in the forward cars of first class, it didn't take long for the guard to get to our compartment.

The door slid open. *"Ausweis und Fahrkarte, bitte."* Identification and tickets, please.

Brown suit handed his over and I retrieved mine from my handbag. Feinberg checked the interior pockets of his overcoat to no avail. He shot me a wide-eyed panicked look. I subtly patted my right hip before handing my papers to the waiting officer. The sergeant unbuttoned his overcoat and found the papers in his suit pocket. I could feel his breath against my cheek as he sighed in audible relief.

The officer asked what my business was, where I'd be staying, and when I'd be departing. The prearranged answers rolled off my tongue. My papers were stamped and returned, and I waited with bated breath as he turned to Feinberg. To my surprise, the sergeant's hand didn't quiver as he passed the documents over, and he answered all the questions in a flippantly bored tone without a single slipup. Satisfied with everyone's answers, the guard remained no longer, allowing the compartment door to slam shut behind him as he left.

Feinberg didn't make eye contact with me; instead he returned to his newspaper, snapping it up in front of his face in a businesslike manner, as though the entire incident was simply an annoying distraction to his day. He carried himself well, and though I wouldn't have considered Feinberg handsome in the traditional sense, the suit gave him a confidence that made him attractive. You never would have guessed seventy-two hours ago this man looked like a ragged bum carrying a lethal weapon, and I had no doubt he could snap the policeman's neck with one twist of his long fingers.

The train finally pulled in to the Tuttlingen station and we disembarked. A few passengers got off with us, and the platform quickly cleared of boarding travelers heading on to Stuttgart. The only people left were those exiting the train and a handful of SS Stormtroopers. One of them had a dog. Feinberg and I followed the tiny crowd, keeping our eyes straight ahead and walking with a swift gait. A guard patrolling the platform stopped the gray-haired woman in front of us and requested her papers. My stomach plummeted. Feinberg paused his steps, but I tucked my hand into the crook of his arm and, with a gentle pressure, got him moving forward. We ambled around the guard, to the end of the platform, and down the stairs unmolested. It would be bad news for us to be stopped and questioned here. Our tickets were paid through to Stuttgart, and we'd prepared reasons for getting off early, but it would be best not to interact at all.

The small crowd scattered as we reached the foot of the stairwell, but I paused until an older gentleman with a black hat and blue scarf made eye contact with me. Nonchalantly, I pulled a pair of green knit gloves from my pocket and put them on. Blue scarf lit a cigarette, then turned and walked down the street. We trotted behind at a distance while keeping him in our sights.

Footsteps dogged us and I loitered in front of a barbershop window to check for a tail. We waited for a dark-haired woman to pass us before continuing onward. The black hat turned right, and Feinberg increased his stride to catch up, but I tightened my grip to slow his gait. By the time we made the turn, blue scarf lingered halfway down the block. He glanced up, took one last drag, threw the cigarette down, and crushed the butt with the toe of his shoe. Again, we lost sight of him as he swiftly disappeared up a side alley.

I worked to keep my breaths even as we approached the flattened cigarette. This was one of the most dangerous moments in our mission. It was the moment when we determined whether or not the contact was still "our man" and not "theirs." A beige Volkswagen Steyr sat silently on the road next to the butt. Feinberg reached for the door and held it open for me. I hesitated for a moment before climbing inside. The sergeant walked around the front of the vehicle and folded his long legs behind the wheel. One swift tug of the chrome handle on the glove box revealed the keys. I passed them to my partner and unfolded the map that had also been left in the box. His fingers shook so much he couldn't get the key into the ignition.

I placed a hand upon his forearm. "Steady on, you are doing fine," I whispered in German. English may have comforted him more; however, we'd agreed not to speak anything but German once we crossed into Switzerland. I wanted his mind and ear tuned to the language in hopes it would reduce the likelihood he'd make a mistake.

His inhalations were loud in the tiny vehicle. The engine roared to life, he shifted into gear, and we lumbered up the road. Due to strict fuel rationing, very few personal vehicles were on the roads. We passed Wehrmacht vehicles but only one other non-military car. As a matter of fact, I'd argued for the use of a horse and carriage instead of a car, but our time to fetch the injured pilot was severely limited by the train schedule, and I finally agreed a vehicle would be best. I prayed it wouldn't be reported as stolen before we'd finished the mission.

An hour and a half later, we followed the road along the Albstausee, into the outskirts of Sankt Blasien, when the car began making a strange whining noise. The sergeant coaxed the vehicle to the promontory by the lake; however, a loud snap rent the air as the engine cut off.

"What do you want me to do first? Check on the engine or come with you?"

This mission required two people because we didn't know how badly the pilot had been injured, if he was mobile, or if he'd need to be carried. "Stay here, check on the engine. I'll meet up with the pilot and see what his condition is. If I need your help, I'll come back. The signal is two whistles."

My meeting place with the pilot was a little fudgy, represented only by a black splotch on the hiking trail. I'd been shown a photo and given a description of the British lord, but I had a feeling he wouldn't be clean shaven and might look a bit worse for wear.

The snow dampened the sound of footfalls. A twig snapped and my eyes searched the gloomy forest, too reminiscent of my recent past. The hair on the back of my neck rose and I swung around, ready to meet danger head on. A blond man wearing a green Tyrolean fedora, black pants, and tan jacket with a red-banded swastika wrapped around his upper left arm stood a few meters away. It was a style of jacket oft seen worn by the Hitler youth, and though without the beard he looked young enough to possibly fit in with the university crowd, the strawberry-blond beard he'd acquired in the past weeks aged him a good five to ten years. A red-plaid scarf wrapped around his neck, and he leaned heavily on an ivory-headed cane.

"Guten Tag, ob es heute wohl regnet?" Good day, do you think it will rain today? I spoke the words with slow deliberation.

"Nein, es soll Schnee geben." I think it will snow, he said with a cringe-worthy accent making the reply sound more like, "Nine, ist shole snee geebeen."

Listening to the ridiculous words come out of the mouth of a man wearing such a uniform had me rolling my eyes. *"Kommen, Sie mit."* Come with me.

He waved to our left, and I turned in time to see hunched shoulders and a woman's dark coat retreating into the forest. I offered my elbow, but we limped along at such a painfully slow pace I ended up pulling his arm over my shoulder to take more weight off the injury. Finally, the car came into sight. My partner was not sitting in the front seat as I had hoped. The rear hatch was up.

I gave the agreed-upon bird whistle.

Nothing.

There were no other vehicles; however, there was a buzz of voices not far away. I whistled again, and to my relief, the hoot of an owl replied.

"*Steig ins das Auto.*" Get in the car. I helped the pilot climb into the back seat before going round to see what I could do to help the sergeant.

Feinberg had removed his overcoat, rolled up his sleeves, and was elbow deep in engine parts.

"*Was ist los?*" What is wrong?

"The belt is shot." He held up a ragged strip of rubber.

"Can you repair it?"

"I tried. My own belt is too wide and the buckle won't fit in the space. Are you wearing one?"

I shook my head. The clothes I'd been provided had no belts.

"We need something flexible that will fit around these two components." He pointed to a set of round engine parts. "Or I'm afraid we're stuck."

"Wait here." I hid behind a clump of brush to remove my stockings. Goose bumps rose as the cold wind bit into my bare legs. "Can you make do with this?"

His faced showed surprise, and I saw him momentarily glance down at my naked legs before retrieving the stockings. "As a matter of fact, I can."

"I'll be in the car." I returned to the front seat to find our passenger had slouched down in the corner and stretched his injured leg along the back seat.

"What is the matter?" he whispered in English.

I shushed him and shook my head. A trio of chattering young bicyclists pedaled by as the back hatch shut with a clunk. Feinberg folded into the front seat, rubbing his hands on a filthy handkerchief, while we watched as the bicycles continued around the corner out of sight.

He didn't say anything, and I think we both held our breath as he fired up the engine. A new squeaking noise had been added to our already loud vehicle, but the sergeant was able to engage the gears and pull out of the parking space. The "people's car" could use a better muffler system.

Once we were toddling along the road from whence we'd come, I turned to our pilot and spoke in low tones. "Here are your papers. Memorize them. Keep them handy in one of your front pockets."

"So, you do speak English! By gads, it's good to see you. I'm Nigel—"

I cut him off. "*No.* Check your papers. Your name is Jean Degarmo. Learn it. Answer to it. The name Nigel will get you killed. My name is Gisele Sandmeier; this is Johann Kraus. If we get stopped, put on a blank face, and for goodness sakes, don't open your mouth to say anything. Your German is atrocious." Considering his utter lack of understanding and speaking the language, he'd been lucky I was the first one to find him wandering the hiking path. "Your file said you speak French, *oui?*"

"*Oui.*"

"Good. Speak nothing else. Johann is a Swiss banker and I am his assistant. He speaks only German; I speak both French and German. You are an intermediary for a steel company in Switzerland, your leg was injured in the recent bombing of Zurich. We are giving you a ride. Once we get back to the train station we will have to ditch the car and walk a bit. I hope you can manage." I glanced at his leg. "Understand?"

"*Oui.*" He gave a boyish grin, but the car hit a pothole, jarring Nigel's leg, and the smile disappeared to be replaced with a wince.

We passed another bicyclist before I continued in a muted voice. "There's a package on the floor with new clothes befitting your cover. Change out of that kit immediately."

Nigel wrestled into the new clothes with a liberal smattering of moans and groans. "What do you want me to do with the old clothes?" he panted.

"Stuff them under the seat for now," I replied. "We'll dump them in a bit."

For the next half hour, we traveled in silence as John expertly drove us through the hilly region, pausing briefly for a herd of goats to cross the road and occasionally pulling around bicyclists or a farm cart. Nigel said no more. At one point, I glanced back to find his eyes closed and his head lolling against the window. I didn't bother to wake him. The poor thing probably hadn't slept well since his plane went down, and it was clear it took a lot of effort to walk any sort of distance. We were running ahead of schedule, and the idyllic vista of the snow-covered trees and hummocks had my shoulders relaxing. I turned to thoughts beyond the mission.

I'd dressed in the dark as Charlie slept in my bed, his cheek pillowed in the palm of his hand and his face peaceful in the repose of sleep. I memorized the placid lines of his profile—patrician nose, black eyelashes brushing his cheek, the curve of his ear—before waking him with a kiss.

The brass compass, too recognizable, couldn't go on the mission with me, and I folded his fingers around the talisman with a promise to retrieve it when I returned. He balked at my leaving the compass behind and recommended a variety of hiding places, going so far as to tuck it into my bra. In the end, I knew there was no place safe enough to hide the precious piece. It was an unusual pendant for a woman to wear, and a description of it might have passed around. Should I be caught with the item, there would be no talking myself out of the situation, and it would put my comrades in the line of fire as well.

Charlie offered to give the St. Christopher medal back, but I declined. My clothes and accoutrements were strictly chosen for this mission, and deviating from the plan just to carry a good luck charm would be foolhardy.

♠♠♠♠

"Scheisse." The quiet expletive roused me from my daydreams and had our pilot echoing the sentiment in English.

John slowed the car, for ahead of us was a sight that had me tensing with unease. A camouflage-painted German Kübel-wagen had rammed a carriage. The cart was on its side, a red spoke wheel rotated slowly on its axle. The limp form of a woman in a skirt lay in the center of the road, obviously thrown from the impact. Blood matted her hair and her legs sprawled at odd angles. The horse gave a whinnied scream as it tried to dislodge itself from the traces, but its front forelock was clearly injured, and he couldn't push himself into a standing position.

We coasted to a stop before the accident, and I flinched as a Waffen SS trooper shot the horse, silencing its cries and putting it out of its misery. An officer stomped around the back of the Kübelwagen, yelling and waving his arms. He pointed at the wreck, then the lifeless form in the center of the road.

"What should I do? Offer to help?" Feinberg muttered.

"*Nein*, wait." I laid a cautioning hand on his forearm.

The officer said something to the trooper that we couldn't hear, then he turned to our vehicle. "*Komm aus dem Auto raus. Hilf mit.*" Get out of the car. Come help, he commanded, waving us over.

"Stay here." John opened the door and stepped out.

The officer turned and continued to berate the trooper; it sounded like he was accusing his subordinate of being drunk. What happened next had fear sluicing through my veins like an electric current. The trooper raised his weapon and shot the officer at point-blank range.

"*Reinkommen!*" Get in, I screamed as the trooper again shot his superior, this time in the head, before turning his weapon on us.

Two shots rang out. One of them pierced the windshield just above my skull and had me slinking down below the glass as John dived back into the car.

Luckily, he'd left the engine running. Releasing the brake and jamming it into gear, he slung his arm across my seat and glared over his shoulder out the miniscule rear window.

"Get down," he barked at our pilot and barreled down the hill in reverse. Shots twanged off the fender and front bonnet as we made our wild escape. Finally, Feinberg rounded a corner and whipped the car into a dizzying spin. He removed his arm from the back of the seat, rammed the gears, and we jerked forward.

"Are you okay?" I asked in German, peering over my seat to find Nigel crumpled onto the floorboards. When I didn't get an answer, I repeated myself in English.

His head popped up. "Is he gone?"

"I certainly hope so."

"What the devil was that?" He winced, climbing back onto the seat.

"Drunk, disgruntled employee, I suspect." I returned my attention to John. "Excellent driving, sergeant."

It was then that I realized he was driving with one hand. His right hand gripped his left arm so tightly the knuckles had turned white. He stared forward, unblinking, with a painful grimace marring his pointed features.

Chapter Twenty-two
Nurse Nightingale

"Bloody hell, you're hit," Nigel exclaimed.

"I'll be fine," John said through clenched teeth.

We zipped over a hill that had me coming off my seat and my stomach performing a flip-flop.

"Do you know how to use a stick shift?"

"Yes," I answered.

"I need you to shift when I clutch. Do you think you can do that?"

"Of course."

We approached a long curve. Feinberg clutched. "Third," he ordered and I downshifted.

"Nigel, dig up that scarf you were wearing. See if you can wrap it around his arm."

Once we hit a straightaway, John held his left arm above his head while driving with the right, and Nigel did the best he could to wrap up the injury from the back seat. For the next bit of time, the sergeant and I worked as a team—clutching and shifting. He took several turnings to get us off the main route and as far from the accident as possible. However, it wasn't long before his shoulders drooped and energy began to flag. Blood seeped through the scarf, and even though every fiber in my body urged us onward, I knew we needed to stop to take care of the injury.

"Pull off at the next turning." I pointed to a break in the trees, and soon we bumped to a stop along a goat track.

Feinberg's head fell forward onto the steering wheel.

"Sergeant?" I shook his good shoulder but received no answer. "Nigel, pull out those clothes you were wearing earlier. We're going to need them."

When I opened the driver's side door, John slid toward me and his weight almost had us both falling to the ground. With Nigel's help, I pushed John across the seat, untied the bloody scarf, and set about removing his overcoat and suit jacket to finally get down to the white shirt, also covered in blood. A little hole stood out among the stains. The bullet hole. Using two fingers, I ripped the shirt apart to reveal a gruesome gash where the gunshot had left behind a jagged trench, about three inches long, burrowing across the flesh of his bicep. Blood pumped out of the injury.

I'd seen gunshot wounds before but never in such proximity. Bile rose in my throat. I held a hand to my mouth and, pushing Nigel out of the way, staggered off the track but didn't manage to make it more than a few steps before folding over and vomiting.

"Sorry," I mumbled. The red armband with the swastika appeared in my line of vision, and I used it to wipe my mouth.

"Knew we'd find a good use for that." Nigel snorted. His hazel gaze studied me. He was so close I could see the freckles dotted along his nose. "You look pale."

"I feel better. I'll be fine now." Breathing through my mouth, I girded myself to look at the wound again. The second time wasn't as bad as the first—though still a ghastly sight. The contents in my stomach remained there.

"Do you have field medical training?" I asked Nigel.

"Sorry, no. What about you, any nursing?"

I shook my head.

Luckily, the bullet had not buried itself in his arm, and a

visual inspection of his coat showed a secondary tear where it must have exited. I needed to do something the stop the bleeding and try to close the wound. Nigel's brown shirt came in handy. I used the sleeve to tie a tourniquet above the cut, slowing the blood loss to an anemic ooze.

"Nigel, in my handbag you'll find what looks like a green coin purse with little flowers embroidered along it."

"This?" He held up the miniature sewing kit.

"Yes, and check under the hood to see if there is anything else we can use."

While Nigel searched the bonnet, I used my lighter to sanitize the needle.

"Here's something that might come in handy." He hobbled over with a roll of tape, and together we stared at the injury. "Poor sod."

There was no sulfa or penicillin to give John, not even a shot of medicinal whiskey to disinfect the wound. Truth be told, I could have used a shot of the Dutch courage myself. There were, however, mounds of untouched snow along the banks of the track we'd turned down. My tote bag revealed a forgotten half-full bottle of fizzy lemon drink, which Nigel happily finished while gathering small dry sticks and laying them out for a fire. Unfortunately, John had left the newspaper behind on the train, and I resorted to tearing pages from my book—a sacrilege—to use as kindling.

Eventually, the snow melted and bubbled merrily in the glass. I gave Nigel my gloves to pick up the hot bottle, and we used it to disinfect the thread. Once the water cooled down to a bearable heat, we poured it into the gash, which, unfortunately, jolted John out of his stupor. He proceeded to mutter expletives, and apologies for his language, through gritted teeth as Nigel held the arm steady and I fumbled with my amateur suturing skills. My hands shook as I sewed the appalling laceration, cringing every time I worked the needle in and out of his skin. The stitches ran a bit uneven, reminding me of Frankenstein's monster, but they held together and stopped the bleeding. I prayed infection wouldn't set in. We made a pad with my handkerchief, and Nigel held it in place while I wrapped it up with tape. Surgery complete, John flopped across the front seats, his face white and damp with perspiration.

Nigel leaned against the hood, looking a bit green around the gills. "Have you a pack of fags?"

"Check my handbag." I stared at the blood on my palms and in the cracks of my trembling fingers; it reminded me the downed air force pilot I cut out of the trees. I fell to my knees and buried my hands deep into a snow mound. The wintry crystals turned pink and numbed my hands. I scrubbed, using the pant leg from Nigel's former outfit, but no matter how hard I wiped, there remained remnants of the blood around my cuticles.

"Give up, love. It won't wash without soap." Nigel stared up at the sky. He must have found the cigarettes, for smoke wafted upwards, creating a cloudy halo above his head. "We had best get moving if we are to make the train."

I brushed a stray wisp of hair from my eyes. "I am afraid that plan is shot. Even if we can get John back into the overcoat and make him presentable, I've no idea where we are. We'll never make the train in time."

Nigel took another drag as he digested the revelations. "Now that the original plan is buggered, what is the new plan?"

I rose and dusted the snow from my knees. "It will have to be the car. Let's hope my stocking holds up and the petrol holds out. We'll have to see if we can find our location on the map."

With help, John was relegated to the back seat and bundled into his overcoat. I thanked the heavens his overcoat was black, hiding the telltale blood. Nigel and I pored over the map.

"We turned here." I pointed.

"Yes, but I can't figure out if we took this turning or the next. Which would either put us somewhere around here or farther north." Nigel's square finger tapped against my knee.

"No, no, we turned left, then right."

"Are you sure?"

I stared at the crossroads and turnings, uncertain if the streets we drove were marked on the map. "No, I am not sure of anything." I sighed, rubbing my eyes, and pictured Charlie's fingers curling around my pendant. "Oh, what I wouldn't give for a compass right now."

"How about a kiss?" John mumbled from the back seat.

"I think you're right, Nigel." I refocused on the map. "We are somewhere around here."

"Would you give a kiss?" John asked again.

Nigel and I shared a puzzled expression. "Are you hallucinating, Yank?"

I turned in my seat. "John?"

"You said, 'What I wouldn't give for a compass right now.' Would you give a kiss?" He spoke in a thready voice, but his brows wiggled as he fumbled with the top collar button on his coat. With a tug, he pulled it free. "You'll find the compass inside. Compliments of your British friend, Captain Fitzgerald."

I plucked the petite brass button out of the palm of his hand and pulled the two pieces apart. I'd heard about compass buttons but had never seen one in person. It was even smaller than Charlie's. The little black arrow bobbed cheerfully in its liquid casing, and for the first time since I agreed to this mission, a smile spread across my face.

"Oh, you beauty." I pushed myself over the dividing seat and planted a smacking kiss on John's mouth.

John beamed and it brought some of the color back into his cheeks.

"All right, now, if we are handing out kisses, what about me?" Nigel whined.

"What about you?" My brows rose.

"I helped you sew this bloke up, didn't I?"

"Oh, for heaven's sakes." I grabbed Nigel's ears and gave him a kiss on each cheek, which brought a ruddy blush and grin to his face. "Now, let's get out of here."

"I hope the car restarts."

"Shush." I pushed the clutch and brake, cranked the key, and like music to my ears, the Volkswagen roared to life.

The petrol marker wiggled dangerously low, and as much as I wished to put my foot to the floor, I kept the Volkswagen at a staid forty-five kilometers per hour. It was just one more reason my body was as tense as an overstretched violin string. The sun dipped lower in the sky by the minute, and I worried about driving the slick roads at night without lights. The increase of military presence didn't help my nerves either; twice I pulled to the side of the road to allow military cavalcades to pass. We now headed south on one of the main roads leading to the town of Bad Säckingen, where we could cross over into the Swiss village of Stein am Rhein.

All of us had proper papers to get into Switzerland—at least they seemed up to snuff, considering there were no problems on the train. I'd compared the falsified stamp on Nigel's papers to the stamp we received on the train. The differences were negligible and could easily have been attributed to an older stamp pad. I debated taking the vehicle into Switzerland or abandoning it in Germany. I still didn't know if it had been reported stolen, and if so, would the border guards have been notified? With the Allied fronts moving forward so quickly, communication breakdowns were on the rise. Additionally, even though Nigel and I had done our best to clean up after suturing John, remnants of his blood remained on the seats and floorboards. If we were asked to get out of the car...

However, all my concerns would become moot if I ran out of petrol. As the only able-bodied member of this troupe, I was now in charge of the lives of two injured men, neither of whom were particularly mobile. I had no idea how long either could hold up if we had to walk, and the thought of rowing across the Rhine in another leaking boat held zero appeal.

Finally, signs for the town of Bad Säckingen came into view, and I coasted to a stop as we entered the village.

"It's time to wake John," I said quietly.

"I'm awake," he whispered and leaned forward so we could speak in low tones.

"Nigel, speak nothing but French, and both of you watch out for English. If they become suspicious, they'll start throwing English words at you to try to catch you. Do. Not. React."

"Are we expecting trouble?" Nigel asked.

"One never knows. Our visas should be fine, but our transit papers..." I shrugged. "Just let me do the talking as much as possible." I wrestled to loosen the money belt beneath my skirt.

"What the devil are you doing?" Nigel asked.

"Preparing to provide a little extra incentive in case we need it. Pull out a handful, Nigel, and stick it in your pocket."

"Where did you get it?" John whispered.

"Compliments of Mr. Blaus. It's probably counterfeit."

A few of the buildings crumbled with bomb damage, and with the sun having disappeared behind the tree line, pedestrians were few and far between. Most were likely sitting behind blackout curtains, eating whatever miniscule evening meal their ration cards had purchased for the day. Nigel turned out to be an excellent navigator. The ancient covered bridge that would lead us into Switzerland soon came into view. A Volkssturm border guard stood next to a small, square shack.

The sight of the elderly Volkssturm had me breathing a sigh of relief, and I pulled up to the empty checkpoint with a smile and papers at the ready.

"*Ausweis, bitte.*" Identification, please, the white-haired gentleman said in a bored tone.

I handed them into his rough, liver-spotted hands.

The sunken sun left only a few of its gentle rays in the waning dusk, forcing the guard to hold the papers close to his face. "Johann Kraus?" He stuck his globular nose into my window.

"*Hier.*" John leaned forward so the guard could see his face.

The man grunted, then perused Nigel's documents. "*Wo wollen Sie hin?*" Where to?

"On to Zurich," I answered and the car gave a funny cough. *Please don't let us run out of gas. Not here.*

He gave another grunt and was about to return the documents to me when another voice paused his hand.

"*Ich habe dir Abendessen gebracht, Onkel.*" I have brought your dinner, Uncle. The voice came from a younger man. "What have we here?"

My side mirror showed an SS soldier approaching.

"*Nichts,* two Swiss businessmen and their secretary returning home. Put the plate on my bench. I will get to it in a moment."

The soldier came to stand by the Volkssturm. I studied his blond hair. My breath hitched and beads of cold sweat popped out all over my body. It was the young Sturmmann from the bus to Dornstetten. Surreptitiously, I used the seat back to push my hat farther forward down my forehead, and I rolled my shoulders forward to present a hunched appearance.

"Guten Abend." Good evening. The Sturmmann bent to look in the vehicle. "Ach, why does the secretary drive two men? The Swiss way, *ja?"* he asked in a jovial needling manner.

Our gazes met straight on, for I didn't want to allow him time to survey my profile, knowing he'd spent the better part of the Dornstetten bus trip studying it. "Unfortunately, my colleagues were recently injured in the Zurich bombing and can't manage on their own."

"Those American *Schwein*, think they are bombing us and end up bombing you. Maybe they need new maps, eh?" He winked. "Or perhaps you Swiss are not so neutral after all? Soon we will come for you."

I didn't wish to provoke an altercation, so I schooled my features into a blank face. Nobody in the car spoke up to defend against the insults.

The young officer studied me for a moment. All the hairs on the back of my neck stood at attention. I laid my hand on the stick shift, ready to pop it into gear and run them down if need be. I desperately wanted to request our documents be returned, but I held my tongue. And prayed my disguise went deep enough.

A bike wheeled up behind the vehicle and caught the soldier's attention. "Be on your way," he grunted and strode to the back of the car, where I heard him greet the bicyclist.

The old man returned our papers and we motored forward. The boards creaked beneath the weight of the vehicle and thunked over every seam as we drove through the two-hundred-and-fifty-year-old covered bridge into Switzerland, but I didn't relax until the Swiss border patrol stamped our papers and waved us forward into the village of Stein am Rhein.

We ran out of gas fifty meters past the checkpoint. The vehicle coasted to the shoulder. John shifted and a spring creaked. Nigel slipped a cigarette into his mouth. The match scraped against his boot and flared briefly.

I could feel it bubbling up my throat. I swallowed in an effort to press it down and held tight to the steering wheel. To my dismay it shifted, presenting as a quiver in my shoulders, which turned into an uncontrollable quaking. I could no longer hold it in, and the hysterical laughter burst forth. In the darkness, I felt my seat mates' stares.

"That's right, love, let it out." Nigel patted me awkwardly on the shoulder. "We've done the thing and you were brilliant. For a moment, I thought that Nazi boy was going to cause us trouble."

The laughter shook my whole body and came so forcefully I had trouble catching my breath. Soon my cohorts were chortling right along with me.

Eventually, the hysterics died down and I pulled myself together. Sucking big gulps of breath, I wiped the tears away. "You don't understand"—my voice grated hoarsely—"I recognized him. He tried to get friendly during my first escape. He gave me his handkerchief."

The vehicle went as silent as a spigot turning off. Nigel's cigarette glowed brightly and I heard the crinkle of the burning tobacco. Its smoke surrounded us like a hazy cloud. Far-off explosions shook the ground and rattled the car.

"I need a goddamn drink," Feinberg murmured.

"Me too, mate."

"And a hospital. Let me see if I can beg, borrow, or bribe someone for fuel."

Chapter Twenty-three
In Need of a Miracle

I traded the car to a local villager for a night's lodging and a ride, the next morning, to the closest train station. By the time we made it to Bern, John's forehead burned with fever, and though he didn't complain, every jostle of the train pained him. Our first stop was a hospital, where his bullet wound could be properly cleaned and re-sutured. I checked him and Nigel in under their cover identities, since that was the only paperwork we had, and made up a story about how they'd acquired their injuries. These were hard times, and the doctors didn't ask too many questions. Even though Switzerland remained a neutral country, Gestapo spies were everywhere, and we risked a knife to the back should we be identified. John's situation did not look good, and I feared the doctors would amputate the arm if he didn't receive penicillin to stop the infection.

I'd been given a phone number to memorize when I took up my post in Oberndorf. If I had to leave Germany and successfully made it into Switzerland, the number was to be used to make contact with the OSS. While Nigel's injuries were seen to, I prowled the hospital halls, finally stumbling across a private office with a telephone.

"Geffen Shipping and Trading," a woman's voice chirped in French.

"The pigeon flew the coop."

"Hold the line please."

A series of clicking sounds happened, then a male voice came on. "Code name."

"Fleur-di-lis."

"Do you have company?"

"I'm alone."

"Your emergency?"

"I need penicillin. Our mission went bad. My partner was injured."

"Where are you?"

"Bern, Switzerland."

"Take him to the local hospital."

"I'm at the hospital. The wound is infected. If he doesn't get the antibiotics, they'll take the arm."

"Go to the Café Turnhalle on Speichergasse 4. Your contact will be wearing a brown overcoat with a white scarf. He'll have a French copy of *War and Peace*."

"Will he have the penicillin?"

"Negative. He'll bring you in."

"I don't need to be brought in. I need the medicine."

"Go to the Café Turnhalle—"

"Forget it, I'm not leaving my partner." I hung up and, with dragging steps, returned to check on my patients.

Nigel modeled a new white plaster cast and reclined on a pair of pillows. The dormitory-style room housed a dozen beds, all full, Nigel's closest to the door. He smiled as I approached. "How is the other fellow?" His French was quite good but spoken with a distinct English accent.

Nigel's French accent should have troubled me more, but for the moment, John's situation remained my uppermost concern. Something in my expression gave my thoughts away.

"Bad?"

"The wound's infected. He needs penicillin or he'll lose the arm."

"Have you anyone you can contact?"

"I just did." I shook my head.

"Bloody hell," he mumbled in English. "Hand me those trousers."

"No, Nigel. What are you doing? You need to rest. Get back into bed," I hissed in French.

"*We* are going to the British Embassy. *Blast.* I can't get these trousers over the cast. They'll need to be cut."

"Nigel. Stop it. You can't get out of bed."

His brows furrowed. "Are you going to get me something to cut these trousers or am I going to have to do it myself?"

I lost the staring contest. "Fine. Wait here."

Two hours later, I walked out of the British Embassy with my hopes flagging. Nigel, or Lord Graydon as I learned, had been treated like the prodigal son returned, and though they were thrilled to have their royalty out of German hands, they claimed not to have access to the necessary antibiotics. I left Nigel enjoying a cup of tea in the embassy's capable hands, the staff readying a room for him for the night. Nigel talked me up at the embassy, and they were kind enough to offer me accommodations as well, but I declined. Instead, I returned to the hospital to check on John.

The doctors had given him something to abate the fever and dull the pain, but the sergeant claimed the wound burned like a firestorm anytime he shifted. His coloring was pale and his brow permanently furrowed with discomfort. I promised him the medicine would be coming and his arm would improve once he had it. The assurances assuaged some of the concern writ over his face.

I resolved to, in the morning, hunt down Allen Dulles, the

head of Bern OSS operations, and wring his neck until he coughed up the penicillin or directed me to someone who would.

I awoke in the middle of the night to find a man in a white doctor's lab coat administering a shot to John. It took me a moment to come fully awake and realize I didn't recognize the doctor. Thoughts of poison had me flying out of the uncomfortable wooden chair at him like an angry tornado.

"*Was ist das?*" What is that? I grabbed his wrist.

"Calm yourself, fräulein. It is the medicine you have been looking for." He responded in German but, with his other hand, held up a vial written in English: PENICILLIN.

I released his arm. "Who are you?"

"You may call me Franz. I apologize. Your message was delayed, otherwise I would have arrived sooner. We have two nurses and an orderly on our payroll who are willing to keep an eye on your patient."

"Thank you." I yawned and rubbed my eyes. "I didn't think anyone was going to help him."

He adjusted his glasses and pulled a piece of paper from his lab coat pocket. "You need to get some rest. Here is the address of a gasthaus. A reservation has been made in your name. You are expected."

The next morning John's fever broke and the swelling dissipated.

Five days after crossing the border into Switzerland, Franz's crew arranged for our safe passage out of Switzerland into Allied-occupied France. We headed toward Mourmelon, where John could return to his company. When Nigel discovered we were leaving, he asked to hitch a ride with us. He had orders to report to Châteaudun, an Allied airbase north of Mourmelon, where he would catch a flight back to Britain. He declared a fondness for our company and determined to continue with us for our last leg of the journey. My own directive remained unchanged—report to Paris. I loosely interpreted the order to mean after I escorted John back to the 101st. Our trio set out with fresh papers restoring our identities.

My first impression of the army city could best be described as brown. Muddy, half-frozen roads were lined with faded brown tents. A platoon of soldiers, dressed in shades of chocolate, marched in precise rows. The tents were occasionally broken up by wooden barrack-style buildings, and in the distance, planes roared overhead as they came in for approach on the landing strip.

The brown city buzzed with activity, and we were misdirected twice before locating battalion headquarters for the sergeant's company. Our ride finally stopped in front of one of the wooden buildings. I helped Feinberg out of the ambulance transport, thanked the driver, and turned to find Nigel in the doorway of the building.

"Must pay my respects to your commanding officer for sending you Yanks to rescue me," Nigel said by way of explanation and crutched his way into a barren foyer with scratched wooden floors and the musty smell that comes with water damage.

A door to our left opened and the foyer filled with male voices. A dozen or more captains, lieutenants, and sergeants filed out of the room. Some milled in the foyer carrying on conversations; others passed us on their way out the front door.

Glassman's eyes alighted on our little troop and he came over to greet us. He was clean shaven and his new uniform sported the gold bar of a second lieutenant.

"Glad to see you've returned." Glassman shook hands with the sergeant, eyeing the arm in the sling. "What happened?"

"Long story, and I'm not sure I can talk about it." His eyes slid to me for direction.

"Maybe over a couple of beers—after the war is over." I grinned.

"Forget the beer. Once this war is over, I'm curling up with a fifth of single malt scotch." Then he turned to me. "You're looking well, Saint James."

"Congratulations seem to be in order, Lieutenant."

His ears turned pink.

"Lord Graydon, I'd like to introduce Second Lieutenant Glassman. This man saved my life. I owe him everything."

"Then, Lieutenant, I, too, owe you my life, because if it weren't for this lady and the sergeant here, I'd likely be toes up by now. Call me Nigel."

As the two shook hands, Jake joined our group, and I made introductions, but my distracted gaze kept flashing past his shoulder in hopes of catching Charlie's eye. He remained in the doorway, his face serious, speaking in low tones with a young captain I didn't recognize. A swell of pleasure filled me.

Nigel bumped my shoulder, and my attention returned to the men in front of me as he joked lightheartedly, "I spent a few days enjoying German hospitality."

"Like that, was it? Then I'm doubly glad you made it back in one piece. You too, Lily. Someone's bad humor should improve with your return." Jake grinned and turned to Nigel. "We can't seem to keep this one away from playing with the damn Nazis. Ungrateful brat went back for more after we worked so hard to rescue her from the Jerries the first time."

I crossed my arms. "Glassman, you mean. If I recall, you were cozily ensconced in your French hotel while P Company did the hard work."

Jake chuckled. "Had I known a beautiful agent waited in the tower, I can assure you I would have been on the front lines of engagement."

"You are quite the Don Juan," I said dryly. It was nice to be back with Jake. We understood each other, and if we made it through this war, I knew I had a friend for life.

"Sergeant, Saint James, in my office." Charlie pointed with two fingers as he crossed the foyer and entered another door. The curt tone he used didn't bode well.

Jake and I exchanged a glance. "Gentlemen, I'm afraid we'll have to continue this conversation later."

I followed Feinberg and Nigel into a cramped office that housed a scarred desk covered in papers and file folders. A tall filing cabinet with chipped green paint was in the corner, and two wooden chairs sat haphazardly in front of the desk. Charlie flipped a few of the papers over as I closed the door.

"So ... you made it back." He walked behind his desk and put his hands on hips.

Feinberg snapped to attention.

"At ease, sergeant." He took in Feinberg's sling, Nigel and his cast, before raking me from head to toe with an enigmatic expression.

He looked better than the last time I'd seen him. His uniform didn't hang so loose, the dark circles of weariness beneath his eyes had lightened, and the curling hair at the nape of his neck had disappeared due to a fresh haircut. A world of good came from time off the front lines.

Nigel cleared his throat and broke my moony-eyed trance. "Major McNair, may I introduce Lord Graydon, Captain in the Royal Air Force."

"Major, I would like to express my sincerest gratitude to you and the 101st for allowing these two to risk their lives to come fetch me."

"Anything for the RAF, Lord Graydon, though I really cannot claim any of the accolades for the mission." An aloof glance pierced me before reverting to the pilot.

"Call me Nigel. All the more reason for my gratitude. I assure you the Royal family sends its appreciation as well. Who would have thought I'd be rescued by a Yank paratrooper and beautiful American spy?"

"Yes … who would have thought?" Charlie said through tight lips. "Tell me about the arm."

I opened my mouth to explain, but John beat me to it. "It's just a scratch, Major." He removed the sling with barely a wince. "I'd like to return to my platoon."

Charlie turned his gaze on me and raised a questioning brow.

I sighed. "He is better but will need some R and R so it can heal properly. It was touch and go for a while and the Swiss doctors were reluctant to release him. I promised he would get some rest."

Feinberg made an irritated grunt in the back of his throat and stiffened. The balloon of happiness that carried me into this room had dissolved as Charlie spoke, so aloof and detached. Now the guilt piled on. The fault for John's injury lay directly at my feet. The poor man wanted nothing more than to return to his unit, and, best intentions or not, my comments would delay that action.

"What exactly happened?" he said through thinned lips.

"Well…" I brushed at a stray hair. The mission involved one of his own men and Charlie should be cleared to hear the details. Personally, I desperately wished to tell him what happened. However, training that had been drilled into me from the beginning of my time at the OSS had me hedging. "We, uh, took some enemy fire." My eyes darted around the room, anywhere but into that disapproving blue gaze that surely knew I prevaricated.

"Bloody drunken SS kid shot his superior right in front of us, then took a couple of potshots at us, didn't he?" The wooden chair creaked as Nigel lowered himself onto it. "Blam, blam." He demonstrated with his crutch. "The sergeant here saved our bacon, driving that old rattletrap of German machinery like a prize filly at Ascot. It was brilliant. First, he fixed the car with the lady's stocking—"

Charlie's brows winged up at that.

"—then he tore through the forest after being shot in the arm. Fellow kept his head the entire time. I fell onto the floorboards, and Gisele here almost took one between the eyes. Missed her by an inch if that." He demonstrated with his thumb and forefinger.

Charlie's jaw hardened and I gasped. Listening to Nigel unfold the story was like watching a train coming at me full speed—I knew I needed to jump out of the way, but I couldn't seem to find the words to tell him to stop talking.

Onward he plowed, "Good thing he missed, because the two of us blokes would have been in a heap of trouble if she'd been shot. Right, mate? We should start calling her Nurse Nightingale, for it was she who sewed your sergeant up with some thread from her shoulder bag. Quite a handy little item. Honestly, I simply did not have the stomach for it. And, boy, did we get an earful, eh?" Nigel elbowed me. "Although who could blame the chap? No morphine or even a shot of whiskey to numb the pain. It's not her fault the wound got infected; after all, that's the risk when you are doing field surgery on the fly. I can't say enough about Gisele. This filly's got gumption, driving us to the border and sweet-talking that German officer who might have recognized her at any second. And the doc said the sergeant's arm will soon be right as rain."

My hands fisted tightly and my teeth were clenched so hard while Nigel recounted our escapade I would not have been surprised if they disintegrated beneath the pressure. He seemed oblivious to Charlie's flared nostrils and darkening expression. Feinberg, too, stood mute with astonishment.

"Yes, well, it … not … so dramatic…" No appropriate words came to mind.

"Feinberg, I'll speak to your company commander and get you sorted out. In the meantime, why don't you take Captain Graydon and see about getting yourselves some chow. I'm sure you're hungry and I would like to speak privately with the lady."

"Oh." Nigel used the crutches to pull himself to his feet. "Brilliant. I would die for a spot of tea. Gisele, I will look for you later. Our journey's end has not yet arrived." He saluted.

"Yes, later," I said weakly.

The door closed. Charlie paced behind his desk like a caged animal. Finally, he came around the front of the table.

His face blazed with fury.

"I'm sorry," I whispered.

"How dare you take him," he said through clenched teeth. "That man is one of our best machine gunners and you almost got him killed. Soldiers like Feinberg don't just grow on trees. I dropped into Normandy with him, you know."

"I know. I am sorry." He said nothing I didn't already know. More guilt piled as heavy as a boulder on top of its predecessor.

"The German Army is collapsing in front of us. I can smell the end of this war, and *you* put this man into a deadly position." He pointed an accusing finger at my chest. "For what? Some lord of the manor?"

He spoke the truth, providing the same arguments I used a week ago that Blaus and Fitzgerald had swatted away like gnats.

"What kind of game is your department playing here? You took an untrained man into the field for your ridiculous spy shenanigans? It's irresponsible!" He grabbed my shoulders.

I'd never seen him so angry. I was both awed by and afraid of his savageness and couldn't seem to get the words past my throat to defend the actions of my superiors or myself.

"Damnit, Lillian! What. The. Hell. Were. You. Thinking?" he shouted, emphasizing each word with a shake that rattled my teeth and loosened my topknot.

Pain speared through my left arm as his thumb dug into one of the still-healing burns, and I let out a yelp.

"Charles!" Jake barked. "You forget yourself."

We both looked over my shoulder to find Devlin standing in the doorway, his face a dark thundercloud. Charlie released me so quickly I stumbled and would have fallen if Jake hadn't leaped forward to steady me.

Mechanically, I rubbed the tender injury.

"What are you doing? Her burns are still healing," he chided.

"My apologies. I don't know what came over me." Charlie turned his back on us, pressed his hands against the desk on stiff arms, and hung his head between quivering shoulders.

"Are you okay?" Devlin turned to me, his brown eyes solemn. "Do you need me to take you to see the doc?"

"No, I'm fine." I pushed the falling hair out of my face. "Thank you all the same." I guided him toward the door. "Give us a moment, would you?"

Jake glanced between the two of us, his mouth turned down. "Are you sure?"

"Yes. We'll just be a few more minutes."

He hesitated, staring at Charlie's back.

"It's all right now." I patted his hand.

"I'll be outside this door if you need anything."

My face softened and I gave a brief nod as I coaxed him over the threshold. The round brass handle turned beneath my fingers, and the snick of the tongue into place sounded loud in the silence of the room. Charlie's back no longer shook, and his shoulders had slumped forward in a downtrodden manner. An internal debate raged within me, and I struggled with the next words. In the last moments of his fury, I glimpsed another emotion. Something beyond the anger. Stark fear. Not fear for the sergeant. Fear for me. And I realized the fear fueled his rage.

"Charlie, come ... sit down." I lowered myself into the chair recently vacated by Nigel.

He swung around—his features drawn and tense.

"Come on, have a seat." I tapped the chair across from me with the toe of my shoe.

He dropped into the chair, pressing careworn fingers against his eyes. "My God, Lily, there aren't enough words to express how sorry I am."

I reached up and pulled those strong hands away. "I know. I understand." Green eyes stared into blue.

"Why did the Brit keep calling you Gisele? Is that your real name?"

"No, it was my cover identification for the op."

"How many different names have you gone by?"

"A few."

"Cripes, do I even know your real name?"

I cringed. "My middle name is Lillian. I started using it in finishing school."

"Saint James?"

"No." I closed my eyes. "It's Jolivet." A sigh of relief escaped as the last lie fell away. "Besides the man who hired me to work for the OSS and a handful of staff members in D.C., you are now the only other person to know my real surname. When the OSS realized who my stepfather was, they changed my name to Saint James. I'm not even sure I know how to answer to my own name anymore. I'm as much Lillian Saint James as Jolivet."

"And have you ever been a photojournalist?"

This man was better at breaking down my barriers and pulling information out of me than any interrogator I'd ever faced. "Sort of ... yes." I sighed. "A cover identity isn't a complete lie. The camera was my mother's last gift to me while I was at boarding school. I was always taking photos, at Mont-Choisi, in Washington, D.C., even on the boat trip home from Switzerland. On the recommendation of one of my Washington roommates, I submitted and had photos published for local newspapers, and even *Life* magazine. I have a knack for photography. The department simply utilized a skill I'd already acquired. But that's not why you're angry."

He stared. Silent. Brows knit. Scrutinizing.

"Charlie, please ... it is okay to be afraid for my safety. Don't you know, ever since Paris, I have spent countless nights fearing you would be killed or injured? When I found out the 101st was sent into the Ardennes, I had nightmares you would be shot." I held a hand up as if to push the idea of his bloodied body away and shook my head. "I think the worst part was not knowing. Not knowing if I would ever see you. Not being able to write, to assure myself you were okay.

"And then, when I'd lost all hope"—an image of the Victory Colt revolver muzzle aimed at my head shimmered in front of me—"that *I*—"

My hand pressed against my chest and I gulped down the rising emotion.

"—would make it out alive to see you again, you came to me in a … a vision. It was nothing short of a miracle that your men arrived when they did, as though you'd sent them to me. And they brought me back to you."

"Oh, Lily." He scrubbed his face. "I've behaved like an ass. I know you were following orders, just like the men I lead. Just as I do. It's the fact that people in our government move you around like … like a pawn on the chessboard. They put you in harm's way and it makes me … go nuts. You're right, it isn't that Feinberg got injured. Nigel said you were almost shot…" He knuckled his eyes. "It's that you … *you* could have been killed…" He fell to his knees in front of me and hung his head. "I hate not knowing where you are. If you're hurt, or even alive."

His hair was soft from a recent washing and I ran my fingers through it. His hands wrapped around my waist and he laid a cheek on my thigh. "I hate the thought of you doing something like that again. Even if it is for the greater good. It's been gnawing a hole in my gut since you left."

I drew a nail around the shell of his ear. "You can stop worrying. This is probably my last mission. They'll want to pull me out for a cooling-off period." My shoulders drooped and a sigh escaped. "Frankly, I'm ashamed to admit … I'm not sure I have the nerve go back in again." I whispered the embarrassing confession.

"Don't." He placed a finger to my lips. "Don't do that. You don't ever have to feel ashamed. You've got more courage than half the army. I should know; I've seen some gutsy moves on the field." In a fluid motion, he rolled back onto his heels, up into the chair, and pulled me forward, tucking me into his lap and wrapping his arms around me.

I confess, I could have happily spent the rest of my life ensconced in his embrace.

"I am exceptionally jealous of Peterson and Grimes ... and Glassman. Do you know why?"

I shook my head.

"Because they dish about their sweethearts. Read their letters. Share pictures. Those girls are working as teachers, secretaries, nurses, or in the factories. Some are taking care of babies. Do you know what they all have in common?"

I bit my lip and shrugged.

"They are home ... safe. Ever since you collapsed at the hotel, I thought, why must it be you? I asked God, 'Why is it my girl insists on putting herself in danger?' Why did I fall in love with a girl who speaks German and French like a native? A girl who voluntarily walks into the lion's mouth? A girl with ... what did Nigel say ... gumption? Don't you understand?" He cupped my cheeks in his hands. "I want to bundle you and your gumption up and ship you back to America. To wait for me in the safety of my family's home."

A balloon of joy expanded and eased the tightness of self-reproach in my chest. "Oh, but I do understand, Charlie. Don't you think I want to do the same with you? Just as the women back home want to do with their own sweethearts. My darling, you are experiencing what every mother, wife, and girlfriend back home is feeling. We all pray for the same thing." I twisted my head to kiss his hand. "Bring our loved ones home ... alive. American men are spoiled. There are so many soldiers here who have sweethearts in dangerous situations serving as nurses or ambulance drivers in France. Not to mention, every British soldier who's left behind a loved one who could die in a German bombing raid on any given day. It is a fear we all share, and the sacrifice we make to keep our country safe."

Charlie snuggled me close and laid a cheek atop my head. "I know. I know what it means to serve my country. I also know I wouldn't have fallen in love with you if you weren't exactly who you are. Fearless, brave ... a bit reckless?"

"Never fearless ... and not so brave. Don't you realize, fear is the enemy sitting on my shoulder every day of every mission?" I inhaled. "I cannot tell you how relieved I am to be in the relative safety of the rear."

"Not nearly as relieved as I." He took my hand in both of his, flipped the palm up, and traced a finger across the creases, sending shivers up my arm. A moment later he reached into his pocket, withdrew the compass, and coiled the chain into my palm. "I believe this is yours."

I curled my fingers around the talisman.

Chapter Twenty-four
Return to Paris

The train idled noisily behind me. Passengers, busy as an anthill, bustled around us. Charlie held my hand and stared at me as though memorizing every dip and curve of my face. I couldn't blame him; I did the same. How I hated to leave … again. Our meeting had been so short. I'd said my good-byes to Nigel, Jake, and Glassman, and Charlie had personally driven me to the train station.

"Why is it we're always saying good-bye?"

"Our lot in life, I suppose."

"How long do you think you'll be in Paris?"

I have no idea. "A while." *As long as I can.*

"I'll try to get a forty-eight-hour pass. Where will you be staying?"

"At Colette's apartment."

"Write to me." He lowered his head and touched my lips. The kiss—too brief.

I boarded the train and leaned out the window, like a child, waving and watching his figure shrink into the distance.

My first stop in Paris was the headquarters of the Special Operations Branch of the OSS. My code name got me a front-row seat with the director, and his feelings for me could best be described as … mixed. The intelligence I'd provided while undercover in Oberndorf was unparalleled, and he genuinely seemed pleased that I'd made it out of enemy hands alive and "unscathed," as he put it. I didn't deign to correct the assumption.

However, my unorthodox delivery of the film and other materials directly to the army was frowned upon, to say the least. Much like what I'd experienced on Capitol Hill, even though we were all supposed to be working together for a greater cause, there were multiple agendas and turf disputes. Even though the information I provided the army would have eventually made it into their hands, it wasn't "filtered," as Devlin would say. I got the proverbial hand slap for my deviation. Despite this, the rescue of Nigel Graydon won me a personal telegram from the King of England, which was tough to argue with. I left the prickly interview with the King's telegram and a request that I return the following morning for a debriefing.

The streets were dark by the time I found the spare key to Colette's apartment under the flowerpot where it had always been. Dishes clanked. The smell of garlic filled the small flat and made my stomach grumble.

"*Bonjour*, Colette," I called.

Colette's head peered around the kitchen wall. "*Mon Dieu*, who is that? Lily … is that you?"

"*Oui,* my friend."

"Lily!" She enfolded me in an exuberant embrace and danced us about the room. "I thought you dead. Weeks ago, Philippe learned from an SOE agent that your mission had gone wrong and you were taken by Gestapo pigs." She squeezed again. "We were devastated and drank a toast in your honor. Philippe fell into a melancholy."

I laughed. "Poor Philippe, he wasn't far from wrong."

"How long are you staying?"

"Until they send me on a new mission."

"Where are you staying?"

"Here ... if you'll have me."

She clapped her hands. "But of course. It will be like old times. Oh, I can't wait to tell Philippe he was wrong. It will raise his spirits so. *Mon dieu*, this hair color is terrible. Is this what you've been wearing for your cover?"

"Only recently. I had one last mission into Germany that required a change of hair."

Her direct green gaze scrutinized me. "You've lost weight since I saw you and your face ... you look tired."

"In other words, I look old and ugly."

She clicked her tongue. "No, never ugly. But, yes, you look older. Your eyes ... they are not so ... guileless. I'm afraid you have seen much in these past months. I recognize that look, for I have seen it in the mirror myself."

Even though Colette was a year younger than I, the atrocities she'd experienced aged her in ways I thought I'd never comprehend. It gave her wisdom beyond her years and made her seem the elder. I knew the look of which she spoke. It was the same one I'd seen in little Dieter's eyes. It was a look of knowing too much. Too much for a lady. Too much for a woman in her twenties, and I couldn't bring myself to answer her unasked questions.

"What are you cooking?"

"Where are my manners? Have you eaten? Come, I am making rigatoni. Let me pour you a glass of wine."

After dinner Colette suggested we go out and meet up with some of our old friends. "I can't wait to see the looks on their faces when they see you are still alive. We'll have to arrange it just so. I'll begin lamenting your loss, then you walk in..." She chattered on with her brilliant plans to reintroduce me like the Ghost of Christmas Past.

Exhaustion closed in, and I couldn't do it. I'd been going

nonstop for too long now, and I paused her prattling with a hand to her shoulder. "Yes, Colette, we can do your little scenario, but not tonight. I beg you … not tonight."

Colette said no more and instead ran me a bubble bath scented with lavender. A treat, to be sure. As I lay back, my pink toes peeped up to the surface. Colette entered, closed the toilet lid, settled herself on the seat, and began filing her nails. The rasping scratch of the metal board filled the room. Self-consciously I sank farther below the surface and brushed the bubbles up to my neck.

"I have already seen the scars, Lily. Do not hide. Tell Colette what happened to you. Do *not* allow the Nazi demons the power to eat you up inside. It will help to let it out." She paused her filing to look at me. "I promise."

I remembered in our early days of living together Colette had woken me with her screams. The visions of the invading army, the burning countryside, bombs, death, the rape replayed in her nightmares. She told me later that confessing the horrors to me helped her sleep better.

At her urging, I confessed my own nighttime terrors. She remained silent while I divulged my story, and by the time I finished, sympathetic tears tracked down her cheeks.

"Now that you have told me, they cannot haunt you as they have done. We have taken away their power."

So many horrors had I seen in the recent weeks, I wanted to believe Colette's assurances. I prayed she was correct and the dreams wouldn't haunt me tonight.

"Tell me more about Charlie." She pronounced his name *Shar-lee*, making it sound sexy and very French. "You are in love with him, no?"

"*Oui.*"

"And he must be in love with you."

"What makes you say that?"

"What man does not fall in love with the charming Lily? Even with that awful hair color, which we must change tomorrow, you will have men falling at your feet. You are like that American actress ... what is her name?"

"Ingrid Bergman?"

"*Oui.*" She snapped her fingers. "*Exactement*, she is just the one. How did you know?"

"Charlie once called me a Bergman look-alike."

"And have you shared yourself with him?"

"Colette!" I was stunned by her audacity. "How can you ask such a thing?"

She tsked. "You Americans and your sensibilities. Such prudes. We French know the value of love, passion, and ... sex." She whispered the last before falling into a peal of laughter.

I threw a handful of bubbles and joined her mirth.

"Is that a yes?"

"If you must know ... *oui.* Right here in this apartment, as a matter of fact." I grinned slyly, which sent her off into another giggling fit. It pleased me to see her like this. The laughter and lightness made her look younger, closer to her real age. What I imagined she would look like if the war hadn't intervened.

My confessions to Colette must have worked; I slept the night through and then some. The bright sun flooded the room, and the clock read past noon when I finally woke to an empty apartment. A note leaned against the cold percolator.

Will return by 4:00. Told the driver who came to pick you up this morning that you were ill and could not go in today. Madam Géroux is expecting you at 3:00. Apartment 8, she will make your hair beautiful again.

- C

The following day I returned to OSS headquarters, in one of Colette's borrowed dresses and with a new dark blond hairstyle thanks to Madam Géroux.

Physically, Paris hadn't changed since I left it five months ago. Spiritually, the people of Paris walked with a lighter step, their faces less furrowed. They laughed spontaneously and spoke less with a sense of doom and more with the possibility that soon Europe would be free from the oppression of the Nazis. De Gaulle's Army along with the Allies had recaptured almost all of France, and though behind closed doors, there were deep concerns that the German National Redoubt would rally, the daily radio reports brought good news of troops moving closer to Germany.

I spent the morning with a man, ostensibly from the Research and Analysis department. He grilled me about the National Redoubt and what I'd learned in my flight across the forest. Goebbels' propaganda machine continued to churn, and even in the face of continual losses on both the Russian and western front, the refrain "Germany will come out victorious," could consistently be heard on the radio and in the newspapers.

It wasn't until lunchtime that I realized my questioner's true purpose.

"And you just … found this horse," he read from his notes in a disbelieving voice.

"Franziska. Yes, actually he found me." I crossed my ankles.

"You had no help getting out?"

"To the contrary, I had help getting across the Rhine from Oskar. I had help after I crossed from Masselin's grandmother, and then Lieutenant Glassman saved my life. Help came from many places, to be sure."

"Both your contacts were captured?"

"Yes, I explained what happened to Lenz. I'm assuming Otto has either been shot or sent to a concentration camp."

"Why didn't you make contact in Freudenstadt?" His friendly manner was gone, replaced with suspicion.

"I had no contacts in Freudenstadt. If I had known, I would have certainly continued on past Dornstetten to seek safety. Instead, I spent the night wandering the woods, chased by dogs, almost freezing to death."

"You were given papers to exit via Switzerland. Why didn't you head south?"

"I told you, I couldn't risk returning to the colonel's home to retrieve the papers."

"Why didn't you return to Stuttgart?"

"I met Magda in Stuttgart. It would be the first place out of her mouth. I imagined the Gestapo would be searching high and low for me there."

"Hmm, interesting reasoning," he mumbled as his pencil scratched across the notebook.

"Tell me, when was the last time you were behind enemy lines, Mister … Caldecott?" I pursed my lips. "If that is your name."

Caldecott's gaze slid away from mine and he tapped his pencil against the desk.

"When the wolves are at the door, you have to think on your feet. Perhaps my reasoning, as you put it, was faulty. It was the best I could do under the circumstances. Unlike your radio operators, who seem to have a large network of spies and sympathizers at their fingertips, my position in Oberndorf was limited … to say the least. Neither the OSS nor SOE placed me there. I took an opportunity to insert myself into a high-ranking member's home, at great personal risk. As a nanny, my time was not my own, and I often traveled outside of the home with the children in tow. Every word I spoke, little Nazi ears listened." I enunciated each word.

"There were times I believe I was followed by Gestapo spies. Therefore, my network was limited to two men." I held up two fingers. "If there were others in Oberndorf, they never made contact with me, and I was never informed of their position. Instead, I was given exit papers and bribe money.

"If you are wondering where my loyalties lie, I'm sure you're aware I took another mission, at great risk, to rescue an RAF pilot after surviving my flight out of German territory. Were I a German sympathizer, you can be sure the British pilot would be dead. If you need further proof"—I pulled the dress aside to show the first burn mark on my shoulder—"I have a matching set that runs down my arm, and these scars aren't pretty little bracelets around my wrists." I glared at my interrogator.

He cleared his throat. "You may return your clothing to its proper place."

"Mr. Caldecott." I straightened the dress and rose in my most dignified manner from the squeaky metal chair. "It is lunchtime, and I am hungry. I believe we are finished."

I whipped my coat over my shoulders and opened the door to find the director, a lanky man who towered a good six inches above me, lurking on the other side. "Finished already? Allow me to take you to lunch," he said jovially.

To refuse the director would be unseemly. I had no choice but to accept his pinstriped arm and allow him to lead me to a bistro a few blocks from the building. Winter still held Paris in its grip, and even with my fur-lined collar, the cold winds bit at the exposed skin at my neck and wrists. The director's thinning gray hair flopped in the breeze.

A gust caught the door, pulling it out of the director's hand and slamming it against the wall. "I'll be glad when spring arrives," he grumbled.

Once we'd ordered, he relaxed against the seat back and folded his hands on the table. His gray bushy brows hooded his hazel eyes, and the expression he wore only seemed to enhance his bulbous chin and ruddy complexion. "You must realize that unpleasantness was necessary."

Imitating him, I crossed my hands on the table. "Why should it be necessary? Have I given cause for you to believe I am anything but what I say?"

"Both your contacts are dead."

My brows rose. "Otto too?"

"Otto too."

I chewed my lip. "That is … sad news. What about Magda and the others?"

"The entire household staff was arrested."

My breath whistled out; his revelations were like a punch to the gut.

"Magda never returned home. We believe they are still holding her or she has been shipped off to a camp. We are unsure where the colonel is, but the children were placed with an aging aunt."

"Did they torture Magda?"

He shrugged. "Probably, yes."

Holy Moses, I left destruction in my wake. I had no love for anyone in that household but Magda, and the news that they tortured her hit hard. The waiter laid our sandwiches on the table, but my appetite had vanished, and I left it untouched.

The director appeared to have no such qualms and took a large bite out of his meal. "What happened to Magda is not your fault." His bristly mustache wiggled like a caterpillar as he masticated the sandwich.

I looked away and swallowed hard. "Of course it's my fault.

I placed myself there. I traded on Magda's desperation to position myself in that household. What happens to her can be laid directly at my feet."

"It was your job."

"I am aware of that. The fault still lies with me."

He paused eating to pick at his teeth and then delivered in a quiet tone, "You … are the only one to make it out of the carnage alive."

The manner in which he spoke caught my attention, and I waited with bated breath for the other shoe to drop. I waited for him to accuse me of becoming a double agent and causing the deaths of my collaborators. I waited for the MPs to come through the door to arrest me for high treason.

He chewed with slow deliberation and swallowed. "For that, I am sincerely grateful, because I have no interest in informing your father that his only daughter is dead."

I gaped like a caught salmon. "You know my father?" If this was true, then he also knew my real identity.

"Edward and I worked closely when he was stationed at the consulate in Lyon. I was sorry to hear about your mother. She was a lovely woman. You take after her." He tilted his head. "Only … not so fragile."

I knew what he meant. My mother always appeared so fluttery and delicate, in need of male assistance to get through life. That was what she allowed the exterior world to think. Edward and I knew she had a backbone of steel. Losing her first husband while practically a newlywed with a baby on her hip, and half a dozen moves around Europe—she never would have survived had she not been strong. In the end, it was only her health that was fragile.

"After lunch, I'd like to speak with you about your future in the department. Unfortunately, we've discovered that not only was Anneliese's cover burned, the Gestapo somehow figured out your true identity."

"Lillian Saint James?"

He shook his head. "The name Sarah Jolivet is on their list."

"How?" I asked the question even though I already knew the answer. Herr Heinburg finally put the pieces together. He knew Sarah Jolivet—the young, knock-kneed, daughter of Edward and Maria Jolivet from the American Embassy. Lillian Saint James meant nothing to him.

The director shrugged. "We're not sure, but your name and a fairly accurate likeness has been passed around by the Gestapo. You are a target on their list. We didn't find out until you'd reentered Germany to rescue the pilot. Had we realized … your return would never have been allowed. The SOE pulled the wool over our eyes on that one."

"I knew that Blaus wasn't telling me everything." *I should have listened to my gut.* "It doesn't matter. We got out and saved a life."

"I suggested they give you a medal."

"The Brits? Give a medal to an American agent? I can't imagine it." I laughed at the absurdity.

"You wouldn't be the first," he said cryptically before sipping from his coffee cup.

"Is my father in danger? If they've realized I am Jolivet, they'll be able to link me to my father's time at the consulate in Bavaria and Vienna."

"Don't worry. We have taken care of it. He is safe enough at home. Speaking about home, you've gained so much knowledge. I'm interested in having you work with the Research and Analysis department … back in Washington." He wiped the crumbs from his whiskers.

"R and A? In D.C.? Why would you send me there? You

said my father was fine. Even if I can't return immediately, I can be of more use here. Isn't there something I can do here, in Paris?"

He didn't respond.

"London?" Loathe to leave Europe, I tried to keep the desperation from my voice.

He gave a self-deprecating smile. "I had to try. Your father is worried and has been requesting your return. When was the last time you wrote to him?"

I shifted uncomfortably. "It's been awhile."

He pulled a handful of letters out of his jacket pocket and laid them between us. "He's been writing to you. We supplied your prewritten letters, but I'm afraid we ran out. If you can assure your father all is well, we might find you a position here in Paris."

"I'll write to him tonight."

"Take your time. I believe you've earned a little R and R. I can arrange for you to go to England."

"There is no need. I'm ready to report for duty tomorrow."

"I'm sure you think so, but you need rest." I opened my mouth to speak but he shook his head. "Report back a week from tomorrow... That's an order."

Chapter Twenty-five
Apology

The pile of letters lay at my elbow awaiting a response. Edward had written regularly. Some begged I return for my own safety. Others demanded it. After a while he seemed to realize the demands were getting him nowhere, and the letters turned into chatty missives about life in D.C., the staff, and reminiscence about places we'd lived in Europe with Mother. The letters evoked a painful memory that I'd intimated to Charlie but was too embarrassed to fully explain. My behavior revealed an ultimate lack of maturity in dealing with my mother's death, and it hurt Edward deeply. A hurt for which I had yet to apologize.

♠♠♠♠

January 1939
Washington, D.C.

"I wish you'd rethink this decision. There is no need for you to move out."

Someone had left the door open. The winter chill invaded the foyer where Edward and I stood rehashing the same argument. A D.C. cab idled in front, plumes of smoke puffing out from the exhaust pipe. Its boot was tied down with twine to keep my trunks and overfull bags from bursting forth.

"There is every need for me to move out, and well you know

it, Edward."

He flinched at my use of his first name. "Sarah—"

"I go by Lily now, my middle name."

He sighed. "Lily, a girl your age shouldn't be on her own in the city."

"Then it's a good thing I'm moving into an apartment with two other women."

"If you insist on moving, then at least let me hire you an apartment in a decent section of town."

"The row house I'm moving into is in a perfectly fine location."

He crossed his arms and his mouth flattened. "If that's the case, why won't you tell me where you're going? You're behaving like a child running away from home."

"I'm no longer a child, Edward," I said dryly, pulling on my gloves. "And I'll send you my new address ... once I'm settled."

"Sarah." His face softened and he placed a hand on my shoulder. "I'm sorry I didn't call you back sooner. She went downhill so quickly. I told you, we thought she'd rebound, like she did before, and she didn't want you to see her like that."

The tears, so close to the surface these days, welled up in my eyes. I mashed my lips together to keep them from quivering and breathed deep.

"You know, I miss her too. You're not the only one hurting."

His last statement invoked the anguish and deep sorrow I'd tamped down in the weeks since Mother's death. "You kept her from me," I cried. "I was to come home ... from England. Then you shipped me off to that ridiculous finishing school. She didn't pull the strings to get me in ... *you* did. You were always jealous of our relationship. I was her daughter, for god's sakes." I pounded a fist to my chest and sniffed.

"You resented me. Didn't you? I was tolerated because you loved Marie, and I was her daughter, and in order to have her, you had to take me too. But you were very skilled in getting rid of me. Weren't you? First the British boarding school, then Switzerland. Well, now she's gone and there is nothing holding us together anymore. I suspect you'll be pleased." I couldn't stop the deeply hurtful tirade as the devastating pain that had been burning in my chest since the funeral spewed forth like molten lava at my stepfather.

Edward's mouth dropped as I spoke and his face turned ashen. "My God. Is that what you think?" he whispered.

The tears flowed in earnest now. I shrugged, wiping my face with a handkerchief. My mother's death was so painful I didn't know what to think. She wanted me to go to that school and Edward pulled the strings to get me in. Right or wrong in my blinding grief, I blamed him for that.

"*I* wanted you home. I asked her to bring you home with us. I knew, as an adult, you would be such a comfort to your mother. I begged her to allow me to call you home, especially near the end. She refused me, over and over. She only wanted what was best for you. In the end, I gave in because she became so agitated, and I wanted to placate her. But though you aren't my own blood, you are my only child and I love you. Deep down, I think you know that. And … I don't wish to lose you too."

I glanced away from his pleading gaze. "I can't stay here, Edward. As you pointed out, I'm an adult now. It's time I stood on my own two feet. I've got to make a difference, and it's not going to happen by becoming some politician's wife. I can't be the person my mother wanted me to be. I'm not sure I ever could." I drew a hand down my face, as though doing so could erase Mother's dreams. "Europe is falling apart at the seams.

Maybe I can help. You can reach me at the Senate Foreign Relations Committee office on Capitol Hill."

I turned to go, but he grabbed the cuff of my coat. "Don't leave like this. Please, stay. I can't stand the thought of rattling around this place alone."

His honesty struck a painful note in my chest. Part of the reason I'd worked up the nerve to leave was the exact reason he stated. We'd drifted around the large townhouse like wraiths, speaking in stiff platitudes and trying not to show the other how much the unbearable weight of depression pressed down upon us.

At the funeral, I'd been approached by a distinguished Senator in his sixties who knew my mother before I was born. He spoke fondly of her, gave me a comforting handshake, and told me to let him know if there was anything he could do to help on his way out the door. I thought of him when I could no longer stand the tedium of doing nothing but bouncing between despair and anger. I never realized how busy my life had been until I came home and there was nothing to be done. I hadn't developed local friends, so there was nowhere to go. No more lessons to be learned. And besides allowing me to arrange the weekly flowers, the household staff took care of everything else with minimal direction from me. Beyond my anger at Edward, I envied him his job. At least he had a place to go every day. Somewhere beyond this depressing mausoleum of a house. A constant reminder that I never belonged here and would never see my vivacious mother living here, even though her scent and decorative touches whispered to me at every turn.

"I'm staying on Fourth Street Southeast." I pulled the cuff loose. "Number twelve."

♠♠♠♠

Dear ~~Edward~~ Father,

I'm writing to tell you that I am hale and hearty and I hope that you are enjoying good health as well. I have been working diligently to help the war effort, and I know you are worried for my safety, but you needn't be. I understand it is in a father's nature to do his best to keep his children out of danger, but I am begging that you please stop using your connections to have me sent home. My job is far from the fighting, I am in minimal danger, and my contribution is more valuable here than in D.C. As I'm sure you are aware, our brave boys are doing their best to bring Hitler to his knees and end this war. I have high hopes that all will come to an end by summer.

On a different note, I am glad you aren't here to see the destruction this war has wrought upon the lands and her people. The memories of places you write in your letters have gone to wrack and ruin. The pretty church we attended in Lyon with the cherub frescos on the ceiling... Sadly, it was burnt to the ground. It is not the Europe you once knew, and the Vichy government did its best to tear France apart under Nazi occupation. Although, you would have been proud to see the strength a village farmer or grocer or rural doctor showed putting their lives at risk to defy the Nazi regime. I have witnessed great bravery against an indomitable foe, especially in the face of certain torture and death if caught. Those were the people of France you knew when you were stationed here, not the turncoats and Nazi collaborators.

I don't know what you'll be allowed to read from this letter, but know that I miss you. When I'm in Paris, I think often of Mother and our last shopping trip. She loved this city so much, but when I remember her fragile strength those last days, it is perhaps best she isn't here to be subjected to the misery Europe is witnessing.

Finally, Father, it has been long in coming, but I wish to apologize for my childish behavior the day I moved out of the Georgetown house. You remember what I speak of. I was distraught with grief and blamed you. My conduct was reprehensible, and though you were gentlemanly enough to ignore it, and we returned to speaking terms before I left, things have never been quite the same. I'm embarrassed I never had the wherewithal to say ... <u>I am sorry</u>. I apologize for the deep hurt I caused you.

When my time here is over, I'd like to return to the Georgetown house for a visit, if you'll have me.

Sending my love,

Sarah

Writing words I should have spoken years ago eased my nagging conscience. I'm sure parts of my letter to Edward would be redacted for security's sake, but I couldn't help writing the bit about France. It saddened me that neither it nor the rest of Europe resembled the place I enjoyed during my childhood. I wondered if the beauty and serenity could ever be restored to its people.

My Dearest Charlie,

You'll be pleased to hear that I've been given a holiday. I have a full week at my disposal, here in Paris, and I don't know what I'm to do with it. My roommate tells me to stop moping and take in the sights. She says there is no city to compare to Paris and she is correct. Whenever I look at the Eiffel Tower, I can only think of our time together and I shan't consider doing it without you. I hope things are well with you and the 101st. Send my regards to Jake, Glassman, Peterson, Tank, and the rest of the gang.

If you get a pass, perhaps you would consider coming to visit.

Yours,

Lily

Chapter Twenty-six
Black Widow

"Lily, you must wake up."

"I'm awake," I groaned and rolled away. Colette's petite fingers were icicles against my skin. "Your hands are cold. Go away. I'm still on holiday, you know." Sleep had been long in coming last night, making for a weary morning. I desperately needed another hour of shut-eye.

"Someone is here to see you."

"Tell Phillippe to go away. I'll see him later." I pulled the blankets over my head.

"It is not Phillippe. But if you want me to tell the handsome American major to go away, I will do so."

Her words had me shooting bolt upright. "Charlie? He's here?"

Colette grinned. "*Oui.* You were not expecting him?"

"I … I don't know. I sent the letter only two days ago." I threw the covers off and jammed my feet into a pair of slippers. "I didn't expect him to get a pass so quickly. Help me with these curlers, will you?"

"Calm yourself, my friend." She sat next to me and began unrolling. "You mustn't appear too eager. I will entertain your visitor until you are ready. Wear the red dress and take time to make yourself beautiful."

"Colette, he doesn't have much time. What if it's only a twenty-four-hour pass?" I jerked at a stubborn roller. "Ow."

Colette pushed my frantic hands away and untwisted the curler. "Lily, the most recent memories this man has of you could not be described as your best. Bloodied, burned, bruised, gray-haired, and gaunt. When was the last time he saw the beautiful woman you are?"

Her comments made me pause. "November."

"He deserves to see the glamorous movie star he fell in love with. Brush your hair, wash up, and put on some lipstick. Take your time. He will wait." She tossed the last curler in the box and rose. "I will make fresh coffee."

Half an hour later, I entered the living room wearing the red calico dress and my newly styled hair pulled back with a pair of silver combs. Colette perched on the edge of her chair, but I only had eyes for Charlie.

"Here she is and just in time too. The major and I have finished our coffee," Colette chirped with her French-accented English.

His eyes widened as he rose from the divan. "Lily? Is that... You changed your hair... You look ... beautiful."

The smile I could no longer hold back spread across my face.

"I hope it's all right that I came. I sent a telegram last night, but your roommate informed me you didn't receive it."

"Yes, of course. It's a lovely surprise." An unexplained bout of shyness gripped me, and I couldn't seem to make my feet walk across the room.

Charlie must have felt the awkwardness, because he, too, stood staring and fidgeted with his hat.

Colette broke the tension. "I am off. Charlie, it was lovely to meet you. We will have a little drink tonight. Lily will bring you to our regular place." Colette pinched my arm as she walked past.

"Yes, good day, ma'am," Charlie mumbled but didn't take his eyes off me.

The door closed behind Colette.

"I like your hair," Charlie murmured.

"You look good too." I shifted my weight. My heart yearned to leap into his arms, but thoughts in my head kept my feet from moving. Our last meeting had been fraught with dramatic confessions and swirling emotions. With all my free time, I had, of course, replayed those moments in my head over and over. Today, I didn't want the drama, I wanted it to be like it was back in November, when our love was fresh and untouched by the harrowing times in between.

"Are you sure it's okay that I came? Our last meeting … I didn't know. I mean … I wanted to see you … and your letter … but—"

"Oh, Charlie." His awkward schoolboy stammering washed away my trivial doubts, and I flew across the room into his arms.

After a while, I came around to asking the question I dreaded most. "How much time?"

"Seventy-two hours."

Seventy-two blissful hours. We held hands wherever we went, and I consistently found Charlie watching me, as though he feared to let me out of his sight.

The first evening, I took Charlie to meet the crew at a bar a few blocks away from the apartment. Philippe, he remembered from our meeting at the café, but there was also Alfonso, a former soldier who lost his arm when the Germans invaded France. A farmer hid him in his barn and nursed Alfonso back to health. Afterwards, Alfonso joined the *Résistance*. Mariette, another co-worker in French Intelligence with Colette, also joined us. She originally lived in a little village in Vichy-controlled France, and she helped as part of an underground railroad for Jews and downed pilots. She barely escaped over the Pyrenees herself when the Gestapo closed in and burned her home to the ground. However, it was the woman sitting next to Mariette who gave me pause as I introduced Charlie.

"And I don't think I know who is sitting next to…"

The dark-haired woman turned her head my way. The years fell away and even the change from blond to black hair couldn't disguise her prominent brow, rather large nose, and sturdy chin.

"Camilla?"

"Hello, Lily." She rose.

I went to her and wrapped my arms around her. "But how? What are you doing here?"

"Much like you, I've been pulled in for a cooling off."

My brows rose. "Let me introduce you to Major Charles McNair. Charlie, this is Camilla, a good friend from finishing school."

After the introductions, Alfonso called Charlie to his side, and I had a private moment with Camilla.

"SOE?"

She gave an enigmatic smile.

"I'd no idea. When?"

"Not long after that last letter I wrote to you. I had to do *something*. By the way, I believe I have you to thank for my getaway."

"What do you mean?"

"I've been informed"—she lowered her voice—"you were mistaken for the Black Widow.

"It was you?"

She winked. "Your capture allowed time for my escape. For that, I am both grateful and regretful. What you must have endured at the—"

"Hush." I shook my head and patted her shoulder. "I'm relieved to find my ignoble capture was of use to someone." I frowned. "But they said she limped…"

Camilla tapped her hip. "Fell down a flight of stairs to the Underground during a bombing raid." She grimaced. "Didn't healed properly."

"Tough luck, that. What about your friend Friederich?"

A look of distress crossed her features. "Unknown."

"Lily, come, we need your sage advice to settle an argument," Colette called to me.

I squeezed Camilla's hand and whispered, "I'm sorry," before joining the rest of the group.

At the end of the night, Colette pulled me aside to tell me she would be bunking at Mariette's for the next few nights and sent me home with a wink and a kiss on Charlie's cheek.

The second night I awoke to an empty bed.

"Charlie?" I poked my head into the hallway to find a faint glow emanating from the living room.

Charlie, lit by flickering candlelight, stood in Colette's red and black flowered kimono, hands on hips, staring out the window onto Paris's darkened streets.

"Darling, what's wrong?"

He turned, his face drawn, and enfolded me into his arms. "Did I wake you?" he whispered. "I couldn't sleep."

"Nightmares?"

His chin rubbed against my head.

"I have them too."

"I remember."

"Colette believes when we talk about our nightmares it takes away their power." I rubbed a finger across his furrowed brow. "Come, sit here."

I fluffed a pillow, tossed it on the arm of the divan, and guided him down. I nestled between his legs, back to front, and wrapped his arms around me. My body rose and fell with his breathing for many minutes before he broke the silence.

"We were in the Ardennes. It was cold. A deep-down-to-the-bone-marrow cold. It's not as though we could light a fire, and I often wondered if I would ever be warm again. One morning, early, I climbed out of the foxhole and headed out to take a pi— uh, relieve myself. We'd get this eerie snow fog in the morning—you could hardly see three feet in front, and sounds bounced around. I'd just finished my business when I heard someone else, close by, doing the same thing. Not ten steps away was a Jerry. You have to realize, our troops were stretched so thin there were gaping holes along the line. Sometimes the enemy would wander into our territory. We'd been taught a few phrases in German. I told him to drop his gun and put up his hands."

His thumb stroked the soft flesh of my inner wrist. "I don't know why he didn't follow the directions. Did I say it wrong? I don't know. The kid couldn't have been more than seventeen, and there was something in his eyes that reminded me of a school chum of mine who was on the basketball team with me, Tommy Gundersen. He scored the winning basket our last game senior year and went to Indiana State on an athletic scholarship. He had the smartest, driest sense of humor..."

I was so intent on listening to Charlie's story, I barely breathed.

"Instead of putting down the weapon, the stupid kid fumbled to aim it. I told him to stop. '*Halten sie!*' I remember calling. He got off a wild shot and I dropped him. The bullet hit him in the chest. His gasping sounded like a gurgling water fountain, and I knew it must have punctured a lung. I was about to check on him, even call for a medic, when I heard other German soldiers. I slipped back the way I came, into the fog, and realized I'd wandered farther than I thought into Jerry territory, rather than other way around. They must have found their man because there was some sort of argument. German. I didn't understand ... but the single shot ... that I understood."

"That was the last time I fired my weapon. The following day, I was moved up to battalion HQ."

"What happened to your friend?"

"Tommy? He died on the beaches in Normandy."

I pulled his arms tighter around me. The dawn light rose, and the candle guttered in its socket. We drifted into sleep.

Chapter Twenty-seven
Ennui

The March winds calmed, bulbs bloomed, and winter slid into spring. The Red Army steadily ate up land in the east, and to the frustration of Churchill, the western front slowed. The 101st trained for a jump into Berlin. Charlie was unable to get another pass to visit Paris before his regiment moved out of Mourmelon to assist the Twelfth Army's encirclement of the Ruhr Valley.

I moved through the day-to-day motions at R and A. Even though I'd admitted to Charlie I feared a return behind enemy lines, I found myself confessing to Colette that Paris made me antsy. The only thing that broke up the tedium was the unexpected presentation of two awards. To my embarrassment, in the relatively small office of the director, I was presented with the Croix de Guerre from France for gallantry in the field during the Normandy invasion.

The second award was hand delivered by Lord Nigel Graydon. His cast had been removed and he walked with only a slight limp. He presented me the King's Medal for Courage in the Cause of Freedom for the part I played in returning him home. After the ceremony, he took me out for lunch, and I confessed that I missed the action, and the minutia of office work had begun to bore me. I felt relatively useless doing it, much like my time on Capitol Hill. He laughed and admitted he understood, because ever since the cast came off, he'd been trying to get cleared and return to flight status.

The feeling of restlessness increased once the 101st moved out and Charlie's letters no longer arrived with regularity. One afternoon, I returned home in a foul mood, and when Colette asked if I'd brought home the eggs, I snapped, "Colette, I don't have time to stand in the damn lines. You'll just have to make do with the powdered kind!"

"*Tiens,* Lily! Your clipped conversations give me a headache! You are a poor friend to be out of temper just because your sweetheart is doing his duty."

Poor Colette, she wasn't wrong, and she didn't deserve my irritation. My happiness had become connected to Charlie, a novelty for me since I'd never been in a serious relationship before. The tables had turned, and now I worried daily for Charlie's welfare while he could be content in the knowledge that I remained safe in Paris. I needed the intensity of a mission to keep my mind occupied. I put out feelers to move back into Secret Intelligence or the Operations Department, and after a few strategically placed comments, I found myself approached to train for a new mission.

The OSS remained concerned Hitler's men would launch a guerilla war in the mountains of Bavaria and Austria. He had a home in Berchtesgaden, where the offensive could be headed up. In an effort to incorporate more agents inside Germany, the OSS had identified members of the Free German Committee in London. The agents had been trained and dropped into Austria in February, about the same time as my own flight to get out of the country.

The Free German operatives were sent in to make contact with other resistance groups and to provide intelligence. Unfortunately, a pair of their operatives had gone missing. They hadn't checked in with the radio operator in seventy-two hours, and there was fear the entire team had been, or soon would be, rounded up and arrested. The situation reminded me of my own experience in Oberndorf. The state of affairs wasn't new, and each spy took on the risk knowing the probable outcome. It didn't stop me from wanting to help.

The OSS decided to revive Gisele Sandmeier. I found myself returning to Switzerland. My last letter to Charlie before leaving Paris ended with this cryptic line: *G is antsy and declares she will return to finishing school next month.* I had no idea if he understood the message or if he would receive it without redaction. It was my way of telling him that I would be returning to Switzerland. The change did me good. My mind was finally engaged upon something other than my obsession with Charlie's welfare.

They called the mission Gumdrop. My job—to parachute into Innsbruck, establish contact with the radio operator, who had already moved twice, and identify if our agent had, indeed, been captured by the Gestapo. I would be entering with another agent known to me as Hans. The mission provided addresses for safe houses, courier names, and contacts. I knew it would be dangerous, but resources had already been established and appeared a far cry from spying from within the household of a German colonel.

I expected the fear to regenerate itself. I expected the nightmares to return. To my relief, they did not.

Two days before enacting the mission, Hans and I practiced my hand-to-hand combat and small knife skills in the dining room of the home where he was staying.

"That was much better. Remember to use your weight to draw your attacker off balance and drive upward with the heel of your hand. It's guaranteed to start a nosebleed."

A knock sounded at the front door and the two of us froze.

"Are you expecting anyone?" I asked.

"*Nein.*" With one hand on his knife and the other on the doorknob, Hans asked, "Who is it?"

"I've lost my umbrella," came the reply.

Hans opened the door to a young man in dark clothes. "Umbrellas are sold on the blue stall on the Schwarztorstrasse."

The courier passed Hans a note and disappeared back into the shadows. Hans unfolded the missive and drew his brows.

"What does it say?"

He responded by passing the letter to me. The succinct hand-scrawled message delivered a double blow: *Roosevelt Dead. Gumdrop mission cancelled.*

The paper floated to the floor as I sank into a nearby chair. It was difficult to say which of the two pieces of information delivered the most punch. Roosevelt, the passionate leader who led America into the biggest war known to man. A larger-than-life leader. One of the big three, along with Churchill and Stalin, determined to wrest Europe from the stronghold of the Nazi regime. Gone.

Once I processed the president's death, it didn't take me long to realize, with Gumdrop cancelled, the likelihood of obtaining another mission was slim to none. HQ must have discovered the fate of their man and no longer needed us to take the risk.

I picked up the paper and crushed it in my fist. "This is it. There will be no more missions, not for me."

Hans looked pityingly at me. "Come, let me buy you a drink."

We decided to drown our disappointment with a *bier* at the Schweizerhof Hotel bar in downtown Bern. As depressed as me, Hans stared moodily into his glass. My efforts to engage in conversation were met with brief monosyllables, and eventually I gave up to my own despondency and took to a spy's natural pastime—eavesdropping. My ears zeroed in on three English-speaking journalists sitting at a table behind me.

Hans excused himself to go to the restrooms and I shifted to better view the group.

A man wearing an ugly brown tie bragged, "Believe me, fellows, I heard the frantic Morse code transmission. It said, 'SOS. This is Buchenwald concentration camp," and they were requesting help from Patton's army. It said they were being evacuated."

"Where?" a balding man drinking ale asked.

"It didn't say. And then, very faint, I swear I heard a reply from Patton's staff telling him to hold on, they would be there soon."

"I heard Murrow arrived today. He's going to get the jump on all of us if Blake doesn't get us permission to go in," said a third man sipping from a brandy snifter.

"Do you believe the stories? About the mass killings?" ale drinker asked.

"I heard they had crematoriums to burn the bodies," brown shirt said, "but I think it's an exaggeration."

"Maybe it's to burn the evidence. If it's not an exaggeration, then it's genocide for sure and a blatant violation of the Geneva Convention."

"I don't know. I'll believe it when I see it." Brandy snifter finished the last sip, rose from his seat, and threw money down on the table. "I'm turning in for the night."

I was so intent on eavesdropping I barely noticed Hans' return.

"*Gehst Du jetzt?*" Are you going now? He gathered his coat.

"I think I'll have one more drink. You look tired. You go ahead," I urged.

Hans tossed some francs on the bar and wished me a good evening. The remaining two journalists turned to discussing Roosevelt's death and the job Truman had ahead. But their conversation about the prison camp intrigued me, and thoughts spun through my head.

My mission was cancelled and I had doubts that another would be forthcoming. The Red Army in the east and Allies in the west had Hitler's Wehrmacht on the retreat. My time at R and A had already shown breakdowns in the German Army communication along with a fair amount of surrenders. Goebbels could churn out all the propaganda he wanted, it didn't change the fact that their country would soon be overrun and bring the Wehrmacht to its knees. If I couldn't be of use to the OSS office in Switzerland, I'd likely be returned to R and A in France. I cringed at the thought.

Lily Saint James had a photojournalist cover identification and press credentials. Even though I'd reestablished Gisele, it seemed her moniker would not see a return to action. For some unfathomable reason burning deep in my gut, I was desperate to return to Germany. When I left the apartment in Paris, Colette had handed the camera to me on my way out the door. "It helps steady you," she'd said. She wasn't wrong. I missed my photography, and the Minox was nothing compared to the 35mm Argus A hidden behind the dresser in my room.

I flagged a passing waiter, ordered another drink, then headed to the ladies' room. The transformation took only a few minutes. Luckily, I'd opted for a wig this time. I tucked the gray-brown strands and glasses into my handbag and combed my own hair into a French twist. I washed the dreary makeup off my face, and with a few pinches to my cheeks and swipe of lipstick, Lily Saint James emerged.

To my relief the journalists were still at the table and had moved on to a heated discussion about Stalin and Churchill. A hotel staff member stopped by the table to deliver a missive to the journalists as I returned to my stool at the bar.

"Hot damn, we're in!" The brown tie slapped his hand on the table.

"We're in?"

"Buchenwald, it's been arranged. Pack your bags, we leave at oh-six-hundred…"

I swiveled on my seat, caught the eye of the fellow with the brown tie, dropped my lids, and produced a mysterious half smile. It was an enticing move I'd learned from Colette.

The gentleman paused, mid-sentence, straightened up from his slumped posture, and smiled back. "*Guten Tag.*"

I gave a deep chuckle. "Speak English. I'm an American, like you."

"Would you like to join us?"

I settled in the empty chair and pushed the brandy snifter aside.

"I'm Jack and this is Freddy."

"Lily." We shook hands.

"What are you doing in Switzerland?"

I smiled and whispered, "I'm going to be honest with you fellows." The two men leaned closer to hear me. "I heard your conversation about Buchenwald. I'm a freelance photographer trying to get my foot in the door to Germany, and I thought … maybe I could hitch a ride with you gentlemen to the camp?" I fluttered my lashes.

Brown tie didn't hesitate. "Sure thing, dollface. Why don't you and your camera meet us out front at oh-six-hundred? That's six a-m to those who don't speak military." He'd obviously tied on a few and might not have been thinking straight.

I didn't care. Just like my spur-of-the-moment decision to save little Klara had gotten me the job in Oberndorf, my impulsive move tonight would get me back into Germany.

"Thanks. Why don't you let me pay for your drinks?" I pulled twenty francs out of my purse, laid it under the brandy snifter, and rose.

"Wait," the ale drinker said. "You're leaving?"

"I must get my beauty rest. Tomorrow's a big day." I blew them a kiss and made my escape before they rethought their position.

Chapter Twenty-eight
Buchenwald

April 15, 1945
Buchenwald, Germany

Nothing in the world could have prepared me for Buchenwald.

Human skeletons wearing black-and-white-striped pajamas, eyes much too large in their gaunt faces, stared with little expression as the journalists recorded this atrocity against humanity. I heard they had cheered when troops from the Sixth Armored arrived, throwing their rescuers into the air. By the time I entered with other press colleagues, the harsh reality had been revealed. Even though their tormentors had run off, men were still dying. Their bodies, so far depleted of any nutrition or overrun with Typhoid fever, couldn't battle any longer. I had no idea a human form could survive such conditions.

The spring sun shone bright and warm on my shoulders, its vividness in direct contrast to the blackness of horror before us. Never will I forget the stink, a combination of unwashed bodies, bitter sickness, and rotting flesh that permeated the surrounding air. I wasn't the only one to lose my breakfast, and I'll admit it took more courage to remain and observe the camp than it did to live inside the colonel's home. My senses were overwhelmed. Having the camera was almost a relief. The lens diffused the ghastliness and distanced me from the devastation it filmed.

Citizens from the closest town of Weimar had been rousted early from their homes and marched, escorted by American soldiers, five miles to Buchenwald Camp. Patton, Eisenhower, and Bradley commanded the civilians witness the atrocities the Nazis had committed in their backyard. Prisoners guided them through the camp, pointing out the vileness like docents at a museum. Patton himself oversaw the Buchenwald procession and called for more press to come record the barbarism. Typhus had run rampant through the camp, and though the press and army were sprayed and given pills, Patton took no precautions to protect the civilian population from the disease.

Twenty-one thousand prisoners were housed here, and the morbidity rate was estimated to be one hundred a day—in the winter as high as nine hundred a day. I photographed a wagonload of emaciated bodies piled in preparation to be burned in the crematorium, left there like an unimportant pile of rubbish rather than children of God. Women, dressed in their Sunday best, became physically ill or turned their heads aside in shame. I understood why. Mortification that anyone could inflict this type of suffering upon another human being, much less the tens of thousands, weighed heavily on my heart.

A group of Jewish survivors placed themselves at a table in front of the barracks, a squat building with hard wooden slats, stacked three high, to be used for beds and no stove for warming the room. Still wearing their striped uniforms, they confronted civilians who walked past. A dark-haired man jumped out of his chair and ranted as loudly as his weakened lungs would allow, with finger pointed, at half a dozen men and women who turned their heads aside in shame.

"Do you understand what he's saying?" a frowning soldier asked as I reloaded another roll of film.

"He's telling them they did this to the Jews. They are Nazi swine. He holds them as responsible as the SS. He says they are all murderers and their town should be burned to the ground."

The man spoke more eloquently than my translation, and I pitied the soldier's inability to understand the language. The former prisoner finally ran out of breath, and his colleagues helped him back into his seat. One of the women in the group that had been harangued sobbed quietly into her handkerchief.

"*Ich wusste davon nichts.*" I didn't know. It became a regular refrain heard from the civilians as they toured the camp.

Soldiers looked on with disgust and disbelief.

But I knew.

I knew they knew something wasn't right with the camps. Hitler had done his best to hide the depravity from the general population. But even in Oberndorf, workers had been escorted through the town to the factory under guard. A kind person who was caught offering them food could find himself beaten in the street or hauled off by the SS. I remember one distressing incident when Dagobert laughed and pointed at one of the poor souls digging in the trash for food. I ached to smack him and probably would have had there not been an SS officer watching and grinning at the child's cruelty. Rumors had run rampant through intelligence divisions about the concentration camps, but unless you were standing here, looking at the destruction, you couldn't imagine the real truth.

By the afternoon, my stomach had turned into a greasy lump of distress, and I worked my way over to the commandant's office, a two-story, dark wooden edifice. The air was slightly less putrid over here, and I let myself into the building. Sunlight shafted into the room from the open door to reveal two soldiers at a large mahogany desk piled with ledgers. A safe to my right stood open, its heavy door hanging crookedly by a single hinge.

The men squinted at me as I entered. The door shut behind me and I blinked as my eyes adjusted to the murkiness.

"Who are you?" a lieutenant asked.

His name tag came into focus and read Wentworth. "Press." I held up the camera. "I was directed to take some photographs. What have you got there?"

"Records of the poor bastards who came through."

The sergeant to his left grunted. "You've got to give the Krauts credit, they sure do know how to maintain good documentation."

"Yes, they're sticklers for the paperwork," I murmured as I set up a shot of the two soldiers. The sergeant shifted and I read his name tag, Lowenfeldt.

"Well, it's enough to hang this old bastard, Pister, for war crimes," Lowenfeldt replied, his features drawn and a look in his eye that made me glad I wasn't Hermann Pister, the commandant of Buchenwald.

"If he makes it to trial," Wentworth muttered. "Prisoners are scouring the countryside for SS guards as we speak."

"And finding them. I saw a pair shoot one by the side of the road this morning." The sergeant flipped through one of the black ledgers.

"Will the military allow the … vigilante justice to continue? Will the men not stand for trial?"

Lowenfeldt glared at me, his jaw set and brows crunched together. "You think it's wrong? That these men shouldn't get their revenge? You think it's okay what the Krauts did to them? The POWs, the Poles, the Jews? You know this isn't the first camp we've found. Are you some sort of Nazi sympathizer?" He stuck his chest out and laid a hand on his M1 sitting on the desk.

"Lowenfeldt." Wentworth laid a hand on the sergeant's arm.

It took all my willpower to remain calm after his unfair attack, and my answer came out in a low voice that, to my displeasure, held a slight tremor. "No, of course not. There is nothing acceptable with the horror story that is Buchenwald. I think … public trials can reach much further into the collective psyche of a nation … and the world, for that matter, than the instant gratification of shooting a monster on the side of the road in the middle of nowhere. I would hope some of the top Nazis are caught alive and held up as an example of the depravity of Hitler's rantings. The world will watch while they hang."

My hand had fisted so tightly my fingernails bit into the flesh on my palm. "But it is not up to me, and I can certainly understand why the prisoners are pursuing their tormentors." Lars, bleeding out on the floor, rose to mind. Would I have allowed Glassman and Tank to arrest him with the rest of the German POWs that day? "Trust me, Staff Sergeant, I understand far better than you realize."

Lowenfeldt's posture relaxed as I spoke, and he released the weapon. "Well, you might have a point. But it's not as though we can do much to stop them. They've already lived in the worst prison man ever erected."

"I suppose not." Twisting the lens, I brought the safe into focus, the shutter clicked, and in the flare of light, something caught my eye. I went over to investigate. The corner of a black frame jutted up from behind the safe. It must have fallen off the wall and gotten jammed in there. My efforts to remove it were futile.

"Has anyone a knife?" I asked.

"What did you find?" The sergeant removed his knife, flipped the blade into his hand, and offered me the handle.

"I'm not sure." I jimmied the metal between the wall and

the safe and worked the frame free of the crack. The sound of broken glass tinkled onto the floor as it came loose, and I took it over to the window.

"The Fuhrer and Commandant Pister taken March 1944." I translated the caption for Lowenfeldt, who'd followed me to the window to peer over my shoulder at the photograph of Adolf Hitler, Hermann Pister, and eighteen other SS officers standing tall and proud. Behind them rose the gates of Buchenwald, identifiable by the words within the metalwork "*Jedem Das Seine*," which, translated literally, means "to each his own." However, in the English vernacular, it would be closer to the meaning "everyone gets what he deserves." An appalling sentiment considering the conditions we'd just found. I'd photographed a line of civilians entering through those gates earlier in the day.

It took every ounce of control not to deface the picture with the knife I still held. Instead, I turned it over. The brown paper backing showed no further inscription, but on a hunch, I dug my nails through and pulled it aside. Sure enough, on the back of the photograph, listed by order of rank, every man's name in the photo.

"I'll be damned," Lowenfeldt breathed.

"I believe there is a Chinese proverb about a picture being worth ten thousand words."

Wentworth joined us and let out a low whistle between his teeth. "This should make identification easy. It looks like they've created their own police lineup. The captain is going to want to see this."

"Indeed." I passed the picture into his hands.

"What did you mean?" Lowenfeldt asked.

"I beg your pardon?"

"You said you understood more than most."

I fiddled with my camera. "It's not something I can talk about."

"I apologize for calling you a Nazi sympathizer. It's just ... this place ..." A golden Star of David hung around his neck, its chain intertwined with his dog tags.

My gaze raked the room, taking in the stacks of paperwork. "You realize this is what the war is really about. Not just the maneuvering to depose an insane dictator but to put an end to the murder of innocent civilians whose only crime was to be considered undesirable to their own countrymen. This is why the generals invited all the press outlets to come here. We are witnesses. You, me, him." I pointed at each of us. "We are here to make sure this never again happens in human history."

My little speech silenced the two men.

I returned behind the camera, taking photos of the office and ledgers, half-empty drawers of filing cabinets, and papers strewn across the floor. One of the ledgers lay at my feet. I crouched down, flipping it open to a random page. Rows and rows of numbers with names, birthdates, and deaths lined the columns. All terminated here in this camp. The page I flipped to had an entire column listing the same date under death for each person. More pages revealed the same, and my finger ran down random names that meant nothing to me ... until one did—Friederich Dantzig, violinist from Berlin, Religion—Jewish. The birth year was three years prior to mine and the date under death was listed as January 17, 1945. I sucked in a breath and my knees thunked to the hardwood floor.

Poor Camilla. *What would I tell her? Should I tell her?*

Of course, I knew would have to write to Camilla so she could stop wondering. It's what I would want if something happened to Charlie. It would be better for her to find out from a friend, but I hated to be the one to snuff out that candle of hope she held on to.

Who else did I know who might be listed on one of the ledgers? My girlhood friends, Sacha? Elijah? Was Magda's name on a list here, or another camp?

The appalling thoughts washed over me unbidden and unwanted. I dropped the ledger and stumbled out the door into the bright sunlight.

Chapter Twenty-nine
Trouble Ahead

I stretched, pressing a hand against my stiff back. I'd been on my feet for days, resting only to sleep and eat what little I could force down. Occasionally, in the evenings, I played cards and drank with other journalists while we listened to the radio broadcasts. Every morning, I religiously read the newspapers, searching the killed-in-action list. So far, Charlie's name hadn't appeared.

By April twenty-fifth, Buchenwald was inundated with press answering Patton's requests to send their brightest stars to cover the Nazi atrocities. I'd made deals with reporters from the *Boston Globe, Iowa Dispatch, Milwaukee Evening Post,* and a few smaller newspapers, who couldn't afford or didn't have the ability to get their own photographers into Europe, to provide photos of Buchenwald and surrounding camps. In exchange, the *Globe* supplied me with film and materials to process it, and the rest paid me outright. Lodging had been arranged for the press in surrounding towns, and I bunked with another female journalist named Marguerite, Maggie for short, from the *New York Tribune.*

Clouds drifted across the late-afternoon sun, and I paused from photographing the locals digging graves to change my lens.

"Hello, there." A man dressed as a fellow photojournalist— two cameras hung from his neck and a large pocketed bag off his shoulder—approached me.

I didn't recognize him, but there were so many of us now it didn't surprise me.

"You are Lily, right?" His rolled-up sleeves revealed sinewy muscles, and he walked with a stiff, upright bearing.

I focused the camera on him. "Yes?" The lens clicked.

"Fleur-di-lis? The company is not pleased with your abrupt departure."

I lowered the camera. "I was informed my mission had been cancelled. I believe my resignation explained my reasons for leaving."

He glanced at the workers. "Let's take a walk."

We wandered uphill to a grassy hummock overlooking the gravesite, away from listening ears.

"I don't think you understand, you cannot simply quit the OSS."

"Actually, as a civilian agent, I've never been contractually obligated to remain." I crossed my arms over my chest. "Unlike you military agents."

His eyes flickered but he didn't acknowledge the hit. "The director isn't pleased, and you're lucky you're a civilian and not military, or you would be brought up on charges," he said in a low voice. "As it is, we'd been warned that you were prone to impulsivity."

"Forgive me. What are you implying?"

"Your country still needs you."

"My country needs to see this." I flicked a hand at the diggers. "What can I do for the OSS besides sit behind a desk and analyze intelligence, receiving the occasional pat on the head like a favored family pet?"

"There are other missions. The war isn't over yet."

"It will be soon. The Russians will be in Berlin within the week. What other missions are there for a woman like me?"

"We'll be hunting Nazis for years to come. You have the capability of identifying many of them."

"I'm not a Nazi hunter, and you will have hundreds, if not thousands, of innocent civilians willing to help in the arrests. There's already a strong contingent right here in Buchenwald, ready to provide testimony." I raised a brow. "Though I'm not sure the enemy will make it as far as the courtroom, much less the hangman's noose. Besides, you know where I am. Show me a picture when you find someone I should know. I will verify their complicity."

"There will be negotiations with the Russians. Soon enough, Berlin will be the place to be."

"You realize I don't speak Russian. I can't be of help in that quarter. The peace talks in Berlin will be up to politicians, not spies like us." I kicked a stone in my path.

"You're wrong, and there will be other nations at the table besides Russia."

"Oh? Sure, there will be machinations on all fronts with whispered backroom conversations, but I am no politician. Besides, I've spent too much time in the company of politicians to know how my opinion will be valued." I pursed my lips remembering the senator's dismissiveness. "Minimal, to say the least."

"We still need people on the ground to gather intelligence."

"I am sure you do. However, I am not up for listening in corners or sweet-talking drunk attachés with wandering hands to find out what Russia plans for Eastern Europe. I am fairly certain Churchill, and Truman if he's listening to his advisors, know exactly what kind of devil they were getting into bed with when they made the pact with Stalin. My intelligence gathering is in here." I held up the camera. "My pictures will be circulated to thousands of Americans. My work is no longer secret. I am providing important information directly to the public. They deserve to know what we've known, or guessed, for years."

"There are protocols, a debriefing is in order."

I sent him an arch look.

"All right then, the head office in Bern would like a report on what you've found here."

"Fine, I'll prepare one tonight."

He sighed and scratched his neck as if realizing he'd taken the wrong tactic with me. "If another mission came up, would you take it?"

I gazed past him and watched an elderly man and woman carry another withered body to the grave. Baby leaves, new in the rebirth of spring, rustled in the breeze behind them, and I lifted the camera to photograph the juxtaposition of life and death. "I don't know. Perhaps."

A soldier approached us. I twisted the lens and his features came into focus. Lowenfeldt hiked up to our knoll. "Good afternoon, Sergeant."

"Ma'am." He tipped his hat and nodded at my companion. "I wanted to let you know, that picture you found ... it was used to identify some prisoners."

"Pister?"

He nodded. "He and four others created false identities. They were found at a detainee camp outside Munich."

"Thank you for telling me. I'm pleased to know they'll stand trial."

The sergeant glanced over his shoulder at the workers as he slipped a cigarette between his lips. "What a fuckin' mess." He lit the fag and sucked in a deep breath.

"I couldn't have said it better myself," my companion replied.

I did not introduce the men.

Lowenfeldt surveyed the two of us and must have realized he'd interrupted something. He took his leave, and I felt the agent watching me as I focused the camera on the soldier's retreating back.

"Sounds like you're already hunting Nazis."

"Contact me again … if there is an actual mission. Otherwise, the OSS can consider me on vacation. I think I've earned it."

"Funny place to take a vacation," he said to my retreating back.

The next morning, I packed my bag and caught a ride out of town with a pair of Czechoslovakian POWs from Buchenwald, Ludvik and Jiri. Ludvik spoke broken German, and from what I gathered, they'd acquired some German rifles and "borrowed" the American Army jeep to hunt down another camp guard. They'd heard about a farm that might be housing an SS guard in the countryside south of Buchenwald. Initially, the men seemed hesitant to take me with them. However, after I showed them my photography equipment and offered them some of the cash in my pocket, they welcomed me.

I didn't have much of a plan, but I knew I had to get away from the hoary cloud of Buchenwald for a few days. The compass hung heavy around my neck, and I had a vague notion of catching up with the 101st.

Jiri, the driver, wore a black beret and an olive American Army coat over a pair of black trousers. His square face and bushy brown eyebrows remained intent on watching the road. Ludvik wore a black knit cap, wool coat, and his black-and-white-striped trousers. Occasionally, he would turn to ask me a question in his broken German such as, "Where from?" or "How get here you?" A telltale tic had his left eye blinking and cheek twitching so much he would subconsciously place a hand to it when he spoke. Over all, the two men were in better condition than many of their comrades, and I gleaned they had been part of the camp rebellion launched two days before the Americans arrived.

We headed south on one of the major autobahns reserved only for Allied military traffic; Jiri had no problem entering the convoy in our commandeered jeep. The three of us watched in astonishment as blocks of surrendered German foot soldiers marched north along the grassy median; some still carried their weapons. American and British military trucks, tanks, and jeeps crowded the highway and made for slow going. The disintegration of the German Army was happening right in front of me. I'd never seen anything like it and spent half a roll of film capturing it. Jiri remained on the autobahn for an hour before taking an exit, my compass showed, turning southeast. Three transport trucks, filled with troops, took the same turning.

We'd only been on the road for a few minutes when the rumbling squeak of a tank had Jiri pulling us up short. I barely had enough time to throw my hands up to keep from slamming into the back of Ludvik's seat. Jiri shifted into reverse, but when he glanced back, we realized there was nowhere to go, as the three transport trucks stopped immediately behind us. I didn't recognize the style of tank, but it was surely German and grinding straight for us.

"Enemy tank!" went up the cry.

Jiri, Ludvik, and I hopped out, abandoning the jeep. The Czechs took to the surrounding woods while I hotfooted it behind the larger truck, where soldiers were dismounting. Two men set up a machine gun in the gully next to the road while the rest exited and scrambled for cover. I hunkered down behind the machine gunners as the weapon let out a *whap-whap-whap*. Bullets spanged against the front of the tank, setting off sparks as they hit, doing little damage. The tank rolled to a halt. I think we all drew in a collective breath.

"It's a Panzer Tiger. You got those mortars ready, Sully?" someone called out.

"Working on it."

The top hatch opened and a white piece of cloth tied to a rifle rose out of the turret.

"Hold your fire," the machine gunner called.

The rifle continued to rise, followed by a hand and then a hatless head. "*Amerikaner? Ich gebe auf,*" the German called.

"What's he saying?" the machine gunner holding the shell rounds asked.

"He said, 'I give up,'" I translated. "Don't shoot." I got to my feet.

"Who's the dolly with the great gams?" one of the soldiers mumbled from behind me.

"*Wie viele Männer sind im Tank?*" I called out.

"*Nur ich,*" the tank driver replied.

"He says he's the only one in the tank." The camera still hung around my neck, and I pulled it up to snap a shot of the surrendering soldier.

The machine gunner with his finger on the trigger stared over his shoulder at me. "Tell him to throw down his weapon, exit the tank, and come forward with his hands above his head."

I repeated the message in German.

The tank driver did as he was told. Once he was a few feet from the tank, five men scrambled forward. One held the German at gunpoint while the others surrounded the vehicle. A private moved up from the rear and took a knee beside me, his weapon at the ready.

The German looked at the men, then at me. "*Nur mich*," he assured me and continued with a spate of German.

As the soldiers checked the tank, I explained to the machine gunner what the German said. "He says he traveled across Czechoslovakia and Germany on his own so he could surrender to the Americans and not the ... *untermensch.* Um, I think he's referring to the Russians. It means something like subhuman ... pigs, maybe?"

The gunner's gaze shifted to the private beside me. "Janssen?"

"Yeah, she got it right, Sarge."

"I'll be damned. I guess that means we just got ourselves a new Kraut Tiger, boys. Load the prisoner in the back of second squad's truck."

The machine gunner and his partner retrieved their weapon while a pair of soldiers climbed into the green-and-brown camouflage-colored tank. Three more soldiers mounted the vehicle, and one straddled the large gun. The tableau was so perfect I couldn't help dashing up to take another photo. The soldiers smiled and cheered as though they'd won the homecoming football game.

"What paper are you with?" a private perched to the left of the gun asked in a thick New England accent while he lit a cigarette.

"I'm freelance. I have pictures appearing in *The Boston Globe, Iowa Dispatch,* and others. I hitched a ride with two Czechs who are on the hunt for a Nazi guard from the Buchenwald concentration camp." I indicated with a thumb over my shoulder.

"Boston, huh? I'm from Boston, the North End. What about you?"

"Sorry, I'm from Washington, D.C."

"Um, I hate to tell you this, D.C., but I think your ride just left without you," the soldier said, pointing with his cigarette.

Sure enough, I looked back to find my bag, with my limited worldly goods, dumped on the side of the road. "Hey," I called to no avail. Jiri zipped away, steering the jeep down the shoulder past the troop trucks. I took a few half-hearted steps before realizing the uselessness of my actions.

"Where are you headed?" The machine gunner stood over six feet tall, with the heavy weapon slung over his shoulder.

"Trying to make my way south, to Bavaria."

"We're headed to a town outside of Nuremberg." He glanced uneasily around at the dense trees lining the road. "Lieutenant," he called over his shoulder.

A lieutenant who'd been speaking with the driver of the front truck came over to where we stood.

"What's up, Gunny?"

"The lady's ride took off without her. It's not safe around here. The Ruskies aren't far off."

I licked my lips and shot the young lieutenant a toothy smile. There were no lines in his round face, and he looked like a ninety-day wonder from West Point. "I'm a freelance photographer. My credentials are in my bag if you want to see them. I'm headed south. Would it be possible to catch a ride with you boys as far as you're going?"

He didn't hesitate. "No problem at all, ma'am. You can ride up front with me."

"I'd be honored."

The machine gunner grabbed my bag and the lieutenant assisted me into the cab. I was more than relieved the boys from the Twelfth Infantry hadn't left me behind to fend for myself. The Red Army was close, and rumors of their ghastly treatment of the local women had been discussed by the journalists one evening over a bottle of schnapps. It wasn't a pretty story and one that had chills running up my spine.

Chapter Thirty
Solomon

It took me four days to catch up with the 101st. They were heading southeast into the mountains of Bavaria toward Berchtesgaden when I finally tracked down their convoy. The trucks lined the road as they waited for the Army Corps to rebuild the bridge over the Bischofswiesen River, a little present left by the retreating SS. The mount I'd acquired in Prien am Chiemsee, a lovely chestnut thoroughbred named Solomon and nothing like the hulking Franziska, ambled lazily past soldiers relaxing along the riverside. I knew I'd found what I was looking for when, instead of catcalls and comments like, "look at the dame on the horse," I heard my name.

"Lily Saint James! Can it be?"

I pulled Solomon to a halt. "Tank?"

"In the flesh." He held a new tommy gun in his hand, and the ever-present stogie shifted upward as his lips curled.

"Heavens, it's good to see you. Hold Solomon's head so I can get down?" I slid off the horse's back and was scooped, laughingly, into a bear hug the moment my feet hit the ground. When Tank let go, I found myself surrounded by soldiers. Some I recognized, Whiskey and Peterson, and there were a few new faces interested to find out who the lady on the horse could be.

"Looking stunning as ever." Tank grinned.

"Look at you. None the worse for wear, I see."

"What are you doing here?" Peterson asked.

"Why, I've been searching for you handsome fellows."

"Are you on a mission?" Whiskey whispered.

I whispered back, "Yes, I'm on a mission to find the 101st. I've just accomplished my mission objective."

The men whooped and Whiskey got a slap on the back.

"She wouldn't tell you if she were on a mission," Tank guffawed. "The boys scrounged up some fresh eggs this morning and are making helmet scramble. Would you like to join us?"

I wanted nothing more than to continue moving forward until I reached the battalion staff. However, the entreaties to remain for lunch ballooned into a rowdy chant of "stay, stay, stay," and I gave in.

Whiskey dusted off a rock for me to sit on, and I searched the faces, looking for one in particular. "Where's Feinberg? Didn't he move out with you?"

The jovial voices went silent.

"What happened?"

Tank removed the cigar and shook his head. "Took a shot to the neck. He didn't make it."

No. My lips moved, but the denial turned into a simple gasp of disbelief. I pressed fingers against my temples and shook my head. After everything we went through to retrieve Nigel, and then at the hospital in Switzerland.

I cleared my throat and swallowed the lump that arose. "He was a good man who knew how to keep his wits about him."

"Here, here," a soldier behind me murmured.

Whiskey handed me a metal mess kit bowl with a small pile of scrambled eggs and what looked to be a charred slab of Spam.

"Thanks." Feinberg's death seemed to have turned my appetite, and I simply held the meal in my lap.

Tank patted my shoulder. "He had a great respect for the work you two did together."

"I held him in high regard as well. His skills saved our butts more than once during the mission. Did he ever tell you how he got injured?"

Tank shook his head.

The men gathered closer as I told them about Nigel, the SS soldier, and our wild ride through the mountains of Germany. When I finished, I knew Feinberg's reputation had increased tenfold and his story would become legendary among the men. It was the least I could do for him.

"Tell us what you've been doing since we saw you last." Whiskey hunkered down at my feet, with his own meal in hand.

I told them the story of Jiri and Ludvik and soon had them laughing over the German who'd hightailed it across Czechoslovakia in his tank so he could surrender to the Americans.

"And then the Czechs took off in their 'borrowed' jeep without me, so I hopped a ride with some boys from the Twelfth Infantry." I didn't mention that it had been a good thing I'd hooked up with the Twelfth, because we soon ran into a ragtag group of Russians who looked rather savage. I don't think it would have gone well for me had I been alone.

"Sounds kind of dangerous, traveling alone these days. You never know who you'll come up against," Tank drawled.

"True. It's why I carry this"—I pulled a fully loaded Walther PPK out of my coat pocket—"wherever I go."

"Very nice." Whiskey whistled. "Can I see it?"

"I assume you know how to use that?"

I gave Tank an arch look, shook my head at Whiskey, and returned the weapon to its place.

"What were you doing with a couple of Czechs?" Whiskey asked.

"POWs at Buchenwald concentration camp. They had

gotten a line on an SS guard and were pursuing him for execution." My comments effectively shut down conversation.

The men shifted uncomfortably and wouldn't look me in the eye.

"Did I say something wrong?"

"We came across one of those camps outside Landsberg," Whiskey murmured.

"Like nothing I've ever seen." Tank's cigar shifted and he glanced away.

"I heard Dachau was bigger. Worse." Whiskey picked at a hangnail.

"What were you doing at Buchenwald?" another soldier asked.

"Freelance photography for a couple of newspapers. They estimated twenty-one thousand prisoners lived there."

Someone from behind let out a low whistle.

"Patton forced the locals to march from miles away to witness the depravity."

Tank nodded. "General Taylor made the locals dig graves for the dead at the camp we saw."

"Buchenwald too."

"I heard the Russians found one even bigger. With gas chambers." Peterson joined our group, sitting on a tuft of grass across from Tank.

"Miss Saint James." My head rotated to find Lieutenant Glassman standing with hands on hips. "Your presence is requested up front."

"Glass!" I hurried over, threw an arm across his shoulder, and kissed his cheek. "You are a sight for sore eyes." I echoed the same sentiment from when he first found me.

He took a laughing step back and wrapped a hand around my waist to keep us from toppling over. "It's good to see you too, ma'am.""

It took a few minutes for me to untether Solomon and say my farewells to the men. Glassman and I walked shoulder to shoulder along the roadside, passing DUKW boats, jeeps, and troop transports. Solomon snorted and shook his head.

"Nice horse," Glassman said.

"Thanks. How did you know I was here?"

"Grapevine. Good news travels fast."

"Do you think he's angry that I'm here?"

"He doesn't know. Captain Devlin overheard the men and sent me to find you. But if you ask me, I think he'll be pleased to see you."

"How much farther?"

"Just around the curve there."

"Wait. Hold up a moment. Here, take Solomon's reins for me." My duffle bag lay slung across the front of the saddle; I unclasped the front pocket that held a comb and other toiletries.

Glassman watched in patient amusement as I primped. The brown slacks I wore were dusty and smelled of horse, and the jacket wasn't in much better shape. I slapped away as much of the dirt as I could and plopped my hat between Solomon's ears. "Lieutenant, do you have a sweetheart back home?"

"As a matter of fact, I do. A fiancée."

"What's her name?" I combed out a snarl.

"Melly, short for Melanie."

A few swipes of lipstick and I smacked my lips together. "She's lucky to have you."

"Well, ma'am—"

"Lily."

"Lily, I'd have to argue with you there. I'm the lucky one."

A smattering of purple wild flowers on side of the road caught my eye, and I plucked a few to place behind my ear. "Will

I do?"

"As pretty as a picture."

"Always the gentleman. That … is precisely why your Melly is lucky to have you." I tapped the brim of his hat. "Lead on, Lieutenant."

We rounded the corner; the shade from the trees broke into shimmering sunlight. Its rays flooded the landscape and my heart. He stood with his back to me, but I would recognize that figure anywhere. One foot rested on the jeep's running board, his elbow on the windscreen while the other hand held a pair of binoculars to his eyes. I only vaguely registered Jake sitting in the passenger seat of the jeep.

"Major," Glassman called.

Charlie lowered the glasses and turned. His face initially registered surprise and then turned to delight. I surged forward into his embrace. I was home.

"How can this be?"

"I've been searching for you for days."

"I don't understand. You said you were going back to Switzerland."

"You understood the message?"

"Of course."

"I've been with the press corps in Buchenwald and decided to take a vacation."

He laughed. "A strange place to go on vacation."

"Are you kidding me? Berchtesgaden is supposed to be one of the premier vacation resorts."

"Lily"—he held me at arm's length—"the war isn't over. We don't know what we're going to find over this bridge."

"I imagine you'll find a bunch of empty houses. You must be a member of the Nazi Party to live here. They'd be fools to remain."

He didn't argue and his hand slipped from my upper arms down to my palms.

"Why did you come?"

"I thought I'd take Jake up on his offer to become his secretary." I grinned at the captain, who unabashedly watched our reunion.

"You're hired. It's good to see you."

"You too. Have you been staying out of trouble, or are you still losing your paychecks in poker games?"

"I only lose when you're in the room. You're the opposite of a good luck charm when it comes to poker." His gaze slid past me. "Where did you find that fine specimen, Glass?"

"That is Solomon, and he's mine." Glassman passed the reins and I laid a cheek against his roan and white muzzle. "Isn't he a beauty? I liberated him from an abandoned stable up the road. I think he belonged to an important Nazi or military officer."

"An interesting choice of transportation." Charlie ran a hand down the horse's neck.

"How much longer before you can cross?"

"The engineers tell us another hour."

"Are you expecting trouble?"

"Probably not. The district head of the local Volkssturm turned in his weapon and officially surrendered to Third Infantry yesterday in Winkl. But we can't be too careful. We're too close to the end to make mistakes."

My predictions proved correct. An hour later the men entered the ghost town of Berchtesgaden. The sun had dipped below the mountains when Charlie tracked me down. I'd tethered Solomon to a tree and set about taking pictures of the town.

"I see you're back to using your photography cover again.

What's the assignment this time?"

As usual, my body filled with a heightened sense of well-being whenever Charlie was around, and I couldn't help the smile that spread across my face. "Actually, I wasn't joking when I said I was on vacation. I'm not on assignment. To be honest, I turned in my resignation. Although I'm not sure they accepted it."

"What happened?"

"I didn't feel there was much more I could provide to the OSS. My last mission was abruptly cancelled and the opportunity to go to Buchenwald fell into my lap."

His brows knit. "Are your press credentials phony?"

"No, they're real enough. I thought I could get permission to stay and get some photographs for the papers."

He grinned. "I'll see what we can work out."

Chapter Thirty-one
Berchtesgaden

Berchtesgaden—a soldier's paradise. Once the Allies crossed into Germany, the conquering army kicked civilians out of their homes and billeted soldiers under warm roofs. However, as I overheard Whiskey say, "the houses didn't compare" to the lavish resort Minister Speer conceived and built in the Obersalzberg for Hitler and his high-ranking officers. In late April, some of the complex had been bombed; however, much of the town and its buildings were still intact, and the 101st took no time settling into the Alpine Village. Checkpoints were set up, patrols still ran shifts throughout the day and night, but hot showers, three squares a day, and comfortable beds lifted everyone's spirits.

I requested and was granted permission to remain with the 101st as a member of the press corps after assuring the colonel, who had luckily never heard of me, that my reporter colleague would be joining me as soon as permission was granted. Immediately following that conversation, I phoned to beg Maggie, my roommate at Buchenwald who'd moved on to Dachau, to come to Berchtesgaden. It didn't take much to convince her to leave the tragedy of concentration camps for the beauty of the Obersalzberg for a few days. She promised to arrive as soon as she could.

Being in Berchtesgaden gave me something I hadn't had in a while—time. I took to writing letters that I'd been remiss in doing.

Dear Father,

It is good to be back in Bavaria. The land is as beautiful as I remember from my childhood. The Allies have conquered Berchtesgaden and the men couldn't be happier. A Maypole festooned with banners of swastikas stood tall in the middle of a fountain at one end of town. The banners flapped in the spring breeze when we arrived. By the following day the streamers had been stripped from the pole, hidden in pockets as souvenirs. The swastika and eagle topper were knocked down and replaced with an American flag. I have enclosed a photo for you to see. The town is rife with Tyrolean architecture and the Gasthof Neuhaus, where I am staying in a miniature room in the attic, is as quaint as a Swiss chalet, but it is nothing compared to the estates of Hitler's high-ranking Nazis.

I'll admit the men loot anything not nailed down. Lugers and first editions of Mein Kampf are popular with the enlisted men, whereas the officers tend to enjoy the finer things in life, and more valuable items such as silver platters, china, and flatware go into their coffers.

Little did I realize I would wind up being the recipient of some of the looted bounty. The second morning, I awoke from the best sleep I've had in months to find a trunk full of women's dresses, shoes, coats, and underthings outside my door, pillaged from a variety of households. When I asked about it, I was told I not look a gift horse in the mouth. Secretly, I'm pleased to be rid of my slacks and into a fresh dress.

All my Best,
Sarah

♠♠♠♠

It was early afternoon by the time I left the regimental photographer behind in his dark room and spotted Charlie eating on the patio of a nearby hotel.

"There you are." He wiped his mouth and pulled out a chair for me. "Where have you been? My orderly has been searching high and low for you."

"I made friends with Staff Sergeant Gerard." I laid a pile of photos at his elbow and flopped back against the wrought iron chair. "This reminds me of Paris." I yawned. "Is it too early for a drink?"

"Funny you should mention that." He flipped through the pile. "These are good. Very good."

"Thanks. What is funny about wanting a drink?"

"The five-oh-sixth discovered Hermann Goering's private wine cellar today."

"I thought his estate was bombed."

"Some of it is still intact. Including the subterranean levels."

"Wine cellar, hm. Goering, the fat gourmand... I imagine it holds some of the best wines Europe has to offer." The breeze had me tucking a stray tendril behind my ear.

"Hundreds of bottles of some of the finest wines and champagne from Austria, Germany, and France. Or so I'm told. But it's not the wine cellar that I think will interest you."

I fingered the compass at my neck as he spoke. "Do tell."

Charlie surveyed my fidgeting as he spoke. "They've found secret tunnels beneath his home housing an art collection worthy of a museum."

My interest piqued, I dropped the compass and sat forward. "It's well known Goering fancied himself a superior art connoisseur. The Nazis have been pillaging the finest Jewish-owned artworks all over Europe ever since the *Anschluss*. Speer oversaw commissioning *das Führermuseum*, in Linz, Austria. Colette told me, when the Germans invaded France, the Louvre crated and filled armored trucks with artworks, such as the *Mona Lisa*. The trucks were constantly on the move to keep them away from Goering's greedy hands. How many paintings did they find?"

"I'm not sure. They're moving it now. You seem to know quite a bit about it."

"Oh, I am not an expert by any means." I waved my hand. "But on rainy days at finishing school, Madam Frischon would have us gather in the parlor for art lectures. I can identify the significant artists of their time. Cezanne, Da Vinci, Picasso, Monet." I listed them off on my fingers. "And the different styles, impressionism, realism, cubism."

"Someone needs to document the find. We suspect most of the artwork is stolen."

"Most likely. Stolen from the Jews, Poles, Czechs, Austrians. By thirty-nine, Jewish citizens had no right to own property. The Nazis basically downgraded Jews to" —I tapped my chin trying to think of an appropriate adjective—"enemies of the state, subhumans. Everything they owned belonged to the government as far as the Reich was concerned. When the *Anschluss* happened, the Germans immediately began pillaging from wealthy Austrian Jews too, claiming they owed the Reich taxes and taking anything of value to pay those 'taxes.'"

Charlie stared meditatively at me.

"What?"

"How do you know all this? Your work at the OSS?"

"Some. And I read."

His brows rose.

"A lot of reading. Most of it was gleaned in letters from finishing and boarding school friends. Camilla remained at Mont-Choisi long after I did. At night we'd listen to the National Swiss Radio station, one of the few German-speaking stations telling the truth about what the Nazis were up to."

"Are you up for the task?"

"The army will allow me?"

"I think I can arrange something." He winked. "After all, you are an expert."

"Stay right here. It'll take but a moment to get my camera."

Charlie laughed and seized my hand before I stepped away. "What about lunch?"

"Not hungry." I shook free of his grasp. "How do I get to Goering's place?"

"Go get your camera. I'll find someone to take us."

Stacks and stacks of paintings and statues lined the walls of underground tunnels Goering had built between his home and Reichsleiter Martin Bormann's. The men carried out canvas after canvas. I identified at least one Botticelli, a Klimt, and a possible Renoir. Two days later, troops found locals looting a train car, hidden in a blocked-up tunnel; it held more of Goering's stolen artworks including statues and tapestries of unimaginable value. The artwork gave me a purpose, and Marguerite, when she showed up three days later, dove into the project with gusto.

Chapter Thirty-two
Surrender

The Tuesday morning dawned bright and chilly. Cream-puff clouds played hide and seek with the Untersberg. I awoke at sunrise. Remorse over neglecting Solomon for the art find of the century plagued me. I donned a pair of slacks and a jacket to ward off the dewy cold and hiked the mile to the barn where he was stabled. We could not have asked for a better morning to ride.

Charlie had taken to breakfasting with me at *Gasthof Neuhaus*, and it was with surprise and a little discontent that I found Jake alone at our regular table following my ride.

His face broke into a welcoming smile as I approached.

I masked my disappointment. "All alone today?"

"Not anymore. Have a seat."

He began to rise, but I waved him down.

"Did you go for a ride? How was it?"

"Couldn't have been better." I pulled off my leather gloves, tossed them on the table, and folded into the chair across from him. "Solomon is a darling. Do you ride? You should try him out."

"Perhaps I'll give him a run this afternoon. I never did hear how you got ahold of such a magnificent animal."

"I suppose you could say I liberated him," I said with a wink and grin. "I found him in a stable about a hundred meters from a house that had been decimated by bombs. The stable was in top-notch condition, like something from a well-to-do Nazi family."

Jake's brow rose.

"I only mention it because of the red swastika painted on the barn door. I heard the poor thing whinnying and went to investigate." I nipped a piece of toast off Jake's plate and took a bite. "Don't know how long he'd been there, but his water bucket was empty and he drank the entire thing once I refilled it. The saddle and reins hung on the wall."

"Why Solomon?"

"There was a plaque above his stall. Three other stalls were empty. Only Solomon remained. Have I ever told you about Franziska?"

He shook his head and so I gave him the highlights of my trek through the Black Forest on Franziska's back, making the harrowing ride and escape far more humorous than it was. Jake laughed over my makeshift reins when Charlie arrived at my elbow.

"Something funny?" He took the chair on my left.

"Your beloved," Jake said.

I flinched at his reference and glanced at the nearby tables to see if anyone had overheard. Charlie and I hadn't advertised our relationship, although many of the men knew we were sweet on each other. My first night in Berchtesgaden, Charlie and I had come to an agreement. Unlike our time in Paris, there would be no public displays of affection in front of the men, and we both agreed it would be in poor taste to broadcast our relationship. We slept in different buildings—stolen kisses happened rarely and always in secret.

Jake continued, oblivious of my reaction, "She has a way with the horses."

"I have news," Charlie said, his face serious, his voice low.

Our smiles disappeared and I stiffened, bracing for bad news.

"Germany surrendered."

Nobody moved.

"Are you pulling my leg?" Jake asked.

Charlie's lips curled and his face lit up. He held two fingers in a V. "Victory in Europe. Hitler's dead. The war is over."

"Hallelujah." Jake whooped and jumped out of his chair, knocking it to the ground. The dozen or so men in the dining room turned to stare. "Germany surrendered, boys!" He pulled me up and danced us around the room in a wild polka. "Victory is ours."

I laughingly twirled with him only to be passed into the joyful arms of one soldier after another until I finally found myself in the arms of the one man who mattered most.

"Major, can we spread the news?" someone asked.

"Shout it from the rooftops." Charlie swooped me into a waltz, propelling me around tables and chairs. The room emptied as the men scattered to spread the word. Our dance slowed, Charlie's face split in a smile so wide his eyes crinkled at the corners, and his face shone with delight. He'd never looked as blindingly handsome to me as he did at that moment.

"Is it really over?"

"Yes, my love, it's finally over." His face softened. "Lillian—"

Hearing the words "finally over" produced an explosion of emotions. Relief, joy, sorrow, and guilt flooded my body at once, and to my dismay, they boiled over in the form of tears that soon turned into racking sobs. Poor Charlie. His consternation mirrored my own, but he pulled me close while I babbled incoherently into his shoulder about Magda, Friederich, Feinberg, Lars, and I even threw in Masselin's grandmother, finally culminating with the atrocities I'd witnessed at Buchenwald. All the pain I'd buried deep and ignored, or held inside, seemed to burst forth like a broken dam. Charlie, bless him, simply stroked my back as the cries shook my frame. Finally, the river came to an end and I dried off with Charlie's handkerchief. My mind and soul, purged of their surplus of baggage, were left behind with a feeling of wrung-out serenity, a catharsis of sorts.

I wiped away the final remnants of the tears and cleared my throat. "I apologize. I am not usually a watering pot. Honestly, I don't know where that came from. Perhaps I didn't get enough sleep last night."

He stared at me, his blue gaze solemn. "You've witnessed a lot during this war."

I glanced away in embarrassment. "Haven't we all?"

He tilted my chin with his finger, and I searched his face for disgust. "Some of us have seen more than others. Perhaps you more than most." His jaw flexed and he drew in a breath. "Lillian Saint James, will you marry me?"

My heart fluttered and I produced a watery smile. "You mean that pitiful display hasn't frightened you off?"

"Oh, my darling, one word that could never describe you is pitiful. You carry a strength so deep it constantly amazes me." He kissed the back of my hand. "So, what do you say? Are you willing to hitch your wagon to this broken-down soldier?"

"A broken-down soldier and an emotionally impulsive spy? Sounds to me like a match made in heaven. Where do I sign up?"

He lowered his head and his lips descended into a kiss that made me ache for more.

"I love you," I whispered when we came up for air.

He tilted his forehead against mine, "You'll be Lillian McNair."

I couldn't help the bright smile that spread across my face. Just one more moniker to add to the list. Only, this one would be of my own choosing.

Chapter Thirty-three
Honors

The ruby ring glittered in the morning sunlight, and once again, I took a moment to admire its beauty on my finger. Charlie presented the ring to me, on bended knee, a few days after VE Day. Its presence still filled me with delight.

The men stood at parade rest, in lines of formation in the middle of a grassy field across the street from the café where I sat. They looked smart in their uniforms, each man's boots polished and pant crease crisp. The camera at my elbow was already filled with a dozen shots of the troops as they waited patiently for General Eisenhower to arrive. Charlie's battalion received word yesterday that the great general was making his rounds of the regiments. The 502nd was on his list and rumors abounded the regiment would be receiving a unit citation.

It had been two weeks since my crying jag. The emotional purge seemed to have provided a catharsis, for I slept well—no longer lying in bed with my mind racing and guilt-ridden or plagued with bad dreams. However, VE Day and the initial excitement had dissipated among the men. Japan had yet to surrender, and fighting in the Pacific raged on. The military issued a point system based on time served, combat awards, and if they had dependent children at home. Enlisted men needed eighty-five points to be discharged. Even some D-Day veterans didn't have enough points, and the officers returned to a training regimen that dampened the initial exultation of the German surrender.

I took another sip of coffee and returned to the half-written letter I'd been penning to Colette, letting her know that I would be returning to Paris, on my way back home to Washington, D.C.

America. A place I was finally ready to return. The surrender and my engagement to Charlie seemed to have lifted my desperation to remain in Europe. A few days after VE Day, I finally admitted to myself that my incessant need to find a purpose to remain in Germany had to do with my shameless pursuit of Charlie and persistent concern for his safety. Luckily, Charlie had enough points to be discharged and we hoped he would be home by fall.

Three days ago, I received a letter from Father assuring me that I was forgiven for my thoughtless words and would *always* be welcome in his home. After I finished the letter to Colette, I planned to write Father, informing him of my engagement, and to ask if we could hold the wedding at his home in Georgetown. Fall was a beautiful time in Washington. If I couldn't convince Colette to come to the States for my wedding, I'd ask either Evelyn or Jane to be my maid of honor. There was enough space to house Charlie's family, and my father could walk me down the aisle. Even though Mother would not be there, I would wear her dress, and she would be with me in spirit. With her grand plans, my marriage to Charlie wouldn't be what she envisioned, but I think, in the end, she would have wanted to see me happy above all else.

A covered army jeep zipped up the road, pulling my thoughts away from wedding plans. The great man finally arrived. His jeep parked to the side of the field, and I strained to catch a glimpse from my vantage point. Lieutenant Glassman must have been hailed by someone in the jeep because he left his position in front of his platoon, and he, too, disappeared from my sight line, but it wasn't long before he returned to speak briefly with Whiskey.

This is it. I rose and positioned my camera so I could catch the perfect shot of Eisenhower as he came around the wall of men. To my surprise, Whiskey broke ranks to jog across the green space in my direction. It occurred to me perhaps there were rules against photographing the general, and I lowered my camera as Whiskey came even with me.

"Ma'am."

"Hello, Whiskey," I whispered. "What's the matter?"

"Nothing, ma'am. Lieutenant Glassman requested that you come closer for a better view of the proceedings."

"Am I allowed to take photos?"

"Yes, ma'am."

Regimental and some battalion officers, including Charlie, were seated on a recently erected platform in front of the troops, and I followed Whiskey over to the viewing area. Expecting to be allowed to stand to the side of the stage, it surprised me when Whiskey indicated I mount the stairs.

"There's a chair for you next to Lieutenant Colonel Kincaid."

A thrill of excitement zipped down my spine at the honor I was being afforded. I wondered if Charlie had arranged it for my benefit. He winked when I glanced up at him as I made my way to the empty seat at the end of the front row.

The men were called to attention. As one, their heels snapped together, and those of us in the reviewing stand rose. I positioned the camera and waited with excitement. The general approached the stage and my shutter clicked.

It wasn't Eisenhower.

The face seemed vaguely familiar to me. He mounted the steps, followed by his driver, shaking hands with the top brass in the front row, then turned to the microphone.

"At ease, gentlemen."

Those of us in the viewing stand took our seats and the men in the field relaxed into parade rest.

"As you can tell, I am not General Eisenhower. I regret to inform you, his plans unexpectedly changed, and he will not be joining us today. My name is General Magruder. General Eisenhower asked me to share these words with you." He pulled a folded sheet of paper out of his pocket, adjusted his glasses, and commenced to read Eisenhower's speech.

Magruder. That name also rang a bell, but I just couldn't place it. I forced myself to retain the genial smile on my face, though I felt such disappointment on the men's behalf. After all, they'd given so much for their country. I listened to the address with only half an ear as I gazed on proudly at the fine-looking group of soldiers in front of me.

They all deserved medals.

The General finished and returned the paper to his pocket. "Now I would like to move on to the main reason I've come to be here with you today."

He surveyed the troops and crooked a finger at his driver, who handed over a small black box. "I'm here to present the Distinguished Service Cross to one of you who showed gallantry and determination against all odds. Someone who not only risked life and limb for their country but also provided vital intelligence to the Allied cause, which saved hundreds, if not thousands, of lives, including innocent civilians back at home."

I listened with interest.

"This person's selfless acts saved not only American lives but foreign ones as well. I'm pleased to be able to present this award today in front of you men because it is my understanding, if not for the precise actions from certain men in the five-oh-second, this person might not have survived to continue work so valuable to the Allied cause."

My brows furrowed as I searched the ranks, trying to figure out who the general spoke of.

"Today it is my honor, as Deputy Director of the Office of Strategic Services—"

Of course, General John Magruder! We'd never met, but I'd seen his photograph at OSS headquarters on Navy Hill in D.C. next to Director Donovan's…

"—to Lillian Saint James."

My head snapped up at that. My musings had distracted me so completely, I missed the rest of Magruder's speech. It was Lieutenant Colonel Kincaid, on my left, who took my hand and helped me rise, propelling me to where Magruder waited, holding a brass cross that hung from a blue-and-red-striped ribbon between his fingers. Thunderous applause rang in my ears, and I stood in mute astonishment while he pinned the prestigious award to the lapel of my jacket. Officers in the stand came forward to shake my hand. My head reeled. I staggered and would have fallen if Charlie hadn't come to my rescue.

Scooping up my elbow, he escorted me back to my seat. "Congratulations."

"Did you know about this?" I asked.

He shook his head. Pride shined through his eyes and his warm grip settled my whirling confusion.

The rest of the ceremony went by in a blur. Many of the troopers, including Charlie, were awarded for their actions in combat. My heart warmed when Magruder posthumously awarded Feinberg the same British Medal Nigel pinned on me in April. Finally, the ceremony wound down and the men dismissed.

I gathered my things and straightened to find the general at my elbow. "Miss Saint James, I've got to be moving on, but I was wondering if you could give me a moment of your time before I leave."

"Of course, General."

He drew me away from the crowd to an empty bench at the far side of the grassy field. "I understand you turned in your resignation after Operation Gumdrop was canceled." He didn't look at me as he spoke, instead stared at the American flag fluttering in the breeze.

"I did, sir."

"Why?"

I sighed. *What could I tell him? I couldn't stand the thought of returning behind a desk while my beau battled Nazi's?* "Well, sir, I felt that my … usefulness at the OSS had run its course. I knew you would never send me back in, and when the opportunity to see the inside of one of the concentration camps came up … I took it. I'm sure my file tells you everything you need to know."

"As a matter of fact, it does. It also tells me that your impulsive actions acquired some unparalleled intelligence. That you're quick on your feet. Did you really fix a car with your stocking?"

My cheeks burned. "Well … *I* didn't fix the car, Sergeant Feinberg did.

"The man who you performed field surgery on with a sewing kit from your handbag?"

I fidgeted with the medal and cleared my throat. "Yes, that's correct."

"And is it true you escaped the Black Forest riding bareback on a German Army draft horse?"

"Yes, sir."

Finally, he turned his gaze on me, and those piercing eyes raked me up and down, pausing for a moment at the ring on my finger. "You are an incredibly resourceful young woman, aren't you?"

"I suppose."

"I understand congratulations are in order. You're to be married."

"Hopefully in the fall, yes."

"Will you be returning to Washington?"

"In two weeks."

"I hoped I could convince you to return to work at the OSS offices there."

I folded my hands over my knee. "I'm not sure how useful I would be."

"I can find a dozen jobs for a resourceful woman like you. But I would consider it a personal favor if you would help me out."

I twisted the ring on my finger.

"At least until your wedding. Afterwards ... well, I suppose that would be up to you and your husband to decide."

How could I refuse the man in charge of OSS Intelligence this favor? I imagined I'd go back to manning a desk, maybe providing translation services. It wouldn't hurt to continue to help out. I'd be safe at home in America, which would make Charlie happy, and it would give me something to do until he was released from the army.

"Who do you need me to report to, General?"

"When you return, contact your old roommate Jane."

"Very well."

Magruder rose and offered his hand.

"I look forward to reconnecting with Jane. Who does she work for these days?"

"Me."

My eyes widened at his revelation.

"Thank you for your service, Miss Jolivet. I'll see you in a few weeks." He tipped his hat, pivoted on his heel, and strode to the waiting jeep.

Charlie found me standing in the same position, watching the empty road where the general's car once stood.

"What did the general want?"

"To offer me a job in D.C.

"What kind of job?"

"I'm not sure, something in his office. A desk job." I turned to Charlie, whose furrowed brow told me everything I needed to know. Cupping his cheek, I assured him, "I agreed, but only until the wedding, darling. After that, it'll be smooth sailing. I'm all yours."

Charlie's features lightened, and he took the compass at my neck in his fingers, rubbing a thumb across the glass face. "I have a feeling with you, quiet and calm is never going to be in our future."

Afterword

Lily Saint James is a fictional character inspired by the actions of real female spies from WWII. An amalgamation of three women in particular formed the basis of her background and traits.

Virginia Hall, an American, initially worked for the SOE and then the OSS. During college, Hall studied multiple languages and finished her schooling in Europe where she traveled all over the continent, much like Lily. Ultimately, she ended up working for the American Embassy in Poland. At the start of the war she worked as an ambulance driver in France. Later she joined the SOE and returned to France where she successfully organized resistance fighters in acts of sabotage and guerilla warfare. She also worked the underground helping downed pilots escape into Spain. Eventually, when the Nazis closed in, she herself fled over the snow-covered Pyrenees Mountains. She did all this with a prosthetic leg. The SS labeled her "the limping lady," and considered Hall one of the most dangerous Allied spies.

Violette Szabo was a French born SOE agent recruited after her husband was killed fighting in North Africa. Szabo trained in weaponry, cryptography, radio communications, and escape and evasion tactics. Like Lily, she parachuted into German occupied France, prior to the Allied invasion of Normandy, to organize local resistance groups and sabotage German communication lines. During one of her missions, Szabo was captured, tortured for information, and for eight months was shifted from one concentration labor camp to another. Eventually, she was executed at the age of twenty-three.

Noor Inayat Khan was born in Russia to an Indian Muslim father and American mother. During her childhood, she lived in London and a suburb of Paris. She studied at the Sorbonne and the Paris Conservatory. When the war broke out, her family fled to England where she joined the Women's Auxiliary Air Force and from there was recruited into the SOE. She trained as a wireless operator. Her fluency in French and knowledge of Paris made her a desirable candidate to serve in Nazi-occupied France. While in France, the network of spies and resistance fighters for whom she relayed messages were arrested by the Nazis; Kahn barely escaped the round up. Constantly on the move, she would transmit for only twenty minutes at a time to keep from being detected by the enemy. In October 1943, a French double-agent betrayed Khan leading to her capture, imprisonment and eventual execution.

Szabo and Khan were both posthumously awarded the British George Cross and French Croix de Guerre for their contributions. Hall, the lone survivor, was presented the Distinguished Service Cross—the only WWII civilian to receive this award. In addition, England made her an honorary Member of the Order of the British Empire.

Attributes from each woman went into creating Lily's character. From Hall, her background traveling the European continent and multi-language fluency made her a desirable agent. Additionally, Hall returned behind enemy lines multiple times, this tenacity gave Lily the determination to return to Nazi-occupied territory. Szabo's daring, extensive training, and resolve under interrogation gave Lily her resourcefulness. Finally, Khan's refined education provided Lily her knowledge of artwork and protocol.

Glossary

Ausweis – Identification card.

Danke – Thank you.

Ersatzkaffee – Coffee made from wheat or other grains, not coffee beans. Drunk during the war due to rationing and lack of access to imported coffee beans.

Frau – A title for a married woman. Equivalent to the title missus.

Fräulein – A title for a girl or young unmarried woman. Comparable to the title miss.

Gasthaus – An inn or tavern providing lodging and food.

Gestapo – Hitler's private militarized police force used for interrogation and infiltration to ferret out spies and other dissidents against the Nazi Party policies.

Hauptmann – German Army Captain.

Heer – German Army.

Herr – A title for a man. Equivalent to the title sir or mister.

Luftwaffe – German Air force.

Maginot Line – French first line of defense, it was built in response to WWI and as a defense against future invasion from the east. It was made of concrete fortifications, obstacles, an underground bunker system, and weapon installations. Construction began in 1929 and continued until 1938. In WWII the invading German Army simply went around it by going through Belgium.

Marken – Ration coupons made for specific items, e.g., eggs, bread, meats.

Marktplatz – A marketplace or town square.

Oberst – German Army Colonel.

Reichsmark – The money created and used during the Third Reich.

Reichseierkarte – The Third Reich's ration card booklet.

Schutzstaffel – Also known as the SS. Specialized paramilitary troops within the Nazi Party responsible for general policing and enforcing the policies of Nazi Germany. Waffen SS were combat troops within the Army. The SS was also responsible for running the concentration camps. The Gestapo was a subdivision of the SS.

Schwarzwald – Black Forest region in southern Germany bordering France. Known for its dense evergreen forests, rolling hills, and quaint villages. Its western boundary is the Rhine River.

Siegfried Line – A mirror to the French Maginot Line, it was the Germans' first line of defense against invasion. Built during WWI along the west German border, it included concrete barriers, defensive forts, tunnels, and anti-tank ditches filled with water. After the D-Day invasion, Hitler commanded able-bodied civilians and children to reinforce its construction.

Sturmmann – Stormtrooper rank within the SS.

Volkssturm – Also known as "The People's Army," it was the German national militia, established near the end of the war by the Nazi Party as a last resort to guard the homeland. It was comprised of old men, young boys, and women who were not already a member of the German military. Training was limited, organization and communication haphazard, and uniforms were often makeshift paramilitary or simply civilian clothes with an identifying armband. They played many roles including police, border guard, and frontline fighters.

Wehrmacht – The Armed Forces of the Third Reich and Nazi Germany. It includes the Heer (Army), Kriegsmarine (Navy), and Luftwaffe (Air force).

Zigaretten – Cigarettes.

Acknowledgements

The Brass Compass has been a long time in coming and, as my first foray into historical fiction, couldn't have come about if it weren't for the help and support from many people. My gratitude and love goes out to my 93-year-old grandmother, a member of the "Greatest Generation," and patron supporter of this publication. I am indebted to Oscar Burchard, a teenager able to escape a Nazi work camp with his integrity intact when others would have turned on their fellow man in order to survive. Your story, memories, and historical knowledge of Germany were invaluable to my research. The wonderful accounts of Army Air Corps Veteran Charles L. Childs stoked my imagination and gave me an insight to the minds of military personnel of the times. Historical knowledge from reenactor Robert Arnett gave a me both a reason and location to base my heroine. A heartfelt thank you goes out to Michaela Johnson and Alice Rachel for your translation services. To my content editor, Kelly Eadon, who talked me off a cliff and steered me in the right direction when I felt the manuscript rudderless, and my copyeditor, Amy Knupp, thank you for being a part of this journey to publication. As always, I am indebted to my family, for their constant support for *The Brass Compass* and encouragement even though it took over ten years for the kernel of an idea to become a published novel. Thank you all for your input, love, and support.

About the Author

Ellen Butler is an award-winning novelist writing critically acclaimed suspense thrillers, and sassy romance. *The Brass Compass* was inspired by the brave women who served in the OSS, British Special Operations Executive and French Resistance. Ellen is a member of The OSS Society and her original interest in WWII history piqued when her grandfather's role as a cryptographer during the war was revealed. Ellen holds a Master's Degree in Public Administration and Policy, and her history includes a long list of writing for dry, but illuminating, professional newsletters and windy papers on public policy. She lives in the Virginia suburbs of Washington, D.C. with her husband and two children.

You can find Ellen at:

Website ~ *www.EllenButler.net*

Facebook ~ *www.facebook.com/EllenButlerBooks*

Twitter ~ *@EButlerBooks*

Goodreads ~ *www.goodreads.com/EllenButlerBooks*

Novels by Ellen Butler
Suspense
Poplar Place

Contemporary Romance
Love, California Style Trilogy
Heart of Design (book 1)
Planning for Love (book 2)
Art of Affection (book 3)
Second Chance Christmas

Readers Group Guide

1) What did you think of the title *The Brass Compass*? Why do you think the author chose this title? Do you feel the compass played an important enough part of the story to use it as the novel's title? Can you think of a different title?

2) Did you find the plot engaging? Did you find yourself looking forward to turning the pages, or did it drag? What kind of emotions did the story evoke as you read—interest, sadness, anger, joy? What would you have changed? What history or storyline did you want more of? Less?

3) Many WWII soldiers brought home foreign brides and there are stories of OSS agents finding love within the agency. What do you think of Lily and Charlie's love story? How difficult would it be for you to be married to someone who worked for the government and kept secrets from you because of national security purposes?

4) Discuss the dynamics between the characters as they relate to Lily—Charlie, Devlin, Glassman, Feinberg, Colette, Camilla, and her parents. Who is your favorite character? Who is your least favorite character? Why?

5) At one point, Lily calls Masselin an enigma. Is that a good description? Discuss your feelings toward him. What do you think his motivations were? Was he a good, bad, or something in between? Do you think he would have helped Lily if he'd survived? Why do you think the author created this puzzling character?

6) Were there scenes or passages that you found insightful or profound? Was there a snippet of dialog that you found captures a particular character's essence? Is there a passage or scene that made you cry or laugh out loud?

7) Throughout the book we see flashbacks to Lily's earlier life, before the war. What do you think of that life? Is that a life you can connect to? In the end, General Magruder called Lily resourceful and impulsive. Did she change to become the spy, or do you think her personality was always impetuous, resourceful, and secretive? Do you believe Lily when she tells Charlie she wants to settle down and have children, or do you think she will be drawn back into the life of spying?

8) Do you think you could live the life of a spy, constantly keeping secrets from friends and neighbors and those you love? Does deception come easily to you?